THE ★ CHINA CONNECTION

MARK DALE

I wish to thank my wife and children
for their support while writing this novel. Without
their encouragement and understanding, this endeavor
might not have been possible

I would like to dedicate this book to all
the brave soldiers who did not return and to their
families and friends they left behind.

PROLOGUE

March 2003
Two days before NATO forces invade Iraq-

Curt motioned to Vic that it was time. Vic knew this was the day he had trained the past three weeks for. He stood and stretched his aching joints, then looked into the cracked piece of glass that these people called a mirror, straining to see his reflection in the poorly lit room. The glass was shattered in several places, but he could still make out his American looking face.

He was about 6'2", taller than most in this area, and he had a well-built form that was muscular, but lean. He took the dark camouflage make up from the bag and began to apply it to his face to hide his somewhat lighter, olive colored skin. He was always naturally tan, but he knew that he had to look much darker to blend in well with the Iraqi crowd.

He traced his square jaw line with the thick paint with his weathered tanned hands that had witnessed too much of war. He began skimming the camouflage up and over his straight and prominent nose that was lightly covered with freckles, which made him appear boyish at times. He smoothed the paint over his suntanned cheek bones that rested adjacently to his protruding nose. His chiseled mouth was set slightly wide, especially when he smiled revealing his perfectly white teeth. He remembered being told several times to conceal his mouth as much as possible because his teeth were "obviously American".

His lips were chapped from the rough weather conditions, but still held the charm they once did when the girls used to stop and look at him as he passed by, stunned by his attractive looks. However, women always seemed surprised by his complete lack of interest in his appearance; he was always focused on more important tasks at hand.

This task was going to be difficult, this time he would be working in a brightly lit room, potentially with many other people nearby. He did not want anyone noticing his facial features, he had to blend in. As he finished applying the makeup to his forehead above his eyebrows, which seemed to arch slightly inward above his deep-set eyes, he put down the tube filled with the dark colored paint and looked into the mirror. "I am committed to this mission, it will save many of our boy's lives; can't let them down," he said to his reflection.

He placed his sturdy hands on either side of the sink and picked up the contact lenses to hide his most Caucasian like feature, his eyes. They were icy-blue, almost silver, with a piercing stare that could mesmerize a person. His deep-set eyes seemed shadowed by his past, making his appearance even more mysterious. He placed the dark brown contacts into his eyes blinking to make sure they were properly positioned.

Then he took out his black temporary hair dye and began to run it through his wavy sandy-blonde hair, just enough to ensure that no one would notice his hair line under the hoods that both men would wear over their heads and necks called kaffiyehs, by the locals. They were white with black and gray zigzag lines. The white cotton robes they were wearing were made of a material that felt like tent canvas and was held at the waist with a braided rope.

His hair was somewhat short, and rested just above his ears. He glanced at the mirror one last time before he left, smirking in satisfaction that his disguise was a success. He looked Persian, except for the fact that he was taller than most of the locals; so he slouched down to hide his well-built form. He walked out into the sun-dried landscape and started the perilous journey that was his mission. Maybe this time, everyone can make it out alive, he thought.

Vic followed Curt to the building that the CIA pencil pushers had determined where the primary computer was supposed to be located. They could hear the morning prayers beginning as Curt opened the large doors and Vic went to work.

After completing his objective, the two men snuck out of the building and started walking north. Two hours later Vic looked up and saw the sun. Not seeing a cloud in the sky, he knew it would be another hot day in Baghdad.

Vic watched the last of a dozen or so compact pickups, all loaded with armed soldiers wearing the official tan-colored uniforms of the Republican Guard, whiz passed him and Curt. They were on their way into the central part of the city in an attempt to bring down low flying aircraft as the enemy planes targeted strategic military sites in the area.

A couple of the guards were smiling, though most had long serious faces as though they knew what the outcome of the war would be. They passed by the two men standing on the side of the once paved road, who were waving and yelling encouraging slogans to the soldiers. The caravan was creating a dust cloud which was drifting over the two United States espionage agents, as if a huge vacuum cleaner bag was being dumped over them. The agents watched the pickups disappear around a sand dune; they continued walking along Highway 1 toward the last checkpoint ten kilometers north of the city.

The yellow dust was stifling; sand was in the agent's nostrils and mouths creating a paste, making it difficult to breathe. Their mouths were dry and parched even though they had drunk some brown water from a plastic jug Curt had purchased from a street vendor an hour earlier. The city's water system was out of service, ever since the coalition forces began bombing the city.

Vic noticed the heat shimmering in the distance as the dry humidity and solar radiation caused the air to appear as if it were vibrating and dancing above the desert floor. He knew that by noon he would have difficulty just getting his breath. He slapped at a sand flea that bit his left arm, cussing softly under his breath.

The two men had passed the guard shack at Az Kazimiyah two hours earlier, without incident, a full hour before sunrise. Vic's kaffiyeh was loose and constantly slid down over his eyes; he had lost the black braided band that had kept the cotton material in place on his head. He would push it up with his right forearm not realizing he was also wiping the dark face paint off his forehead.

Curt looked around to ensure no one could hear him as he spoke quietly in English to Vic, "That was a really good idea you had of displaying 'The Bird' on the monitor when they select the fire sequence for the bio-weapons."

Vic grinned, "Yeah that ought to confuse them. These rag-heads will probably think it is an omen from Allah. I wasn't sure we were going to get out of there before the morning prayers finished though."

"And out of here is where I want to be," Curt said uneasily, looking over his left shoulder for unwelcome observers.

Vic laughed softly, "Yeah, that will complete a successful two week mission in Baghdad and I'm tired of this bag-the-dead city."

"Well, if they can't take a joke…" Curt trailed off.

Vic tensed his muscles, realizing that Curt spoke quieter, he leaned close and whispered. "What is it?"

Curt faced Vic and whispered, "According to my map the last guard shack is just passed this next dune, no more talking, your Farsi is not good enough and I don't want anyone to hear us speaking English."

This was not the first mission for Vic, but it was the final mission for Curt, being more used to the cloak and dagger style activities, was older and more experienced of the two agents. He was scheduled for retirement upon his return to the United States and Vic was learning all he could from his mentor.

The mission had started with their midnight high-altitude, low-opening (HALO) clandestine insertion fifty miles south of Baghdad. They had parachuted from a muffled engine, U.S. Air Force C-130 Hercules aircraft at 25,000 feet elevation and performed a free fall to 1300 feet elevation before opening their parachutes. After landing they had buried their uniforms and gear; then changed into the clothes they were now wearing.

It was Vic's responsibility to sabotage the firing sequence of the scud missiles that were armed with Sarin gas, which stood pointed at the coalition forces from the underground bunkers, before Saddam could launch them.

Flight 637
DFW to Mariscal Sucre Airport

Elena concentrated on the passengers she remembered seeing when she boarded the plane two hours earlier. She was the last passenger to board on purpose and was searching for a man, a man who might unwittingly assist her.

She remembered the man wearing the blue polo shirt, in first class, with the vacant window seat. She thought he was her best chance. He seemed to be traveling alone and had a carry-on bag at his feet.

She held the white onyx turtle in her clammy fingers, knowing if she were caught at customs in Quito; her brother would suffer, might even be killed. She felt Juan pressing against her left shoulder again as he leaned closer, smelling his foul breath.

"Like I said, I can help you with Señor Cordova if you will sleep with me when we arrive in Quito. I have a cozy house in Perucho."

Elena felt that sick feeling in her stomach return and knew she might throw up. She stood to go to the lavatory, when the seatbelt sign came on. She imagined, her brother Eduardo being beaten and tortured by Señor Cordova's thugs. She felt the tears welling in her eyes as she thought; I must get this turtle to Cordova. She set back down again with fear racking her body.

She felt Juan softly stroke her upper arm and thought of the repulsiveness of him touching her body, of him lying near her. She squeezed the turtle, and hesitantly stood in the darkened cabin, hoping she wouldn't be told to take her seat. She smoothed her blouse and slowly stepped forward, moving cautiously past a flight attendant passing out pillows and blankets.

Baghdad

The two men rounded the curve in the road and approached the checkpoint guard shack. Vic felt himself falling into the training regimen, deep breaths to slow the heart rate, thinking calming thoughts to help relieve the stress of the situation. His training was so complete his current actions were happening like the autonomic nervous system controls a body's breathing and heart rate. He had hated the training, but now appreciated the mental control he had learned.

Vic saw the shack in the distance as the two men rounded the sand dune, it was a wooden structure that had once been painted white, but now most of the paint had peeled off, the remaining paint resembling ruffled feathers on an undernourished chicken. The building was perhaps eight feet from the front to the back wall, and about six feet wide. There were two, three foot windows on each side and a small window in the rear. The door way was actually door-less allowing for ventilation of the structure.

An eight foot long, two inch diameter, steel pipe painted a bright yellow, blocked the road's access past the front of the shack. An Iraqi stop sign was welded to the center of the pipe and the end of the pipe closest to the shack was mounted on a tripod with a counter weight on the end of the pipe so a guard could easily raise and lower the gate with one hand.

Vic observed two guards, one standing out front and the other squatting just inside the door of the guard shack, taking advantage of the morning shade. Both guards were wearing the olive drab green military uniforms of the regular Iraqi Army, not the tan uniform of the feared Republican Guard, and both guards were armed with AK-47 assault rifles. The squatting guard was holding his weapon over his knees and the standing guard had his weapon's sling resting on his right shoulder. An old faded yellow Toyota pickup was parked behind the guard shack, no one else in sight.

Vic started thinking about the days left in hostile country. One more stop, then a twenty-mile hike towards Samarra. We'll meet the Kurdish resistance tomorrow night; then a three-hour-long camel ride to the extraction point where a chopper will take us to Turkey and then home, he thought to himself.

Vic watched the guard who was standing, step away from the shack, raising his left hand, keeping his right hand firmly on the pistol grip and his index finger on the trigger. "What is your name?" he demanded.

Curt stopped three feet from the guard, smiled and answered in flawless Arabic. "I am Ahmed Sawasha and this is my brother Abraham."

The guard looked at both men holding the rifle muzzle pointed at Curt. "Where are you going this morning?"

"We are leaving the city. Our father lives in Samarra and is ill; we are going there to care for him. We want to leave before the Americans attack."

The guard relaxed his grip on the weapon and adjusted his sunglasses with his left hand. He took his hand off the pistol grip, letting the rifle hang near his waist.

The guard sighed loudly and said, "Yes the bombings are becoming more severe each night. I believe Satan's armies will attack soon, but the great Allah will crush them when they attack us," he replied with a grimace that made Curt wonder if the guard really believed that, wondering why he had said Satan's armies, ignoring his mention of America.

The guard stood with the sun at his back causing the two Americans to squint as they looked at him, he now seemed more relaxed, appearing bored and wanting to chit-chat. Curt responded with small talk for a minute or so, as Vic grew more uncomfortable with every word that was spoken.

Vic stood there, feeling hot, his head dress slipping down; he wanted to go home. The guard and Curt were laughing when the guard looked more closely at Vic's face and saw something that should not have been. The guard stepped closer to Vic, slowly moving his right hand back to the pistol grip.

Vic was not aware that his brown face paint was smearing and rubbing off his forehead just below his kaffiyeh each time he pushed it back up over his eyes, the pushing motion exposing a slightly paler skin tone, resembling a tiger-stripe camouflage pattern. Curt turned to see what the guard was looking at, his first thought was to ignore it, but instinctively knew the guard would question why Vic looked like a brown zebra.

Moving quickly, Curt shoved the guard with his left hand, forcing him back into the small building, while reaching for the long bladed knife in his waist band with his right hand. The guard raised his weapon as he was stumbling and falling backward against the second guard who was squatting in the doorway, impulsively squeezing his trigger finger. Curt, feeling the impact of the bullets, felt himself losing control of his legs, felt the shock as though being hit with Babe Ruth's homerun bat, realizing he was sinking to the sand.

When the guard fell backward, with complete loss of balance, firing the rounds, he landed against the second guard. The second guard, hearing the gunfire, raised his weapon, snagging the barrel of his gun on the first guard's rifle sling, jerking the weapon out of the first guard's hands.

Curt was collapsing to his knees as Vic lunged over him drawing the Kurdish, curved-bladed dagger from his waistband and slashed the first guard's throat from left to right as deep as he could, severing the larynx and both carotid arteries. The guard immediately stopped trying to retrieve his weapon and quickly put his hands to his throat attempting to stem the massive flow of blood which was spurting and flowing over his hands, down his uniform and onto the sand in front of the small guard shack. His legs began to fail him as he attempted to stand and flee from Vic, falling backwards onto the floor of the shack. Vic noticed that the first guard was now lying on the second guard's legs, pinning him down, and saw that the second guard's assault rifle had skidded under a stool in the rear of the guard shack.

Vic dove into the guard shack clawing and climbing over the first guard as he lay on his back gagging and gurgling. Vic stretched his arm out as far as he could and plunged his knife into the second guard's left leg burying it a half inch into the guard's upper left thigh bone. The guard yelled in severe pain, drawing up his legs and the knife out of Vic's reach, trying desperately to reach over his head for his weapon to fight off the vicious attack.

Vic noticed the first guard's weapon in the front corner and rolled to his right, grabbing the weapon, he tried to rise up on his knees for a good shot, but slipped in the pooling blood. He rolled over on his back and rotated the selector from single-shot to auto-matic with his right thumb, then lifted the rifle two inches from his chest and pointed it over his head at the second guard, as he lay in a prone position and pulled the trigger. Firing a three-round burst, the first bullet entered the guard's left hip and lodged in his pelvis, the second and third bullets entered the guard's abdomen just under the left lower rib lacerating the liver, puncturing the stomach and left lung before lodging in the heart. Vic rolled to his left and onto his knees, and saw the second guard twitching a couple of times, then heard him gasp and watched as he died.

Vic crawled back over the first guard whose blood was still flowing from his throat wound, and spreading out the door of the shack, dripping onto the parched ground. The air from his lungs was mixing with the blood, creating a pink froth as the guard made gurgling sounds through the jagged open wound. Vic could smell the blood which was mixing with the smells of his stomach as he bled out.

Vic turned his attention back to Curt, who was bleeding slowly from his stomach wounds and seemed unconscious, crawling out of the guard shack, Vic knelt on both knees inspecting Curt's wounds. He found two small entry wounds an inch apart and two inches below his ribs just left of his sternum. Vic gently rolled Curt onto his right side and inspected Curt's back and discovered one exit wound about three inches in diameter with lacerated intes-tines exposed, bleeding badly.

Vic removed his kaffiyeh and used it as a compress on Curt's exit wound, then rolled Curt onto his back, taking Curt's kaffiyeh, he applied pressure to the entry wounds, desperately trying to stop the flow of blood. Vic noticed Curt's eyes flutter and open slightly, looking at him.

"Vic, leave me here, save yourself, don't let them cap—capture you," Curt stammered in a hushed tone. "The mis—the mission is too important."

Vic tried to be strong and offer encouragement with his voice, but it cracked as he said, "The mission is over, it's successful, there is nothing else we can do here," he choked on the tears and stopped talking.

Vic noticed blood beginning to trickle from the right corner of Curt's mouth as he coughed, confirming that internal bleeding was severe, and knowing that Curt was hemorrhaging into his stomach or lungs, perhaps both.

Vic could not speak; he felt the stinging wetness on his face from tears, picked his best friend up in his arms and began walking north to the Kurdish rendezvous point.

He felt someone pushing his left leg and knew one of the guards must still be alive. Turning, he instinctively reached out, feeling the guard's throat. He placed his thumbs on the soft area of the larynx and began squeezing. Vic felt the guard grab his wrists, pulling and tugging attempting to free himself from Vic's firm hold, hearing him gasping for air, knowing the guard would die soon, feeling long fingernails pressing and digging into his flesh. Long fingernails?

FINGERNAILS!

Vic opened his eyes and realized this was not an Iraqi guard, he was not in the desert, and he was not choking an enemy soldier. He was choking a passenger on the plane. Her eyes were tearing up and her mouth was open, her tongue was protruding between her lips in a final attempt to breathe and scream for help.

Vic loosened his grip and removed his hands, realizing she was now falling. He tried to catch her as she crumpled to the floor. The best he could do was to keep her from landing too hard on the floor in the aisle between the seats of the airplane.

PART ONE

Day One
Flight between Dallas and Quito, Ecuador

Vic grasped the arm rests with his fingers, pressing the soft padded leather until his forearms begin shaking, then quickly unbuckled his seatbelt and slid to his knees leaning into the aisle. He clamped his jaws tightly, gritting his teeth and muttered, "Damn it!" more to himself than anyone else.

He thought back to that fateful day in Baghdad, wondering if the memory would ever get better, knowing the death wasn't totally his fault, but still felt the twang associated with 'survivor's guilt' syndrome.

He noticed the lady's eyes were closed and she appeared to be unconscious. He put his right hand to her neck, feeling for a pulse. Oh God, did I kill her? He thought.

Vic swallowed hard and quietly asked, "Miss, Miss are you okay? I am so sorry, it wasn't on purpose!"

The young lady opened her eyes and tensed her body; she tried to scoot away from Vic, pushing with the heels of her shoes against the legs of the seat. She felt dazed, light headed and confused. She saw the man who owned the backpack. Had he caught her putting the turtle inside the zippered flap? She tried to remember, but only remembered his hands around her throat, then darkness, until waking on the floor.

Vic reached out and put his hands under her right arm to help her to her feet. Her body tensed and she jerked away, putting her hands on the floor trying to scoot further from him. Vic could see the fear on her face. He swallowed and hung his head.

Vic slowly lifted his head, looking into her eyes, feeling lower than snake shit, he softly said. "I'm trying to help."

She looked at him, her eyes locked on his. She looked at the blue backpack beside his knees and leaned forward reaching out her left hand.

"Miss, I'm so sorry, I didn't mean to hurt you."

Elena realized with his apology that he was not aware that she snuck the turtle into his backpack. She looked at the backpack again, and then looked at Vic, then pulled her hand back.

She felt the shame of smuggling, the responsibility of her brother's life resting on her performance. She was told this was to be her final shipment for Ithaca Exports and Señor Cordova. That Eduardo would be released if she delivered the turtle. Have I been discovered she thought as tears began to flow down her cheeks.

Vic saw the overhead lights come on and saw the flight attendant kneel down in the aisle. He looked at her and said," It's my fault."

"What did you do?" she asked.

Elena quickly reached out and grabbed the Flight Attendant's arm and tugged as though she would help her to her feet, while looking at Vic and thought I can't let him find out.

Elena cleared her throat then hoarsely whispered, "I tripped."

Vic looked at the young lady on the floor, trying to sense why she lied; perhaps she is oxygen starved and really thinks she tripped. He noticed her fixation on his backpack or at least on the floor near his knees. He heard the long, silent pause and saw her looking at him again. "I tripped," she finally announced again in a stronger sounding voice.

Vic jerked as though snapping to attention, feeling a spark of hope. "What the hell?" he sighed with a feeling of relief in his voice.

The flight attendant stood and helped Elena to her feet and asked, "What is your name?"

"Elena, my name is Elena."

"Would you like something to drink, perhaps a bottle of cool water?"

"Si, por favor, yes please, water would help I think," Elena answered in a raspy voice.

"Here, sit in this seat for moment and make certain you didn't hurt yourself," she instructed, pointing at Vic's seat then walked to the galley.

Elena looked at Vic's aisle seat, but moved to the vacant window seat. I hope I can pull this off, if she makes me move back to coach, I will lose sight of him when we deplane. Oh, this might have been a bad idea, she thought.

Vic took his seat and noticed her staring at his shoes and wondered why she was protecting him, but found no answers that made sense.

What the hell was I thinking! Vic thought as he watched her rub her throat. Crap, this is all I need, a scandal in the papers, and on the TV.

Vic knew if Elena told the flight attendant what had actually happened he would be placed under guard by the Air Marshal. After landing he would be arrested and escorted to jail. Vic also knew that an assault on any flight carried a potential five year prison term and if he were arrested he could kiss the multimillion dollar deal with Ecuador goodbye; rendering the past three months of work fruitless.

The flight attendant returned and leaned in to the seat, getting Elena's attention.

"Do you feel well enough to return to your seat?"

Both Vic and the flight attendant saw the panic on Elena's face. Vic saw her turn her head and look at him, as though she would tell if she was forced to move.

Vic turned, looking at the flight attendant and said. "You know, that window seat was empty, I have the frequent flier miles to upgrade her or I can purchase the seat, if you will allow it."

The flight attendant looked at Vic and then at Elena, shrugged her shoulders and said, "Go ahead and stay in that seat, it'll be okay, Mr. James."

Vic pressed the button on the arm rest, reclined his seat back and closed his eyes. He began remembering back to Iraq and the long trip home with Curt's body on the plane, that long flight in the C-130 sitting in a jump seat next to a casket which was anchored to the floor. He remembered resigning his commission after Curt's funeral and how he tried to forget that time in his life, throwing himself into his work, but the memories would creep back like an incurable disease. The doctor's called it Post Traumatic Stress Disorder, but he simply referred to it as "the shits". Every time he began that stroll down memory lane it would culminate with tears on his cheeks and some sort of physical act. This time he choked an innocent, helpless, small, female passenger. "God, what evil lurks inside me", he thought to himself; searching for answers, wondering if his actions were solely from the intense training or if they had awakened and trained a hidden part of his soul, an evil soul.

Vic heard the rustling and clinking sounds of the curtain between the coach and first-class compartments being opened. He watched the flight attendant hurriedly walk past him toward the rear of the first-class compartment.

"Do you need something?" he heard her ask.

"I need the lavatory," a man said in a thick Spanish accent.

"You should use the lavatory in the rear of the plane. This lavatory is for first-class passengers only."

"But, I have to go now!" he demanded and heard her exhale quickly as though she was hit in the chest.

Vic heard her voice change from her normal tone to a strained growl, as if she were lifting weights at the gym.

"Sir, please use the lavatory in the coach compartment, you are not allowed in this section of the plane!"

Vic felt his seat back being pulled backward by the man trying to force himself past her. He unbuckled his seat belt and stood up, turning, he saw the man holding the red curtain to the side with his right arm, trying to look over the seat back into Elena's seat. He noticed the man was wearing a gray, long sleeve shirt and a blue ball cap with the Dallas Cowboys logo on the front. He had shaggy hair over his ears and it was apparent he hadn't shaved in several days.

She was standing with her right foot back, leaning on it for support, holding the back of Vic's seat. "Sir, if you do not step back I will call the Captain," she groaned.

Vic stepped into the aisle and noticed the man had forced her backward two rows from the curtain and was holding the seatback where he was sitting and pulling it backward as he leaned forward looking down at Elena.

Vic stepped forward and grabbed the man's left wrist, twisting it and pushing the ring and little fingers down towards his elbow with as much pressure as he could muster while standing in an awkward position leaning around the flight attendant.

"¡Ay!" he squealed in Spanish, glaring at Vic with tears in his eyes.

Vic saw his lips form a small "O", displaying yellow stained teeth and exhaling loudly, blowing a foul breath, laced with beer and tobacco. The man relaxed his arm in a surrendering gesture, followed by Vic releasing his grip allowing the man to retreat back to the coach cabin.

Vic watched him return to an aisle seat about mid-cabin area of the coach section, before relaxing. He stepped backward away from her, realizing he was applying force to her left shoulder as he leaned over her.

"He seemed intent on using this lavatory didn't he?" Vic exclaimed.

"Yes, but he wanted something else. He did not go to the lavatory in the coach cabin either, very strange. Thank you for helping me."

She picked up his empty glass and looked up at him for a moment. "He scared me..." she trailed off and walked back to the galley.

Vic took his seat and closed his eyes again, remembering Ralph's office; seeing a photograph of the Oval Office, surrounded by several military ribbons and medals, on the wall behind Ralph's desk reminding him of his meeting at the White House with the

President. The two Bronze Stars and the Silver Star from the Air Force were in his display case on his mantle in his home in Austin, and the Distinguished Intelligence Cross from the CIA he received for heroic duties during Desert Storm was still in the vault at CIA headquarters in Langley, Virginia.

Vic remembered the meeting with Ralph and instinctively knew it was not going to be a standard presentation, especially when Ralph asked that one question.

"Mr. James, are you proud to be American? I mean, are you really proud to be an American; would you stand up for Freedom, Lady Justice and Apple Pie?"

Ralph continued probing and prodding for sensitive information and finally asked point blank what Vic's military duties were. Vic remembered responding that he was assigned simple duties trying to offer general terms and avoid the conversation.

"What were your duties in the Air Force?" Ralph pressed again.

"Simple duty, nothing important."

"Oh, nothing important, huh? Are you familiar with the Air Force's Official Security Investigation, better known as the OSI?" Ralph asked.

Vic remembered that old feeling coming back, knowing he was being recruited. The pilot's voice woke Vic from his snooze. The pilot announced that due to wind speeds in excess of forty miles per hour it was too risky to attempt a landing at the Mariscal Sucre International Airport in Quito at this time.

Vic straightened his seat back, looking to his right he noticed Elena watching him, he smiled.

She leaned over toward Vic, her blouse sagging open, with the top two buttons unbuttoned, revealing a clear view of her perfect cleavage and a glimpse at the top of her breasts.

"Excuse me, Señor. Have you traveled to Quito before?" she asked in English with only a slight Spanish accent.

Vic noticed her now, really for the first time. Her hair was dark brown and seemed to sparkle with natural streaks of amber, creating a healthy, glossy look that rested just below her shoulders. She had large honey-brown eyes and a beautiful Latin complexion that highlighted her perfectly smooth skin. Her face was heart shaped with high cheekbones and the corners of her mouth were curled up with the top lip showing white teeth when she smiled. Her figure was…well, something I would like to explore further he thought. She was definitely model material, reminding him of a model in Sports Illustrated Swimsuit Edition. She was wearing tight jeans and a pink, long-sleeve cotton blouse with the top two buttons open. The blouse was tight and he could make out the contour of her bra cups as she leaned forward, straining the cloth material.

Were both buttons open earlier? Vic shook his head, bringing his attention back to her question. "Yes, I've been here many times, my company has an office in Quito," Vic said, watching her sit back in her seat, perhaps more relaxed than before, noticing her eyes darting from his eyes to his feet.

"Look, is there anything I can do to make up for the trip, chok-, uh, incident?"

"Like what?" she asked.

"I know a doctor in Quito who can look at your throat and make sure you're going to be okay."

"Perhaps that would help," she said, placing her left hand to her throat and grimacing slightly, then making a slight guttural sound as she cleared her throat.

Vic looked at her for a few moments and realized he was staring at her. She was so pretty he had difficulty breaking his gaze from her. He had a desire to rest his eyes on her as though she was therapeutic.

Elena watched him, hoping he would make a pass at her. Vic fought against the draw her sensuous beauty was having on him. He wanted to ask why she lied to protect him, but thought it best to leave it alone.

She turned to him and asked, "You know a doctor who could help me?"

"Yes, I could ask that he look at you."

"I am feeling much better now," She briefly looked down at the backpack, then back into his eyes. "Perhaps a doctor is a good idea though," she said.

The pilot announced more bad news. "Ladies and gentlemen, we cannot land in Quito tonight due to the high winds that are common at almost ten-thousand-feet elevation. We have been diverted to Guayaquil, a city about thirty minutes southwest of Quito on the west coast of Ecuador and at sea level. I apologize for the inconvenience this may cause, but remember, safety first."

Twenty minutes later the plane landed with a thump, Elena turned to look out the window, while fidgeting. Vic noticed she was very nervous, even more than when Heather questioned her seat assignment.

She turned back toward Vic and leaned way over, allowing the blouse to sag seductively again, with the top three buttons unbuttoned now.

"Excuse me again Mr. James, I am not prepared to stay in a hotel, I was expecting to be home tonight. Do you know if the airlines will help with a hotel?"

"I'm certain they will; it's not our fault we didn't land in Quito." Vic replied while looking down her open blouse, which revealed well shaped breasts in a very sexy bra.

She slowly, with movements of a strip tease artist, sat back in her seat, buttoning the third button as though she could reveal her treasure again for him when she was ready.

She looked out the window, watching the airport traffic as they taxied on the tarmac. Her hands, busy buttoning and unbuttoning the third button on the blouse.

She leaned over once again looking into his eyes and leaning slightly to her left to provide an even more seductive view down her open blouse. Sensing that he was almost ready to explode, she softly and in a raspy voice said, "My name is Elena Torres"

"My name is Vic James," he replied and offered his hand. He shook her hand and noticed it was soft and delicate. She is so tiny he thought, as he felt her hand and fought to break the mental tug to drop his eyes to her breasts again.

She looked at him for a full minute as though she was inspecting for insects. She saw that he was very good looking, handsome in a rugged sense. The light blue polo shirt and jeans seemed to remind her of the kind of men you see in catalogs. His smile was friendly, displaying perfectly aligned teeth and his blue-grey eyes were very soft and comforting.

The plane pulled slowly to the terminal gate of the International Airport at Guayaquil, Ecuador, Vic felt the front dip slightly and knew the pilot had set the brakes. He heard the rustling and clicking as the other passengers released their seatbelts and Vic stood up in the aisle. He reached down for his backpack, placing it in the seat and reached into the overhead luggage compartment for his brief case and Elena's bag and placed them on floor.

Vic looked at her and felt a pang of guilt. "It has been interesting traveling with you," he said with an awkward feeling, noticing her nod slightly and briefly glance his way, but seemingly not fully aware of his presence.

Vic turned to his right and took two steps, when he spotted the man who attempted to force his way past the flight attendant. He turned back to Elena to watch her reaction as the man shuffled closer to the first class compartment. He saw a frightened and shocked face, a pretty face with fear on it, as though she wanted to run for help and knew there was no help, even in a crowded plane.

Vic watched as the wide eyes seemed to break away from the cowboy, and focused on him now. He stood in the aisle waiting for her to go first. He noticed she now seemed to realize he was on the plane, as though the cowboy caused her mind to do a reset. Then he heard her say, "Yes and very painful," as though the lapse in time was common for her.

She reached out and lightly caressed his right forearm with her fingernails in an obvious gesture, smiling very seductively again.

He fought the urge to pursue the gesture which she was making, feeling as though it was more of an offer than a simple gesture. He turned and began to shuffle back towards the open door from the first-class cabin. Stepping onto the jet-bridge, he saw the Spanish man in an obvious hurry, about thirty feet in front of him and walking fast.

Vic felt the warm sea breeze on his face as it was blowing in from the coast, whipping through the openings between the jet-bridge and the plane's body.

He turned to ask if she wanted to have her throat checked here in Guayaquil or wait until she reached Quito. He was shocked and had a feeling of relief at the same time, as she quickly slipped around him pulling her bag behind her, obviously ignoring him as though she was rushing to meet someone. He noticed the bag making a clacking sound every time the broken wheel made a rotation, hearing the echo in the long, brightly lit corridor.

Vic followed the other passengers as they made their way into the terminal building to the international flights luggage claim area. The walls were painted a bright white; the room always reminded him of a sterile area, with large overhead lights hanging from the ceiling casting long shadows on the floor. Vic walked to the metal ramps and watched for his luggage to be off-loaded from the luggage cars as the baggage handlers made trip after trip from the plane.

There were no pictures on the walls, only the sign that stated Aduyana, with the word Customs written in English underneath with a large black arrow pointing to the adjacent room through large, heavy metal swinging doors where the steel inspection tables were located. Everyone, it seemed had a large cart, similar to a flat-bed cart at a home improvement store, to put their luggage on so they could roll it to the inspecting tables.

Vic noticed Elena place her carryon bag on a cart and seemingly sneak a glance at him, then exit through the doors, making a mental note that she had no checked luggage.

His suitcase was on the last luggage train delivered from the plane, arriving ten minutes later. He picked up his suitcase and placed it on the cart, with his briefcase and backpack, then proceeded through the door.

He saw the sign for "Non-Residents" and got into the line for "Nothing To Declare". A guard inspected his luggage as Vic answered a few text messages on his satellite phone, then nodded his approval.

Vic walked through the exit doors into the main terminal building, letting out a long sigh of relief, feeling his shoulders relax for the first time since he choked Elena. He started toward the airline ticket counter and saw Elena walk out of the restroom across the terminal and saw her quickly turn her head away from him, almost as if she didn't want him to recognize her.

He realized how tired he felt and decided not to stand in line at the ticket counter for a food voucher and cheap motel. He turned to his left and started for the main terminal exit and saw Elena stop and walk back into the restroom.

He walked through the large double doors, out to the curb; the smell of the sea was strong, a swift warm breeze was blowing in. The faint smell of salt mingled with dead was fish in the air.

"Taxi Señor?" Vic heard a young boy call out from behind him as he approached the curbed taxi island.

"Si, por favor," Vic responded as he continued walking, hearing staccato footsteps as the boy trotted past him to the taxi stand.

The boy waived for the next taxi in line, and waited as a ninety's model, well-dented red Chevrolet, pulled up to the curb. The young boy grabbed Vic's suitcase and walked to the rear of the car, Vic watched him place the suitcase in the trunk and slam the lid.

Vic handed the boy a five dollar bill, "Gracias; thank you sir," the boy said, opening the rear door for Vic.

Vic heard a voice from behind him calling his name, "Mr. James, Mr. James."

He turned and there she was, standing in the darkened shadows of the trees, her sexy silhouette against the white, concrete wall of the airport terminal.

He watched her slowly walking toward the taxi, with a gentle sway in her hips. "Can you give me a ride please, Mr. James?" she pleaded in a very quiet innocent voice.

"Sure, come on get in," Vic said, pushing and stepping back from the open rear door. The boy changed his direction, realizing the young lady was going with him and he gave the boy another five dollar tip, while watching him put Elena's tattered bag in the trunk. Vic then climbed into the taxi behind Elena.

He knew she was following him, but couldn't quite put his finger on the reason why, he answered his paranoid feeling with the fact he had choked her and that she wanted the doctor he had promised.

"Take me to the Hotel Rio de Oro, please," Vic told the driver again as he got into the car.

Vic noticed Elena had not moved to the far side of the taxi and was watching him closely as he stepped into the taxi. Vic pushed against her with his left shoulder until she finally slid across far enough to allow him room to sit and close the door. He placed the briefcase with his computer on the driveshaft tunnel and his backpack on the briefcase, forcing her to move her feet to the left of the tunnel.

She cleared her throat several times with an exaggerated, raspy growl as though trying to cough up a fur ball and said. "My throat is bothering me." She began rubbing her throat with her left hand.

Vic pulled his wallet from his right back pocket and took out two one-hundred dollar bills. He handed them to Elena. "Here, take this cash and get a hotel room and have your throat checked at the hospital tomorrow morning."

"I don't have a place to stay tonight," she sobbed.

"Bullshit, that's not true; the airline will provide lodging and meals for you and fly you up to Quito in the morning, at no charge to you. Besides, I'm trying to give you enough money to buy a room for a week, so I know you can afford one night!"

"You said you knew a doctor who could help me."

"Yes, in Quito or you can take the cash and see any doctor you wish."

The taxi stopped at a traffic light, Elena suddenly leaned forward and grabbed for Vic's backpack, which lay close to her feet and opening the door with her left hand, at the same time. Vic felt the sudden movement, looked at her and noticed she was stealing his backpack. He clinched his left fist and popped her in the side of the head pretty hard, watching as she fell back against the seat with a dazed and defeated look in her eyes and Vic noticed the taxi driver looking in his rearview mirror with fear in his eyes.

Vic grabbed the backpack from her grasp, stuffing it under his right arm, as an NFL running back would secure the football.

"Get out now!" Vic yelled. He watched her open the door wider to step out then pulled her foot back into the cab, slamming the door. She reached for his arm, not to hit, but more as an apologetic gesture.

"Don't touch me, leave me alone! Take the money."

"Please, sir, please help me tonight," Elena pleaded.

"No, I can't help you tonight or any other night. Now leave me alone! Tell the driver where to take you?"

"Drive, damn it!" Vic yelled pulling another twenty dollar bill from the money clip and tossed it into the front seat. "Andale, rapido!"

The driver sped off, running the red light gripping the steering wheel with both hands letting the twenty dollar bill whirl around the front seat in the wind that was blowing in through the open windows. Vic noticed her door was not securely closed, leaned over her, pushed the door open and closed it securely as the taxi was careening down the street.

Vic turned toward the young lady, "What the hell is wrong with you?" he asked.

He noticed she set without moving the rest of the trip to the hotel. He grew concerned that he had hit her too hard and perhaps knocked her unconscious. He couldn't tell in the dark and the street lights passed by to swiftly for him to see if her eyes were open.

Elena felt the panic return. He now knows that I want his backpack. I must convince him that I can fulfill his needs tonight. Oh, I hate my life!

The taxi slowed as they approached the hotel and Vic turned to look at her, noticing she was looking back at him, appearing unhurt, perhaps just dazed or simply laying in ambush for him, many thoughts raced through his mind.

Several moments later the taxi pulled up to the Rio de Oro hotel. Vic watched the doorman jump from his stool, meeting the car when it stopped. He opened Vic's door and walked around the car and opened the door for Elena.

Vic stepped out holding his briefcase and backpack tightly, handing the taxi driver the fare and another twenty dollar bill.

He stopped and quickly turned, leaning through the front passenger window, he said, "Take her somewhere, anywhere, but here."

He walked to the rear of the car as the doorman unlocked the trunk with the key that was in the lock and retrieved both suitcases from the trunk of the taxi, and placing them on the concrete drive way, waiting to follow Vic into the hotel.

"That one is mine the other one, the ripped suitcase; it stays with her! I don't want it!"

The doorman reeled at Vic's angry statement and watched as Elena quickly hopped out the other side of the car and ran around, where they were standing.

The doorman moved her suitcase to the side and put Vic's on the sidewalk. He watched Elena now standing in front of Vic, noticing her demeanor which indicated she was prepared to do battle or beg for mercy, he wasn't sure which. He watched Vic and wondered if he was going to hit her. The doorman was obviously concerned for her welfare and wondered how the battle would end; already thinking he would take her if Vic chased her off.

She stood there looking at Vic and began crying. She looked up at him and he saw the pale redness on her throat, the bump on her forehead and now a bruise on her right cheek bone.

"Elena, you've cost me over two hundred dollars since I met you and I still don't have a hotel room, much less know who you really are or what you want with me. Please, just go away!"

"I haven't cost you any money! I-I didn't take your money and I don-don't want your money. You can't buy me," she sobbed, her shoulders heaving uncontrollably.

"I'm not trying to buy you, just go away."

"I really like you."

"Yeah, I'll just bet you do. What did you slip into my backpack that you want back now? Don't play me for a fool. Customs was looking for something, too many inspectors and guards on duty tonight. They suspected you of having it, but I passed without question, since I come to Ecuador monthly.

What did I smuggle into the country for you? Lady, I don't need trouble!" Vic said and noticed the doorman watching the drama.

"I am sorry, Mr. James. I won't bother you. I can sleep on the street tonight," she said, watching the doorman reach for her suitcase again.

"I'm certain it won't be your first night working the streets."

Elena stood there looking at him with tears streaming down her pretty face. She took a step backward and turned to the doorman, taking the tattered bag that he handed her, when a small, pink makeup bag slipped between the ripped zippers and fell to the ground.

Vic noticed her look down at the makeup bag on the ground and started to shiver and shake as though it was her last straw before a complete emotional breakdown ensued; her feet stomping the concrete.

"Take the money and go," Vic offered once more, extending his hand with the cash.

"I don—don't want your money, I'm sure I will be safe without anyone's help."

Vic waited for a long moment, hoping she would take the cash and leave, knowing that as much as he wanted to, he couldn't force her to stay on the street tonight. Crap there is a new bruise, he thought as he looked at her again. I'm beating the hell out of her, he thought to himself.

"Come on, it's too windy down here to discuss it, besides I feel very vulnerable out here with you, you can understand why, can't you? Your friends probably have me in their gun sights right now," Vic said while nervously looking over his right shoulder into the shadows of the trees against the adobe wall of the hotel.

"Get the lady's luggage," Vic told the doorman.

Vic saw the doorman struggling as he took her suitcase from her and placed it on the concrete. He reached for a small, red cart, resembling a child's pull wagon, like the old Radio Flyer and placed the suitcases on the wagon. He waited for Vic to walk through the door, following both of them, pulling the wagon.

Vic heard a taxi with an extra loud muffler pulling into the hotel's driveway. The car's exhaust was smoking as it pulled up to the door behind them. He looked back and noticed the man from the plane, the same man wearing the Dallas Cowboys cap, who attempted to get past the flight attendant, get out of the taxi. The man paid his fare and seemed to hurry as though he was tailing them. Vic remembered seeing him at the airport as he left customs and again when he walked through the terminal exit.

Coincidence he thought? Vic didn't believe in coincidences, he knew from his training and experience that believing in coincidences will often get a man dead and he was too busy to wind up dead. There's that paranoid feeling again, he thought.

Vic stepped up to the front desk. The doorman placed both suitcases on the floor in front of the desk, Vic handed him a ten dollar bill and watched as he returned to his post at the front lobby door; pulling the wagon behind him. Vic noticed she was now carrying the pink makeup bag in her left hand with her purse.

Elena watched the desk clerk; she was thinking that if he rented one room, it would allow her a definite chance to recover the turtle. If he got two rooms, but different floors, it would pose new challenges. She continued thinking when Vic requested two rooms with an adjoining door.

Elena felt exuberated, thinking she had a shot, that not all was lost yet. The clerk slid a form across the counter he read that rooms 407 and 409 were rented. The clerk nodded to the bellhop who was standing against the wall, who then scurried to the desk and placed the bags on a trolley.

She wanted to be near enough to this man to steal the turtle back. If he makes me stay in a different room, he might leave in the morning before I can get the turtle. She felt the world closing in on her again, feeling as though she would be at the mercy of Juan, who was now in the hotel.

Vic saw the cowboy across the lobby sitting on a sofa, holding a magazine, but looking over the top towards the front desk. Vic knew that he was following them, but not certain if he was following him or her.

Elena felt renewed and smiled at the desk clerk then looked up at Vic, seeing his soft blue-grey eyes as he stood there with a kind of smile that was between a smirk and a grin.

Vic noticed the cowboy was paying close attention to the front desk, but seemed to want to appear nonchalant. He picked up the magazine again, as though he was reading an article, however, Vic noticed the magazine was now upside down.

Vic turned toward the trolley and nodded to the elevator as he winked at the bellhop and grinned slightly, as if to say, it's late and I'm tired and watched as the desk clerk handed him both room keys.

She began thinking that she had to make him feel superior, that he would command her to be his for the night and she would then tease him until he gave her the turtle.

Elena quietly followed Vic and the bellhop to the elevator, Vic noticed she seemed timid, perhaps out of character while standing in the corner of the elevator. When the doors opened, he held back, waiting for her to exit following the bellhop.

Vic waited as the bellhop unlocked her door, concerned that she didn't enter her room, but walked with Vic into his room. The bellhop crossed the room and opened the door between the two rooms and walked back to Vic's door.

"Buenas noches, have a pleasant evening," the bellhop said, reaching for the five dollar tip, Vic was holding, he closed the door behind him.

Vic turned to Elena, nodded toward the open connecting doorway, leading the way he carried her suitcase into her room and gently placed it on the bed. Turning around he saw her standing in the center of her room, arms crossed and smiling, a friendly expression on her face, he quietly stated, "This room is yours for the night."

Vic turned and began walking to the connecting door, she pivoted to her left keeping her focus on him, he stopped at the door and turned around, watching as she backed up a couple of feet against the bed while looking at him. She had the sickening feeling that if he walked into his room all would be lost. She placed her left hand on the bed and smiled at Vic.

Vic, ignoring her, turned and walked through the door, pushing the door gently letting it partially close. He ignored me she thought. She stepped toward the door, peeking into his room she saw him walk to the small square table, while looking at his wrist watch.

Vic noticed the time was almost two in the morning. He felt tired, not only had he lost an hour due to the time-zone change from central to eastern, but he was now saddled with this gal, which was causing extra stress. I'd better find out what I'm smuggling before going to bed, he thought.

He looked at her door and saw her peeking at him. "Elena, would you please come here."

She looked through the crack at Vic, wondering what he was going to do to her, but knowing her only chance was to be in his room. She tensed her muscles, smoothed her blouse and attempted to straighten her hair. She started back to the dresser to look in the mirror when she heard him talking again.

"Lady, get in here, we need to talk."

"Did you want me?" she asked softly, feeling her stomach turning with fear and started into his room.

"Sit down, I want to know what I smuggled into Ecuador for you."

Elena froze, she took two steps back, her eyes were wide with fear and she felt perspiration starting to bead on her forehead. She heard his voice, but the words seemed to be distant, as though from far away. She continued retreating back into her room.

"Get in here and sit down."

"I want to take a bath first," she said, hoping to get him to follow her to her room, allowing her a chance to grab the backpack and make it out the door.

"Not until we get a couple of things straightened out first. So get in here and sit your ass down. Now!" Vic commanded, grabbing his backpack and slamming it on the table. "If you make me break something, I'm going to get really pissed!"

Elena slowly and cautiously walked into his room. She looked at him and took off her high heel shoes, pitching them toward his bed, gauging the distance between the table and the door.

She sat down at the table. Vic noticed that she would not look him in the eyes, but rather stared at a cigarette burn mark on the edge of the table.

"What am I going to find in here that's not mine?" he demanded, taking a seat in the chair across from hers.

She reached out her left hand toward the backpack as though she was stopping traffic in an intersection. "Okay, stop. I put something in there while you were asleep on the plane earlier," she quietly admitted.

"Well, let's see what gifts you bring," Vic persisted, noticing that she was now twirling a strand of her hair in her right fingers, her eyes were darting between the backpack and the door, indicative of a snatch and grab maneuver being cooked up in her mind.

He opened the backpack flap, seeing a small, white Onyx turtle, the same type of turtle for sale in tourist shops for a couple of dollars.

Vic removed the turtle from the backpack and held it up for a closer look, estimating that it was about three inches long and two inches wide and about an inch thick at the hump of the turtle's back.

He turned it over and saw a label affixed to the belly, a white label with black lettering, stating that the turtle was purchased from Ithaca Exports souvenirs and antiquities in Dallas, Texas. The label was torn at one corner, appearing as though it was removed from some other item and hastily placed on the turtle.

He slipped his index fingernail under the label, pulling up, watching it fall to the table, curled up like a tight cash register receipt.

Vic looked up, seeing her move her left hand to the edge of the table, slowly slipping her fingers under the edge and tightening her thumb on the top, her forearm muscles rippling, as they flexed.

"Don't even think about grabbing for this damned turtle, hoping you can reach the chained door before I knock the crap out of you," Vic snarled, watching her eyes for the telltale squint before her move. He saw her eyes widen slightly and relax.

He exhaled slowly and continued, inspecting the turtle again, this time top and bottom, seeing what appeared to be a straight line, like a cut in the Onyx that wasn't part of the original mold.

He reached into the backpack and grabbed his fingernail clippers. He stood and walked to the bed side lamp, which was on the small table, setting on the bed and leaning toward the lamp, he adjusted the lamp shade to shine more light toward him. The bulb was a small wattage causing him to squint, while holding the turtle under the lamp, looking at it closer, slowly rotated the turtle.

"What are you doing to my turtle?" she demanded.

"I am trying to find out why you were smuggling it."

Vic put pressure on the small scratch mark and pushed down with the file blade and noticed a slight give to the line, then pop. The file broke through the thin underbelly of the turtle. He noticed the piece that broke was a small square plate similar to a flat battery compartment cover in a television remote, the edges of the small plate were concealed with glue, then prying up the plate, he removed it.

"Please don't break my turtle, I can't deliver it if it is broken," she pleaded.

He ignored her remark and said, "I sincerely doubt the customs inspectors would have found this hidden compartment, hell I wouldn't have looked if I simply found the turtle, but since you were smuggling it, I am looking a little closer to see what the hell I smuggled for you!"

After removing a thin piece of foam rubber under the plate, he saw the treasure she was smuggling. A tiny Micro SD card was wedged into the compartment and he immediately thought of the recent news reports about the Iranian nuclear facility being attacked by a computer virus which was reportedly delivered by a flash memory card.

He walked back to the table and watched her return and take her seat again, he looked past her, into her room and saw her purse on the bed. He asked, "What do you do?"

"I am a student," she quietly replied, looking intently at the two pieces of the turtle lying on the table and the memory card in his hand.

He stood and walked into her room, turning back, seeing she was focused on the turtle, he opened her purse and saw her passport. He confirmed the picture was of her, and then looked at her name and birthdate. He closed the passport and saw an airline voucher partially folded, including two meals and a motel room in her name. He quickly returned to the table.

He focused his attention on her eyes when asked, "Did you say you were a student?"

She raised her head slightly and softly began, "Yes, I am a student at the Catholic University in Quito. I also attend UT Austin, working on an MA degree."

"What is your Major?"

"Linguistics and International languages, focusing on French, English, Spanish and Mandarin Chinese."

"Linguistics uh? What are your specific courses this semester?"

"I am taking Syntax I and Semantics II. Why?"

"Doesn't matter," Vic said grabbing a pen and writing the classes on a small note pad he carried in his backpack.

"Who are your professors?"

"Dr. Kline teaches Syntax and Professor Stubbs teaches Semantics and Phonetics. Why are you so interested in that? Please just give me back the card, you can keep the turtle."

"Did you receive a voucher for a motel room tonight?"

"Uh…" He saw her bow her head, then look up at him. "Yes, I did," she finally said.

Vic opened his satellite phone and scrolled to text. He typed a message to Lisa, asking her to use her government contacts to verify that Elena Torres was enrolled at UT Austin and was in a class taught by Dr. Kline, and to request a character reference and GPA.

"So why are you smuggling?" he asked, sending the text.

"I am not smuggling," she replied, looking down at the table.

"What do you call this?" he said holding up the turtle.

She set back in her chair without responding to the question, a dejected look on her face. Vic noticed that she was now in a posture as though she was surrendering to him, her shoulders attempting to thrust her breasts toward him, perhaps as a trade he thought, just what a whore would do.

"So what is your real name?"

"I told you Elena Torres."

"You look what, 19?"

"No, I am 24, born in 1989. Why do you care about my age?"

Vic realized she looked up and right when answering truthfully.

She sat quietly holding her slender hand out for several moments, thinking, I must trade for the card, but how? What would he want? He has money and probably a girlfriend. He could buy whatever I could trade, God I hate Cordova.

"Listen, I risked going to jail, maybe even my life, for this thing. I have a right to know what is on it. Do you understand me? I am pissed!"

He watched her for a few minutes, hoping she would discover that she was not going to win the battle.

"Okay, tell me why you snuck this turtle into my backpack."

She bit her lower lip and started, "My brother, Eduardo, was kidnapped by Señor Cordova. If I do not deliver this turtle he will be killed."

"What? What kind of BS are you telling me?" He noticed she looked up and right when speaking about her brother. He then said, "So you sneak items you are smuggling into pockets or backpacks of innocent people, then what, trade them back for sex?" Vic asked.

She looked down at the table and responded, "No, it's not like that."

"Cut the shit lady and tell me the truth!" Vic said turning on his laptop.

She remembered Señor Cordova approaching her on the university campus in Quito one day, informing her about her brother's accident. She went with him to his office and saw Eduardo sitting in the chair with his hands tied behind him, his face was bruised and bleeding, his shirt in shreds. There were large burn marks on his chest and under his right arm, he was crying and pleading for his life.

She remembered Señor Cordova telling her about Eduardo's theft of cocaine and that he was being punished. She remembered Cordova telling her that Eduardo would be executed if he didn't return the cocaine or the money he had sold the drugs for.

She watched as Eduardo begged for them to stop and told them that the cocaine was stolen while he waited for the buyer. Señor Cordova didn't believe his story and smiled at Julio. She watched as Julio hit Eduardo again.

Señor Cordova then offered her a deal to save her brother. Since she had a reason to visit Texas, she could save her brother's life, if she agreed to escort shipments for him. She sadly looked at Eduardo's swollen face, then looked into Señor Cordova's face and realized that he held the power to save or take Eduardo's life. She accepted the trade. She remembered being dropped off at the Catholic Church where she stayed while in Quito, with instructions to be ready for a short trip the next afternoon.

A man met her at her at the church and delivered her to Señor Cordova's office in Perucho, she remembered Cordova leering at her with an evil smile while he drove her to the hotel in Perucho.

He introduced her to Rosita and a policeman who was at the bar. He then told Rosita to dance for him. Rosita began dancing, until he grabbed her arm and slapped her very hard in the face, knocking to the floor, grabbing her hair; he pulled her up to a sitting position on the floor.

"Where is the package from Dallas," he demanded.

"I gave it to Juan when I returned to the airport in Quito," she cried.

"He said you did not have the package and I want my money now!"

He slapped her again then kicked her in the face twice while she lay on the floor, she whimpered for a few moments then lay quiet, moving her right arm slightly to her bruised face.

"I want my money you whore!" he bellowed and kicked her several more times until she stopped moving.

Elena remembered seeing Julio walk into the hotel bar, the ugly scar stretching from under his right eye to his chin, and knew she would never forget his scar or his evil, crooked grin. She remembered thinking that even the policeman seemed scared of Señor Cordova.

"Here Julio, take this whore and convince her to tell you where my money is," Señor Cordova said then stormed out of the bar as the policeman followed. Elena often wondered if Rosita ran away after that night.

Señor Cordova will rape me she thought, or give me to Julio. He will then kill Eduardo, before he beats me more, there will be pain, lots of pain and I don't like pain, I have to get the turtle back, but how she thought. She watched Vic slowly rotate the small memory card he had removed from the turtle.

She felt as though she should speak and tried, but the best she could do was mumble the words as she said, "Eduardo is my brother, and if I do not deliver the turtle he may die."

Vic interrupted her thoughts when he said, "Okay, you are smuggling a Micro SD card, I mean escorting an antique Micro SD card into Ecuador. At least it's not drugs. Do you even know what a Micro SD card is?" he asked.

"Of course, I'm not stupid. I just want to give the turtle to Señor Cordova."

Vic inserted the Micro SD card into the slot and watched the computer access the memory card. It was password protected. "Let's see what antique songs or information you have," he chuckled and activated the anti-virus program that ran continuously in the background.

Vic had graduated from UT Austin with a master's degree in computer science and had written the bulk of the programs for his company, SatCom. He also had spent many hours writing encryption programs to safeguard his intellectual property. The program he was currently using was what he referred to as fifth generation, considering what the government was currently using, the Advanced Encryption Standards, as fourth generation and borderline obsolete.

"Bingo, we are in," he said as he moved the cursor to the Run icon and clicked the Browse button, he noticed Elena looking at him as though he was nerdy, he ignored her.

"PNG files, uh?" Vic mumbled to himself as the program listed all the folders on the memory card.

"Mr. James please, for the last time, please, give me the turtle and the memory card. You don't understand what will happen if I do not deliver the turtle, my brother may be killed or—"

"I'll be a-look at this!" he exclaimed as he opened a folder titled Brazil currency.

He noticed that the folder contained three files; he clicked on the first one. A Brazilian-currency ten Real bill, front and back, was displayed on the monitor. At the bottom of the screen were options for entering serial numbers. The next file displayed a Brazilian fifty Real bill, then a one-hundred Real bill. Each denomination had a serial-number beginning option.

"Interesting, you can not only create authentic counterfeit bills, but can select serial numbers that have never been used or, more importantly, serial numbers that are in the system already. So Ithaca Exports is getting into the Brazilian treasury business? These look authentic!"

He clicked on the next folder entitled Mexico and discovered two folders, the first file in the folder contained the Mexican 20 pesos and the second file contained the 100 pesos denomination. He looked closely and realized they were flawless also.

Vic clicked on the last folder entitled United States and viewed the displayed images. He saw a ten dollar, twenty dollar and a one hundred dollar bill image, again with the serial-number beginning option. He scrutinized all three bills just as he had done to the Brazilian and Mexican currencies, even pulling bills from his wallet to use as comparisons.

"These all look genuine to me, with the correct paper you would be a very rich young lady until you were caught. Now I understand why you used the PNG format, it is a format that doesn't compress the data and prints the exact image of the original. For counterfeiting, that is what you would need. Of course you are well aware of that, aren't you? I can now also understand why you didn't send the data in a file over the internet, any compressing of the files might affect the minute detail of the currency images. Wouldn't take much to lose one bit that would leave a blank where a small green dot should be and only an inspector might catch something like that. So smuggle the memory file to the printing company, or titty bar where you work with the printer in the back room."

"It is not mine," she said dejectedly.

"I can understand counterfeiting the Dollar and perhaps the Brazilian Real, but I don't understand why anyone would want to counterfeit the Mexican peso, their money is almost worthless."

"Please, let me have the turtle so I can deliver it to Señor Cordova. Please!"

"Listen lady, you snuck this card into my luggage and by doing so, you brought me into your world of smuggling. I didn't ask for this, but now that I am involved, I will not allow you to continue with your counterfeiting operation."

Vic noticed that she appeared genuinely afraid of the Cordova character, hell she's part of the counterfeit ring he thought, as he watched her squirm in her chair.

"I'll do anything you wish, anything. I mean anything. I'm not that sort of girl, but I don't want my brother to be killed by Señor Cordova, I'll sleep with you tonight if you wish. Please, just give me the turtle," she said in a very shaky voice, as though she was riding The Zipper at the Texas State Fair.

Vic thought back to the unbuttoned blouse on the plane while noticing her fingers were fiddling with the top button on her blouse suggestively, leaving it unbuttoned and moving to the second button as she seemed to be going through the motions, but not actually looking at him the way a prostitute should be attempting to control him for a better tip.

He slowly forced himself to turn away from the amateurish show and gripped his fists to force himself back into reality.

"So customs was alerted to something being smuggled into the country tonight and figured you had it. I just happened to be a convenient mule that suited your purpose at the time; right so far?" Vic asked, shaking his head in amazed disappointment at his ignorance for being so naïve and equally amazed at her or

Cordova's brass balls for attempting the counterfeit operation, ignoring her sexual suggestions.

"I guess, if you say so," she said in a defeated tone as she continued crying and continued slowly opening her blouse.

"Lady, you must be on their radar and they are probably tailing you," he said thinking back to the guy in the oil burning car at the front door of the hotel. "Listen, it's late, and I don't know what to do about this right now, or you, as far as that goes. Go to bed. We'll decide tomorrow."

Vic stood up from the table and slipped the Micro SD card into his right jeans pocket. He noticed she continued setting with her blouse unbuttoned and appeared to be in shock. He started the shutdown procedure on the laptop and walked over and put his suitcase on the table, opened it and removed clean underwear and a shirt for the next day. He walked back to the table and closed his laptop.

He noticed she was still sitting at the table, with a very saddened face. He reached down and grasped her shoulders, pulling her up to her feet. She seemed dazed as he walked her to her room and put a battery-powered alarm on her doorknob, he wanted to know if she tried to leave her room as well as if someone attempted to get in.

"Please, Mr. James, please give me my turtle. I will do anything," she pleaded softly, then opened her blouse fully and pulled it off her shoulders.

"I thought you weren't a prostitute," Vic said, watching her slip her blouse off.

"I am not a prostitute!"

"Then put your blouse on. You are very attractive and damned sexy, but it's not going to work on me," Vic announced.

He returned to his room, closing, locking the door. He heard her begin crying. The gentleman in him wanted to reopen the door and help her, but the OSI agent in him insisted he stay clear. He knew though that she seemed to be telling him the truth about her brother. He looked at the mirror and acknowledged he wasn't sure what the truth was, but the memory card was definitely illegal.

Vic stretched dental floss between the adjoining room door and his outside door and balanced a chair against the floss with an ash tray on the seat of the chair, then placed his pocket change in the ash tray, balancing the chair so that if either door were opened the ash tray would slide off the chair and the pocket change would jingle.

He set the alarm on his phone, undressed and got into bed, putting the Micro SD card under his pillow. Vic lay there unable to sleep, thinking about the smuggling and the pretty lady in the next room, thinking out several scenarios, his primary fear was that the smuggling would be associated to him and SatCom. If he simply turned the memory card into the authorities, questions would be asked, and then President Mendoza's attorneys might view it as a potential problem and cancel the deal. If he alluded to the lady that he might return the memory card and turtle to her she wouldn't go to the police, at least not until the deal was finalized and that was his short term goal. He fell asleep dreaming about a complete failure because of her.

Chengdu Military Base
Sichuan Province, China
General Yi's Headquarters

General Yi, a Chinese man with a slight paunch, standing just over five and a half feet with his shoe lifts, walked into the building where his office was located. His slightly overweight frame diminished the extra inch of height which he coveted. His receding hair line caused him to appear slightly older than his age of thirty-seven years and he dealt with it by always wearing a hat or cap.

He was the base commander at Chengdu Military Base and Officer in Charge of "Clandestine Operations" for the North and South American continents. He dreamed of having the responsibility of all seven continents under his control, knowing that he could then manipulate the western powers, or more explicitly the United States, into his wishes with more control than the Chinese President seemed capable of doing.

He had learned to be a shrewd, savvy negotiator, always winning the pot on the table. Rarely walking away from a deal with a win-win, he strived for the win-lose every time, eager for the kill move against his opponent. He also knew how to read people's body communications when they were being interrogated or questioned, detecting when someone was lying to him; never allowing a second lie.

General Yi reviewed all intelligence information from his agents stationed on the two American continents, with close scrutiny of the intelligence from the United States. He offered ideas and suggestions for counter-intelligence being fed back to the CIA, FBI, NSA and Canada's Security Intelligence Service, the CSIS. He also monitored the intelligence data from the Latin American countries, but only kept close eyes on Panama, due to the canal, knowing that control of the canal was paramount to the shipping between Asia and the rest of the world.

General Yi had met with Microsoft and asked, or demanded that he be given the source code for all of their products. The request was denied until he announced to Microsoft, that China would develop a new operating system called Kylin[1], which would be based on the open operating system utilizing the Linux platform that would then be marketed as a competitor to Microsoft and sold worldwide. After he won the negotiated demand, his programmers and hackers spent over thirty months searching for and discovering many flaws in the code.

He subsequently convinced Cisco, Google and many other companies, to provide their source codes also, which allowed his programmers and hackers to make changes to the giant software products, allowing for closer scrutiny and control of the content of the web in China.

General Yi's programmers, led by Professor Szu, were now intimately knowledgeable with the source codes of the entire web's platforms; however, he needed unfettered access to the computers in the United States, all computers, not just the computers in the Washington D.C. area.

Laboratory 257
Plum Island, NY

Plum Island is located off the East end of Long Island and is accessible only by ferry. Laboratory 257 is one of the few buildings on the island and is one of two locations in the world which house the smallpox virus.

Many other viruses are also stored and researched in Lab 257, such as Ebola, Hemorrhagic fever, Congo, Lassa, and the Hanta virus to name a few.

John Bellamue, a service technician working for BioTech Solutions, was dispatched to Plum Island to install a chemistry analyzer. He drove to Cross Sound Ferry where he parked his company's van and unloaded his tool box and spare parts cases. He noticed a chill in the air as the sun was setting. He had been informed that the installation was to be performed during the evening shift at the lab.

He placed the strap of the oscilloscope over his shoulder and lugged the two cases to the ferry gate and showed his company identification along with his Pennsylvania's driver's license to the security guard at the window.

John's credentials were checked against the list on a clip board. The guard then helped John load his equipment onto the small ferry which was waiting to take him to Plum Island. The ferry was painted blue with red trim and was completely enclosed. The heaters were on which made the trip bearable as he set reviewing the latest technical bulletins regarding the C-4900 analyzer he was to install. He had confirmed the equipment arrival yesterday before driving out that afternoon. John thought it strange that he was the lone passenger on the ferry, he noticed that the floor was clean and even the benches in the cabin were cleaner than other ferry's he was on. Perhaps not many tourists visit Plum Island he thought.

John had never been to Plum Island and had never heard of the island until last week when he learned he was to install the analyzer. He was instructed to bring a change of clothes with him in case he misplaced his clothes which sounded ludicrous. How can I misplace my clothes he wondered? Perhaps his tools, but he didn't plan on taking his clothes off.

The ferry's engines slowed and he heard a voice over the loud speakers advising him to remain seated until the green light was lit. When the green light was illuminated he stood and picked up his delicate oscilloscope and exited the ferry cabin. He walked to the right side of the ferry and saw that someone had placed his tool box and parts case near the exit gate. He picked up his equipment and walked down the gang plank to the dock, feeling better once he was on solid ground. He was met by another security guard wearing sunglasses and was told to walk to the waiting van in the parking lot. As he got close to the white van he read the stenciled lettering on the door, "Department of World Health". The sliding door opened and another guard helped him load the equipment into the van, Ray then got into the front seat and fastened his seat belt. The van sped off on a narrowly paved road over a small rise. John noticed that there were no trees or vegetation except a few patches of fresh cut grass. He noticed that there were white rocks, perhaps an inch in diameter, in beds around the few trees and lining the few buildings and sidewalks. He wondered why there was such sparse vegetation. It was definitely not typical for an island in New York. He wanted to ask the guard, but the guy seemed as though he didn't want to talk, so John sat with just his thoughts. He had the strange feeling that the island was some sort of prison or perhaps a convent for monks.

The van stopped at a large building that was painted a dull white with no signs except a number over the door which read 257 in black. Another guard walked from the building and opened the door, helped John carry his equipment into the building, and placed it on a waist high counter.

The guard checked the cases for cameras and recording equipment. The guard recorded everything that John had brought with him on a form attached to a clip board; even the extra box of small screws and nuts, then nodded his approval. Another guard placed the equipment onto a flatbed cart and said, "Follow me". John followed him through a door with a sign that read 'Men's locker room'.

The guard stopped and turned, looking at John's coat and tie, then smiled, "Strip down and put your clothes in this locker," he said, while pointing to a metal bank of lockers against the wall, with the locker on the end standing open. John noticed all the other locker doors had locks securing the handles, he wondered if he would receive a key for his lock.

"I'm here to install equipment not work out."

"Yes sir, but the equipment you are installing is located in the lab and you can't wear clothes in the lab so empty your pockets and put everything in this tub, then strip and place all your clothes in that locker," the guard said holding out a plastic tub with his left hand and pointing to the end locker with his right index finger.

John began taking off his clothes, stripping down to his skivvies, he stood waiting for the guard to turn back around, feeling cold.

The guard turned back around and looked at John standing with goose bumps on his arms and legs and smiled, "Everything comes off. You have to shower before entering the lab."

John took off his boxers and put them in the locker and slowly closed the door with a feeling of dread. He followed the guard to the door under the sign reading 'Showers'. The guard held the door open and John passed it hesitantly, watching the guard close the door. John heard water dripping then jumped when warm water hit him from all sides, even under his feet which tickled. The water warmed his body, he started rubbing his chest as though he had a bar of soap in his hands, feeling silly and thinking about an article he had recently read about learned behavior. The water lasted less than a minute then a female voice over a PA system instructed him to pass through the shower and lift his arms over his head. He walked through the door with his arms raised, the female voice told him to close his eyes tightly. He was then hit with high pressured hot air which dried him fairly quickly.

Please exit, the female voice instructed and John walked through a heavy opaque plastic curtain. John watched a different guard walking toward him and felt very conscientious, dropping his hands for modesty and saw the guard holding his eyes at face level and hand him a thin, blue set of coveralls and a grey plastic suit. The guard helped him put the coveralls on followed by a suit which included a masked headgear and latex gloves. As John struggled into the coveralls and plastic suit he wondered if the woman could see him in the shower.

After dressing the guard stepped back, then walked completely around John, tugging and pulling at the plastic suit, "My name is Ray. You look secure, follow me I'll take you to the lab and stay with you all day. If you find that you need anything that you didn't have checked at the front door, I'll get it for you. The cafeteria serves a meal at midnight."

"Would that be lunch?" John asked.

"Yes and we have to go back out through the showers to eat in the cafeteria."

John felt his wits begin to reemerge; he had felt very intimidated since taking off his clothes. He slowly did a complete three-sixty, "What the hell is this place?" he asked, feeling the echo of his voice in the plastic hood.

"We do research here," Ray replied.

John saw the C-4900 sitting in a corner. He walked over to the analyzer and noticed his equipment was on the floor beside the analyzer.

"Is it okay to start?"

"Sure, I'll be here if you need any help," Ray said then walked to a table, set down and started reading a magazine.

John began the installation procedure. Removing the panels was difficult with the gloves he was wearing. He worked until noon.

"Do you want to break for lunch?" Ray asked.

"Yeah, I guess so," John replied, looking at the clock on the wall, confirming why he felt so tired.

He followed Ray to the changing room then through the shower and into another changing room where he was given white coveralls to wear. He dressed and followed Ray to the cafeteria and selected the meatloaf and potatoes meal option from the serving line and set with Ray at a long table with several ladies who were visiting and talking, while they were eating.

"I do not want to move to Kansas, too many tornadoes and besides my husband said Dorothy died," the other ladies laughed and one of them eyed John as he ate his meal.

"Who do you work for?" she asked.

"I'm with BioTech Solutions, and here to install the C-4900 analyzer," she made a face of despair, rolled her eyes and shook her head in disbelief.

"Ray, why are they installing a new analyzer if we are relocating?" she asked.

"The old one cratered and they couldn't get some of the parts to repair it so someone decided to install a new analyzer. It doesn't make sense, but that's our taxes at work," Ray announced with authority in his voice.

"Typical. Well I saw Dr. Lewis rolling the smallpox trays back into the vault. I guess he completed his testing and inventory."

"Smallpox?" John quizzed.

"Yes, he was doing the same type of testing on the Ebola virus two weeks ago," the lady replied.

John was fascinated with the conversation between the lab workers and wanted to hear more about the deadly viruses. The thought that he was in the same building with the most lethal viruses known to man was very stimulating. His imagination was in high gear as he envisioned someone dropping a vial of smallpox and he saved everyone in the lab by risking his life to contain the spill.

"It was scary when the vent fans quit last week, I mean I don't think there would be any type of contamination with the suits and all, but still-" she stopped speaking when she was interrupted.

"The new facility in Kansas will have all the newest safeguards so we won't be exposed to any vent failures," Ray confidently announced.

"When is the facility relocating? I mean someone from Bio-Tech Solutions will have to come in and shut the analyzer down. You can't just unplug it and ship it and expect to start up again," John announced.

"The latest I heard was sometime soon, the facility is completed and we are waiting on the delivery of boxes for our equipment. Of course Dr. Lewis will probably ride the train his viruses will be on.

"Train?" John responded.

"Yeah, the viruses will be transported via ferry to Long Island from there to Kansas by rail."

John was thinking about all the viruses, when he heard Ray excuse himself and watched Ray walk to the restroom near the door. John read the signs on the walls about how one mistake could endanger the entire complex. He felt the excitement growing in his mind and how he wanted to work in a place that had danger.

John overheard the ladies talking about Ray in hushed tones. One said that he was Dr. Lewis's pet and that he would break his neck if the Dr. made an abrupt stop, another stated that Ray was as smart as a sick goose, and then he heard all of them laugh.

John saw Ray walking across the room and noticed how the conversation turned to testing protocols. John wondered if Ray was as slow as the ladies had said he was and thought that perhaps he himself could apply for a job at Plum Island.

John finished his meatloaf and followed Ray back through the showers and into the lab again. He continued the system installation.

John was testing the final procedures when he detected a failure. One of the tests revealed a printed circuit board was defective. He had spare parts in his case, but had not anticipated this type of failure during the installation.

"Ray, I need a part from my van and the van is not on the island."

"I can have one of the security guards take the ferry over and get it for you, if you don't mind them unlocking your van."

John described the van for Ray and told him which key on the keychain would unlock the van. He also described the metal case the spare parts for the C-4900 were in. Ray walked John back through the showers to the cafeteria and John found a stack of old magazines to read at one of the tables, while the parts were retrieved.

He was thumbing through a "Field & Stream" when two men walked into the cafeteria and set at the table next to John. They began talking quietly about a new strain of disease they were designing. A disease that would affect only cloven hoofed animals. Ray could faintly hear them talking and began concentrating on their conversation.

"This will be the most lethal strain of Aphtae epizooticae ever known. That last test proved it exceeds the specs required by the Omega Agency."

"Do you think they would actually disperse the virus or is this simply trying to keep pace with other governments and next we will be required to find a vaccine for Hoof and Mouth disease again?"

"How should I know? The people coming up with these ideas must be super paranoid though."

"Yeah, or they are complete nuts!"

"I'm still not sold on the name of "Aph-Zoot 27", but it is the twenty-seventh test and hell I guess it doesn't matter what we label it, they'll probably rename it anyway."

Ray walked into the cafeteria and announced that the parts case was inspected and already in the lab next to the analyzer. John followed Ray back through the showers again and completed the installation.

John completed the installation and drove home. He couldn't wait to get online and tell his friends about Plum Island. He didn't know such a place existed, where deadly viruses were played with, and that they were moving to Kansas. All this in one day, he would be popular for a week or two with this information he thought.

PART TWO

Day Two
Hotel Rio de Oro
Guayaquil, Ecuador

Vic woke up the next morning feeling pretty good, considering the circumstances; he hadn't gotten much sleep, and was stressed to the max. He looked at his watch, Pablo ought to be up by now, he said to himself.

He sat on the edge of the bed and called Pablo's cell phone in Quito. Pablo Vasquez was Vic's best friend and worked for the Ecuador National Police in their drug enforcement division when they first met. Vic was in Bogota, Columbia assigned to the DEA while still a Special Agent for the OSI with the Air Force, he briefly thought back to a time, a time when they were both wild.

The two men had become close friends and their friend- ship had lasted for years. Vic had called Pablo when he bought the sat- ellite and formed the company SatCom Ecuador. He hadn't been certain if there would ever be a profit in Ecuador, but he wanted Pablo working with him and Pablo had recently married and did not want to move from Ecuador, so he began managing the new Quito office.

Pablo was about Vic's height and was on the slender side for his six feet. A very handsome man, and was the most sexually active man Vic knew. Pablo was two years younger than Vic and his wife Gaby, had given him twin boys who were now four years old.

"Hola," a sleepy voice answered.

"Pablo, mi amigo," Vic said.

"Early isn't it?"

Vic felt himself gaining confidence after hearing Pablo's voice, "Yeah, sorry about that, listen, I'm in Guayaquil, the plane couldn't land in Quito last night."

Pablo explained that he was aware of the flight change and was at the airport when they announced the flight diversion. He also told Vic that he had called Rachel and let her know about the change. "So what are your plans?" Pablo asked.

Rachel was Vic's secretary and office manager in Austin. "Thanks for calling her, she mothers me like an old hen. Sorry I didn't call you last night."

"Listen, I want you to call President Mendoza's office this morning and try to reschedule the meeting until this afternoon. We can't afford to not close this deal. A multimillion dollar contract for the next several years will keep your ass employed. Have one of the secretaries check the shuttle flight status and call me, okay?"

Vic then vaguely told Pablo about meeting Elena and that he wanted them to have seats together on the morning shuttle.

"What's her name?"

Vic provided Elena's name for Pablo and started to hang up. "Oh, Vic, hang on, Manuel called late last night and told me that the SNOOP beta test is ready for you to pull the trigger."

"Call Manuel back and tell him bang. Start the test," Vic said, terminating the call.

Vic felt a sense of accomplishment and anxiety. His R&D team of engineers had recently designed SNOOP, it was an eavesdropping device based on the parabolic microphone used at sporting events, but SNOOP had a software package he had designed which was miraculous, or so he thought.

"I hope this thing captures voices a mile away, it'll be worth millions, and we need the millions," Vic said to the wall.

Vic called Rachel and told her that Pablo was attempting to reschedule the meeting with President Mendoza.

"Vic, Lisa at DIR called last night and asked if you could call her, she was cryptic, something about contract issues. I didn't know we had a contract with DIR," Rachel quizzed.

"We currently do not, but might soon," he lied and terminated the call.

He hadn't noticed any boogie men prowling around during the night and hoped that all parties involved thought that the lady, or he, did not have the turtle. He noticed the rigged alarm was still tied to the door and the change was still in the ash tray.

His satellite phone chirped, he answered, Pablo told him he had two hours before the shuttle flight.

He picked up the room phone and called for a bellhop with a cart. He then called her room.

"Hola," she answered groggily.

"Buenos dias," Vic announced, and immediately visualized her lying in bed and the memory of her removing her blouse the night before popped into his head. He was tempted by her offer and knew there was a good chance of him succumbing to her sexual beauty if she offered herself again.

She shook the cobwebs from her brain, "What do you want?" she asked.

"The shuttle flight leaves in two hours, we need to leave within an hour. Can you be ready?"

"Si, yes, I'll be ready in thirty minutes," he heard her drop the phone receiver as she attempted to hang it up.

He plugged the charger into his satellite phone. He personally had designed the software for his satellite phone, which was the size of the smart phone; however, the difference was that his phone could connect to satellites, cell towers, and standard land lines if they were equipped with a special router. His phone, the prototype of a true universal phone, was a highly sought after and equally guarded technical phenomenon.

Vic opened the satellite phone and scrolled down to DIR, then pressed the green call button. "DIR, how may I assist you?" Lisa asked when she answered.

Vic briefly explained that he was in Guayaquil and hoped to be in Quito later that morning. She told him that Ralph was very interested in his SNOOP project test and wanted to know if it was successful. He told her the tests were scheduled for that morning in Panama City, Panama.

She explained that Ralph wanted him to know that something was brewing in Panama with the Chinese, but he had no specific details.

"What does that mean?" Vic asked.

"That's all Ralph said, just to tell you to keep your ear to the ground while you are down there."

"I'm not in Panama, but I will stay alert. Listen I need you to check on a company called Ithaca Exports which is located in either Quito or Perucho, Ecuador, and possibly an office in Dallas. They are apparently an import/export business. Did you get my text?"

"Yes, I'll send the request over to the FBI."

Lisa then told him she would get on the Ithaca Exports thing as soon as she got to the office. "The office phone is on forward during the night," she volunteered, anticipating Vic's next question and hung up the phone.

Vic looked at the mirror and asked, "What does China have to do with Panama?" He knew he had no answers and began thinking about that and how sexy and pretty Elena was as she removed her blouse, he visualized her chest again and the deep contour of her bra. That has to be the thinnest bra in the world, he thought, as he stepped into the shower. The water was warm and his thoughts kept drifting back to her, until he reached down and turned the hot water off. He stepped out shivering grabbing a towel.

John Bellemue's Home
Philadelphia, Pennsylvania

John Bellamue set down at his computer terminal and started typing. "You won't believe where I was last night. There is an island called Plum Island a brief ferry boat ride east of Long Island, New York. I was installing a chemistry analyzer there and they have many deadly viruses in the laboratory at that location, like Ebola and Smallpox.

I had to strip, walk into a shower stall, and then I was sprayed with funny smelling water that left a white residue on my skin. I was then instructed to walk through the door and was dried with warm air, no towel was used." John continued detailing the day's events, unaware that his email was being intercepted by the program at Tsinghua University.

Hotel Rio de Oro
Guayaquil, Ecuador

Vic checked under his pillow; yes the Micro SD was still there, he got dressed and cut the floss string from the two doors, then banged on the connecting door to the adjoining room and grabbed the Micro SD and the turtle and put them in the backpack while waiting for the door to open.

The door slowly opened about two inches and stopped; he could see her through the narrow opening as she peeked at him and seemed to be very hesitant about opening the door.

Vic placed his hand on the door to push and thought a moment; no, he didn't want to force her. "Lady, open the door please," he asked.

She slowly opened the door the rest of the way and stepped back, Vic was stunned. Her beauty was much more than he was expecting, even though he had seen her last night without her blouse, she was even prettier this morning fully dressed.

She was wearing a royal-blue mini-skirt that was more mini than skirt; a very tight white cotton blouse with the top couple of buttons open, revealing a perfect cleavage and black high heels. Her hair was pulled up in a French twist. She noticed Vic's eyes moving up and down and felt a spark of hope that he would be interested enough to make a trade today.

Vic knew he did not want to be alone with her again, she was too sexy. He realized how disarming she was, as he walked into her room, not stopping until he heard a knock on his door. He stopped abruptly and turned, walking back into his room, realizing he had thoughts of a sexual nature on his mind. He opened his door and let the bellhop gather the luggage.

Tsinghua University
Beijing, China

Professor Dexin Szu had taught computer science, logic and cryptology for over ten years at Tsinghua University.

General Yi, with the aide of Professor Szu, had taken the idea of computer hacking to the next level, expanding it to be used as a weapon, a cyber-weapon. With his leadership and Professor Szu's technical knowledge, the team had released many "botnets", robotic networks, controlling "zombies", computers which "virused" or "wormed" cyber warriors against China's adversaries.

Those actions fell right in line with his other clandestine operations. He had assembled key personnel to perform the operations and had designed it with such secrecy, that very few people including Beijing, knew of the in-depth capabilities of the hackers.

He took his responsibilities seriously, formulating plans for the past four years, plans which would cripple the United States. His primary plan, "Sun-Chang", was simple enough that even if portions of it were discovered, it could still be successful, however, he needed a third prong. He was hoping the hackers could find that third prong. General Yi was scheduled to present his plan, at least the plan "they" were aware of, to the National People's Congress in Beijing tomorrow.

Tsinghua University
Software Lab

Li Meu and Mi Quan, were students in Professor Szu's computer science class. Li's hacking software was using a filter to key on many words, one of them was smallpox. It was randomly searching emails on the internet and keyed on John Bellamue's email to his friends. He continued monitoring and discovered that John passed on the information regarding the impending relocation of Lab 254 to Kansas and that the smallpox virus that Li was searching for was being relocated to Fort Leavenworth, Kansas. It was a simple process for Li to find that the lab contents would be transported via rail on two different ship dates. The first shipping manifest stated that only one container was scheduled and the second ship date listed three rail cars containing office furniture and other contents one week later.

Li accessed CSX freight lines and started his password detect program and logged on as a CSX employee. He received detailed information including times and the type of rail car to be used for the Plum Island equipment relocation.

Li forwarded the information to Professor Szu who forwarded the information to General Yi.

Hotel Rio de Oro
Guayaquil, Ecuador

Vic led Elena, keeping a close eye on her, stopping at the front hotel desk. He signed the bill for him to check out and noticed the government tail in the lobby setting on a couch, reading the morning paper. Vic sensed Elena tense up when she noticed him.

Vic started thinking that if the guy was a government tail, he would not be stupid enough to allow her to recognize him or to do something that would make her scared of him. No he is someone who is tailing her, but doesn't work for the Ecuadorean government or even a police department, perhaps he reports to that Cordova character. Vic thought as they got into the taxi.

Vic began working on a plan for Elena. He knew he had to get her to Quito, keep her with him at least until after the meeting, then following the meeting drop her at the police or bus station. He knew he didn't have the time nor the inclination or resources to help her and besides, he thought to himself, she is a criminal and should answer for her actions.

President Yang's Office
Beijing China

General Yi concluded his presentation to the small group of hand-picked men from the National People's Congress and Professor Szu from Tsinghua University.

"Operation 'Sun-Chang' which was designed by many attendees in this meeting will ultimately bring the economy of the United States, to a complete and abrupt halt. The testing phase of the computer hacking of the giant internet conglomerates has been a complete success and the counterfeiting operation is on schedule. The printing of the currency will begin in Ecuador within three days. I will now turn the meeting over to Professor Dexin Szu."

"Thank you General Yi. Yes we have been working tirelessly and have successfully hacked into computers at the Pentagon, the Federal Reserve and the United States power grid, and I add, completely undetected. We backed out of all three, but left a pass code or trapdoor as we call it, to enable us to return when we are prepared for the final phase. We have several more projects scheduled which should make headlines in the newspapers in the United States.

I would also like to add that we have been able to download worms via pornographic web sites to privately owned computers as well as government owned computers. The vast majority of the emails which we have reviewed, thanks to the worm programs, are of no value to the Sun-Chang project, however, some have proven to be very interesting. Such as the recent email, that originated from a computer located in Pennsylvania, which alluded to a new virus designed at Plum Island, New York. That island, referred to simply as Lab 257 is one of a few locations in the world that house many of the deadliest viruses known to man, such as smallpox, Ebola and hoof and mouth disease. Hoof and mouth disease is deadly to cloven hoofed animals, such as cattle, sheep and pigs.

Hoof and mouth disease, known by the term Aphtae epizooticae in the scientific world, we believe is alluded to in an email using the term Aph-Zoot 27. The email does mention this term along with the term "hoof and mouth" in the same sentence and goes on to state that it is more deadly than the current virus. We believe this means a new disease has been designed. That concludes my report."

General Yi stood and looked at each of the men in the conference room and smiled, then said, "I will not bore you with details, but we have located your originator, an American by the name of John Bellamue. We will be interviewing him in the very near future," General Yi stated, then slowly turned to face the president again and continued, "We are ready for phase two to begin, which is great news. We are starting to tighten a giant vice on the United States. This operation not only targets the U.S. dollar, but also currencies in several Latin American countries as well. The purpose for the other currencies is obvious. A large quantity of cash will be required to pay for increased drug cartels in Mexico, Brazil and Panama. Funneling drugs across the borders is expensive and cash that should be returned to the seller is often confiscated before it crosses the border.

I offer a word of caution though. Do not underestimate the resilient nature of the United States. History teaches us that the country is very slow to respond, but when she hits back she can hit hard, so we must weaken the United States financially first.

The People's Republic of China will control the world economy within two years, and the Chinese currency will be the only cash in people's wallets, the entire world over," General Yi displayed a confident smile, bowed slightly, then walked closer to Professor Szu.

The members of the congress stood, then began to file out of the conference room and General Yi intercepted Professor Szu at the door.

"I have assigned several agents from General Chen's Zhongda Bram to assist you with your future computer hacking tests. They will be available for you to ensure the students do not hesitate when they need to act."

"Yes sir," Professor Szu simply replied, not certain what he meant by the statement, and felt the twinge in his gut at the mention of

Zhongda Bram. He personally knew several programmers in the secret organization. They were not only trained as superb programmers, but he also knew them as being cold-hearted and ruthless, led by the little known, but extremely paranoid General Chen.

"I want all the information you can provide for that computer in Pennsylvania, and I want it soon. I also want access to the computers at Plum Island, specifically everything regarding that "Aph-Zoot 27". What is the purpose of the new strain of hoof and mouth disease? Why are the Americans designing new viruses? Those are questions I want answers to. Get it soon! Do you understand me?" General Yi ordered as he walked out of the room with a smile on his face.

He walked to the office he used while in Beijing and started his computer and began a new email to Colonel Hon, his adjutant. I want agents assigned to John Bellamue immediately. He resides in Stroudsburg, Pennsylvania. Monitor his activities, do not confront him, and contact Professor Szu for details.

Guayaquil Airport
Guayaquil, Ecuador

Once at the airport, Vic and Elena walked to the ticket counter and were issued boarding passes for two first-class seats.

Elena took her seat near the window, she hesitantly asked, "Why did they move me to first-class?"

Vic didn't look at her, but focused on the door, looking at the passengers entering the plane, "Do you want the seat or not?" he quipped.

Elena ignored his remark and fastened the seat belt. She was puzzled about why she was moved to first-class, but didn't want to ask too many questions and risk the airlines moving her back to coach, separating her from Vic.

He was looking for the government tail and saw him board. Vic noticed him intentionally ignore them as he walked past their seats to the coach section. Vic also noticed that Elena intentionally looked away as he walked past. Vic saw that he was wearing the same grey shirt and ball cap, noticing he hadn't shaved in perhaps five days and was sporting an odor of week old gym shorts.

Vic knew he was being tailed for certain now, or perhaps they were tailing her, he thought. Perhaps the tail is working undercover. No, he knew an undercover policeman would not be so obvious, even a private legitimate tail wouldn't be this stupid. Vic kept thinking about the tail, no this cowboy had to be tailing the turtle. Now that son of a bitch is tailing me and SatCom. Shit, if questions are asked, SatCom and I will definitely be tied to a smuggling and counterfeit ring. His mind was racing as he conjured up reasons for President Mendoza to cancel the contract. No, the tail was definitely not a government employee; he was simply a goon for that Cordova.

Once the plane lifted off, Vic attempted to relax a bit, but realized he was too stressed; he was thinking about the cowboy and how he could lose him after landing in Quito. He turned to Elena. "Do as I tell you and I will consider giving you the turtle. Do you understand me?"

"I think so. You will give the turtle to me, yes?"

Tsinghua University

General Cheng and Professor Szu's team established a dialog with John Bellamue as an old buddy from the Army using the chat feature on Facebook. John was pleased that he was the center of attention, responding to the inquiries regarding his work with the deadly viruses.

The primary information the team was searching for was the name of a current employee at the lab who might be wormed and tracked as a potential piggyback to the server or main computer at the lab, and John inadvertently passed that information on as Ray Ballinger, the guard.

The team planted a worm onto Ray Ballinger's home computer and began recording each keystroke made from his computer until the password was discovered for the login sequence to the server at Laboratory 257 on Plum Island.

A worm program was downloaded and the entire memory for that computer was then uploaded to Professor Szu's research lab.

A team of scientists at the Tsinghua University began evaluating the chemical structure for the new designer virus Aph-Zoot

27. The virus could be spread either from the sky via plane or on the pants leg of a visitor to an infected location. The difference between the original hoof and mouth disease virus FMDV and the Aph-Zoot 27 was that there were seven serotypes and vaccines for each one of the original FMDV, but the Aph-Zoot 27 was a completely new serotype with no vaccine available. The new virus was also more potent than the typical forty percent morbidity rate for FMDV; the Aph-Zoot 27 would have a morbidity rate of ninety percent. Resulting in the decimation of a country's beef and pork industry in a matter of months, thus leading up to wholesale starvation of a population in a very short time frame.

Unfortunately, a major stumbling block was found. The chemical structure was encrypted in such a multi-layered fashion the DNA of the virus was not recognizable to the scientists and it could not be replicated.

General Yi's hotel room
Beijing, China

General Yi opened the email received from Professor Szu regarding the possible new virus from Plum Island. He read it twice. It confirmed that Aph-Zoot 27 was only mentioned one other time in all the hacked computers in the United States, and then only mentioned as a possibility. It also detailed the extremely tight security of the island.

The last sentence of the email intrigued him though. He was informed that the lab would be relocating to Kansas soon, but no details were available for the move. He began formulating a plan to seize the new virus. He knew he needed a place to secure the virus after he stole it.

He sent an email to his counterpart in Tehran requesting information and availability of Iran's laboratory ship, the Milanian.

Quito International Airport
Quito, Ecuador

Vic was looking behind him for the cowboy as he and Elena exited the plane and walked up the jet bridge to the terminal in Quito.

Vic saw him following them out of the gate area and stop to talk to another man who had not been on the plane. Vic noticed both of them look in his direction and turn to follow.

Okay, he thought, she tensed up at the sight of the cowboy at the hotel. So was she scared of him or was she afraid he would expect delivery of the turtle and she couldn't deliver? So now is he keeping tabs on her, me, or the turtle? Which one though?

He saw Pablo on the far side of the terminal speaking with a young lady; he felt better knowing he would not have to wait on him.

Vic touched Elena's arm and nodded toward the near wall and quietly said, "Elena, come with me to that water fountain."

"I am not thirsty."

Vic changed from a whisper to a low growl and said, "If you want that damned turtle, you better stay with me and do exactly what I tell you!"

She quietly gulped for air, her eyes darting from left to right, knowing that if she was taken by Juan without the turtle she would surely be raped and praying that Vic would give the turtle back to her if she followed him.

When they arrived at the fountain, Vic grabbed Elena's arm and quickly jerked her around to face him with her back to the cowboy. He positioned her so he could see Elena, the cowboy and the other man at the same time. The cowboy continued walking toward them, then stopped to watch.

Placing his backpack on the floor, he reached inside and retrieved the turtle, then stood and held it out for Elena. Making certain the cowboy could see it clearly. He noticed the cowboy reach out to the other man to stop him.

Vic continued holding the turtle in plain sight of the cowboy as he watched him and waited to see if the cowboy would rush him to try to steal the turtle. He moved it from side to side keeping her from being able to grasp it. The cowboy watched intently, but kept a distance of about twenty feet. Vic quickly pulled the turtle back from Elena again.

He realized he had the cowboy's full attention with the turtle. "I'll keep it the rest of the day and give it back later," Vic said, still watching the cowboy. He heard her squeal with frustrated anger, ignoring her.

The cowboy motioned for the other man to walk to his left, and the man started to make a wide arc as though the two men would try to flank Vic and Elena.

Elena's pupils dilated, she squinted, her voice edged up an octave when she spat, "I thought you were giving it back to me?"

Vic kept his focus on the cowboy and said, "Shut up!" He stooped over and put the turtle back into the backpack, then picked it up and grabbed Elena's wrist, looked at the other man and saw what he thought was an escape route toward Pablo. He started walking, pulling Elena with him.

She balked and he yanked her wrist, twisting it. She jerked her arm and yelped, "You are hurting my arm!" He released her wrist and quickly grabbed the back of her left upper arm, keeping her close.

Vic looked at the other man again and realized they were not going to confront him, yet. "Be quiet!" he ordered.

"Elena, do you see the man wearing the white shirt with the green tie?" he barked. He turned his head and saw that she was looking at the front doors. He jerked her arm getting her attention. She lifted her arm in an attempt to break his firm grip. He simply tightened his fingers. "He is your ride, you are going with him. Do you understand me?" Vic snarled.

She tried to pull her arm free from his grip and stepped to her right, he tightened his grip, jerking her close to him again.

"No, I do not understand. I don't understand what you want. You are hurting me," she cried fearfully as she began looking for a way to escape from Vic.

Vic turned his head and noticed the cowboy getting closer and the other man staying even with him, but about ten feet to his left. Vic began walking faster pushing Elena with his right hand as he approached Pablo.

Pablo held his right hand out to shake hands and noticed Vic's firm grip on Elena's arm with his right hand, instinctively sensing something amiss and quickly pulled his hand back.

"Pablo, it's good to see you! I have a situation here," Vic announced quietly.

"What's up?" Pablo responded looking around for potential trouble.

Vic turned his head, directing Pablo's attention behind him, "See the guy probably twenty feet behind me wearing a grey shirt and a Dallas Cowboys ball cap?"

"Yeah," Pablo said, looking out the corner of his right eye.

"He has a friend to my left about ten feet, in a brown shirt."

"Okay," Pablo said, as he looked to his left and nodded slightly.

"They are following me and I want to lose them and I don't want them to tie me to SatCom."

Vic fished the luggage claim tickets from his shirt pocket and glanced again at the cowboy.

"Here are the claim checks for our luggage," he said, handing the checks and Elena's arm to Pablo.

"Take her with you and meet me at that little bar on the east side of town, the Casa del Sol," Vic ordered.

"Okay," Pablo said, looking at Vic. He took the claim checks, but did not take her arm. He looked at Vic instead.

Vic realized he was putting his friend in an awkward situation and yanked Elena's arm again, getting her full attention.

"Stay with him, if you signal to your buddies you will never see your turtle again! I mean it, stay with him!"

He lifted her arm again toward Pablo. She hesitantly stretched out her fingers in a gesture to hold his hand. Pablo raised his eyebrows and looked at Vic.

"Damn friend, you have good taste," he said looking into her eyes and taking her hand.

Vic rolled his eyes. "Call me before you get there," Vic said, ignoring Pablo's comment and shoving his brief case towards him.

Elena looked at Pablo with disgust, feeling as though she were being sized. She wasn't sure if staying with Pablo was a good idea or if she should attempt to break and run. Where would she run? She tried to think of a way to steal the card, but wasn't certain where he had hidden it. She tried to think of a different plan, but she had difficulty focusing on the current problem.

Vic made a show of holding up the backpack hoping the cowboy was after the turtle and not Elena. He then immediately started walking to the terminal exit. He looked back and ensured the two men were following him, and ignoring Elena and Pablo. He quickly walked through the front terminal exit, and hailed a taxi.

Vic, hopped into the backseat of an old brown station wagon, "Here is twenty dollars, now drive," he said.

"Señor, I do not know where to take you," the driver said, pulling slowly away from the taxi stand.

Vic looked out the rear window and saw the two men running and getting into the next taxi. "Do you see the silver taxi pulling away from the terminal building?" Vic asked.

"Si, err, yes," the driver said, looking in the mirror.

"They are following me and I do not want them to catch me. I'll give you two hundred dollars, U.S. currency, if you lose them, Vic said pulling the two bills he had handed Elena last night from his wallet, letting the driver see the bills.

"Yes sir!" the driver yelled as he floored the throttle, squealing the tires as he made the next left turn.

Vic looked out the rear window and saw the silver taxi falling behind. "They either don't have two hundred dollars or their driver doesn't want to play chase," Vic chuckled to the driver, relaxing slightly.

Research Lab
Tsinghua University

Professor Szu walked across the university campus from his room in the administrative dorm to the research lab. The lab had cinder block walls and always felt cold; they were painted light beige with several murals of President Yang leading armies into battle on the walls.

He entered the lab and saw General Cheng leading the Zhongda Bram as the next hacking exercise was underway. A large fifty-seven inch plasma television was mounted to the wall and students were at computer terminals, some were typing commands on their keyboards and others were watching the monitor while working their joysticks. The exercise was being managed by Professor Honghui, the lead professor in the mechanical engineering department.

"Shift, let the Zhongda Bram take over now," Professor Honghui announced to everyone in the lab.

The students operating the joysticks slowly moved so the military personnel from General Chen could assume control. Professor Szu observed the monitor and saw three mini-submersible submarines. All were painted a bright yellow with contrasting blue paint, labeling them Ocean Studies 2, 3 and 5. The subs were ten meters long and two meters in diameter.

Professor Szu saw the legend on the far right of the monitor stating that the mini-subs were over a mile below sea level and the location was simply stated as Longitude 23° and Latitude 90°.

"Ocean Studies 2, supply additional cable from your side," Professor Honghui commanded.

Professor Szu observed the large monitor and saw the vague water crafts through the murky sea water as they hovered close to what appeared to be a large pole on the bottom of the sea floor.

"Hold that tension."

The joystick operator made another loop with the cable around the large pipe and waited for Ocean Studies 5 to maneuver in closer to the vertical pipe.

"There, right there between those two coiled loops," Professor Honghui said.

The operator of 3 worked the joystick and Professor Szu saw the sub move forward slightly, getting closer to the pipe.

"Now, start your saw."

The operator of 3 squeezed the trigger on the joystick and Professor Szu saw a whirl of bubbles emanating from a large saw blade as it spun and inched closer to the vertical pipe. The saw blade made contact with the pipe and Professor Szu watched as the submersible began vibrating violently.

"Steady, hold your craft steady."

A small black stream of liquid began spurting horizontally from the right side of the pipe. The stream grew larger as the saw continued cutting, until the pipe began vibrating viciously, side to side. Then the pipe separated, but not smoothly, leaving both ends of the vertical pipe very mangled. The upper section of the large pipe began to wobble and descend to the bottom of the sea floor. The black liquid that was now gushing from the severed bottom pipe slowly clouded over the mini subs.

"Now! Reverse your propellers," Professor Honghui ordered and observed as the upper pipe began gyrating and seemed to be pulled upward and to the right, as though it was falling over.

"Excellent work men," Professor Honghui said. "Blow the ballasts and allow the subs to sink."

Quito International Airport
Quito, Ecuador

Pablo and Elena walked to the baggage claim area and waited for the luggage train to begin unloading. Pablo felt that he should have helped Vic with his situation more than escorting this lady. He looked at her and felt the desire to get to know her, hoping that she wasn't Vic's girl.

"My name is Pablo Vasquez," he said.

She looked around the baggage claim area for an exit and responded without looking at Pablo.

"I am Elena."

"Vic said he met you on the flight from Dallas last night."

"Yes," Elena replied, looking for her bag on the carousel.

"That one," she said, pointing at the tattered bag.

He noticed she seemed very nervous, but wasn't sure why. He continued trying to get her to talk to him, noticing she offered one word responses, if she said anything. He asked what happened to her luggage again and she ignored him.

He saw Vic's bag, which had the SatCom luggage tag through the handle and grabbed it from the carousel. He turned and saw her hurriedly walking toward the exit, pulling her bag. He grabbed Vic's bag and caught up with her.

"I don't know what is going on, but I trust Vic. He told you to stay with me, you will stay with me. Do you understand?"

He reached down and took the bag from her hand. She turned it loose, but he noticed she seemed to want to run to the exit. Pablo pointed to the Jeep, a blue 1997 Cherokee, "This is my car, give me a moment to put the bags in the back then I'll unlock your door," he said.

Elena stood at the passenger door, waiting and not saying anything. She was frightened of Pablo, especially after the rough treatment from Vic at the airport. She was scared to go with Pablo and scared not to go with him.

Pablo noticed the frightened look of a deer in the headlights in her eyes. He wanted to know what the hell was going on, but trusted Vic without trepidation and decided he would be informed when the time was right.

Pablo walked around and opened the passenger door.

"Here, hop in."

He drove out of the airport parking lot taking highway 10 to Miraflores where Casa del Sol was located.

....

Vic turned and looked out the back glass for the silver taxi, feeling better that his driver had lost them. He paid the two hundred dollars when they arrived and walked to the door of the blue and orange painted building.

He stepped to his right after entering the door, allowing his eyes to adjust to the dimly lit bar. He noticed the walls had several beer signs and clocks on them. The aroma was rife with stale beer and empanadas. He walked to the bar and ordered a beer and took a seat near the wall, facing the door. If the cowboy showed up, he wanted to see him before being seen.

He nursed his beer and looked at his watch, waiting for Pablo to call.

....

Elena noticed Pablo looking at her often as he drove, she kept looking out the window and saw the exit to the Catholic University coming up, feeling the desire to hop out and run for help, not certain who could help her now.

Pablo looked over and wanted to know if she was Vic's girl, but didn't want to horn in if she was.

"What do you do?" he asked her.

"I'm a student," she replied.

"Oh, what are you studying?"

"International languages, I am hoping to get a job at the Ecuadorean consulate in the United States after I graduate."

Pablo noticed she was perhaps starting to thaw a little bit, and asked if she had ever been to the United States. She nodded and said that she was an exchange student at UT Austin.

He exited the highway, then opened his cell phone and dialed Vic's satellite phone. Pablo told him they were two minutes from the bar. He hinted that he and Elena didn't mind coming in for an early lunch.

"No, I'll meet you in the parking lot." Vic said, paying for his beer and walking out the door.

Pablo pulled into the parking lot and parked in the nearest empty space. Elena saw Vic walk out of the bar; she hopped out and walked toward Vic.

"Where are you taking me?" she asked.

Vic started walking toward the jeep. "To my office, I have a meeting in a couple of hours, and then we'll discuss your turtle.

She started thinking about her first trip to Austin and how she felt when the hotel clerk where she stayed that first night treated her because her English was not spoken well. She made a vow that night that she would learn the language well enough to pull off the idea she was a citizen and not be called a wet-back or illegal.

Elena noticed a couple boxes of technical equipment in the seat beside her. She saw several green panels with many black and silver things stuck to one side of each panel, and wondered what exactly Vic did.

Vic began thinking about the purpose for his trip to Quito. He knew SatCom was over extended financially and had to sign a deal with President Mendoza today or lose millions of dollars in the very near future and be out of business soon.

"What time is the contract meeting with President Mendoza?" Vic asked.

"It has been rescheduled for 12:30 p.m. today."

"Are they pissed about the delay?"

"No, actually one of the attorneys working for President Mendoza was on the same plane and they were going to request a delay also," Pablo said.

Vic spun his head to the left. "Shit! He was on the same plane I was on?"

"Yeah, no big deal, though. They understood and agreed with the delay. What's the problem?" Pablo asked, looking at Vic as though he were nuts.

Vic turned around and glared at Elena, "Damn it!" he barked.

"Don't you look at me, it wasn't my fault!"

"Like hell it wasn't!" Vic yelled back at her.

"Hey, what's going on? Sounds like I missed something important. Come on spill the beans."

"It was nothing. Elena caused a scene on the plane last night," Vic said.

She tensed her muscles and knew she was losing control. "A scene? A scene! Is that all it was? A scene! You asshole. Tu pindejo!"

"Settle down, it's over," Vic yelled back.

"You tried to kill me! Now, it's just over?" Elena grabbed a printed circuit board from a box in the seat beside her and threw it at Vic. The board missed him and hit the windshield with a crash.

"Hey damn it. I'm trying to drive up here!" Pablo yelled.

"Lo siento, I'm sorry, but I hate that man, he is a killer, he tried to kill me!"

Pablo turned to his right and jerked the steering wheel to the left, "You tried to kill her?" he said, correcting his mistake.

"No, I didn't try to kill her."

"He choked me!"

"You choked her?"

"No, I didn't choke her, err, well I choked her, but it was a dream!" Vic yelled again.

"She dreamed you choked her?"

"He did choke me, it was no dream."

Vic snapped his head around, "Elena, shut the fuck up!" he yelled. He turned around and faced the front of the Jeep, closing his eyes, trying to make the entire fiasco disappear.

Elena looked out the window. "You are a mean man, a very mean man and a rude gringo," she said.

She began thinking of a plan, anything is better than this she thought. He makes me so mad. I will never get the turtle back. Oh, I hate him. She clinched her teeth so tight she envisioned breaking a tooth. "Oh!" she screamed through gritted teeth.

Vic slowly turned around and looked into her blood stained eyes. He knew he should drop her at the police station, but kept imagining the repercussions if he did and what she might say about the Micro SD card. He looked at the bruise on her forehead and the bruise under her right eye. He finally said, "Elena, I'm sorry. It wasn't your fault. Please forgive me for yelling at you and for hitting you."

She wiped tears from her eyes and clinched her fists. She wanted to tell him to go to hell, but knew that would not be helpful.

"I apologize for throwing that, whatever it is at you," she said.

"That's fine, no harm done," Vic said, looking at Pablo and seeing the confused look on his face. Vic promised to explain everything to him someday.

Pablo looked in the mirror and now noticed two bruises on her face. He looked at Vic, wondering what the hell was going on. He had known Vic many years, but had never seen him be physical toward a woman.

Pablo asked about the two guys at the airport, Vic started to tell Pablo and heard Elena softly crying and turned and saw her staring out the window. He turned back around to face the front of the vehicle without saying anything else.

It was very quiet for a few minutes until Pablo asked, "So where the hell did you stay last night?"

Vic heard Elena as she attempted to control her emotions. He felt a twinge of guilt for the entire situation, but knew he couldn't do anything different until after the meeting.

"We stayed at—".

"It was on the plane, he choked me on the plane!" "Wait, you choked her on the airplane?"

"Just one minute, it was an accident and she is not hurt! Just drive! Okay?"

"Okay, I'll drive, Señor jefe, ugly Americano."

"Shut up, Pablo," Vic huffed.

Vic turned around to look at Elena. "I said, I was sorry and I truly am. Please, forgive me. Elena, you don't understand, I have a meeting today worth millions of dollars and one of the attorneys that will be at that meeting was on the plane last night. He may have seen what happened. I can't afford to have an accident affect this meeting. Do you understand that?"

"No, I don't understand!"

"Hell, it doesn't matter if you understand or not! Just calm down, damn it."

Vic noticed Pablo looking at her in the mirror and told him it was none of his business. Pablo kept glancing in the mirror as she silently cried.

Elena began thinking that Vic was only concerned with some meeting and she was concerned for her brother's life and perhaps even her own life was in jeopardy and the two things were very different. The thoughts began to make her feel nauseas. She couldn't stop wondering what would happen to Eduardo if she didn't deliver the turtle intact.

Elena wanted to scream and cry as she watched the city traffic while they drove to the SatCom office. She wondered if Eduardo would be able to see the traffic or if he were already dead. She thought she had perhaps delayed too long and that Señor Cordova was even now torturing Eduardo again.

She heard the two men speaking as if their precious meeting was the only thing in the world that mattered to anyone. She wanted to attack Vic, but knew that would not force him to hand the turtle over to her. She thought that she had only one thing to barter with and that was her body. She had always hoped she would remain pure until she met that special man, but Eduardo's captivity changed everything.

Pablo drove past the recently purchased SatCom office building in the downtown business section of Quito and pulled in to the parking garage and parked the Jeep. Vic and Elena got out, she looked at him with questioning eyes.

Pablo started thinking as he watched Vic and Elena, now why the hell does Vic keep her with us if he choked her on the plane last night, and even stranger, why is she even here with Vic? If someone choked me, I'm sure as hell not going to stay close, no, Vic wouldn't have done that, but he said he did, this is really strange.

There's got to be a juicy story behind all of this. I'll bet she is a good lay though, he thought while looking at Elena.

Ithaca Exports Office
Perucho, Ecuador

"Señor Cordova, this is Juan calling."

Señor Córdova relaxed a bit as he set down at his desk. "Yes Juan, is Elena in Quito?" he asked.

"Yes sir, she is in Quito, but I don't know where."

He gripped his cell phone and stiffened, "What?"

Juan swallowed hard then cleared the frog from his throat, "Sir, she changed seats, I think to put the package in a different bag like she often does. Now the person she sat next to has the turtle. I saw him holding it at the airport. Then he got in a taxi and left her at the airport. We tried to follow him, but the driver was too slow. I do not know where he is and we didn't follow Elena either," he reluctantly admitted.

"You were supposed to stay with her and deliver the turtle to me!"

"I am sorry sir, I will find him."

Señor Córdova gripped the cell phone so hard in his left hand he heard a crack, "Bull shit! Quito is a large city, are you going to stop everyone and ask if they have seen someone with a turtle?"

"I am not sure yet what I will do."

"Do you know his seat assignment on the plane?"

"Elena moved to first class and I saw her in seat 12F, he was in seat 12D."

"You are certain it was 12D?"

"Yes sir, I am certain of the seat number," Juan said.

"I will contact our friends and get his name. I'll have Julio visit with him, I won't need you the rest of the day," Señor Cordova said before slamming the cell phone closed.

Señor Cordova called the number he had for his contact at the Tsinghua University in Beijing.

"Can I help you?" the voice said.

"This is Señor Cordova, I need to identify a passenger on a flight from Dallas, Texas to Quito, Ecuador last evening; the flight was 2356 and the passenger was in seat 12D. I need this information quickly."

"I will perform the search and return a call to you," the voice said, then terminated the signal.

SatCom Office
Quito, Ecuador

Elena touched Vic's left arm, getting his attention.

"So what am I to do here today?" she asked, looking at his backpack, wondering if she could run faster than him.

Vic leaned near her and said, "I'll introduce you to the office personnel, you can read a few magazines, or whatever."

Vic grabbed his briefcase and backpack and closed the rear door of the Jeep, then headed for the elevator with Pablo; he turned to ensure Elena was following. They took the elevator to the seventh floor of the SatCom building.

Construction was incomplete and workers were still on the job. The remodeling contract of the building was signed less than four weeks earlier. World Telephone & Telegraph had moved out two months before that and left the building in poor condition and in need of remodeling.

"Pablo, quite a bit of work has been done since I was here last month; the place is looking real snazzy."

Pablo looked at Elena, winked and said, "I personally handle all the decisions here regarding the entire company of SatCom in Ecuador."

Elena looked down the hall, noticing that the walls were painted a cream white and many pictures were hanging on them making the office appear homey and comfortable.

"Come on," Vic said, rolling his eyes as the three walked toward Isabella's office.

When they entered her office, Vic noticed Isabella wiping donut crumbs from her mouth; she stood and walked around the desk, "Mr. James, I hope your flight was enjoyable."

Isabella was the office manager for SatCom Ecuador. Elena noticed her petite frame was accented by her ample bosom. Her Latin complexion was a delicate golden; her hair was dirty blond and held back with a large hair clip. She was dressed in a modest length, brown skirt and golden colored blouse. Elena knew at first glance that she was the perfect, dedicated employee.

Everyone heard a giggle as Lucy came bouncing into the office, "Mr. James, Mr. James! Oh, it is so nice to have you visit us again!" Lucy said.

Elena watched Lucy as she seemed to bounce with each step, looking like a college student, wearing a short black skirt and tight pink blouse. Her complexion was fair with a few pimples on her cheeks.

Pablo noticed Vic as he stood quiet for a moment, as though he were trying to get past an awkward moment, uncertain what his next move should be. Pablo saw him acting as though he had a deep secret and began thinking about what his boss and best friend had gotten himself into.

Vic cleared his throat, then said, "Isabella, Lucy, I would like you to meet Elena Torres. She is accompanying me on this trip at least for a day or two. Will you ladies please see that she is made comfortable?"

"Si Señor," Isabella winked at Lucy as she spoke.

Vic saw something in the two lady's behavior that made him uncomfortable and looked at Elena very sternly, she responded by wrinkling her nose. Pablo watched Vic's head turn quickly, when he noticed Elena's facial communication, almost as though the fat lady had started singing.

Pablo wondered if Vic had fallen for this lady. She was definitely sexy and damned pretty, but not his type. Hell, she is more my type, he thought to himself. He saw Vic open his mouth as if to say something, but Pablo interrupted the moment when he gently waived his right hand motioning Vic to go with him and said, "Isabella, we'll be in my office." He turned and led Vic out of Isabella's office into the hallway.

Vic stopped and turned back toward Elena, he noticed her hair was beginning to unravel slightly from the French twist on the back of her head. He realized he was walking back toward her and stopped, then placing a hand on each of her shoulders. He leaned close and whispered. "Elena, these two girls can help with anything you need today, anything, just ask."

She looked up into his blue eyes and whispered, "Thank you." Then continued, "How can you be so nice to these two ladies and be so cruel to me?" while stroking his left arm softly with her fingernails and smiling.

Vic leaned closer and whispered, "I haven't been cruel to you and the turtle has illegal contents that I just can't allow for you to sell or whatever you were going to do."

Elena stopped stroking his arm and trembled slightly then pinched his left forearm as hard as she could.

Vic immediately stepped back, "Ouch," he quietly said.

"There!" she whispered, looking at him.

Vic shook his head in disbelief, and walked toward Pablo, who heard what Elena said and saw the stroking followed by the pinch.

Vic saw the quizzical look in Pablo's eyes and the smiles from Isabella and Lucy as though they saw something in the conversation that he hadn't been aware of. He turned back to Pablo and asked, "Have they completed remodeling the conference room?" trying to keep Pablo from asking questions.

"A couple more days of work left yet, come on I'll show you," Pablo said, leading Vic down the hall. Vic walked with Pablo listening to the chatter from the ladies.

"Do you drink coffee, Elena?" Lucy asked.

"Yes, I do thank you," Elena replied.

"Oh don't you just love Mr. James? He is so thoughtful and sweet. He is every girl's dream at SatCom. We were wondering who would capture his heart," Isabella said.

"We knew it would have to be a lady as beautiful as you," Lucy commented, as the sounds of their conversation receded while the three ladies walked down the hall to the break room.

Ithaca Exports
Perucho, Ecuador

Señor Cordova's cell phone rang. "Hola."

"I have the information you requested for Brian Stevens," the voice said.

He quickly straightened up in his chair, "Yes?"

"The passenger's name who was in seat 12D on flight 2356 is Brian Stevens. He stayed at the Hotel Mena in Guayaquil, Ecuador last night and has reservations at the Marriott Hotel downtown location in Quito, Ecuador for tonight and two more nights with a return flight to Dallas, Texas in three days. Do you require additional information?" the voice asked.

Cordova leaned back and relaxed, "No, that is all I need," he said, pressing the terminate button. That bitch gave my package to him and she will pay for betraying me, he said into his phone as he closed the cover. Brian Stevens will not keep my turtle and he will beg for mercy he thought, as he began formulating a plan to retrieve the turtle.

Señor Cordova reopened his cell phone again and called Julio, his most trusted employee and explained that Elena had given the turtle to a passenger on the plane. The passenger's name was Brian Stevens and he is staying at the Marriott in Quito. "I want you to pay that son of a bitch a visit and get my turtle. Elena's probably with him, so have fun with her too, but make certain she suffers!"

"What should I do with them after he returns the turtle?"

"I don't care, just get my turtle back! He may have opened it and I do not want the contents to be seen by anyone. Do you understand?"

"Yes, I will speak with him this evening," Julio said.

Research Lab
Tsinghua University

Professor Szu watched General Yi enter the lab, speaking with several of the students who sat at tables gazing at their computer monitors as he made his way to the desk at the front of the class-room.

Three of the students were preparing to activate valves and pumps which operate a gasoline pipeline in Texas. The pipeline initiates at the Slaughter gasoline plant near Sundown, Texas, terminating near Chicago, Illinois. The pipeline is over 950 miles long, it is constructed of eight inch reinforced steel pipe. The pipe is buried four feet below ground level for safety purposes and had made many turns to avoid populated areas, however many towns have grown into cities near the pipeline, since it was built in 1968.

A computer monitors the pipeline pressure and fluid volume, adjusting pump speeds to maintain a constant pressure of sixty pounds per square inch and a volume of four hundred gallons per minute moving in the pipeline. The hackers had left a trap-door in the software code when they initially hacked into the computer operating the pipeline. The trapdoor allows access not only to view and monitor the gauges, but to open or close valves and adjust speeds of the individual pumps.

General Yi took a seat near Professor Szu's desk and nodded that he was ready to watch the show. The Professor typed a command on his keyboard and the large fifty-seven inch monitor on the wall instantly displayed several panels.

The left panel displayed two pumps with the name and speed of each. The top pump was labeled Lubbock, the second pump was labeled St. Louis pump. The Lubbock pump's speed was operating at 5300 rpm and the St. Louis pump was operating at 5370 rpm.

The center panel had a satellite image of the central portion of the United States from Illinois to Texas. The image was from a hacked Google Earth satellite and updated every fifteen seconds, like a time lapse camera. The satellite was 412 miles above the earth and traveling at a ground speed of 600 miles per hour.

The right panel on the monitor listed two valves. The top valve was numbered 36 and corresponded to the Lubbock pump. The second valve was numbered 159 and corresponded to the St. Louis pump; both valves indicated they were open.

Professor Szu waited a few minutes until the satellite image displayed Lubbock, Texas on the right side.

"Close valve 36 and advance the Lubbock pump to a maximum speed," he said, watching the monitor.

The speed began increasing and displayed the speed at 5960 rpm within a minute, with the pressure indicating 136 pounds per square inch and the volume indicated 335 gallons per minute. The message "ALERT" in red flashed across the screen, one of the hackers pressed a key and the message disappeared. The pump speed continued to accelerate and topped at 6370 rpm. The pressure now indicated 178 pounds per square inch and the volume had dropped to 2 gallons per minute.

Professor Szu typed a command on his keyboard and the satellite image zoomed in to a cotton farm near Ropes, Texas with a resolution of 22 centimeters. The pump speed was now oscillating between 6450 rpm and 6730 rpm with the pressure holding at 169 pounds.

General Yi turned to his left and frowned at Professor Szu for a moment, hearing a whoop from the students, he turned back to the monitor and saw the pump speed was now stable at 7200 rpm and the pressure was at 136 pounds and rapidly decreasing.

The satellite image showed an explosion with a plume of dirt and mud shooting skyward. Fifteen seconds later the plume was on fire shooting flames two hundred feet into the air.

Professor Szu watched the monitor and said, "Close valve 159 and advance the St. Louis pump to a maximum speed and kill the Lubbock pump."

General Yi smiled as he saw the pressure beginning to climb at valve 159.

SatCom Office
Quito, Ecuador

Vic checked his watch; it was 12:20, the morning was proceeding faster than he wanted, and realized the meeting with President Mendoza was scheduled to start in ten minutes. Walking down the hall, he thought of the incident on the plane and felt beads of sweat forming on his forehead.

Vic used his satellite phone and called DIR, he waited for the phone connection to complete while he continued thinking about the turtle and Elena. He began thinking about Elena and how sexy she was without her blouse. Vic's thoughts were interrupted when he heard the phone ring at the DIR office.

Lisa told him that Ralph was on the phone with the White House. Vic explained that he stumbled across a possible counterfeit ring; or at least their mule and the counterfeit images while on the flight from Dallas to Quito.

He told her to update Ralph on his discovery as soon as she could and went on to explain that the counterfeit images were the property of Ithaca Exports and asked if she had any information on the company or Elena Torres.

"I made the inquiries, but haven't received anything yet."

Vic grimaced, expecting more information than her answer. "I don't know what I'm going to do about the images right now, but I have a meeting starting. I'll call you later," Vic said, closing the satellite phone.

Vic ensured the laptop and Pico projector were powered on. He thought, hell maybe if they are aware of the incident, I can dazzle them with some bullshit. No, if they know about it, the deal is already over, he thought while wiping away more sweat.

Pablo peeked around the corner of the door, "We're on, chief, the players are all in the lobby," he said walking in carrying the contracts in a manila folder. Pablo noticed the quizzical expression on Vic's face and told him there were three men with Mendoza and one was his personal assistant. Vic nodded to Isabella to escort President Mendoza and his team in.

Vic looked at Pablo, "I'm more nervous than a virgin at a prison rodeo; I just hope he was sitting in coach, not first class."

"We'll find out real soon. Here they are," Pablo said, watching the entourage file into the room.

Vic walked forward and extended his right hand. "President Mendoza, it is a pleasure to meet with you again, sir," he said.

Vic looked closely at both of the attorneys as they entered the room, but didn't recognize either man as one of the first-class passengers. All the men shook hands and Vic felt a little better.

Vic briefly revisited the history of SatCom, and explained the anticipated cell phone usage for remote areas in the steep mountains of central Ecuador and the jungle areas in eastern Ecuador. He concluded his statement with, "Mr. President, Pablo and I agree with the small changes you suggested in the most recent round of contract negotiations, it is ready for your signature."

Vic felt a major weight being lifted off his shoulders, seeing the president nod his acceptance.

President Hemmati's office
Tehran, Iran

"Sir, we have received a request from General Yi at Chengdu Military Base in China, requesting the availability of the converted ship, the Milanian. How should we respond to his inquiry?"

The Milanian, originally the USS New Orleans, a 10,000-ton Cleveland class light cruiser built at Newport News, Virginia, was commissioned in June 1954. The ship was delivered to the Iranian navy in 1976 as a goodwill gesture. The gesture turned sour following the fall of the Shah and the hostage crises.

The ship was reconverted to a floating laboratory ship during the Iran and Iraq wars in 1983. It was used to manufacture poison gas and other biological agents, which were launched against the Iraq forces. The ship was 286 feet long and 42 feet wide and originally carried a crew of 1,136.

The armament was removed and the below decks area were totally refitted to house a crew of 336 including six scientists and fifteen laboratory technicians working with the latest equipment.

The original ship propulsion design was recently updated to include four diesel engines generating a combined 7,200 horsepower that powered two electric generators which could move the ship at the speed of 37 knots.

"They have been extremely helpful with our nuclear program. Reply that the Milanian and crew is at their disposal for six weeks."

The Strait of Juan de Fuca
Thirty miles West of Puget Sound
Seattle, Washington, USA

The luxury liner 'Northwest Princess' was scheduled to dock at Pier 66 at the Port of Seattle on Saturday afternoon returning from a maiden seven night voyage cruise to Alaska. The ship was at capacity with 6,700 passengers and a crew of 1,850. The 'Northwest Princess' is the newest and largest ship of the Northwest Passage Cruise Line. It is larger than those normally allowed to enter the port at Seattle, approved primarily because of the latest in maneuvering controls. The ship uses three Azimuth Thrusters instead of propellers and has no rudder, the thrusters are lined up on the keel of the ship, one at the bow, one at mid-section and the third at the stern, and each are on separate pinion gears and bearing housings which work independently from each other. By utilizing the thrusters, which can be rotated a full 360 degree radius; the ship won the approval of the Seattle Harbor master to dock.

Most ships measure their stopping distance in miles, however with the new thrusters the 'Northwest Princess' can stop from full speed in 1200 yards, about three quarters of a mile.

The ship is 1,210 feet long and weighs 228,000 tons and is powered by six diesel generators supplying over 6000 horse power and 30,000 Kw of electricity to the ship and thrusters. With the captain at the joystick control, he can literally move the ship sideways at four knots or reverse at 10 knots and can achieve a top forward speed of 36 knots in three miles.

Over 400,000 tourists depart from Port of Seattle each year with approximately 80,000 tourists in Seattle on any given day, and today was no different with tourists and residents rubbing elbows on the piers and in the markets.

Captain John Lytle was on his final trip as captain for the Northwest Passage Cruise Line and would retire three days after docking and fly back home to Houston, Texas. He thought it very ironic that it was his last and the 'Northwest Princess's' first voyage.

He could make out the tip of Neah Bay off to his right as the ship entered the Strait of Juan de Fuca. It was a typically overcast day in the Northwest United States; however, he could see the lush dark green color of the forests on the Makah Indian Reservation.

It is customary for a maritime pilot to board a ship when it is coming in to dock and since this was the first time for the 'Northwest Princess' to dock with passengers at the Port of Seattle, a computer generated email was sent to the Seattle port authority alerting the maritime office of the ship's location. The ship's company monitored all of its ships with GPS technology, the resolution was so detailed it could measure the distance between the ship and the dock to the inch.

Captain Lytle was informed that the maritime pilot, Sam Musky, was assigned to pilot the ship while docking and was in route and should be arriving via helicopter within five minutes. He had worked with Sam many times previous and knew him well.

He heard the typical thump, thump, thump of rotor blades as the helicopter began hovering above the helideck of the large ship. A few minutes later the door opened and Pilot Samuel Musky was escorted into the room.

"John, how did she handle?" Sam asked.

"Like a dream. I love the new thrusters. In the training classes there was a lot of concern about not having rudders anymore, hell, with thrusters, you never miss the rudders," John replied.

"I have brought two ships equipped with thrusters into port, neither as large as this one, but they almost dock themselves," he chuckled as he took the cup of coffee offered by a steward.

John looked off to the right and saw the entrance to Puget Sound as he witnessed Sam expertly steer the large ship into the narrower waterways.

The ship passed the large tank farm at Wells Point where the massive oil tankers unloaded their black liquid cargo. He felt a slight vibration through the ship as though the azimuth thrusters increased their RPM.

Sam leaned over the seaman at the controls, "Decrease the speed from fifteen knots to ten knots," he commanded as he looked at the digital reading on the display as it slowly decreased below fourteen down to ten.

John noticed the terrain on the beach as it seemed the ship was actually increasing speed and considered saying something, but thought it was his imagination, so he remained silent. The ship shuddered again as they were passing by the light house and sewage plant at Fort Lawton

"Sam, the ship's increasing speed, I can sense it. Look at the shoreline; it is moving too fast for five knots."

Sam looked at the digital display again, "We are at five knots," he said.

The ship vibrated again as the large diesel generators increased to maximum RPM. The chief engineer called from the engine room and reported that the diesel generators were running wide open; however, the gauges all read dead slow RPMs.

Sam looked at John with raised eyebrows and felt his voice squeak a little as he said, "What the hell is wrong with your ship?"

The ship was picking up speed and nearing the top speed of thirty-six knots as it veered hard to port causing John Lytle and Sam Musky to lose their balance as they grabbed each other and the bolted down furniture for support.

Sam shoved the seaman out of his chair, knocking him to the floor, "Hard to starboard!" he yelled, grabbing the joystick and twisted it hard to his right. He shoved the throttle lever hard to max and back to dead slow.

The ship maintained its course toward the Port of Seattle at top speed. John weaved as he walked forward and grabbed a pair of binoculars hanging on a hook near the front windows and saw the coastline two miles away, just making out the Seattle Waterfront Marriott Hotel.

Sam was now pushing all the buttons and flipping all the switches on the instrument panel, trying to find anything that would cut power to the thrusters.

Both men felt the ship as it veered slightly to port and lined up with Elliott's Marina on the north coast of Puget Sound. John saw many people as they were oblivious to the destruction headed toward them as they walked to and from their docked boats.

Elliott's Marina is one of the largest marinas in Puget Sound and has the capacity to dock over 1,500 boats. It was near capacity today, Captain Lytle could see the boats and the people, as he looked through the windshield.

"Sam you're headed for Elliott's Marina."

"I'm not piloting this ship, someone else is,"

Sam grabbed the radio handset and yelled Mayday, then dropped the handset and used both hands on the joystick. John reached for his cell phone and frantically began calling, but all his preprogrammed numbers were for the Houston area, he scrolled through his numbers and found the Seattle office and pressed the call button.

"Northwest Passage Cruise Lines, can I help you?" the operator announced.

"This is the Northwest Princess calling, we are in the sound and have lost control of the ship, call Brett Banks in Galveston, tell him I need him to call me on my cell phone. I need technical support for this ship."

Brett Banks works for Maritime Shipyards in Beaumont, Texas, the company who built the ship and trains all the captains for the new class of ship.

"Who is this again?" she asked.

"Never mind!" he said and started searching for the direct number in his phone for Brett.

The switchboard operator turned to her coworker and told her it was another prank call about a rogue ship in the sound and stated cruise line ships don't crash into ports they park themselves with the auto-pilot.

Captain Lytle found the number for Brett Banks and dialed it, leaving a message that he was in an emergency situation and needed a call back, then next called the Seattle Harbor Master office.

"Harbor Master," the voice identified after answering the phone.

"This is the "Northwest Princess. We are in the Sound and out of control. Sam Musky is trying to pilot the ship, but she will not respond!"

"We are dispatching tug boats now. Please cut your engines," he said.

"Hurry!" John said, ignoring his request.

"John call tech support, we need help!" Sam said still trying to operate the joystick.

"I tried. I left a message for Brett Banks."

John pressed the #3 key on his phone and held it for several seconds to activate the speed dial on his phone again.

"Hello," a sleepy voice said on the cell phone.

"Who is this?" John asked into the phone.

"This is Donna Lytle. John is that you?"

"Donna! Donna! The ship is out of control!" he told his wife.

She felt her body tense and she set straight up in the bed, "What do you mean out of control? Where are you?"

"I am in Puget Sound, the ship won't respond, we are going to crash if we can't gain control of the ship. Call the Seattle office; have them call me on my cell phone! Quick it's an emergency. Do you understand?"

"No, not really, but I'll call your office," Donna Lytle, John's wife of twenty-six years said, as she placed the phone on the receiver. She searched her cell phone's memory for the Northwest Passage office number and pressed the call button.

"Nana, what's wrong?" John and Donna's four-year-old grandson asked, as he walked into Donna's bedroom.

"Nothing is wrong, Johnny, go back to bed."

Donna waited for the call to go through and listened as the phone rang several times, then heard a prerecorded announcement that the Houston office was closed.

Donna said and swung her feet out of the bed and stood up, "Seattle, Seattle!" she said, redialing the phone with the Seattle number.

"Northwest Passage Cruise Lines, how can I help you?" the operator asked.

"This is Donna Lytle. My husband is Captain John Lytle, he is Captain of the Northwest Princess. He called me a couple of minutes ago and said he was entering Puget Sound in Seattle and the ship was going to crash. He wanted me to call you!" Donna said.

She noticed her hands were shaking and her knees were very weak, she sat down on the edge of the bed and began to cry, helping Johnny climb up into his grandmother's lap.

"Who did you say this was?"

Donna took a deep breath and slowed her speaking, "This is Donna Lytle! My husband is Captain John Lytle! He is captain of the Northwest Princess and is crashing into the Seattle harbor!"

"We have had several reports and are handling the situation, we have everything under control."

Donna terminated the call, and she then hugged Johnny closer and cried.

John leaned over Sam's left shoulder and pressed the button, sounding the ship's horn. A few of the people at the west end of the marina looked in the direction of the horn and saw a huge ship traveling at top speed directly for their location.

John grabbed the intercom and called the engine room and waited for a response, "Paul here," Paul Williams, the chief engineer said.

"I want you to manually cut power to the diesel engines."

"I can't, all six generators are running past the red line on the tachometers and do not respond to any of my manual override attempts to kill the engines."

"Close the fuel valves!"

Paul Williams an employee with the cruise line for fifteen years, was considered the top chief engineer of the company, working his way up to engineer from fitter.

He instructed the assistant engineer to manually close the valves between the diesel generators and the mammoth fuel tank, knowing the ship still had fifty percent of the 61,000 barrels of diesel oil on board.

The assistant engineer started turning the fuel gate valves. He closed the valve to generator number one then moved on to the second generator. Paul saw him struggling to close the twenty turn valves and ran to generator number 3 and started closing the fuel valve.

Paul expected to hear the large diesel engine of generator number one start to sputter and cough as it ran out of fuel. The engine kept running at maximum RPM, he called Captain Lytle and delivered the bad news that the engines were apparently running on air. He remembered that each of the generators, which were enclosed in their own large eight feet by twenty feet metal cabinets, had a 100 gallon fuel tank in each cabinet.

He knew that the 100 gallon tanks would allow the diesel engines to run at maximum RPM for about ten minutes. He grabbed a large screwdriver and yelled at the assistant engineer to close the other valves. He started removing the panels on the generators. Paul wanted to disconnect the fuel lines from the enclosed tanks to the fuel injector manifold. He tried to loosen the clamp on the manifold input and realized that would take at least five minutes. He ran back to the large tool cabinet and grabbed a pair of wire cutters and ran back to generator number one.

Paul noticed that the assistant had closed all the fuel valves and had removed the panels from generator number 2. Paul reached in to the cabinet feeling the heat from the overheated engine and placed the cutters on the metal shrouded fuel line and squeezed.

Diesel fuel started squirting on the hot engine which was reaching a temperature of 300 degrees in the engine block. The fuel started smoking; it then burst into flames before Paul could jump back to a safe distance, the diesel fuel that had soaked his coveralls burst into flames.

Paul started running, knowing that he should drop and roll, but the metal deck in the engine room was now covered in oil and diesel fuel. He was hoping to reach the watertight door and make it to a carpeted floor in the next room. The flames were burning his hands and face and the pain was unbearable, he couldn't make it to the door and dropped to roll on the metal deck. The flames burning his uniform and his skin ignited the fuel on the floor and the flames followed the fuel back to generator number one and ignited the 100 gallon tank. The tank exploded, shrapnel from the tank pinged off the ceiling and walls in the engine room. The assistant engineer saw the explosion on generator number one and started running to the watertight door to escape the immediate danger. He saw Paul writhing on the floor, as he ducked through the door, then panicked and slammed the door closed.

John grabbed the ship to shore radio handset and pressed the talk button. He announced Mayday, Mayday and hoped to raise anyone from the Harbor Master's office. There was no reply to his distress call.

He looked out the front window again and saw the ship was less than one thousand yards from the marina and still traveling at maximum speed even though the instrument console panel was reading five knots and the thruster at five thousand RPMs.

He pressed the horn button again and saw people pointing at his ship as it narrowed the distance to less than five hundred yards. He looked at Sam and both men knew the collision was imminent and braced for the crash.

The bow of the large ship hit the west end of Elliott's Marina and crushed the first row of boats and the wooden pier the boats were docked to. Thirty people had seen the large ship approaching and had begun running along the pier trying desperately to reach the safety of land. The ship crushed the second pier and then the third pier. People were screaming and trying in vain to flee.

Captain Lytle felt a hard pull as all three of the ship's thrusters rotated to the left and began moving the ship away from the marina. The ship crushed eight of the fourteen docks of the marina and began moving almost sideways to the right away from the marina. The forward momentum of the ship slowed, throwing both John and Sam into the glass windshield.

The ship began moving away from the north edge of Puget Sound and back into open water narrowly missing the concrete

pier of Smith Cove waterway. The bow of the ship turned to the right then the thrusters lined up to pick up to a speed of 32 knots with one of the six generators out of commission.

John crawled on his hands and knees to the console and stood up, he looked out the front window and saw the ship was now heading in a south easterly direction even though the compass in the console registered due south. He could hear the passengers screaming and the door burst open as the purser raced through. "What the hell are you doing?" he asked.

The forward thruster turned ninety degrees to the left and the aft thruster turned ninety degrees to the right, forcing the ship to a new heading of 180 degrees, due south. The ship continued at full speed for another four minutes then the forward and aft thrusters reversed and forced the ship to turn to a due east direction again causing the ship to list to the right at a thirty degree angle. The purser was angry and demanding that they stop.

"Captain, we have passengers overboard, stop the ship!" he said watching the two men attempting to stop the ship. He left to go to the aid of a passenger who was screaming.

John looked out the front window and saw the ship was lined up with the Seattle Aquarium and still traveling at near top speed. He sounded the horn again and saw people at the aquarium pointing at the ship and starting to walk away from the edge of Puget Sound. He could see tourists along the harbor waiving and screaming that he should stop, he could see the dockworkers pointing at his ship. John noticed a ferry boat carrying over one-hundred people bobbing like a fisherman's cork in the huge liner's wake. He could see the fear on their faces; and knew the same look of fear was on his own face.

He saw five tug boats and a couple of police boats coming toward him. Their lights were blinking and the horns were blaring, the tugboats were positioning to push him from his port side to attempt to turn him around. "That's it. Turn me around. Point me back to sea," he prayed.

John could see as the tugs began to make contact and began to try to steer him to starboard and was thrown to the deck as the ship made a hard sixty-degree turn to starboard. The huge ship leaned dangerously to the left as it made the hard turn. "Yes, keep pushing me!"

"Do it again, damn it. Come on, line up again!" John said and noticed that the ship had made a turn without the assistance from the tug boats and was now headed for Queen's Pier with the Star Ferry beside the pier. Thousands of people were in that small crowded area.

"No! What the hell is this?" he asked no one in particular.

Sam answered his cell phone on the second ring. "What!"

"Sam what the hell is happening to your ship?" the Harbor Master asked.

"I don't know. The ship is not responding to any of our commands, even the compass is reading incorrectly. I don't know what the hell is going on!"

"We are trying to turn your bow, but the ship's thrusters have too much power for the tugs! Can you decrease power?"

"What the hell do you think we are doing? We are trying to stop the engines! Keep turning us. Force us into tight circles!" Sam ordered.

Sam closed his cell phone and concentrated on the console panel trying to get a handle on what was causing the ship to respond the way she was. His phone chirped again and he opened it, realizing Brett Banks was calling him.

"Bret, the ship is not responding to any commands, the generators are running wide open and the thrusters seem to be following a predetermined route. I need help!"

"Okay, try resetting the computer by pressing the Escape and Insert keys at the same time, then hold them down for three seconds."

Sam reached and pressed the keys and released them, he noticed the console lights blink then reset momentarily with all the digital readings at zeros. He felt the ship's momentum slow down.

"That's doing it!" Sam said, feeling relieved.

Sam saw the monitor which was controlled by the main computer as it started displaying the systems that the computer controlled. He felt the shudder again.

"She's picking back up to full speed again. That didn't work!" Sam said into the phone while looking at the console.

"Disconnect the console! The primary computer is located in the control room, three decks below you. Have someone power it down. There is a Molex connector for the console under the monitor. It is a direct link to the primary computer. Disconnect it."

Sam told John to send someone to power down the ship's main computer and dropped to his knees and looked under the console and saw the bundle of wires with a large gray plastic connector. He started tugging on the connector and pulled it away from the underside of the console. Then he pressed the connector tabs and pulled the connector loose. He immediately felt the powerful thrusters start to diminish their power. He stood up and looked out the front windows.

"She's losing power. That did it!" Sam said, while looking through the front window, realizing it was too late.

The bow of the ship hit the ferry boat and crushed it. Then the ship smashed into the aquarium dock while many commuters, tourists, and workers were still scrambling and running for their lives. The large timbers and concrete that constructed the dock broke into small pieces of wood and concrete dust under the massive cruise ship's weight. The heavy concrete footings that the large structure rested on was pulled up as the ship crashed past the dock. The ship's momentum carried her past the buildings and up onto solid ground, digging up the asphalt of highway 99, the Alaskan Highway Viaduct. The ship destroyed the Green Tortoise hotel and office buildings. Three minutes later the ship was still moving, finally stopping as the bow was eighty meters past the dock destroying the Pike Market Child Care Center and listed seventy degrees on her starboard side with the aft thruster still turning slowly. The engines began to overheat due to the listing of the ship allowing oil to seep from the engines.

Suddenly all was quiet except for the occasional sound of people crying for help. The morbid sounds increased to a loud crescendo for perhaps twenty minutes before the sounds of voices began to fade away. Seattle Harbor was not prepared for this magnitude of disaster. Mangled piles of junk lay beneath the cruise liner.

John Lytle lay on the floor under Sam Musky. He rolled Sam off to his right, hearing Sam moan slightly. He felt sick to his stomach when he saw Sam's massive head injury and saw the hole in the windshield with blood and hair stuck to it. He began trying to make sense of what had happened.

Chengdu Military Base
Sichuan Province, China
General Yi's Headquarters

General Yi looked out the small window of the private aircraft. His new personal plane was awarded to him by the National People's Congress two weeks prior to this trip to Beijing. He felt confident of his role in Sun-Chang and even more confident in his ability to maneuver people into doing things they might not want to do.

He observed the green, fertile agricultural land growing rice and soy beans as the plane banked to the left and vectored in for final approach.

Chengdu Army base was located in south west China in the Sichuan Province and in the Chengdu military region. The base was located seven miles south of the city of Chengdu, a city of almost eleven million people. The city recently enticed the world's leading computer chip manufacturer to open an R&D center and a large manufacturing facility there. The city was becoming the country's leading pharmaceutical R&D center with the aid of General Yi and Colonel Hon.

He was returning home to the Chengdu Army Base from a three day meeting in Beijing where he had made his final pitch to secure approval for his plan, "Sun-Chang" to force the United States government to its knees.

The plan outline began by devaluing certain Latin American currencies, then devaluing and destroying the U.S. dollar's value. The second phase would begin with the systematic remote controlled destruction of the power grid.

He knew the power grid could be destroyed and it would immediately affect the vast majority of the population. The concern he had with that phase, however was the close proximity of fuel supplies for residential and industrial generators.

He continued searching for a better plan, hoping to discover a foolproof way to actually destroy at least fifty percent of the population in the United States.

I will be promoted to Chairman of the Central Military Commission, he thought, then only one step to General Secretary. I will be admired and loved for my bold and brave actions. No longer a dog for anyone else, they'll see.

He heard the squeal of the tires as the Chinese built Harbin Y-11 twin engine prop plane's wheels touched the concrete runway. The RPM's of the two 550 horsepower engines slowed as the pitch of the propellers were rotated slightly to a flat angle adding drag to the plane. The pilot applied the brake and taxied to the hanger.

General Yi knew his driver would meet him at the bottom of the cabin stairs with his limousine as always. He descended the plane's ladder and saw his car being brought to the foot of the ladder, and waited as the driver ran and held the door for him without speaking. General Yi didn't appreciate idle conversation and the driver as well as all his subordinates had learned to keep their mouths closed unless spoken to. He took his customary seat and watched soldiers scamper out of the way as the car drove quickly to his office.

The car stopped at the base headquarters building, which was converted from a munitions bunker to his office complex. The bunker, painted light brown, had several trees planted near the front entrance. General Yi commanded the base and the twenty thousand infantrymen stationed there. He waited while the driver opened the rear door and stood at attention until he entered the building.

The interior was completely gutted, now filled with twenty-two desks for secretaries, cute secretaries and one office, his office.

"Welcome home, sir, how was your trip to Beijing?" Colonel Hon asked as he clicked his boot heels, the way General Yi liked as he walked past the colonel into the office.

Colonel Hon was his closest friend at the Chinese Military Academy located in Fengshan. General Yi ensured he was always one rank below him and always assigned at the same base he was.

"It was uneventful," he replied as he walked through the ante-room directly into his office.

"Come in and close the door," General Yi commanded as he rolled his chair back from the desk and sat down.

"Hon, I was so busy in Beijing I have not been updated on local news, is there anything I should be aware of?" General Yi always addressed the colonel with his first name when they were alone.

"The American ship crashed in Seattle and the disaster is even more than we had hoped for. Hundreds of people were killed and the destruction is devastating, it may be weeks or even months before the cause of the crash can be determined."

"Do you have satellite photos?" General Yi asked.

"Yes, I have over two hundred Google photographs and our satellite photos, during and after the crash," Colonel Hon stated, placing a packet of stapled pictures on the desk.

General Yi had spent the better part of the past four years developing Sun-Chang and knew that it could unravel quickly if things didn't go as planned.

He wasn't comfortable having to depend on Cordova for the counterfeit phase, but Professor Szu was on schedule with hacking into the computers in the United States, but wasn't comfortable with Cordova, but had no true complaints with the man.

Even so, why did he not feel as confident as he wanted to feel? Why was he constantly expecting a phone call alerting him to a disaster? He knew that even though Sun-Chang was approved he could always make tweaks and changes as needed if he could just find that ace-in-the-hole idea.

He wasn't certain if he should attempt to steal an unconfirmed virus. It might be a ploy from the American's to test his hacking capabilities. He discarded that idea as simple paranoia.

He needed to confirm if the new virus was real or fabricated. He had responded to the email requesting additional information, specifically how to obtain the virus. That generated a response with an employee's name at Plum Island who might be questioned. He was concerned about alerting the American's that he knew about the new virus, so he decided not to have his agents speak directly to the employee.

"Everything is proceeding as planned isn't it?" Colonel Hon asked.

"Yes, so far, but we have many more obstacles to get past and any mistake can bring everything we have worked for crashing down."

General Yi started his computer and accessed his email account. He was searching for a response from the Tehran embassy and noticed the email. He hesitated before opening it wondering if he should proceed or not with his plan and decided that only bold men can be leaders and he wanted to lead China to world domination.

He read the response from Tehran informing him The Milanian was at his disposal for the next six weeks. He responded and asked that the ship be sailed to Havana, Cuba as soon as possible and wait there for instructions.

"Would you like a cup of tea?"

"No, I want to be alone for a few minutes, have my driver bring Choon-Yei to the office, notify me when he arrives."

"Yes, sir," Colonel Hon said as he saluted, then left the office and closed the door, relaying the orders to General Yi's orderly.

General Yi leaned back grinning broadly; he thumbed through the satellite pictures in the packet, then closed his eyes and imagined the destruction as it must have occurred at the Port of Seattle.

"General Yi, your car will be out front in two minutes," Colonel Hon said opening the door.

His counterpart in North Korea, General Maeng, had sent him a gift for his last birthday. Choon-Yei was fifteen and was by far the best birthday gift he had ever received, she was very cute and her large dark eyes had a sparkle even when she was crying.

She was taller than most North Korean women at five foot two inches and weighed just over thirty kilos. Her most important attribute was that she had superb training as a sexual entertainer.

"She better have missed me," he said out loud, imagining how she would jump from the staff car and hug him.

General Yi stood and walked to the door, opened it and looked out past Colonel Hon's desk at the two new secretaries who had recently been transferred to his command. He wondered which one he should take first, while briefly remembering the encounters with many of the other girls.

"I am going home now, I haven't seen Choon-Yei in over a week," General Yi said as he watched the two cute secretaries across the room, hoping for an embarrassed reaction, but saw nothing.

Colonel Hon remembered how the general was at the academy, and how he was ignored by the pretty girls who came to the dances. He remembered how the general had changed over the years, how he had become more sexually aggressive with each promotion.

"I'll be at my quarters the rest of the evening if there is an emergency; walk with me to my car," he said as he walked through the anteroom and out the front door.

Colonel Hon walked a step behind and asked, "Seattle went perfectly as planned. Do you think the American's suspect anything other than an accident?"

"No, I don't think so. They want world peace so badly they will believe anything we feed them. Yes their government is very naïve, and they must continue to be until Sun-Chang is implemented, and then it will be too late. Their major problem is they will do anything to be liked, they are complete fools."

General Yi watched the limousine stop at the curb in front of him. The orderly ran around and opened the rear door, he felt embarrassed standing there with Hon, when he did not see Choon-Yei hop out of the car and hug him.

General Yi waited for a few moments and stepped into the back seat, noticing Choon-Yei was wearing the dark plaid, short skirt he liked and the loose fitting white blouse, it was unbuttoned just as he had instructed her to wear it. The skirt reminded him of the school uniforms the high school girls wore.

"Choon-Yei, you couldn't wait to be with me, could you?"

"No, sir, I came as I was told," Choon-Yei said quietly.

General Yi waited for the driver to close the door, then quickly backhanded her in the face.

"Bitch, you will want me! Haven't I made that clear to you? You are such a stupid bitch whore!" he said as he unbuttoned his fly.

"Yes, I do want you sir," Choon-Yei said as she wiped away tears and rubbed her bleeding lip.

"Then show me!"

SatCom Office
Quito Ecuador

Vic's satellite phone rang. Manuel was calling to update him on the beta test for SNOOP and informed Vic that the test was completely successful. Vic felt a shudder of exhilaration race through his body.

Vic had met Manuel Martinez two months before meeting Pablo. Manuel was a citizen of the United States and Columbia, he had moved with his parents to Columbia when he was in grade school from El Paso, Texas. Manuel worked for the Colombian National Police at the rank of Undercover Agent. Unlike local police forces in Colombia, the National Police was a military armed force and was part of the Ministry of Defense the largest police force in Colombia.

Manuel was kidnapped and held for ransom by one of the cartels, the Columbians had written him off as already dead, but Vic had not given up on him and located the jungle area where he was being held captive. He then led a daring raid on the hideout and rescued Manuel from a certain death. Manuel vowed to never forget that he owed his life to Vic.

The three men, Vic, Pablo and Manuel, became close friends protecting each other's backs while fighting the drug cartels in Ecuador and Columbia. When Vic created SatCom Panama, he moved Manuel to Panama City to operate the existing communications company he purchased and renamed it SatCom.

Vic walked down the hall, meeting Pablo halfway. "Pablo, this is turning out to be one of the best days I have ever had in my life, we finalize the contract with Ecuador worth a quarter of a billion dollars, and the SNOOP beta test is a success in Panama. Damn it, it just doesn't get any better than this!" Vic said, noticing he could not suppress the grin on his face.

Vic's satellite phone rang again and he saw that Ralph was calling. "Pablo, will you excuse me for a few minutes?"

"Sure, Vic. Mendoza's attorneys are in the lounge with Lucy and Elena, I'll take them to my office," Pablo said as he walked down the hall.

Vic stiffened with a look of fear on his face, "With Elena? Crap, go get them away from her!"

"The contract is signed, it's a done deal," Pablo said.

"I know, but... shit! Never mind. I'm just paranoid," Vic waved at Pablo to go on.

Vic walked back to the conference room and listened as Ralph brought him up to date on intelligence which was received from a CIA handler agent in China regarding a new coziness between Panama and China. No details were passed on and the handler's pigeon hadn't reported as expected at the last two drop locations. The handler was sent in as a salesman for a computer company and had in turn recruited, selected, trained, and paid a pigeon who was a Chinese citizen.

Ralph explained that it was too risky to attempt to locate the handler and that the company he worked for had no idea he was a CIA agent. They would have to wait for the company to ask for assistance in locating their employee.

"Listen, we have information that China is preparing something, but we are not sure what yet. It appears that it somehow has something to do with the Panama Canal. The company has assets in Panama City, but so far they have no intelligence on this situation. We don't have any reliable assets in the government itself at this time. What can you put together on short notice?"

"Can you give me a little more detail here?" Vic asked.

"I don't have any detail other than, it involves China and the Panamanian government, and I'm not even certain which part of the government."

"You said the canal."

Ralph felt his voice raise a notch in pitch and his frustration growing. "The canal is in Panama, hell I'm just trying to line up ideas here; the only thing we suspect at this time is that it involves the Panamanian Government," he said.

"The government huh? That's not much to start with. I need a little more to go on here, like maybe a key word to look for or something a little more concrete than Panama and China."

"I know you have an office in Panama City and SatCom is the primary phone company in Panama. I was wondering if you could, well—"

"No way! Vic said, feeling his back stiffen and felt the anger growing to a crescendo. "I am not going to use SatCom or the employees as an intelligence network for you or anyone else!"

"I wasn't asking that."

"Then, what the hell are you asking?"

Ralph knew he stepped into dog shit and lowered his voice back to a normal volume, "I need information and I don't know where else to get it except through you and your company," he said.

"Give me more. Something between Panama and China really doesn't give me more than perhaps a business deal between the two countries."

"Okay, even a business deal shouldn't be a secret and the United State has vast interests in Panama that may be effected by a deal between the two countries."

"Tell you what I'll do. I will ask the SatCom manager in Panama City to listen for anything that he might hear on the street regarding a potential deal between Panama and China. How's that?"

"That's not exactly what I had in mind—"

"Hey Ralph, like I said, I operate a legitimate worldwide company and I am not going to jeopardize the employees or the profits for you. You are asking me to lower my ethical standards to simply feed your paranoia and I am not going to do that!"

"That's why I hired you, so you could help monitor the potential situations in Latin America—"

"Hired me!" Vic felt himself going ballistic. "You didn't hire me. You don't even pay me. I agreed to help you when I could, but not at the expense of SatCom!" Vic pressed the terminate button and slammed the cover closed. Hearing footsteps in the hallway he looked up and saw Pablo walk in out of breath, "What is going on? I heard you yelling from my office."

Vic violently shook his head from side to side, trying to relieve the immense tension that had invaded his happy day. "It's nothing, sorry for the screaming."

He stood and walked past Pablo into the hall, then turned and took the elevator down to the street level and walked out through the front door. He noticed a few cumulus clouds in the sky and knew the daily light rain would start around noon. He walked down the street and saw a vendor selling hand crafted beaded necklaces on leather straps and woven woolen blankets. Everything on the small cart had bright colors and appeared to be made locally. He heard the sounds of traffic and the people talking as their lives continued, oblivious to the potential threats to their country and way of life if China got a foothold on the continent.

Vic stopped and thought back to when Curt was dying in his arms at that guard shack in Iraq. Could Saddam have been eliminated without that war he wondered? Could he have helped to prevent all the civilian casualties and the American boys and girls who died to free the civilian population in Iraq? Curt most definitely would have taken him out, if that were the mission objectives. He would do this for Ralph if he were here today, Vic admitted to himself.

Vic performed several mental exercises to throw off some of the stress for a few more minutes, watching the Indian women on the sidewalks selling their handmade crafts. He pressed the speed dial for DIR on his satellite phone and waited for the call to be processed.

"DIR, how can I help you," Lisa asked when she answered the phone.

"It's Vic; I need to speak with Ralph."

Vic heard clicking as he was transferred to Ralph's phone.

Ralph changed his demeanor to one of kiss ass. "Vic, I apologize, I had no right to put you on the spot like that and I know you do not work for me, it was totally uncalled for on my part," he said trying to wipe some of the dog shit from his shoes.

"That's okay. I'll see what I can find out regarding Panama and China. No promises, but I will keep my ear to the ground and see what turns up."

"Thanks Vic," Ralph said, feeling his voice crack slightly.

"Okay, let me work on it and I'll get back to you."

Ralph relaxed and felt his ass unclench. "Fair enough. Now what the hell is this about counterfeit money down there?"

Vic related the story of meeting Elena on the plane, minus the choking. He told him how he discovered the turtle in his backpack and finding the secret compartment in the belly of the turtle. He told Ralph about the counterfeit images on the Micro SD card and how authentic they appeared to be. He also mentioned that Elena was scared of some guy related to Ithaca Exports and that Lisa was running a check on the company now. Vic didn't tell Ralph how absolutely beautiful and sexy Elena was.

Ralph felt a chuckle slip out as he said, "So what are your plans for your new treasure?"

"I'm not sure yet, I'm thinking about monitoring the mule for a day or two, you know, see where she leads. Listen, from what I can glean from her story, she is being blackmailed; forced to smuggle for Ithaca exports, her name is Elena Torres. Can you do a check on her? I don't want to force her to return empty handed causing her brother to be hurt worse," he said remembering Manuel's kidnapping.

"I'll start a check and see where it goes," Ralph said.

"Okay, I'll call you back in a couple of hours," Vic said, closing his satellite phone.

He next dialed Manuel in Panama. "Manuel, I need you to set up SNOOP to monitor the capital buildings there in Panama City. Can you do that for me today?"

"Yeah Vic, I can have the microphones relocated this afternoon and perhaps start monitoring before the end of the day."

"How many microphones will it take to monitor all the buildings?"

Manuel briefly calculated the area of the city which Vic wanted to monitor and suggested that the six microphones, which were available, might do the job. He quickly calculated the location, approximate size and height of the buildings from memory and estimated that approximately eighty percent of the buildings could be monitored.

"Once all microphones are set up, two of them are already in the area and simply need to be re-tasked with new angle directions, but I estimate we can capture the bulk of all conversations. I can't be certain until I start receiving data."

"Okay, start the process."

"Should I target and record everything?"

"No, we'll actually start by only targeting conversations regarding China, Chinese languages, or anything else relating to relationships between China and Panama," Vic instructed.

"That can be done easy enough."

"Transmit everything to me via the broadband burst transmission and make sure all transmissions are secured," Vic instructed.

"Vic, I'm not certain this is legal. We are eavesdropping and unless we have a court order—"

"Manuel, we don't have any court order, but it is very important to me that this be done. I'll understand if you don't want to be part of it though," Vic explained, allowing an out for Manuel.

"Vic, if you say it is important to you, then it is important to me also, we go back too far to let little things like a court order affect our relationship, amigo."

"Thanks, Manny," Vic said.

"I'll start the new task immediately," Manuel said as he began formulating plans to have the microphones in the area re-tasked and the others relocated closer to the downtown area close to the government buildings.

Vic terminated the call and started walking back to the SatCom building. He dialed Rachel in Austin and had her reschedule his calendar to allow him several additional days in Ecuador. Vic also instructed her to contact Pablo and write several press releases regarding the new contract between SatCom and Ecuador.

"Got it, I'll get on that as soon as we hang up. When are you coming home?" Rachel asked.

"It could be several days yet. The deal with Ecuador was finalized today, but there are irons in the fire to handle while I'm here."

Vic returned to the SatCom building and took the elevator. He walked down the hall toward Isabella's office from the conference room and stopped outside the door when he heard the ladies talking and listened to their conversation.

"What is your job in Perucho?" Lucy asked.

"I actually do not have a job in Perucho. I am a teacher's assistant at the Catholic University here in Quito and I am studying for a Master's degree at UT in Austin in the states."

"What are you studying?" Isabella asked.

"International languages, I'm hoping to get a job in New York with the Ecuadorian consulate or in Washington D.C. with the Embassy," Elena said.

Vic cleared his throat and stepped into the room. He saw Elena sitting in a large office chair with her legs crossed and her miniskirt pulled very high up her thighs and felt himself being drawn toward her as he walked through the doorway.

Elena looked up and saw Vic walking toward her, and noticed him staring at her. He couldn't get his eyes off of her legs and didn't see the loose seam in the carpet which had not been completely installed yet. His toe caught the carpet and he tripped, landing on his knees at Elena's feet with his face planted firmly between her breasts.

He immediately pushed with his legs to stand up before putting his hands on the chair arms; the rear wheel didn't budge, and the chair tilted back too far. He felt they were going over, but couldn't do anything about it, one large crash of the chair in unison with her scream and they landed with his face resting on hers, lips almost touching. He attempted to get up so quickly, he didn't notice his right hand was on her left breast when he tried to push himself off of her.

Elena screamed, "What are you doing? Get off me!"

Vic realized where his right hand was, rolled to his left, and lay on the floor beside Elena, looking up at the ceiling. He couldn't help himself, and began laughing uncontrollably, Elena started laughing also. Isabella and Lucy ran over and stared at them lying on the floor. Isabella's mouth was open and her eyes were wide with surprise, "Mr. James, are you hurt?" she managed to ask.

Vic looked up and noticed that her face was contorted, with her mouth smiling, attempting to stifle her laughter, as the boss lay sprawled on the floor. Elena was still in the chair lying on her back with her legs sticking up in the air. Her skirt was now pushed up to her waist.

"Isabella, please pull Elena's skirt up, no I mean down, no, I mean-" That confused statement was all it took; Isabella began laughing so hard she had to hold on to the chair legs to keep her balance. Lucy was laughing and snorting, which made everyone laugh even harder.

Pablo heard the commotion from his office and arrived out of breath, observing the situation. "Mr. James, I think you ripped our new carpet," he calmly announced.

Vic finally rolled to his right and managed to stand up carefully, watching where he put his hands, he helped Elena up out of the chair.

"Elena, I apologize for being so clumsy."

"No! No! It is okay."

She looked at him and threw her arms around his neck, the hug was more than an accepted apology, he knew it, and she wanted him to know it.

"Okay, that is enough," Vic whispered as he noticed Isabella and Lucy watching the two holding each other. Vic knew he liked it though, as he unclasped her hands from around his neck.

Pablo shook his head and rolled his eyes. "Mr. James, you know you should be more careful, someone could get hurt," he snickered.

"Yeah, well you could have had the carpet installed correctly and this wouldn't have happened," Vic said, realizing he was happy that it had happened, especially the way it ended. The pressure of her breasts against his chest was almost more than he could stand. He felt the urge to pull her even tighter. Elena stepped away from Vic after he unclasped her hands and gently pushed her away.

Laboratory 257
Plum Island, NY

Dr. Lewis completed the third and final inventory of his viruses and bacteria. He was following the transporting protocol that he and the World Health Organization, as well as the CDC and the Federal Government, had devised and agreed on. He slid the smallpox tray back into the vault; he referred to the large incubator as the vault. The vault was temperature controlled and double locked with a digital keypad lock and a timer that disarmed the digital keypad for twelve hours following the closing of the door.

He had provided the contractor with the dimensions of the vault and received the special container, complete with a heating and cooling system which was operated with propane. The container was built to transport the vault during shipment to Kansas.

The container was built with an outer steel shell, one half inch thick, painted gray and an internal case of composite material made from silica and carbon steel. There was a third layer of foam inside the silica shell that was impregnated with a chlorinated chemical designed to destroy any virus or bacteria that came in contact with it.

He advised Ray Ballinger again of the dangers regarding the viruses in the vault as he supervised the loading of the vault into the container by the men from the moving company. Ray was selected by Dr. Lewis to accompany the vault during the trip. Dr. Lewis was told that the container would be shipped via rail from Long Island to Fort Leavenworth, Kansas. He was supplied with a rail car number that the container would be loaded on and he could access the location of the rail car at any time with the log on and password information he was given. He was also given a secure laptop computer that could only be accessed via Wi-Fi on the train. The laptop could be used for daily email updates to the doctor and would provide GPS data while en route. Ray knew he was important now and had the complete trust of Dr. Lewis.

Dr. Lewis had selected Ray from the list of security guards to accompany the shipment. Ray had shown an eagerness to perform his duties and seemed to want additional responsibilities. He sensed that Ray tended to have a normal IQ, even though he appeared perhaps slower than the other guards. Ray could at least follow directions and Dr. Lewis was comfortable knowing the shipment protocol was written out and all Ray had to do was pay attention.

"What if there is an emergency and I need to access the vault?" Ray asked.

"There will never be a need to access the vault during the shipment. No matter what you think the emergency is, there will never be a sufficient reason to open the vault. That is why you will not have the code. There is an alarm that will sound if a leak is detected, however, even then do not attempt to access the vault. If you hear the alarm simply vacate the area and contact me immediately. Do not access the vault! Do you understand?"

"Yes sir, I understand," Ray said, watching Dr. Lewis close the container door and secure the anti-theft container lock through door bolt and thread the green tamper proof cable around the lock and bolt the mechanism.

Dr. Lewis tugged on the lock to ensure it was locked. "That will deter anyone from peeking inside. Here is a binder with the detailed route the container will follow. I have even provided a checklist and place for the date and time of each stop," Dr. Lewis explained, as he put the book and the laptop into a black, canvas shoulder bag and handed the bag to Ray.

"Don't lose this bag! It is your communication vehicle with me. Do not use your cell phone to contact me. The communication with the laptop will be using secure transmissions. You do not need to do anything but turn the laptop computer on at every scheduled stop, this responsibility sounds simple, but I am trusting that you understand how important the job is. I don't think anyone even knows we are relocating, but I have been told not to take any chances. These are not my orders to you; they are orders from the Center for Disease Control and the National Security Agency. You don't want to piss those guys off!"

Ray stood there absorbing the information and feeling a little intimidated by what the doctor was telling him. He slung the bag over his shoulder. The two men watched the movers load the container on a forklift and slowly maneuver it through the laboratory to the loading dock where they loaded the container onto a large flatbed truck. Ray walked to the passenger door; he shoved his suitcase in and climbed up with the canvas bag. He waved to Dr. Lewis and called back, "I'll see you in Kansas, Toto."

Ray noticed Dr. Lewis shake his head side to side and thought he detected a grin, but wasn't sure. It might have been a grimace, well it was a stupid thing to say, he thought.

The driver started the truck and pulled slowly away from the dock, then drove to the ferry landing on the west side of the island and backed up to the ferry which was waiting for his cargo.

Three men with the moving company guided the truck to the ferry boat gang plank. One of the movers started the engine of a forklift and the container onto the ferry. The ferry captain blew the whistle as Ray grabbed his suitcase and bag, and stepped aboard.

The ferry backed up, then turned toward Long Island and started to increase speed for the short trip.

SatCom Office,
Quito, Ecuador

Vic was feeling excited, but yet a slight rumble of fear was in his gut following the fiasco with Elena and the tripping on the carpet. He knew he liked the closeness it provided to the pretty young lady, but also knew he couldn't allow any type of relationship to start with her, not being certain if she really was smuggling against her wishes or not.

He returned to the conference room and clicked on his email icon. He thought she seemed to be telling the truth in the hotel room, but an experienced liar can get away with almost anything.

He noticed there were twenty-three new emails, and scrolled down until he found the first of three emails from SatCom Panama and clicked on the first one that had SNOOP listed as the subject.

There was an attachment titled conversation- capital buildings 12:04 p.m. He clicked on the attachment. The laptop display switched to a screen that stated 'two voices' and with two panels each containing voice data recognition graphs. Vic moved the cursor to the play button and clicked. The first voice began;

"Are you ready for lunch?"

"Yes, what about Chinese today?"

"Great, let's go."

"Damn, that doesn't help anything," Vic said to himself. He deleted that file and returned to the email, wondering if Ralph's paranoia was a trumped up claim. He clicked on the second attachment titled capital buildings.

The display returned to the SNOOP screen, he positioned the cursor and clicked on the play button.

"President Sanchez I trust all is well with you and your family. President Yang sends his best wishes and has asked that I convey to you that the Chinese Government has agreed to all of your requests listed in the canal operations contract."

Both voices were speaking Spanish and Vic started taking a few notes on a pad that was lying beside the computer.

"Thank you Minister Yon. Please relay my best wishes to President Yang for me."

Vic noticed the voice recognition graphs began plotting the voice patterns as the two voices were analyzed and stored in the SNOOP's memory.

"I will as soon as I return to Beijing."

"Let's begin. I have question and I need to be specific, has your government agreed to Panama's requirements that China will pay the payroll for all employees related to the Canal for the life of the contract?"

"Yes, the Chinese government has agreed to all payroll requests and in addition will make monthly payments to the Panamanian government which will total ninety million pesos per year for three years, and as discussed, all employee salaries will be paid in cash."

"This is a great day for not only the citizens of Panama, but for citizens the world over. If the Chinese government had not made their first offer to finance the daily operations, the Panama Canal might have been in great jeopardy."

"The Chinese government is only interested in the support of the Panama Canal. The vast number of ships that traverse the canal each year transporting Chinese manufactured goods, number in the thousands and if the canal were to close, the Chinese economy would be greatly affected."

Vic heard a cell phone chirping, and then what appeared to be an oriental language being spoken by the person who answered the phone. He felt the frustration of not understanding what was being said, he could tell by looking at the SNOOP screen that the voice was the second voice in the room.

Vic heard footsteps in the hall. He paused the SNOOP playback and walked to the door and saw Elena standing in the hall outside the conference room.

"What are you doing, spying on me?" Vic demanded.

"No, I heard someone speaking Chinese and I was curious."

Vic quickly thought about the playback and remembered someone said the Chinese government in Spanish. "Why do you think it is Chinese?" Vic asked.

"Like I told you last night I am majoring in that language."

"Can you tell me what is being said?"

"It was rude and sounded like a phone conversation. The person speaking Chinese was in someone's office and referred to that person as being stupid," she replied, shaking her head side to side as she slowly walked toward him.

Vic looked at her wondering if she was being honest about everything else, he then suggested she return to Lucy's office.

"Okay, it is not often I hear that language in Ecuador. I didn't mean to offend you," she said looking into his eyes.

"Elena, you didn't offend me, it's just that, well, I'm not sure what to believe at this time."

She turned and walked away. Elena walked into Lucy's office, grabbed her purse and walked to the bathroom. She dabbed at the tears as they started rolling down her face and felt utter despair about the situation.

She looked at the saddened face in the mirror and asked, "How can I get the turtle and the memory card? Eduardo, please hold on for another day."

....

Vic returned to his computer and moved the cursor to the resume button.

"I think we are ready to sign the contract, however, as I previously stated, this must remain confidential. I do not want the Panamanian people to lose face due to this agreement."

"President Sanchez, I promise it will remain our secret."

"Son of a Bitch!" Vic said out loud.

He moved the cursor and clicked on the play button and listened to the captured conversation once more. Vic returned to the email screen and forwarded the attachment to lisa@dir.com then opened the final email from Manuel. He started the playback and heard voices switching between Spanish, Chinese and English. It was a classroom setting for Chinese as a second language. He deleted that email attachment and closed the laptop; he then opened his satellite phone and dialed DIR in Dallas.

"Lisa, this is Vic. I sent you an email with an attachment. Make certain Ralph hears the attached file. Before you open it, I want you to wait for a second email from me; I will type the word voice in the subject line.

Open it and save the file to your computer then open the first email. Ralph needs to review the email as soon as he can. He's waiting for this intel."

"Okay," he heard Lisa saying as he closed his phone.

....

Elena felt her knees as they began to shake and felt herself falling to the bathroom floor, grabbing the sink for support. She tried to think why Mr. James was keeping her at the office, feeling as though she was being forced to stay, but was afraid to just walk out the door, knowing that would cut all ties to the turtle. *If he will get another hotel room, I will seduce him; make him want me so badly he will give me the turtle.* She felt anger at herself and Cordova. She looked up and said, "Ayúdame a la Beata Madre". *Who can help me now?* She thought as she slumped to the floor and cried.

....

Vic opened his laptop and clicked on Visual Basic then began writing a short routine to automatically load and install the SNOOP program on Lisa's computer. Then he emailed the routine and the SNOOP program to her address.

What the hell does China have to do with the canal? Whatever it is, it can't be good for the U.S. No, no good can come from having them in our back yard, Vic thought.

He put away his laptop, grabbed his backpack and walked to Pablo's office.

Elena heard Lucy walking in the hall and shook off the emotion, steeling herself to be strong and left the restroom.

Orient Point
Long Island, NY

The ferry slowly pulled to the dock at the east end of Long Island, the mate threw the two ropes to the men on the dock. They secured the anchor ropes and lowered the ramp across the three foot gap between the ferry and the dock.

One of the movers climbed onto the forklift and started the propane engine, then lifted the container and slowly moved to the ramp, starting onto the ramp, the container suddenly shifted to the left and started rocking back and forth. Ray ran to the forklift operator's right waving his arms wildly, trying to get the forklift operator's attention.

The operator felt the wild gyrations of the heavy container and quickly lowered the container to the deck to keep it from sliding off the forks. The right end of the container hit the deck with a loud crash and Ray wasn't sure whether to check the damage or run for safety. He cautiously moved to the container, listening for an alarm. The forklift operator moved the gear to reverse to attempt to reposition for a better balance of the container, the reverse alarm sounded and Ray hollered, "It's leaking! Run!" Ray tripped on one of the mooring lines and fell. He dropped the canvas bag with the laptop and binder and watched it slide off the end of the pier into the water.

Ray realized the alarm was from the forklift and reached for the bag, watching as it began sinking below the surface and jumped into the water. He landed on the bag forcing it deeper under the water, reaching down to his feet, he felt it and grabbed the strap with his left hand and began treading water with his right hand trying to reach the pier. The bag was now full of water and very heavy, Ray felt himself being pulled under water, he was kicking his legs as hard as he could and clawing for the pier which was about three feet away, but just out of reach.

One of the movers reached down and offered a hand to Ray; he grabbed the outstretched hand and pulled closer to the pier. Ray struggled to lift the bag strap up a foot for the mover to grab with his other hand. Ray saw the mover pulling the bag from the water and placing it on the pier as another mover stretched out a hand for Ray.

Ray felt the wooden timbers securing the dock with his feet and swam to his right several feet to a ladder and climbed onto the dock.

He stood shivering, feeling the slight breeze and thinking it felt more like a subzero wind from Canada, "Man, that water is cold!" he said as he retrieved the wet bag from the mover.

The mover grinned broadly, stifling a giggle. "What the hell did you do that for?" he asked.

"I can't lose this bag."

"Why did you run though?"

"I thought it was leaking." Ray sheepishly admitted.

Ray heard the two movers laughing as he walked to the forklift operator who was still attempting to reposition the load for a better balance. Ray saw the truck that was to receive the container backing up to the edge of the dock; the driver set the air brake and climbed down from the cab.

The driver looked up and down at Ray with questions in his eyes, "Are you Ray Ballinger?" he asked.

Ray nodded affirmatively.

"I'm Tom Matthews with Clovis Transportation. I'll be taking your container to Brookhaven; it'll be loaded onto a rail car from there."

Ray walked to the ferry and grabbed his suitcase and noticed that the forklift operator had the container up again and slowly advancing toward the truck, he expertly set the container on the truck and three movers started throwing web straps across the top and securing the container to the truck bed.

Ray walked to the cab of the truck and climbed into the passenger seat and closed the door; he noticed the truck was a new F650 Ford truck, with the new smell still in the cab. The engine was running and the air conditioner was blowing, causing him to shiver.

He inspected the binder and found every page was wet and some of the pages were torn. The ink was smearing on every page and illegible on many of the pages. He flipped to the last page, the one with emergency contact information, hoping it was not ruined or at least legible. It wasn't. He felt sick to his stomach and wanted to quit the job. He checked the laptop and poured water from the keyboard, knowing the computer was totaled.

The driver opened the door and climbed in without saying anything. He looked at Ray and snickered, making a comment under his breath about how wet he was. He put the truck into gear and pulled onto the narrow paved road.

General Yi's apartment
Chengdu Military Base

The phone beside the bed rang and General Yi rolled over to answer it on the second ring. His bedroom was paneled with Agarwood. An expensive, dark wood from Southeast Asia, primarily harvested with slave labor. General Yi, often imagined that female prisoners were forced to hand polish the wood to its deep shine. The only light in the room was from lamps that gave off a faint yellow glow and the walls were covered with nude porn models, many in action.

"This is Professor Szu, we have discovered the routing information for the contents of Lab 257 on Plum Island."

"When is it being moved?" General Yi asked.

"It is in route now."

"Can it be intercepted without calling attention?"

"Perhaps, but I will need to know the new delivery location."

General Yi couldn't think of a place to deliver the contents and wasn't even certain how it was being moved.

"I'll be in my office in ten minutes, I'll call you back," he said.

He pushed himself off the bed and quickly dressed as he grabbed the phone again and dialed the number for his aide. He told him to be at his door as soon as possible. He finished dressing and watched Choon-Lei laying there nude, he thought that he would get a new girl in a month or so then walked out of the apartment.

SatCom office
Quito, Ecuador

Vic walked into Pablo's office and the two men congratulated each other on contract negotiations. Pablo told Vic that he had spoken with Rachel and had written press releases for all the newspapers and technical publications.

Vic sighed loudly then said, "I dodged that bullet, I was certain one of the attorneys would have known about the plane fiasco".

He told Pablo about the dream he had while on the plane. Pablo knew about Curt and the relationship Vic and Curt had. Pablo also knew that Vic had difficulties sleeping at times and was prone to react violently when he was surprised, especially when he had that 'thousand-yard-stare' in his eyes. Pablo knew many military veterans with combat experience who suffered the same affliction.

"You won't believe what she was smuggling into Ecuador."

"Smuggling, you choked her and she is a smuggler. This is getting weird."

Vic related the events on board the plane and the hotel room, detailing how he had discovered the Micro SD card. He showed Pablo the turtle and asked if Pablo knew of Ithaca Exports. Pablo admitted he had never heard of the company.

The two men discussed the possible problems that the smuggling could cause for SatCom. Vic loaded the Micro SD card into Pablo's computer and showed him the images. Pablo confirmed he couldn't see any problem with the counterfeits either.

"So…what are you going to do?"

"Shit, I don't know. Keep an eye on her for right now, I guess. Hell, why don't you keep the turtle and memory card in your wall safe until I decide what to do?"

"Why, you want to go into the counterfeit business on the side?" Pablo winked.

"No, shithead. I need to turn it over to the authorities, but not tonight. I just don't have the time right now and I want to make certain SatCom can't be connected to the ring or whoever it belongs to."

Vic explained that the two guys at the airport were following the turtle and probably looking for him now.

Vic knew that counterfeit rings were often associated with other illegal activities such as drug smuggling, assassination groups or even prostitution. He thought that would definitely fit this situation as he thought about Elena.

Pablo raised his eyebrows and said, "You show up and bring all kinds of trouble with you, but it is exciting," he chuckled.

Vic began thinking of the dangers that might come with Elena. He suspected Cordova was already scouring the city for him and the turtle. He knew he didn't want to meet the cowboy or Cordova on their own turf and not certain how many friends they might bring to the party. Vic also knew he didn't want to be tied to a prostitute or whatever she was; he continued thinking of the easier ways to simply dump her someplace.

Vic's phone chirped and he opened it, seeing it was from DIR. "What's up?" he asked.

"Vic, I have a response from the FBI on your Elena Torres," Lisa said.

"Go ahead."

Lisa began reading the report from her monitor, "Elena Torres is enrolled in Syntax I, Semantics II and Phonetics at UT Austin, currently holding a GPA of 3.86. Dr. Kline reported that she is an excellent student with no absences or character infractions. She speaks, English, French, Spanish and Chinese. Vic that concludes the report, anything else?"

"What about Ithaca Exports?"

"Nothing yet," she said.

Vic slowly closed his phone, shaking his head. He thought about Elena and how he had treated her. Knowing she had been mostly honest with him, and now wanting to know more of her story, and wondering how he would apologize for his actions.

He watched Pablo press the digital code to open the safe and started piecing together her statements about Eduardo and how she was so scared of Cordova and the cowboy. He wanted to confront her and get the rest of the truth about what she knew and why she lied to him in the beginning.

Pablo placed the turtle and the small Micro SD card in the safe and closed it. He turned back around and said, "Hell, if she lives in Perucho you can put her ass on the bus. Perucho is less than an hour north of Quito," lifting his hands in a problem solved gesture.

"No, I just found out that part of her story is true, perhaps all of it."

Vic thought about the bus option, but knew he couldn't do that. He wasn't comfortable since she now knew that he was SatCom and suspected the two guys from the airport would come knocking as soon as she told them where the turtle was. Even if he turned the memory card over to the police, it might not keep them from bothering the girls in the office.

Pablo turned toward him, raising his eyebrows. "What part is true and how do you know?"

Vic started to reply and caught himself, he knew Pablo did not know about DIR and also knew he could not tell him about his relationship with Ralph or Lisa. "Well, her story checks out with UT, she is a student there," he said.

He continued trying to decide what to do, when he heard Isabella tell Lucy good night. He looked at his watch, confirming the day had sped by. "Did you reserve a room for me tonight?"

"Yeah, you're set," Pablo said smiling.

Vic thought now was as good a time as any to talk to Elena. He walked to Lucy's office and saw her sitting in a chair, watching Lucy shutting down her computer.

"Elena do you have a moment?" he asked.

She stood from her chair, smoothed her blouse and stared at Vic. "I guess." She felt the anger bubbling inside her stomach. Angry that he had stolen her property and yet knowing that she had gambled on sneaking it into his luggage and lost the bet.

Vic stepped aside as Lucy walked past him to the hall, then stated, "It's late and the office is closing, but I want to stay here and listen to your story if you are willing to tell it me. I confirmed that you are a student at UT."

"Okay," she replied.

Vic led her to the conference room. He pulled a chair from the large table for her to set and took a seat himself.

"How did you check on me?" she asked.

"The how is not important, but I know you were honest about that part of your story. I want to know the rest and I want you to be honest with me. For starters, you said your brother was kidnapped and that you are being blackmailed to rescue him. Is that accurate?"

"Yes, Eduardo either stole money or drugs, I don't know which or how much," she said.

"Okay, why didn't you go to the police and report it?"

"Señor Cordova has policemen working for him. I don't know who to ask for help or who to trust."

"Start at the beginning and tell me everything about Ithaca Exports and your friend Cordova. I want to know about that guy with the cap and how you play into their deal.

She then told him how she was a Teacher's Assistant for a Professor Martinez in the language department at the Catholic University in Quito. She told him that she had a student visa and was also studying at the University of Texas in Austin, which was the reason Cordova wanted her to work for him.

"What else do you want to know?" she asked, feeling confused and scared, wanting to run away. "Cordova will kill Eduardo and probably me as well," she said, standing up and walking to the door.

"Wait," Vic said, reaching out and putting his right hand on her arm stopping her.

She turned and looked into his eyes, then said, "Just give me the turtle and the memory card and let me go," she demanded, while staring at him.

"I'll give you the turtle and I'll let you go, but I can't give you the memory card."

"You don't understand!"

"No, I think I am beginning to," he said, looking at her and seeing someone that was in over her head and couldn't stop or back out of the trouble she was in. He sat rigidly in the chair; his back perfectly aligned, trying in vain to hide his obvious curiosity. He looked at her face, the bruises he had caused and wondered if things were different, would he have the same feelings.

"How is she doing this to me?" He thought defiantly.

Sweat began to form above his brow; he had never felt this nervous with anyone, or anything before. In desperation he closed his eyes and leaned his head forward, cupping his chin in his hands. Then with one last exhale, he surrendered.

Slowly, he reluctantly turned to face her with the most wounded expression, almost unsure of what he would find in her face.

She noticed his eyes were filled with guilt, fear, worry, and for a moment, his eyes seemed to open a small window into his inner soul. She had never seen him this way before. He, a man who had never been defeated in battle, who was fearless, was now displaying weakness before her. And for the briefest of moments, she thought she saw a hint of emotion, hoping for a hint of compassion. She wanted the emotion to be something, anything would be better than the stone cold attitude he had displayed to her in the hotel.

He opened his mouth, afraid of what might come out.

"I'm sorry." That was all he could manage to say, yet his expression said so much more than words ever could, and that was all that mattered. That was the only thing that mattered to her.

Vic saw the distraught ridden face of a young lady, who was being forced into actions beyond her wants and wishes. He saw the self-guilt of her knowing if she didn't perform to expectations she would be responsible for her own brother's death.

He couldn't fathom that responsibility and thought back to Curt. He knew that he wasn't responsible for Curt's death, but still felt guilty for not driving that old pickup, which was parked behind the guard shack to Samarra and perhaps, just perhaps, saving Curt's life.

She stood there not backing away from him and not trying to put on a show to win his affections so she could somehow steal the turtle back from him. She was standing in front of him now with nothing else to do, but surrender to her fate as she saw and understood it.

"Tell me more, I want to hear everything," Vic said looking into her very pretty brown eyes.

Elena could not hold the emotional weight of the situation on her shoulders any longer. She began crying with such a release that her shoulders heaved with huge sobs.

Tears were streaming down her face streaking the mascara and dripping on to the floor. She began thinking that perhaps, just perhaps, he was going to help her. She felt her strong shoulders, which she had attempted to build, but knew they were a simple façade, now beginning to crack.

She knew that she still had to be strong to save Eduardo, but the thought of Vic helping her was too much and she felt everything come crashing down.

"I can't continue! I have killed my brother. I was supposed to deliver the turtle to Juan when I arrived in Quito. It has been days now and I know Julio or Señor Cordova has killed Eduardo. I did that!" she said and continued sobbing, then started coughing and choking.

Vic stood and put a hand on each shoulder and drew her closer to him as he gently put his arms around her. She inched closer, fearing rejection once more and yet knowing she needed a strong shoulder to cry on. She coughed again and Vic stretched to his right and reached the box of tissues, pulling a couple out, he held them to Elena's face; she wiped her eyes and blew her nose.

Elena slowly put her hands to his waist pulling closer to him, she grabbed handfuls of his shirt and pulled tightly as though she would fall into the abyss if she let go. The longer she stood close to him, the tighter she held on and the harder she cried. Vic stood there allowing her to vent the huge emotional stress for a few minutes.

He dropped his head a couple of inches putting his mouth near her right ear and whispered,

"Elena."

"What?" she finally answered.

"I want to talk more, but not here. I know a place we can talk and not be disturbed, the office is closed and Pablo needs to go home. I want to hear more, I want to hear it all."

"Okay," she said, releasing her tight grip and stepping back slightly, expecting Vic to push her away and walk out the door.

He stepped back and said, Listen, I'll check if Pablo is still here. He has our luggage in the Jeep.

"What are your plans for the night?"

"I don't know, I can't go home and I can't go to Cordova without the memory card."

Vic expected a response of I'll just go home or something like that, but was surprised at her response. It just seemed strange for her to accept that she had no place to stay, he thought back to when he saw the voucher in her purse and wondered if she actually had a place tonight, but was keeping it secret.

He opened the door and walked down the hall, walking into Pablo's office he told Pablo he needed a ride to the hotel.

Pablo was ready to go and drove him and Elena to the Patio Amador Hotel.

Brookhaven Rail yard
Long Island, NY

The truck pulled to a stop under a large gantry crane, the driver climbed out of the cab and signaled to the crane operator. He loosened the straps securing the container to the truck bed and waited for the cranes trolley to stop above the truck. The operator lowered the cable and the driver grabbed the hooks and connected one at each corner of the container. Ray was trying to decipher the smeared print on the wet sheets of the binder. He remembered that the rail car that was purchased for the container had four numbers and the last two were 93. He climbed out of the cab and watched the container being suspended twenty feet in the air as it was moved to the rail cars sitting on the spur. The operator slowly lowered the container over a flatbed car and two yard workers disconnected the cables and secured the container to the flatbed rail car.

Ray couldn't see the number on the car so he climbed up on the truck and felt better when he saw the rail car's number was 5593. He hopped off of the truck and walked to the driver's door. "I'm supposed to stay with the container," he announced to the driver.

"Hop in, I'll drive you around to the office or you can walk over and stand by the car," he chuckled sarcastically.

Ray walked back to the passenger door and climbed back in the truck. The driver started the truck and drove several hundred feet to the yard office, then Ray climbed out of the truck, grabbed his suitcase and the wet bag, and walked up the steps to the office door. He walked in and saw several men sitting at desks behind a counter talking on telephones. He looked around for someone to help and saw a man in the rear of the office putting paper in a printer.

Ray looked around and noticed the office seemed rather old. The walls were repainted at least three times. He counted the different colored layers of peeling paint, counting at least three different colors. The walls were now a putrid looking white. A couple of framed photos of the rail yard through the years were on the wall.

"Excuse me," Ray said loudly, watching the man as he walked away from the printer toward him.

The man slowly looked up and to his right in a 'you are bothering me pose' "What do you need?" he asked.

"I am supposed to accompany rail car 5593 to Kansas."

"Hang on," the man said, and walked back to the rear office and started typing on his keyboard. He waited for several minutes, then picked up the telephone and dialed a number and spoke to someone on the other end of the phone, then waited for several more minutes, finally listening to instructions. He hung up the phone and walked back to the counter.

"A strange request, but you will be in a coach car being delivered later this evening from Amtrak. Is your name Ballinger?"

"Yes."

"I'm Frank. The car will be here around 6:30. You are welcome to all the coffee you can drink while you wait," motioning to the pot on the table under the front window and noticing the wet clothes.

Ray walked to the table where the coffee pot was and poured a cup then set down and opened the binder. He used several of the paper towels lying beside the pot to dry the pages in the binder. He reached into his pocket and removed his cell phone, realizing it was soaked; he put it in the wet bag. He felt the wind from a fan that was oscillating and blowing on him from across the room, his clothes were still wet and he was now starting to shiver. He finished the cup and poured another.

General Yi's office
Chengdu Military Base

General Yi arrived at his office and immediately called Professor Szu's cell phone, who explained that the transportation information was located on the computer at Lab 257 in a print file.

"General, the virus and bacteria have been loaded into a self-contained locker and the locker is in some sort of special container. That container is already in route to Kansas on railcar 5593 and the car is scheduled to be coupled with an Amtrak coach car number 30117 for some reason, the team has searched the records, but can't find any other time when a coach car was coupled to a freight train."

General Yi looked at a map of the eastern United States and decided to have the container delivered to the Philadelphia ship yards if possible.

Professor Szu promised to track the location of the rail cars and hack into CSX and reschedule the container as quickly as possible.

"What about the coach car?" Professor Szu asked.

"I don't care about tourists," General Yi responded, terminating the phone signal and shutting his computer down, he set for several minutes wondering if he had made the correct decision, he felt himself nodding off to sleep and lay his head on his arms on the desk.

Joint Intelligence Meeting
Washington DC

Joint intelligence meetings were held every Tuesday evening in the White House and was normally attended by the directors of the CIA, NSA, and the FBI, and of course the president and his chief of staff. The topics discussed included any hot spots in the world that might affect the United States. There was an unwritten understanding that senior department heads can sit in on the meetings if they might have information regarding current issues. Ralph had called prior to the meeting and had requested to be included in this week's meeting.

The meeting began with several bullshit reports presented by uninvited attendees wanting to be heard and further substantiate their reputations for being first rate ass kissers.

Ralph held back until the meeting was noticeably winding down, then he made his interruptions, stating his name and current location in Dallas. He started with the bold statement that one of his agents had intercepted information implying that Red China, he still referred to China as 'Red China', was preparing to offer Panama an undisclosed amount of cash and possibly other aide to help operate the Panama Canal.

"Where the hell did you get that information?" asked Director Greene of the NSA.

Director Waters of the CIA, Ralph's boss, interrupted his response and asked Ralph how the information was delivered to DIR and by-passed Langley. Ralph felt pressure and quickly realized that he had inadvertently placed his boss in an embarrassing position. Ralph knew that Director Waters was keen on micromanaging and would not appreciate being blind-sided by his subordinate. Ralph felt a slight smirk appear at the right corner of his mouth as he continued with his statements.

"I received this information via an operative currently in Ecuador,"

Ralph introduced Vic's name to the team on the phone, detailing his many accomplishments while in the Air Force.

"He reports to me and is reliable!"

"How was the information obtained," Waters asked.

Ralph began hedging, attempting to dodge the question. He knew the President was a stickler for proper protocol when it pertained to monitoring phone lines and wiretapping. Even though the Patriot Act was questioned by some, the government was using the same processes it had used for many years to monitor organized crime, but once the processes hit the news media people became paranoid.

"Has the information been verified?" Waters asked.

"I'll have verification tomorrow," Ralph said and felt his ass pucker hoping Vic would be able to accomplish that.

"Mr. President," Director Pierce interjected, "that intelligence from Panama goes along with our latest information that the Panamanian government is broke, virtually bankrupt. The United States would be the last country Panama would ask financial help from. With that said we sure as hell don't want China running the canal."

"Perhaps we could speak with President Sanchez and offer a deal ourselves," Director Greene with the NSA suggested.

"No, they won't talk to us regarding their finances. If word got out that they were strapped for cash they would look like fools, especially considering what the critics said about the return of the canal," Director Waters said.

Ralph cleared his throat loudly, "Mr. President, this is Ralph again, considering the bankrupt statement, the CIA field office here in Dallas received information just this morning of a mule being intercepted carrying counterfeit currency digital images for several Latin American countries one of them being Panama," he said.

"Who do the currency images belong to?" Director Pierce with the FBI, asked.

"We think they may belong to a company called Ithaca Exports, but we do not have confirmation of this. We are looking in to it though," Ralph said.

"Ithaca Exports? That's interesting, they were added to the list of suspected terrorist businesses recently," Director Waters with the CIA, stated.

"The company may have ties with Al Qaeda, but we are not sure yet. They have offices in Quito, Ecuador and Dallas, Texas," Director Pierce with the FBI added.

"Ok, gentlemen, let's see if we can connect the dots we have so for," the president said. "Panama is broke; the Chinese are offering to help them financially and perhaps help themselves to the canal and Ithaca Exports is a company, which may have close ties to Al Qaida with offices in Dallas, Texas and Quito, Ecuador and may have the means to counterfeit the currencies in at least one country in Latin America. China is positioning themselves to be Panama's savior from financial ruin. Does that sum up what we know so far?"

"Yes, Mr. President."

"Well this is scary, but I don't see a clear enough picture here to justify calling China and telling them what we know and telling them to cut the shit out. Hell, if I lost sleep simply because I was not aware of something, I would never get any sleep."

"We are still working on acquiring additional intelligence," Director Waters said, waiting for Ralph to chime in with a comment and disappointed when Ralph was silent.

"Does the CIA have any operatives in China that can provide additional information?" the President inquired.

"At this time all agents have their ears to the ground, so-to-speak but, no additional information has been received. We have lost contact with an agent who had some intelligence, but not enough to actually help us analyze anything that might be concrete," Director Waters replied, hoping Ralph would not have more information.

"Then stay on it and I want to reconvene soon, this issue will be assigned the name…?" he looked at his Chief of Staff.

"Jupiter, Mr. President," the Chief of Staff said.

"Okay, Jupiter it is. I do not want to be caught unawares here. Do I make myself clear?"

"Yes Sir," stated the group as they left the room and Ralph hit the terminate button on his conference phone on his desk.

Patio Amador Hotel
Quito, Ecuador

Pablo pulled up to the drive and stopped, nodding to Vic as he hopped out, grabbing both suitcases from the back and walked to the front desk, leading Elena.

"I should have reservations in the name of Vic James," he said.

"Yes sir, a room for two, for one night."

"No, it should be a room for one and I would like to get a second room for her, Elena Torres," Vic said nodding at Elena.

"Sir, I apologize, but we are at maximum occupancy tonight."

"Okay, I'll take the room," Vic said.

He saw Elena looking at him, she wondered if he was going to expect sex for the room or perhaps sex for the hard work of listening to me, she thought to herself.

The clerk handed the key to the bellhop who was standing nearby. Elena followed the two men to room 447. She knew he wasn't going to return the memory card and did not want to be placed in a situation to be expected to owe him anything.

Vic walked into the room, leaving the door open for her. He noticed she hesitated in the hall before entering, leaving the door open behind her.

Vic opened his phone and dialed Pablo, getting Lucy's cell phone number from him; he then dialed her at home.

"Lucy this is Mr. James. I am having a difficult time finding a room for Elena for the night. Can you help me find a room?"

"Sir, I made a reservation for her at the Patio Amador Hotel with you. Pablo said to book one room. Is that not right?" she asked.

"Elena is not sleeping with me; she and I are not together."

"Oh sir, I am sorry. The city is booked for the night; the only rooms available are in, well in the seedier side of town."

"I'll figure something out."

"Sir, she and I really enjoyed each other's company today. If she doesn't mind she can stay in my guest room tonight."

"Are you certain? I can have her at your apartment in thirty minutes," Vic said, hoping to confirm her suggestion, before she backed out.

Elena heard the conversation and wondered why he didn't make a promise to return the card for sex. She had promised sex for the memory card last night and would have fulfilled the commitment tonight for a promise. She did feel better, knowing she would not be pressured into doing something she did not want to do. She relaxed, walking in and taking a seat at the table.

Marriott Hotel
Quito, Ecuador

Julio walked in through the front door of the hotel and spotted the house phone on the table. He crossed the lobby and picked up the receiver, then placed it back in the cradle, with a new idea. He slowly and deliberately walked to the front desk, cementing his new plan as he walked. He knew he was the most trusted man in Cordova's organization and he had confidence he could recover the turtle for him. He was wearing his favorite clothes, Levis jeans and a cotton shirt with Hawaiian floral print. He saw a man in the lounge that stood up from his stool at the bar and walked to the rear of the bar toward the bathrooms, leaving his suit coat on the bar stool. Julio walked over and grabbed the coat and walked to the hotel's front desk.

"I'm looking for a business associate, Brian Stevens, who is staying here. He left his suit coat at the office and I need to give it to him," Julio told the clerk, holding up the coat.

"I can connect you to Mr. Stevens' room if you like," she said.

He held the coat up for her to see he was legitimate, "I am in a hurry, the taxi is waiting and I just need to give him his coat," Julio exclaimed.

She walked to the other end of the desk to give a guest his key, then returned to Julio as two other guests walked up to the desk, she looked at Julio and returned to the center of the desk to answer their questions. Julio waited, looking at his watch several times waiting for the clerk to return and working on a backup plan.

"Well, I shouldn't give out the room number, but since you work with him, I guess it will be alright, we are so busy, he is in room 541," she said and returned to the next guest.

"Can you go ahead and ring his room and let him know I am on the way up," Julio asked. "That will save me some time and make you feel better that he knows it is me," Julio said, seeing the clerk agree to the request, seeming more confident of her decision.

He walked to the bank of elevators and took the first elevator to the fifth floor, then walked out when the doors opened and looked both directions to make certain no witnesses could identify him. He knocked on the door at room 541 and waited, the door opened a few inches and he saw a lady in her late twenties looking at him.

"There must be a mix up. Brian was wearing his jacket when he returned a little while ago," she said.

Julio smiled at her and watched her seem to slightly relax when she saw his smile. He pushed hard against the door, shoving her back and started into the room, slamming the door closed behind him. He saw that she was a very attractive lady, wearing a dark blue, pleated skirt and a contrasting, light blue, button down blouse. Her brunette hair was a little past her shoulders.

"Please do not come in, Brian didn't leave his jacket anywhere."

"What is your name?" Julio growled.

She gulped for air, focusing on the scar from his right eye to his chin, imagining that he must be tough to have a scar like that, "I am Carrie Stevens, Brian's wife. Who are you?" she managed to ask in a quivering voice.

Julio quickly looked around the room, "I need to speak to him about the package."

"What package?"

"Where is he?" Julio demanded.

"You can't just barge in here like this, I will call hotel security!" she announced sternly, feeling her knees starting to buckle slightly as fear began to take control of her body.

"Shut up, bitch. Where is he?"

"He's not here. Get out!"

Julio heard the bathroom door open a few inches, "Carrie, where would you like to eat this evening?" Brian hollered.

Carrie froze when she heard Brian's voice and saw Julio turn and slide the deadbolt and hang the chain on the door. He started for the bathroom.

"No! Get out!" Carrie screamed.

Julio quickly spun and hit her in the face with his fist. She fell to the floor dazed and bleeding from a cut under her left eye.

Julio waited a moment and saw Brian in the mirror, looking at his face as he shaved. Julio waited until he wiped the shave cream off and grabbed a towel to dry his face. He leaned toward the door, "Carrie, I didn't understand you. Where did you want to eat?"

Brian stepped out of the bathroom holding a towel around his waist and froze when he came face to face with Julio. "Uh, who are you?"

"Were you in seat 12D from Dallas to Quito last night?" Julio asked.

"What? 12D, uh…, yes, that was my seat, but we landed in Guayaquil instead. Why?"

"You have my package and I want it back."

"What package?" Brian asked.

He noticed Carrie lying in the floor at the foot of the bed. "Carrie!" Brian said; rushing past Julio to Carrie as she slowly eased up onto her left elbow. Brian knelt down and touched her bleeding left eye.

"Ouch," she whimpered, as she looked up at him. She stiffened again when she saw Julio's shadow.

Julio kicked Brian in the stomach and rolled him over on his right side. "Where is the package Elena gave you?"

"What-what package?" Brian sputtered and coughed trying to breathe.

"The turtle! That white turtle, you know what I'm talking about. I know she gave it to you and if you want to live you will give it to me now!"

"I don't have a turtle. I don't know anyone by the name of Elena. Wait, you said seat 12D?"

"Yeah, seat 12D, the seat you were in."

"No, I changed seats with a guy from seat 9C, I think. I was in seat 12D, but I swapped with 9C so Carrie and I could set together. You have the wrong guy. He must have your turtle."

"Now you are lying and making up stories. Give me the turtle!" Julio demanded. He walked to the closet and slammed the door open.

He grabbed Brian's leather belt that was hanging over the hanger bar and walked back to where Brian and Carrie were lying on the floor. He raised his right arm and struck Brian on his back with the belt's buckle. The force was hard enough that it ripped into Brian's soft skin and left a two inch gash just below the rib cage, which started bleeding.

Brian rolled into the fetal position expecting another blow when Julio reached down and grabbed Carrie by her hair and yanked her to her feet.

"Get up, bitch!"

He slapped her hard enough to knock her back down, then pulled her back to her feet again as she whimpered. He pulled a fist full of dark hair loose from her head.

"Were you on the flight too?" Julio demanded.

"Yes, b-but we don't have any turtles!" she said, putting her right hand to her head.

Julio slapped her and she fell to the floor again, he then kicked Brian again and rolled him onto his stomach. Julio walked to the bedside table and picked up the telephone and ripped the cord loose from the phone and the wall. He walked back to Brian who was still coughing and trying to catch his breath.

Julio grabbed his arms and pulled them tight behind him. He tied a loop in one end of the cord and placed it on Brian's right wrist and tied it to the other wrist tightly. He grabbed a wash cloth from the bathroom and rolled Brian over and hit him hard with his fist and stuffed the cloth into Brian's mouth forcing a broken tooth in with it.

Carrie was starting to regain consciousness when Julio forced Brian to stand and walked him to a chair, using the remainder of the phone cord; he tied Brian's feet to the chair legs and walked back to Carrie as she looked up at him with fear in her eyes.

"Get up Carrie," Julio demanded.

"What," she whimpered, trying to stand, but felt wobbly and fell onto the bed.

"That's better, now where is my turtle?"

"I don't have your turtle," Carrie sobbed.

"He does though and I want it back," Julio said, pointing at Brian.

"No, we don't have it. Why would we lie to you?" she pleaded, as she stood up looking at Brian.

"You can either give it to me and I will walk out or you can continue lying to me. Either way I will leave with the turtle. The turtle was given to him. It was probably put in his luggage when he wasn't looking, so I want you to go through your entire luggage now and find the turtle. If you don't find the turtle, you and I will have a little party," Julio ginned.

He walked closer to Carrie and she took a step back, he grabbed her blouse with both hands and ripped it open as she opened her mouth to scream, then he slapped her again, knocking her to the floor.

Julio walked to the closet and took out two suitcases and unzipped them, then dumped the contents onto the bed. He rummaged through the clothes, but found no turtle. He walked to Carrie and grabbed her hair again as she tried to stand to keep him from ripping the hair out. "Get into the bathroom," he growled.

Carrie walked slowly into the bathroom ahead of Julio then she broke into a run hoping to lock the door. He was too fast and shoved her into the tub, causing her to hit her head on the faucet. She lay slumped over the edge of the tub while he poured the contents of the makeup bag and Brian's toiletries bag onto the counter, but found no turtle.

Julio walked back to the bedroom and over to Brian who was sitting with wide eyes and making moaning and whimpering sounds through the wash cloth stuffed in his mouth. Julio noticed the rag was turning red with fresh blood.

Brian's eyes grew larger as he watched Julio turn the round wooden table over and bust one of the legs loose. He walked slowly back to Brian and removed the wash cloth.

"Tell me where the turtle is."

"I don't have a turtle. I wasn't with anyone to put a turtle in my bags. Please, I don't know what you are talking about!"

Julio took a baseball batter's stance and cocked the table leg like a bat, aiming at Brian's head, when a noise was heard from the bathroom. Julio could hear Carrie trying to get out of the tub and crying.

"I have something better for you," Julio told Brian as he pitched the table leg onto the carpeted floor and walked into the bathroom. "Carrie, I need your help for a few minutes," Julio chuckled.

Carrie managed to stand. Julio heard Brian scream that he had no turtles. Julio led Carrie back to the bedroom and stood her at the foot of the bed facing Brian, and then Julio stuffed the rag back into Brian's mouth.

"I want you to convince your husband to tell me where he hid my turtle. You can do that for me can't you?"

She saw Julio staring at her and felt his eyes boring holes into her chest, "Yes," she murmured as she saw Brian looking at her.

Julio motioned with his index finger for her, "Step forward please. I want Brian to see everything so he will feel more compelled to talk. Of course it all depends on whether or not he loves you doesn't it?" he asked.

Julio turned and stepped toward Brian and pulled the rag from his mouth, then stepped behind Carrie and opened her blouse and slid it off of her shoulders. Next he unhooked her bra as she started crying and trembling with fear. "Tell him, please tell him," she cried.

"I don't have a turtle!" Brain yelled.

"Perhaps you are just a pervert and want to see your wife having sex with a stranger," Julio smiled, as he removed her bra.

"No, please don't," Brian said, with tears running down his cheeks.

"Talk to me Brian. You can stop this at any time with just a few honest words. Tell me where the turtle is!"

Carrie was shaking uncontrollably now and Julio reached to her waist and unbuttoned and unzipped her skirt. He started pushing it down over her hips.

"Tell him!" she screamed, reaching down and trying to stop Julio from pushing the skirt lower.

"Tell me!" Julio mocked her as he shoved the skirt down and flexed his knees slightly letting the skirt fall to the floor around her feet.

"I don't know anything about a turtle! I don't have any turtles!" Brian said as loud as he could.

Julio stepped from behind Carrie and closer to Brian then another step closer, close enough to whisper into Brian's ear.

"Once I stick my dick into her mouth I won't stop, so you better tell me before I do. Do you understand?"

"Yes, I understand," Brian acknowledged, shaking his head.

Julio walked back to Carrie and pushed her on to the bed.

"No!"

"Talk Brian!" Julio commanded turning back to face him.

Brian was crying so hard he was having convulsions and Carrie was crying and shaking so badly she was almost falling off the bed.

"Get the panties off bitch."

"No, please no," she whimpered softly.

Julio grabbed her feet and pulled the panties completely off and she rolled onto her side wrapping the bedspread around her.

Julio loosened his jeans and slowly pushed them down and set on the bed to take them off, he looked at Brian as he took his shirt off. He then leaned over the bed and rolled Carrie over and yanked the bedspread off of her. She screamed again and rolled tightly into a ball with her knees up to her chin.

Julio stood up and walked to Brian and picked up the table leg from the floor. He stood in front of Brian and took up the batter's stance again.

"This is it, you can stop this now. Tell me where the turtle is!"

"I remember now. I gave it to a man at the airport, no I gave it back to her and she took it home, no, no the pilot has-"

Julio swung the table leg as hard as he could. It connected with the left side of Brian's head. The force of the impact knocked the chair over and Brian fell to the floor as blood splattered on the far wall.

"Home run! Whoo-hoo," Julio cheered.

Carrie heard the sound of the table leg hitting flesh and bone and screamed as loud as she could that they had no turtles.

Julio returned to Carrie and forced her to lie on her back as he raped her before bludgeoning her to death with the table leg. He then dressed and walked out of the room.

Julio left the hotel through the back entrance. He was on an adrenaline high and took a taxi to his favorite bar on the west side of the city. He arrived at the Barra de Sexo Caliente where is girl-friend had a room on the second floor.

Brookhaven Rail Yard
Long Island, NY

Ray had dozed off while sitting in the chair waiting for the coach car to arrive. He heard his name being called and looked up at Frank standing at the counter.

"Your coach car is in the yard. I called for someone to take you over there."

When Ray was informed he would accompany the container to Kansas, he had started studying the different jobs and responsibilities of rail employees and how the rail car could be tracked during the trip. Frank hadn't said, but Ray thought that the person to take him to the car would be a Railroad Carman, whose responsibilities included ensuring the car was safe and that the car was in the correct location of the train.

He knew that supply chain management improvements and heightened security concerns had increased the need to track and pinpoint rail car locations at all times, whether the rail car is stationary in a rail yard or siding, or being moved through the rail system by a locomotive. He learned that rail cars are equipped with radio frequency identification (RFID) tags such as Automatic Equipment Identification (AEI) tags that may be read by a wayside tag reader positioned at known locations within the rail system and configured to recognize and report when an AEI tagged railcar passes. Location and a time of passage, including weight of the rail car are reported from the wayside tag reader to a centralized database that may be accessed by shippers or the railroad companies to track the last reported locations of their tagged rail cars.

Ray heard someone walking up the steps to the office door, he looked up when the door opened and saw a man wearing overalls, walk into the office.

"There's your freight," Frank said to the man, nodding at Ray.

"I'm Boots," the man said walking over to Ray.

Ray stood, picked up his suitcase and the damp canvas bag, and walked after Boots through the front door. He followed Boots to a pickup and sat in the passenger seat and closed the door. Boots pushed the floor mounted gear shifter to the far right and revved the engine up to a screaming pitch. Ray looked at the tachometer and saw the needle over four thousand, when Boots let the clutch out quickly. The engine scream immediately dropped to a slow pitch as the pickup slowly started picking up speed.

"First gear is out and they won't replace it," Boots announced shifting into third gear.

Boots was now speeding as the pickup bounded over the tracks. Ray placed his left hand on the dash and raised his right hand to the ceiling trying to keep from hitting the windshield and roof. Ray saw the flatbed rail car with the tag 5593 and an Amtrak coach car coupled in front of it. Boots pulled up to the coach car and slammed on the brakes. The pickup skidded in the loose gravel as it came to a stop. Ray opened the door and stepped out.

Ray looked at Boots and tried to smile, but couldn't get control of the fear that still controlled his mind, "Thanks for the ride," he said and watched Boots rev the engine and force the shifter into second gear, making a loud grinding noise and popped the clutch. The pickup lurched forward, picking up speed.

Ray turned around and saw a man standing on the steps of the coach car. He was wearing the striped overalls, the standard uniform of many years past. "Are you Ballinger?" he asked.

"Yes I am," Ray responded walking to the steps.

"Pitch me your bag. I'm Stevie, the conductor," he said reaching down for Ray's suitcase. Ray handed it up to Stevie and grabbed the handrail as he climbed the steps to the coach car.

"I've been conducting seventeen years and never saw a coach car coupled to a freight train. You must be important," he said, leading Ray through the door into the car.

Ray noticed the car had six rows of seats in front of another door. He walked through the door and saw two bunks on each side and another door. He walked through the third door and saw two booths on one side of the car, and a short counter with three bar stools toward the rear of the car across form the booths. There was a small refrigerator, an electric hot plate and a microwave oven on a shelf behind the counter.

"All the comforts of home," Stevie said putting Ray's suitcase in the drawer below one of the bunks.

"Will you be riding in the coach car with me?"

"Only as far as Philadelphia, then someone else will be with you from there."

Ray nodded and heard a distant train whistle, then felt a bump which made him grab the back of one of the seats.

"That's the engine hooking up. You should be in Pittsburgh at 4:30, day after tomorrow. You'll pull out of there at 12:30 that afternoon. I have some paperwork to complete, so go ahead and make yourself comfortable," Stevie said, walking to the front of the car and taking a seat.

Ray noticed Stevie had a satchel in the seat where he set down and began filling in blanks in a printed form. Ray sat in a window seat and watched the office in the distance as the train slowly moved to the west. He felt nervous and couldn't sit while thinking about the binder. He stood up and walked through the door to the berth section of the car and undressed and lay down on the bottom bunk. He closed the curtain and quickly fell asleep to the gentle rocking of the train's motion and the hypnotic sounds of the clickety-clack from the seams of the tracks.

General Yi's office
Chengdu Military Base

General Yi awoke with a jolt, trying to remember where he was, quickly realizing he was alone in his office. He logged back on to his computer and opened his email account and pressed the 'new' button. He selected Professor Szu's email as the recipient and typed 257 in the Subject line.

I want the container from Lab 257 to be rerouted from the train to a ship destined to Havana Harbor as soon as possible, to the attention of Colonel Garcia. It doesn't matter which ship, as long as you track the location. The container should be transferred to an Iranian ship, the Milanian, when it arrives in Havana, Cuba. I will provide additional information once the Milanian has received the container.

He pressed the Send button, calling for his driver to take him back to his apartment.

Patio Amador Hotel
Quito, Ecuador

Vic led Elena to the lobby and they walked through the front door and to the waiting taxi. Vic opened the door for her and turned, seeing the cowboy near the hotel door looking at them. He saw her eyes widen when she saw the man.

He quickly pushed her in, jumping in beside her. The taxi driver confirmed the address and slowly pulled away from the curb. Vic looked out the back glass, seeing the cowboy running for the parking lot. The taxi took the next left then a right getting onto the highway. Vic looked back, but did not see any car following.

"What are you going to do?" she asked.

"I'll take you to Lucy's and go back to the hotel," he said wondering if he would be lucky enough to lose the cowboy a third time.

"Elena I want to hear more about Cordova, your brother and the cowboy. What if we go to a quiet bar and talk for a little while?"

"Sure," she replied. She looked at him, thinking that he might offer to return the memory card, she started working up a plausible lie that Cordova might believe for the delayed delivery.

Vic leaned forward and passed an extra ten dollar bill to the driver. "Can you take us to the Casa Del Sol bar?" Vic asked.

Research Lab
Tsinghua University

Professor Szu, heard his phone buzz when he received General Yi's email, does the man ever sleep, he thought, and opened the email. He made a couple of notes on a pad on the desk, then activated the decryption program and typed in CSX freight lines. He accessed the login option and began the program to sign on as the system administrator, noticing the logon and password boxes, as characters were automatically typed and retyped while the system searched for the correct information to defeat the current security codes.

He refilled his cup of tea twice while waiting for the hacking program to complete its objective. The screen on the monitor changed as the correct login and password codes were accepted by the CSX computer in Chicago.

He typed in rail car 5593 and saw that the car had passed Newark, New Jersey and was on time for Pittsburgh, Pennsylvania. He typed in a new routing for the car to be sided in Harrisburg, Pennsylvania. He opened a new order for the container to be moved to rail car 6743 and connected to the Penn Eastern Rail Lines and scheduled for delivery at Philadelphia Shipyards the following day. He rerouted a container, with similar weight, which was scheduled for Spokane, Washington to be transferred to rail car 5593.

He logged off of the CSX computer and went home.

Casa Del Sol
Quito, Ecuador

Vic followed Elena through the door, reaching for her left arm, he stopped her, easing her to her left away from the door. He stepped to the bar and ordered two Carta Blanca beers, waiting until his eyes adjusted to the dimly lit room.

He saw the beer signs and several clocks on the dark paneled walls. The bar was crowded with people, a few playing pool in the back and most at tables, where men were attempting to find a sleep mate for the night. The dance floor was crowded and a live band was playing slow music from a corner of the room near the dance floor.

He placed his hand against her lower back and guided her to a vacant table near the far end of the large room, walking past the bar and the several men sitting on the stools as all of them watched her glide past. She felt very self-conscious knowing that she was under their microscope and his. She felt Vic's unwavering hand on her back which gave her the feeling of safety and hope.

Vic pulled a chair away from the table for her and took a seat across from her. He ordered two dinner plates and leaned in toward her. He wanted to ask many questions, but felt the training start to kick in and asked, "Do you know how much drugs Cordova is smuggling,"

"No."

"How are the drugs transported? What is the shipments original departure location?"

"I do not know the answers to your questions," she said, wondering if he was interested only in the smuggling or was he interested in Eduardo.

"Okay. Let's start over. Tell me what you do know."

She told him about Rosita and how Cordova accused her of stealing his money which she had brought back from Dallas, she was silent for a long pause, remembering Rosita on the floor.

Elena explained that she rarely escorted shipments to Texas, but would meet the man at the Dallas office and bring back suitcases or boxes. There was one other time that she was warned about the shipment similar to the turtle, she told him that she had slipped the small package into a man's jacket pocket and let him kiss her after the plane landed until she could sneak the package way from him. She then ran and hid in the bathroom for three hours. She admitted she was trying to do the same thing again by putting the turtle in his backpack.

Vic leaned back, shaking his head attempting to absorb everything she was revealing. He waved for another beer and a couple of empanadas.

Elena felt her body come alert when she heard his next question.

"Tell me about your brother."

Vic realized he was falling for this girl. He kept looking at her beautiful face with the small mole near her left cheek bone that seemed to accent her beauty. He noticed how her eyes were almond shaped and so pretty that he kept looking again to replenish his memory.

She explained that she and Eduardo were raised in an orphanage in Quito and that Eduardo had started a job for a man who farmed in the jungles in eastern Ecuador. It was several years later when she discovered the man grew coca for medicinal use in Ecuador.

Vic knew the coca plant was used by the majority of people in Ecuador, especially when scaling 14,000 foot mountains. The effect of the coca plant when consumed as coca tea keeps people from losing consciousness at extreme elevations. The problem arises with the plant, when it is refined into cocaine.

Cordova had moved in on the man Eduardo worked for and eventually killed him; assuming his business and then began refining the coca and shipping it out of the country, primarily to the United States.

Eduardo had stolen a bundle of cocaine destined to be shipped to the United States via Brazil and was waiting for the buyer when Cordova found him. Cordova had threatened to kill Eduardo unless she worked for him.

Vic finished his empanada and ordered another beer and stammered when he asked if Cordova had forced her to have sex with him. She admitted he had tried, but she was always successful at fighting him off each time.

Vic looked at her now with wanting eyes and felt that he had to take care of her; absolutely had to protect her. He looked at his watch and realized it was almost midnight, then called a taxi.

Vic concentrated on what he had learned from Elena and felt anger at Cordova for her predicament. He called Lucy with an ETA.

The taxi drove the twenty minutes to Lucy's apartment; he had been looking, ensuring they were not being followed. She got out and they walked to Lucy's door. Vic returned to the taxi and rode back to the hotel, deep in thought of how to free her from Cordova.

Research Lab
Tsinghua University

General Cheng moved the cursor to the program start button that was displayed on his monitor. The program activated and started running, the program was searching for a certain traffic computer in Los Angeles, California. The computer was hacked several days previously with a trap door left in the operating software. General Cheng saw the panel that popped up on the large monitor indicating the program was active and waiting for his programmer's input. The large monitor displayed three panels, on the left was the operating program in Los Angeles, the middle panel displayed the status of traffic lights that the computer operated and the panel on the right displayed the street view of nearby traffic from security cameras.

General Cheng motioned to Li, the program manager, to begin and saw that all the traffic lights went to "green" simultaneously. He saw a cement truck entering the intersection from the right and a mini-van entering the intersection from the top which appeared loaded with kids, displaying lettering on the windows, Go Cougars and We are the Best.

Professor Szu waited and watched the two vehicles getting closer. He saw the crash as the cement truck broadsided the mini-van, feeling a sickening twinge that gripped his intestines.

General Cheng looked up and calmly said, "Next location." He watched, as the programmers backed out of the traffic computer in Los Angeles. Next Professor Szu saw an intersection in Dallas, Texas being displayed on the screen in the same format. General Cheng noticed Li entering software code into the new traffic computer.

Professor Szu looked at the bottom of his note pad and saw that there were seven other cities in the United States targeted for the day's exercise. He felt the guilt pangs tightening in his stomach and noticed that Li appeared very pale and asked to be excused. One of General Cheng's programmers took the keyboard.

Tsinghua University
Professor Szu accessed the computer system at Philadelphia Harbor. He had discovered that laws prohibited direct freight from any point in the United States directly to Cuba. He initiated a freight manifest from Philadelphia to Panama, and a second manifest from Panama to Havana. He booked the freight on Guangzhou shipping.

Day Three
Research Lab
Tsinghua University

Li walked into the darkened lab and looked at the large monitor on the wall. The system was turned off, but he kept reviewing
the image of the underwater robots and submarines that was on
the screen when General Yi's men were in the room several days
before. He had uploaded an article from Sky News earlier that day
detailing the catastrophe in the Gulf of Mexico off the Alabama
coast. The article stated that over thirty men were missing and fifteen were known dead from the collapse of the oil rig. He enjoyed
the hacking of computers when he was simply looking at other
systems and learning about encryption codes, however now it was
becoming serious and he had second thoughts about the program.
The cars with the children wrecking and the ship crashing was
much more than he had ever thought would ever happen, and he
wasn't convinced that the killing of innocent people was ever justi-
fied. Soldiers killing each other on battle fields were one thing, but
this wasn't war, it was murder. He wanted nothing to do with it.

He sat down at the terminal in the corner that was rarely used
and logged on. He typed in CIA and started searching the hacked
government agencies for a computer that was currently powered
on and had keyboard activity at the CIA in Langley, Virginia. He
found one and wrote the IP address on a note pad.

He began writing a worm that would target only that computer;
next he found the listing of computers and their operators at the
CIA headquarters. He didn't speak English, but had used a phrase
book earlier in the day to compose a message.

He started the coded message using Python language and
spent over two hours detailing the code, ensuring there were no
mistakes, especially misspellings or words that would be out of
context.

His target computer was assigned to Ed Tatum, a communication specialist, Li completed the code and pressed the enter key,

feeling much better knowing that he had sent the message inside the worm and that he had completed his task without getting caught in the Research Lab without authorization.

Harrisburg Rail Yard
Harrisburg, Pennsylvania

Ray heard the train's whistle and felt the train stopping. He got up and walked to the front section of the coach car and looked out the side window, noticing the train was on a siding as another freight train passed it in an eastern direction. He didn't see anyone in the front section of the car and assumed the conductor was taking care of his work elsewhere. Ray walked back through the car to the dining portion and saw a porter sitting on a stool behind the counter.

"Good morning, sir. Coffee?" the porter asked.

"Yes, please."

The porter stood and poured a cup of coffee from the pot that was under the drip canister, then placed the cup on a saucer and slid it in front of Ray, moving the small cream and sugar packets closer to him at the same time.

"Where are we? I must have been asleep a long time; I didn't hear you come aboard." Ray said.

"We are in Harrisburg, Pennsylvania and I came on board about three hours back."

"Are we still on schedule for Pittsburg today?"

"No, we are being delayed for a couple of hours. We are stopping to unload some of the freight to another train, then moving west. We should still be in Pittsburgh by morning."

Ray saw a stack of magazines in a rack at the end of the counter and selected the most recent "Food and Wine" and started thumbing through it.

CIA Headquarters
Langley, Virginia

Ed Tatum's cubicle was in the basement of the CIA headquarters. Two panels enclosing him against a concrete wall, a picture of the Washington Redskins and several of Ed in his rugby uniform. Ed was assigned to the Western Europe group and noticed his computer acting strange. The keyboard stopped responding to his commands. The monitor went blank momentarily it displayed a full screen picture of flowers along the base of what appeared to be the Great Wall of China.

Ed pressed the Control, Alt, and Delete keys simultaneously to activate the Task Manager, but the keyboard was completely locked out. He called the person in the next cubicle who looked over the partition, seeing the difficulties Ed was experiencing and called the IT manager.

Frank, from the IT department walked up and immediately realized Ed's computer was affected by a virus, he reached down and disconnected the Ethernet cable. He continued trying different things to activate the keyboard, disconnecting the cable several times. He put his finger on the power button and looked at the monitor and noticed that the picture on the monitor appeared to be changing slowly.

He withdrew his finger and set back, watching the screen. A few of the flowers had changed shapes and were now displaying a different image on the screen. He noticed that portions of the wall had changed. Other areas of the picture began the same type of anomaly as the two men watched for ten minutes.

Ed noticed the picture was changing one pixel at a time or perhaps a hundred at a time. He grabbed his calculator and quickly multiplied 1280 x 1024, that's 1,310,720 pixels. Hell that could take hours. He watched the screen fading out, similar to the television screen when the satellite transmission is dropping out. He stopped trying to find the reason for the keyboard being locked out and waited for an hour, noticing that half of the picture was now changed and starting to resemble a typed page with a font size of 16, black letters on a yellow background. He waited for another forty-five minutes and walked to the coffee pot and refilled his cup, he came back and set down and saw the new page on his monitor.

Special message to Ed Tatum, CIA headquarters, Langley, Virginia.

Be advised: Large computer hacking program underway. Ship wreck was not accidental. Oil rig disaster not accidental. Lab 257 viruses loss was not accidental, destination unknown.

Ed grabbed his phone and called Jim, his supervisor.

Jim walked into the cubicle. "What the hell is going on?" he asked, seeing Ed's finger pointing at the monitor.

Jim reread the message aloud; he looked at Ed when he heard the printer start up. Both men looked at the printer and wondered if the problem was affecting the printer also, then a sheet printed out as though someone had pressed print screen. Jim picked up the sheet and looked at the message on the sheet of paper. Both men saw the monitor flicker and go blank. The computer then shut down.

Jim looked at Ed and Frank whistled softly, then said. "I have seen many viruses and problems, but never one this complex."

Jim breathed deeply and said. "Ed, you are not an analyst and neither am I, so don't go off the deep end here. Pass the intelligence on up the chain without journalistic type comments, the pencil pushers will want more data on this so start digging now and don't touch this computer."

"I'm already working on it," Ed stated and started typing on the computer in the next cubicle.

Barra de Sexo Caliente
Quito, Ecuador

Julio stumbled into the bar, he was drinking all night and was now looking for a girl. He climbed the stairs and bumped into the owner. He paid $40.00 for the youngest of the girls and walked into her room. He saw her asleep on the bed and began taking his clothes off. He looked at his cell phone and noticed the battery was completely discharged, he knew his charger was in his apartment, and pitched the phone onto the banana crate which doubled as a dresser. He climbed into the bed and passed out.

Hotel Patio Amador
Quito, Ecuador

The sun was up as Vic hurried to the bathroom to brush his teeth and shave. He called Pablo and told him he would be at the office later in the morning.

He took the elevator down to the lobby and walked to the restaurant. "One for breakfast," Vic told the hostess as he picked up the morning paper from a stand. He followed her to the table and opened the paper.

He was shocked when he saw the picture of the man and woman from the plane on the front page. He read the article about Brian Stevens, an American, on a business trip with his wife and was murdered in their hotel room. Neighbors in the hotel had complained about too much noise and the manager had found them in the room.

He continued reading the article and froze, when he read that neighbors had heard someone screaming they didn't have a turtle. He read the paragraph that described the obvious torture that the couple suffered before their deaths. Feeling rage, wondering if Cordova was behind the murder or not.

He walked to the elevator and as the doors were closing, Vic saw the cowboy watching him from the center of the lobby.

Vic grabbed his phone and dialed DIR. "Lisa, do you have anything on Ithaca Exports?" he asked.

"Yes. It appears they are a front company for a suspected terrorist group called 'World for Ala'. Ithaca Exports is suspected of setting up a counterfeit ring to break the finances of certain Latin American countries. They are suspected to have close ties to the terrorist group Al Qaeda. They are committed to their cause and are considered to be well funded and very dangerous," Lisa finished reading the alert.

"That explains the images," Vic said.

"They have a sister group in Panama called 'El Nuevo Mundo para Ala' or 'The New World for Ala' and that group is believed to be funded by The People's Republic of China," she continued.

"China?" Vic asked.

"That's what the bulletin says. Do you need anything else?" she asked.

"Yes, but you don't have a magic wand, so never mind," he laughed and closed the phone.

Vic walked to his room, looking at his watch, he noticed the time was almost 9:00; he opened his satellite phone and dialed the phone number for the President's office in Panama City.

"Capital building. How may I direct your call?" the receptionist asked.

"This is Vic James with SatCom calling for President Sanchez."

"Is he expecting your call Señor?"

"No Señora, he is not expecting my call, but it is very important I speak with him. Is he available?"

"Wait one moment, por favor, I will check." Vic waited for a minute, hoping he wasn't in a meeting, then heard the secretary announce she was transferring the call.

"Mr. James? This is a pleasant surprise. How may I help you?" President Sanchez asked.

"Sir, I am calling to inquire about the operation of SatCom's performance in Panama. I trust that the phone company is operating to your expectations and satisfaction."

"Yes Mr. James, I am not aware of any complaints at this time."

"Mr. President, I will not take any more of your time and I wish to thank you for allowing SatCom to continue to provide telephone service to the great country of Panama. Have a nice day sir," Vic said, closing his satellite phone.

He called Pablo, telling him about seeing the cowboy, asking him to come pick him up. He started working on a plan to discover how deep Cordova was in with the counterfeiting and how far he would go to get the memory card back.

Harrisburg Rail Yard
Harrisburg, Pennsylvania

Ray heard the train's whistle and felt the lurching motion as the train began moving again. He looked out the window and saw the multiple parallel tracks and various rail cars passing slowly by as the train began picking up speed. He walked back to the forward section of the car and took a window seat, then put his ear buds in and turned on his iPod. He reclined the seat back and closed his eyes listening to the music. He started thinking about the first day and jumping into the water to retrieve the canvas bag. Good thing my iPod was in my suitcase, not the canvas bag he thought.

He opened the binder and tried to read the ink smeared pages so he would know the next stop, but couldn't decipher the words. He attempted to turn the page and realized two pages were stuck together, he cussed himself knowing he had screwed the pooch. He closed the binder and laid it on the seat.

DIR Office
Dallas, Texas

Ralph received a phone call from John Waters, the CIA director advising him on the latest development regarding the company Ithaca Exports. The company was added to the terrorist list and the Dallas office was raided. The office computer was confiscated and was being inspected by the FBI. The proprietor had not returned to the shop since the raid and the home address of the owner was a home owned by the mayor of Dallas. The FBI was working the case.

Barra de Sexo Caliente
Quito, Ecuador

Julio woke up with a terrific headache, sensing that he was passed out way too long and knew Cordova would be pissed if he found out about it. He found his cell phone in his jeans pocket, cussed when he realized the battery was dead. He rolled off of the twin size mattress that was on the floor, holding the cane bottom chair for support, as he stood up. The music on the juke box down stairs was playing, as he stumbled out the door into the narrow hallway of the Bar.

The owner of the bar often let him sleep in a room after paying for the girls when he was too drunk to go home. He was still too drunk, but knew he better let Cordova know about the turtle. He left the bar and walked to a pay phone on the street corner. He called Señor Cordova and informed him that Brian Stevens did not have the turtle.

Butler Rail Yard
Pittsburg, Pennsylvania

Ray felt the train slowing as the whistle blew several long bursts and he set up on the edge of the bunk, attempting to shake the sleep from his brain. He pulled his jeans on and slipped his feet into his shoes walking to the rear of the coach; seeing a new man behind the counter.

"Where are we?" Ray asked.

"Pulling into the Butler yard."

"Butler what?"

"Pittsburg, Pennsylvania, we are scheduled to hook up with another west bound and run three engines to Chicago."

Ray turned around and walked back to the bunk and got back in bed. He was getting cabin fever and wanted off the train.

DIR Office
Plano, Texas

"Ralph, Director Waters is on line one," Lisa announced over the intercom.

Ralph was filling his coffee cup and walked back across the office to his desk. "I wonder what that son of a bitch wants now." Ralph grumbled. He was still upset from the near ambush on Vic during the SNOOP conference call the previous day.

"Ralph here."

"This is Waters. A coded message was received on a computer at Langley and is being given top priority, which will be part of Jupiter. I will forward you a summary of the original email. Is your man still in Latin America?"

"He is in Quito," Ralph said.

"POTUS called an emergency Joint Intelligence Meeting this morning. I'll conference you in when we start."

"You should be receiving an email with the coded message attached, look for it. Use the North Branch code to decode it."

Ralph opened the email from Langley and clicked on the print page ICON, then grabbed his jacket and brief case. He opened the crypto folder from his safe and quickly deciphered the printed message. He read it twice.

> **Top Secret-**
> **All government computers, mainframes and personal desk systems are being inspected for viruses. Norton, McAfee and other anti-virus companies have been notified to search for possible threats. Possible subterfuge currently being employed against the United States.**
> **Jupiter meeting at noon in D.C.**

Ithaca Exports
Perucho, Ecuador

Señor Cordova received a call from Juan and was informed that he had set in front of the elevator all morning and had not seen Elena or the American again since earlier that day.

Juan, gulped and said, "I am afraid they saw me and checked out, I don't think they are here anymore," with obvious fear in his voice.

Cordova was quiet for a couple of moments, he was angry all day and now livid, Stevens must have been the wrong American, he thought, and now Juan has lost Elena again.

"Keep looking for them! Stay all day if you have to, but find that bitch!" he slowly closed the cell phone.

He dialed the emergency number General Yi had given him. He requested they speak in Spanish and asked that a message be delivered to General Yi that the counterfeit currency images were lost and hesitantly requested a replacement be sent to him in Ecuador.

Oval Office
Washington, D.C.

Director Waters of the CIA started the Joint Intelligence meeting by handing everyone a printed copy of the message received on Ed Tatum's computer. He summarized the message as apparently being legitimate, in that it seemed to originate in China, he also cautioned that it could still be a hoax from China. He asked if anyone knew what was meant by Lab 257, no one in the room was aware of that location or had ever heard of Lab 257 as stated in the context of the message.

Director Pierce informed the group that the FBI and the Coast Guard had interviews scheduled with Captain Lytle and Pilot Sam Muskey with the Seattle Harbor Master the following day. They had waited for their injuries to heal slightly before grilling them to why they would crash the ship. Both men were under guard at the hospital in Seattle.

The oil disaster in the Gulf of Mexico was attributed to metal fatigue by engineers and was not being investigated further. The valves on the large blowout preventer were closed, stopping any long term affects from crude oil being leaked into the ocean.

Director Greene with the NSA concluded his presentation with a report that all the government computers were being sniffed for malware, viruses and worms.

Director Pierce's cell phone chirped as he set on the couch. The other men in the room saw his face turn ashen while he received his verbal message. He replied to the caller, "Locate the container and perform a visual on it, today!" he terminated his phone call.

He repositioned his butt on the sofa and said, "Gentlemen, Lab 257 is another name for the nasty stuff on Plum Island. FBI agents will investigate the report of a container of bacteria or viruses in transit from New York to Fort Leavenworth, Kansas. We have no report of it missing, but we are tracking the container and the FBI will assign agents to escort it to Kansas."

FBI Office
Chicago, Illinois

John Roberts, special agent in charge of the Chicago office, received the urgent phone call from Washington. He was provided the routing information for flatbed car 5593 on CSX Freight Lines. The information included a scheduled brief stop at Dearborn Station in Chicago an hour later.

He walked to Steve Logan's office and gave him the information and told him to grab his jacket for a road trip. Steve knew that Dearborn Station was a thirty minute drive from the office that time of day. He wasn't certain why they were going, but knew John would explain it in route.

Chicago Rail Yards
Chicago, Illinois

Ray felt the train cars bumping as the train slowed, he had fallen asleep to the gentle rhythm of the clacking sounds of the track seams. He walked back to the rear of the car and found the porter playing solitaire and asked where they were and how much longer to Fort Leavenworth, Kansas. The porter told him they were scheduled to offload his cargo in two days. Ray ate a sandwich and drank a can of soda while talking to the porter.

SatCom Office
Quito Ecuador

Pablo picked Vic up at the hotel rear doors and noticed during the drive that Vic was deep in thought or was just tired from too much of Elena. He smiled to himself while parking in the SatCom garage.

Both men walked into the building. Vic stopped at Lucy's office; he looked at Elena and acknowledged she was the prettiest lady he had ever known, noticing the puzzled look on Pablo's face when he realized Elena had gotten to the office earlier than Vic. He turned to ask and Vic explained that she had spent the night at Lucy's. They continued on to Pablo's office.

Pablo sat and listened as Vic told him everything that Elena had shared with him at the bar the previous night. Pablo whistled softly a couple of times, asking few questions.

"Do you believe what she told you?"

"Yeah, I believe her."

"What are you going to do?"

"I have a plan that includes you or a taxi. I just need to know who to call."

"I'm your driver, where are we going? Whose ass are we going to kick?"

Vic let out a sigh and nodded his head in an, I thought you would say that gesture. "I like your attitude," Vic said, feeling very relieved.

Vic looked at Pablo, realizing that he was a true friend who was willing to go to battle over something that really didn't affect him, but wanted to go, to help a friend.

"We're going to Perucho, with a stop at the hotel first," Vic said, slowly standing up.

He explained his plan to Pablo and retrieved the turtle from the safe, then found a different Micro SD card in his briefcase and placed it in the turtle's belly and glued the plate in place. Vic noticed a stack of cash in the safe; he rolled it up and put it into his pocket.

"Are you going to trade Eduardo for the turtle or buy him off?"

"I don't know, but I want to be as prepared as possible. I want Cordova to leave Elena alone and to release Eduardo. Either way, I am not giving the real memory card back to Cordova. The cash is SatCom's right?" Vic asked.

"Yeah, for emergency's, I guess this suffices," Pablo smiled.

"Let's move," Vic said putting the turtle into his shirt pocket.

Vic stopped at Lucy's office and asked Elena to join him and Pablo.

Dearborn Station Rail Yards
Chicago, Illinois

John explained the reason for the urgency to Steve as they drove through the Chicago traffic. "What the hell do they mean a missing container?" Steve asked.

"You got me. We need to verify that the container is on the flatbed. If the flatbed is there, then the container is probably alright. Who the hell could steal a container from a moving train?" John asked.

John parked the car at a building at the south end of the rail station, then he and Steve walked up the steps and saw a man sitting at a desk inside.

"Can I help you," the man asked.

John introduced himself and Steve as agents with the FBI, explaining that they were there to inspect a rail car traveling to Fort Leavenworth, Kansas.

"I received a call about twenty minutes ago to side 5593 and the coach car in front of it. They are still on the siding, waiting for you."

"What coach car?" Steve asked.

"The coach car is carrying the guy traveling with car 5593. If the flatbed car is sided, the coach car has to be sided with it. That is on the manifest."

"Then we'll speak to the guy on the coach car first," John said.

The man provided several quick directions to the location of the rail-siding the cars were waiting on. He then resumed his monitoring of a large electronic board on the wall. John and Steve walked back out to the car and realized their Chevrolet Impala would not clear the tracks and they did not see a road in the direction the man had given them. John returned to the building and explained he had to inspect the car and needed transportation across the many sets of tracks.

John returned to the Impala and told Steve a ride was on the way. Ten minutes later a white Ford F-150 pickup pulled up to their car and the driver honked the horn. Steve and John got into the vehicle and the driver started the bumpy trip across the rail yard to the siding where the two cars were located. Steve climbed the steps of the coach car with John close behind and the two men walked inside, a porter was at the counter playing cards with someone.

"Excuse me gentlemen, my name is John Roberts and this is Steve Logan, we are Agents with the FBI," John stated displaying his badge. "I won't waste your time, but we are here to ensure a container is on flat bed car 5593."

Ray quickly stood up, "That's my car!" he announced.

"We simply need to ensure the container is secure. Can you tell us about the container?"

Ray sheepishly admitted he had destroyed the information in the binder and ruined the laptop computer. The porter told the three men that he could show them the flatbed and container, then walked out of the car and climbed down the steps, he led Ray, John and Steve to rail car 5593.

"This is the container I am escorting to Fort Leavenworth," Ray said pointing up to the gray container. He snapped his head hard to his left, taking a second look.

Ray realized the container was a lighter shade of gray and had considerably more rust and dents than it had when they loaded it onto the car. He walked to the end of the car and noticed the anti-theft container lock had a longer shackle and the tamper proof cable was red instead of green.

"This isn't my container!" Ray thundered.

John called the local office and a subsequent call was placed to the FBI headquarters in D.C. and to the local police station.

Hotel Patio Amador
Quito, Ecuador

Pablo drove Vic and Elena to the hotel; Vic told him to stop fifty feet before he arrived, then hopped out of the Jeep and walked the rest of the way. He entered the front lobby doors and waved to Pablo as he drove past the hotel.

Vic looked around the large room for the cowboy and saw him setting on a couch in front of the elevators. He waited near the bar, in sight of the couch while he studied the cowboy for a few minutes to see if he had a friend. Not seeing anyone appearing to be waiting with him, Vic walked to the couch and set down next to the cowboy.

The cowboy did a double take, staring at Vic. He set up straight and glared, then said, "Give me the turtle!"

"Is it your turtle?" Vic asked.

"No, it belongs to Señor Cordova."

"I may give it to him, but not a niño pequeño like you."

Vic noticed the cowboy's eyes narrow, his right hand slowly lowered to his waist. Vic saw a small bulge at his waist, he removed the turtle from his shirt pocket, holding it up, and asked if Juan wanted it.

"Yes, you can give it to me or I will take it from you, it is your choice" he smiled, displaying his yellow teeth.

Vic stood lifting his arms in a mock surrendering gesture and calmly stated. "I'll give it to you outside, come on, are you driving or walking?"

Vic watched Juan get to his feet, then led Juan to the front lobby doors, looking over his shoulder to see if he was following him to the parking lot. Juan stayed with Vic, walking out the doors.

"Are you driving or walking?" Vis asked again.

Juan pointed to the older green Chevrolet. Vic started walking toward the old car and noticed Juan balk slightly, not certain to believe Vic or not. Vic stopped and pulled the turtle from his pocket again.

"You want this or not?" he asked continuing to walk to the car.

He noticed Juan was now eagerly following him. Vic walked to the driver's door, reached in and pulled the hood release lever, then looked at Juan as an instructor would look at his student and said, "I'll show you a problem with the motor on these older cars, it's something you need to pay close attention to or the car will simply stop running someday."

Juan looked at Vic's shirt pocket wondering if he could steal the turtle and decided to play along for a few minutes, at least until there were fewer people in the parking lot.

"Now look at this," Vic said, walking to the front of the car, raising the hood and holding it to keep it from rising completely by the lift springs.

"See that fan belt, feel how rough the belt is where it is frayed on the edges," Vic said watching Juan reach his right hand for the fan belt. Vic slammed the hood down as hard as he could on Juan's right arm.

"Chinga!" Juan squealed trying to withdraw his arm which was tightly wedged between the hood and the radiator, with Vic's full weight on the hood.

Vic leaned over close to Juan. "Listen, shit head, I don't like to be tailed and you have pushed me too far!" he growled aggressively.

"Please?" Juan pleaded, with tears welling in his eyes.

"Where is Cordova?"

"What? My arm, please!"

Vic was leaning on the hood applying as much pressure as he could. He looked at Juan who had tears rolling down his cheeks now, but seemed to still want to be a tough guy.

Vic lessened the pressure on the hood slightly and Juan started to withdraw his arm, then Vic quickly bounced on the hood with all his weight, hearing the bone snap. Juan screeched then started moaning loudly as his knees buckled and he dropped to the concrete.

"I will put your head under the hood! Do you understand me?"

"Yes, yes I understand."

"Then tell me where Cordova is."

"He is at his office."

"Is he in Perucho?"

"Yes, yes Cordova is in Perucho," he cried.

Vic looked down at Juan. He had tears in his eyes and was on his knees. Vic could tell Juan knew he had met someone he could not threaten and push around.

Vic relaxed his body and straightened up releasing the pressure on the hood. Juan hesitantly pulled his arm back and tried to stand, but lost his balance and fell, whimpering again.

"Get up tu hijo de puta, you son of a bitch! You want to hurt Elena? You have to get past me first!"

Vic felt his anger getting out of control. He helped Juan stand up and walk, watching him carry his right arm with his left hand to the passenger door. Vic opened the door, and then quickly reached under Juan's shirt for the bulge, he removed a block of wood, looked at Juan and sneered, then pushed him into the car and slammed it. Vic sternly looked at the two men watching from the corner, observing as they quickly looked away, not wanting to get involved. He walked around the car and got in under the steering wheel, turning to his right, he glared at Juan.

FBI Headquarters
Washington, D.C.

John's call was received and transferred directly to FBI Director Pierce, who had returned from the meeting in the Oval office. He was informed that the container on rail car 5593 was not the same container that had shipped from Lab 257 on Plum Island. The information was then forwarded to the new facility at Fort Leavenworth, Kansas. An alert was generated to find the location of Dr. Lewis.

Hotel parking lot
Quito, Ecuador

Vic looked at Juan, sitting in the front seat of the old car. He held his hand out demanding the ignition key. Juan struggled to get his left hand into his right front pocket and fished out the key, handing it to Vic.

"Tell me how to get to Cordova's office. If he is not there you are going to lose the use of both arms," Vic said.

He reached for Juan's right arm. Juan jerked back and hit his elbow against the door, whimpering again.

"You've got one chance to get this right, I broke that arm and I will break the other if you lie to me, or if Cordova isn't at his office."

Juan looked at Vic as though he was the judge and executioner, but offered no indication that he understood.

Vic felt his anger welling up. "Do you understand?" Vic demanded.

Juan set stoically still; looking at Vic as if he could whip him with only one arm. Vic tightened his right fist, and then he back-handed Juan hitting him in the stomach. Juan leaned forward coughing, trying to get his breath.

Juan struggled to breathe finally inhaling deeply. "Yes, take highway 35 toward Tanda, hurry, he is leaving early today," he said with obvious pain in his voice.

Vic started the car and pulled into traffic, then opened his phone and dialed Pablo. He told Pablo to follow, but to stay back so no one would assume they were traveling together. Vic closed the phone and looked at Juan again.

"What about Eduardo? Is he there?"

"Who?"

Vic hit Juan in the mouth with his right hand. "Are you lying to me?"

"No, Eduardo is there, working in the back, he is there," Juan cried, wiping blood from his busted lip with his left hand.

"Please, no more!"

Vic held the steering wheel so tight his arms were shaking. He glared at Juan and said, "You are a real pussy, a weak bully who threatens small defenseless women. You piss me off. I hate ass-holes like you!"

Vic hit Juan again in the left temple, wanting to throw him from the car at fifty miles an hour. He drove for forty-five minutes, watching Juan slowly sink lower in the seat.

Vic saw a sign for Perucho to the left in three miles. He slowed down and saw Pablo and Elena behind him at a safe distance. Vic turned left and followed the road into Perucho, then stopped at an intersection and turned to Juan.

"Now where?"

"Through town and three more miles, Ithaca Exports will be on the right."

Vic drove slowly out of town, when he passed two miles he slammed on the brakes. The car skidded to a stop. Juan had not buckled his seat belt and hit the dash with his broken arm and his head.

Dearborn Station Rail Yards
Chicago, Illinois

Ray sat in the seat looking out the window. He felt very humiliated and useless as he wondered if he would only lose his job or if he would be held responsible for the loss of the container as well. He remembered back to the first day, how he destroyed the binder and the laptop, his phone never worked again either. He tried to think of a time when someone might have stolen the container, but couldn't imagine how it could have happened. The rail car is still 5593, but the container looks different, it even has some Korean name on the side. He knew he was going to jail for losing the container. His stomach was in knots and he felt like throwing up.

Ithaca Exports
Perucho, Ecuador

"Get out, now!" Vic leaned over and pulled the door handle, then pushed Juan out of the car. Vic saw him literally fall out and land in a heap onto the gravel road and whimper again as he attempted to move away from the rear wheel as Vic slammed the car back into drive and floored the accelerator spinning the tires in the loose gravel. He threw gravel onto Juan who was kneeling, trying to stand up while holding his right arm.

Pablo saw Vic dump Juan and told Elena to duck as he drove past the guy who looked like a whipped puppy dog. He waved for help and Pablo ignored him, as he drove past.

Vic rounded a curve and saw a building on the right which was almost covered in thick bushes and vines. The faded paint covered cinder block walls, many cracked and chipped. He parked the car next to a blue Kia in the drive and called Pablo, telling him the he was going in to try and find Eduardo.

Vic walked to the door of the building and tried the door knob, it was locked. He knocked on the door and waited for several minutes, then walked around the side of the building and saw Pablo and Elena drive slowly by. He continued to the back of the building and heard people talking. He rounded the corner and saw three men standing beside several long tables with coca plants lying on them drying. They were using long handled pitchforks to turn the stacks of plants over to allow the bottom ones to dry.

Vic surveyed the large area for weapons or anything he might use to protect himself. He was relieved and disappointed that there were no firearms. Vic walked into the area clearing his throat.

"I am here for Eduardo Torres, I am with the United States DEA. He will be arrested for cocaine trafficking and extradited to the United States," Vic said, walking toward the three men.

He noticed all three jumped at the sound of his voice, trying to figure out how he had snuck up on them. The older man was wearing a dark green button shirt which was ripped in several places. The sleeves were ripped off, displaying massive muscles, his jeans were torn at the knees and the left rear pocket was hanging loose. He appeared to be about thirty years old and in very good shape, Vic knew he might not have a chance at an even fight with this guy and started looking for a possible weapon.

"Where is Señor Cordova? He called and told us that Eduardo was here," Vic said trying not to show any fear, even though he was scared.

The older and larger of the three men started walking toward Vic holding the pitchfork as though he would use it. Vic stopped and looked around for anything that might be useful to fend off the pitchfork. He saw an axe handle leaning against the wall fifteen feet away in the corner to his left.

The man was walking slow and deliberate, stabbing air in front of him with the pitchfork, Vic stopped and started backing toward the corner where the axe handle was, he saw the man grin as though he was looking forward to using the pitchfork.

"I am not here to bother you, only Eduardo," Vic advised him, getting closer to the axe handle.

"You are bothering me, this is private property and you are trespassing. I do not like gringo narcs," the man growled getting closer with each step.

Vic feigned to his right and dove to his left, grabbing the axe handle. The man took several steps closer until he saw Vic roll and land on his feet with the handle in both hands. He then smiled as though he welcomed the struggle between his pitch fork and a stick.

The man made several short jabs with the pitch fork tines, swinging it sideways trying to catch Vic's arms with the sharp tines. Vic held the axe handle in both hands, pointing the larger and heavier end toward the man. The man lunged with the pitch fork and Vic parried and hit the fork tines forcing them to his right, the man then thrust again, Vic's handle was only half as long as the pitch fork and he knew he wouldn't be able to thrust with any type of success.

He waited for the man to thrust again and swung the handle like a baseball bat, catching the pitch fork at the handle an inch below the tines. The force knocked the pitch fork from the man's hands. Then Vic quickly stepped forward and thrust the axe handle and hit the man in the chest with a hard blow. The man faltered and tried to breathe, Vic thrust twice more hitting the man in the sternum both times. The man stumbled and fell to his knees wheezing loudly.

Vic turned toward the remaining two men, slowly advancing, holding the handle with the intention of beating both men with it.

"I'm Eduardo," the younger of the two men standing close to the tables said, taking a step forward.

"You can't go anywhere!" the third man said.

The man was wearing jean shorts and a plain white tee shirt, he was very thin and appeared as though he used the coca leaves that he was now drying and processing. He picked up his pitchfork, swinging it at Eduardo.

The tines caught Eduardo on his left arm making three deep wounds about two inches above his elbow. Eduardo quickly retreated from the pitchfork, holding his right hand on the wounds.

The man turned back to face Vic. Vic knelt down near the man, who was now laying on his back on the floor still trying to recover from the hard jabs to his solar plexus.

Vic picked up the pitchfork in his left hand while holding the axe handle in an overhand grip with his right hand. Vic slowly walked toward the third man stabbing at air with the pitchfork and swinging the axe handle. The man began trembling, Vic noticed a wet spot forming at his crotch and spreading down both legs. The man dropped his pitchfork and ran out of the building across the road and into a stand of trees.

Vic turned to Eduardo and saw the blood oozing from his wound. Eduardo looked at him and Vic could see in his eyes that something very wrong was about to happen, Vic instinctively rolled to his right and heard the first man running past him with arms flailing at air. Vic lost the grip on his pitchfork, watching it scoot to the far wall, about fifteen feet away.

Vic regained his stance and secured the grip on the axe handle. The man was wheezing and turned to run at Vic again and Vic lined up the handle with the man's throat.

When the man was less than five feet away he stepped toward him with his left foot and jabbed the handle at the man. The handle caught the man's throat with a sickening smack. The man's momentum carried him past Vic as he stepped to his right. The man slid six inches on his stomach, rolling over onto his back, clawing at his throat with his hands trying to open the smashed wind-pipe.

Vic turned and looked at the remaining man with the arm wound. He was hoping the man had told the truth and that he really was Eduardo.

"Elena's safe and waiting for you."

"Wha-she is? Where?"

"Run to the front of the building. Get in the car and drive around here to get me, I'll be ready to go. Hurry!" Vic ordered.

Eduardo ran out of the building and Vic started turning over shelves looking for anything that would burn, he found a kerosene lantern that had a pint of fuel in the canister and unscrewed the lid, then sloshed the kerosene on the coca plants. He looked for a match but couldn't find one, looking at the dead man on the floor, he saw a pack of cigarettes in his shirt pocket. Vic heard the car's engine as Eduardo drove to the rear of the building.

Vic checked the dead man's pockets and found a lighter in his left front jeans pocket. He lit the coca plants lying on the tables, stoking the fire to ensure it would continue burning. He walked out of the building as Eduardo stopped the car.

Vic called Pablo and found they were two miles north of the building waiting for his call; Vic told them to meet him and Eduardo in Perucho. He watched the plants smoldering and starting to burn, then got in the car and noticed Eduardo's arm was bleeding worse now. He looked around the car for something to put on the wound, not seeing anything, he told Eduardo to change places, then hopped out and ran around to the driver's door as Eduardo slid over to the passenger side. Vic slammed the gear shift into drive, flooring the accelerator and fishtailed as they caught traction and sped away.

Center for Disease Control
Atlanta, GA

Sue Richards was at her desk on the third floor of the CDC building in Atlanta when she received the call from Steve Logan with the FBI. He was sitting in the coach car in Chicago with Ray and briefly explained that he needed to find an emergency phone number for Dr. Lewis at Plum Island. She refused to give out the number until he explained the emergency.

"What do you mean, missing?" she asked.

"The only facts we currently have indicate there is some mix up with CSX freight. They were transporting a container to Kansas and the container was somehow swapped with a different container, I have no other information at this time."

She opened her iPhone and retrieved the phone number for Dr. Lewis and read it to Steve.

"Thanks I'll keep you updated on the investigation."

"Wait! What do you…," she said, realizing he had hung up.

Dearborn Station Rail Yards
Chicago, Illinois

Ray looked out the train coach window and saw several police cruisers with their red lights flashing, a S.W.A.T. truck, a fire engine, and one ambulance. He overheard someone saying everyone was waiting on the HazMat team to arrive before opening the container. Ray felt a sickening knot in his stomach and walked to the small bathroom again.

Ray saw the large HazMat truck arrive, men dressed in white vinyl suits and hoods got out of the back of the truck. He couldn't see the rail car, but knew they were preparing to open the container, he could see that the firemen had positioned their hoses strategically to douse water on the container if it was needed.

A second large fire truck was pulled up close with even larger black hoses, he could hear a motor that was pressurizing a large tank on the truck that would spray foam on the container if it was decided that water wasn't the correct retardant.

Ray felt the coach car bump as an engine coupled to it to move it a safe distance from the flat bed rail car. He watched several men with hand radios giving commands and felt the coach car bump again as the engine stopped one hundred feet from the flat bed rail car. Ray felt that sickening feeling again and hurried to the bathroom once more.

Ray looked out the window and saw a man carrying a large bolt cutter who was flanked by other men with different tools to remove the container lock walking toward the rail car. The man with the bolt cutter had a cable secured to a harness he was wearing and moved slowly toward the flat bed rail car carrying the bolt cutter in one hand and pulling the cable with the other. He continued until he was out of sight. Ray bent over the toilet again and lost his lunch.

Ray waited for the explosion, bracing himself as he made it back to his seat. He waited for several minutes listening intently for the expected bang, imagining what it would sound like. He remembered hearing of windows that shattered when an explosion was set off near buildings and slid off the seat onto the floor.

Ray heard people yelling as he peered over the window seal and quickly ducked back to the floor. He tightened his grip slightly on the seat and pulled up to look out the window again, seeing the man with the bolt cutters returning to the truck. Ray watched several other men walking toward the rail car. He noticed one with a radio who was talking with animated gestures, waving his hands. Ray felt hope and dread when he held a thumbs-up sign with his right hand to someone Ray could not see. Ray heard someone climbing the coach's metal steps and saw the door open.

"The container is full of ship propellers," the man said then quickly turned and left the coach.

Ray felt nauseated again and knew deep down he didn't want everything to blow, but he didn't want to go to prison for destroying the laptop either.

Perucho, Ecuador

Vic arrived in Perucho with Pablo close behind, he pulled over at a small grocery store, telling Eduardo to hop out and get in the Jeep. Vic saw the local police station a block down a narrow cross street and drove to the station, then parked, leaving the engine running and ran to the Jeep.

Elena had moved to the back seat beside Eduardo who had climbed in behind Pablo. Vic hopped into the passenger seat as Pablo pulled back onto the road and picked up speed after leaving Perucho.

Elena kept crying while attempting to keep pressure on Eduardo's wound, using an old cloth diaper that was in the Jeep. Vic noticed Elena kept touching Eduardo as though she couldn't believe he was rescued and was now safe with her. Vic heard Eduardo relating the fight scene to Elena with a slightly different twist than what actually happened. He listened and discovered that he had cowered in a corner while Eduardo had defeated three men with his bare hands, mano a mano.

Vic leaned back and wondered what would have happened if things had gone differently. He noticed the beautiful sunset as Pablo drove back to Quito, feeling his body crashing as the adrenaline rush wore off.

He wanted to ask Eduardo where Cordova was, but thought it might not matter any longer. SatCom was safe, he had the memory card, Elena had Eduardo and she was finally free. What else mattered he thought.

He turned around and looked at Elena still holding the cotton cloth diaper on Eduardo's wound. "Maybe we should stop at a hospital," Vic said to Pablo.

"That's where I'm going," Pablo replied, driving to the Los Andes Hospital, on the north side of Quito, parking near the emergency room.

Elena had calmed down and wasn't crying any longer, she helped Eduardo out of the Jeep and walked with him through the doors.

Pablo walked with Vic to the waiting area, "What the hell are you going to do with him?" he quietly asked.

"How the hell do I know?" Vic said, mulling the same question over in his mind.

Vic was still concerned that he hadn't dealt with Cordova like he had wanted to, but was relieved knowing that the only witness was really scared. He knew the guy from the coca barn would not remain scared and would eventually report back to Cordova, he wasn't certain about Juan. He thought he had a few days before Cordova started looking for him again.

Dearborn Station Rail Yards
Chicago, Illinois

Steve Logan dialed the emergency phone number for Dr. Lewis again; he was trying to reach the doctor since he was provided with the number earlier that afternoon.

"Hello," Dr. Lewis said.

Steve introduced himself and briefly explained the situation. He noticed Ray was squirming and looking ill as he spoke with the doctor.

"I don't understand what you mean by missing?"

"Ray Ballinger is here and said the container on the rail car is not the same container he started with in Long Island."

Dr. Lewis asked to speak with Ray after gaining his composure and tried to allay his own initial fear of a loose virus.

"Ray, are you certain my container has been replaced?"

"Yes sir, the container is different. The original was much newer and this one is faded, rusty and has some oriental writing on it, also the tamper proof cable is red instead of green."

"Let me speak with the FBI guy," Dr. Lewis said.

Dr. Lewis briefly explained that the container had to be located quickly and that it should not be opened by anyone but him. He repeated the statement several more times; rambling as though he was in shock. Steve assured him that the container would be located soon and terminated the call with the doctor.

Steve next placed a call with CSX freight lines to get the latest information on the computer tracking for the railcar. He was assured the container had not been removed from car 5593.

"Every car has a number that is electronically tracked, we have a record of where that car has been and can show the location at all times. In fact the weight is similar compared to when it left Philadelphia," the CSX representative stated.

"Similar? What is the difference?"

"We are still running the program to compare the original weight with the current weight. Are you certain the containers are different?" the rep asked.

"We will know for certain when we open the container. Right now it is simply a report and suspicion of the cargo being changed, nothing more. You will be contacted as soon as possible, until then, please review your records to determine the possibility of a swap and where it could have happened."

Main Office
CSX Freight Lines
Chicago, Illinois

Jason Holder, the manager of operations, for CSX typed a new query command on his keyboard for the computer to perform, he wanted a history of rail car 5593 and car 6097, since Long Island. He wanted to use rail car 6097 as a standard, if the data for it was the same at each check point, then he had confidence in the data. He typed commands in the query program for the past five days, including sidings, stops and layovers. He also requested the weight for the two rail cars at the seven different stations it had passed through since leaving Long Island.

He waited for the program to complete, knowing that it should only take a few moments to track the history of one rail car for five days. He heard the high speed drum printer's whirring sound as it printed off the three pages for his report. He walked into the print room and pressed the Top of Form button on the printer and tore the report from the basket of printouts. Then returned to his desk and started reading the report. It listed each of the wayside tag readers locations that rail car 5593 passed. He verified the tracking information, by comparing the data for 6097. No discrepancies were seen. He then turned the page and looked at the weight of the rail cars. Car 6097 was identical at each check point; he scanned the report for 5593. He read the Wheel Report twice and saw the glaring error; rail car 5593 began as an empty car in Long Island with a weight of twenty-nine tons. The car read thirty-seven tons when it left Long Island, the car was the same weight at each station until it was weighed leaving Harrisburg and there it weighed sixty-three tons a difference of twenty-six tons.

Jason called his manager and reported the error. The two men discussed the probability of it being a scales problem and decided the rail car's weight was probably accurate. They decided to report it as a simple tracking error and that the container should be located within twenty-four hours and delivered to Fort Leavenworth no more than a day late.

He called Steve Logan and informed him that CSX would locate the container within twenty-four hours and of course discount the shipping cost appropriately.

General Yi's Office
Chengdu Military Base

General Yi arrived at the office and informed Colonel Hon of the latest status regarding Sun-Chang. They discussed the possibility of failures and concluded that the plan was still transparent to the Americans and was proceeding at the best possible speed.

He opened the door and stood looking at the girls working at their desks in the large office. He transferred in new female recruits after their initial training, keeping them under his command until he tired of them, then transferring out. He noticed the two new girls typing at their keyboards and imagined how grateful they would be if he promised them an early promotion, he began walking in their direction.

"General, an email was just received from Professor Szu," Colonel Hon said.

General Yi grimaced slightly and returned to his office and slammed the door. He set down and opened the email, it was a status update on the container.

> **Container was loaded onto a Chinese registered freighter, the Tiangong Kaiwu, which belongs to Guangzhou lines.**
> **There is no, I repeat no shipping from Philadelphia to Havana. The container will be in Panama in six days. It can be redirected to Havana from Panama if you wish.**

General Yi smiled as he read the email the second time, feeling confident he had found what he was searching for, the third prong of the plan. Now Sun-Chang cannot fail. We will devalue the dollar, shut down their power grid and use their new virus against them. I will explain the virus to Beijing later, he thought, no reason to tell them now, at least no reason to tell them until I am certain the virus is as deadly as they think it is. I will be a hero, he thought, smiling as he imagined himself being heralded as the next president of China.

Los Andes Hospital
Quito, Ecuador

Vic was walking, trying to de-stress in the hospital parking lot; attempting to find a resolution for Eduardo. He looked over and saw Pablo on the phone lying to Gaby, hearing him explain that a major catastrophe had occurred in Guayaquil and he might have to travel out of town tonight. He walked into the hospital and saw Elena sitting by herself in the waiting room.

She turned to him, he could see she was still teary eyed and quite nervous while waiting for her brother to be cared for and released.

She looked at him and scooted over on the bench making room for him to sit; he set down next to her. She looked up and said, "Vic, thank you for everything, I know you took a huge risk to rescue Eduardo. You not only rescued him, you also released me from Cordova's grasp. You've saved our lives." She wiped away a tear.

"That's okay. Listen I need to know what to do with him. Where can I take him and I guess you too?"

"I know a church, Saint Jude's, it would be a safe place for him," she said looking into his eyes and seeing genuine compassion.

"What about you?" Vic asked.

"I'll leave that, up to you," she offered.

She sat looking at him for some reaction to her response for several moments, then turned away and wiped another tear from her eyes. She had a compulsion to be held by him, to feel safe in his arms, but hesitant to make any unwanted advances.

Holiday Inn
St. Louis, Missouri

Dr. Lewis checked in at the motel on I-70 with his family, after getting the luggage into the room, he called Sue Richards, letting her know his location for the evening. He had kept in constant contact with Sue and Steve Logan after the abrupt call informing him of the missing container, he then called Steve to let him know that he was in the Holiday Inn. Steve informed him that the container on the rail car was definitely not the container he had loaded at Plum Island, "Ray Ballinger said there was a procedure to open the vault inside the container safely. Is that accurate?" Steve asked.

"Yes, if the vault is opened incorrectly an alarm will sound and the lock is designed to de-energize, not allowing any code to be accepted until I enter an override code, this could potentially damage the contents, the propane tank is designed to maintain the proper environment for eleven days, no longer. Do you understand all my work could be destroyed?"

Dr. Lewis pressed Steve for any information he had regarding the location of his container and reiterated several times the danger involved if someone else opens the vault and how many thousands of people might be adversely affected if any of the viruses or bacteria is released.

Steve explained that CSX had assured him it was a simple misplacement which would be corrected within a day, perhaps less.

Main Office
CSX Freight Lines
Chicago, Illinois

Jason Holder started another query for rail car 5593, this time he was looking for changes in the work orders for the car. He ran a second program searching for any emails in the CSX server referring to rail car 5593.

His office phone rang, his manager told him to call him back using his cell phone. Jason called and the two men discussed a strategy to down play the situation if the media heard about it.

He heard the drum printer whirring again and walked over and took the reports back to his desk. There were no work order changes; however, there was one flag. A flag is generated when a work order change is made and reversed back to the original order.

There were no emails in the system referring to rail car 5593. He returned to the work order report and printed the flag report. The one flag was for a removal of the container from rail car 5593 to rail car 6743 in Harrisburg, Pennsylvania. The work order was cancelled six hours later.

Jason ran a history report on rail car 6743 for the past three days, he waited for the query to finish running then tore the report from the printer. He scanned the report and saw that a work order was initiated which mirrored the work order for rail car 5593. He dropped to the bottom of the report and read that the rail car was delivered to Penn's Landing in Philadelphia and the container transferred to a south bound ship scheduled to depart earlier that day. He made a note of the ship, the Tiangong Kaiwu which belongs to Guangzhou freight lines.

Jason opened his cell phone and called his manager again, they decided to report the discovery to the FBI. He called Steve Logan and told him the bad news and started a query program attempting to locate the CSX computer where the work order changes were generated from. An employee ID number is required when entering any type of work order or shipping changes and he was now searching for the employee and the office that initiated those changes.

FBI Office
Chicago, Illinois

Steve contacted John Reynolds at the office downtown Chicago and forwarded the information he received from Jason at CSX. John then contacted the FBI office in Philadelphia, relaying the information and requesting they stop the ship from leaving port. He next contacted the FBI office in Washington, requesting further instructions.

Oval Office
Washington, D.C.

"What the hell do you mean it was delivered to a Chinese ship in Philadelphia?" FBI Director Pierce yelled into the phone and slammed it closed, then turned to the president.

"Mr. President. I believe we are at war with someone, I'm not certain who, it appears to be a cyber-war," Director Pierce announced slowly.

He explained that the container from Plum Island was transferred to a Chinese freighter, the Tiangong Kaiwu. The ship was already at sea and destined for Hong Kong via the Panama Canal. He noticed the president seemed to have a look of bewilderment on his face as he set at his desk.

Ithaca Exports
Perucho, Ecuador

Señor Cordova arrived back at his office and discovered the entire shipment of cocoa plants received was destroyed. One man was dead and no one else at the office.

He immediately assumed Elena was somehow involved and that she had recruited the assistance of the man she was now traveling with. He contacted the local police, who had worked with him several times before and was well compensated for their efforts. He told Captain Garcia about the murder of his employee, Felix Sanchez, by another employee, Eduardo Torres.

Captain Garcia promised he would track down the murderer and notified him of Juan's abandoned car at the police station. Cordova suggested the police locate Juan, the he had a description of Eduardo's accomplice.

St. Jude's Church
Quito, Ecuador

Pablo parked the Jeep in front of the church and looked over at Vic, waiting for some sort of confirmation that Vic knew what he was doing and saw Vic shrug his shoulders.

"Got to put them somewhere," Vic sighed, shaking his head.

Pablo nodded and helped Eduardo out of the car as Vic held the door for Elena, then they all walked into the church. Vic saw a Padre cleaning up, following evening mass.

"Elena!" Padre Martinez said, and hurriedly walked to her as she entered the front doors.

Vic noticed a broad smile on the Padre's face as he walked to her.   She had a quick reunion with the Padre, he smiled politely at Eduardo, and Vic noticed a definite attitude cooling when he spoke with Eduardo.

The Padre told Vic a brief history about Elena and Eduardo, how they were raised in the orphanage at the church and how Eduardo had left for a job. Two years later Elena had entered the Catholic University. He included how Eduardo was usually in trouble and Elena was always a perfect child. Vic noticed Eduardo's obvious embarrassment, which seemed to confirm what was being said.

Vic told Padre some of what had happened at Ithaca Exports and asked if Eduardo and Elena could stay with him for a week or so, until it was safe for them to go home. Padre was hesitant until Vic pulled a roll of cash from his pocket. Padre agreed the two could stay as long as they wished while stuffing the cash into the pocket of his robe.

"Gracias, Padre," Vic said as he turned and started to leave with Pablo.

Elena inhaled quickly feeling panic closing in and almost screaming said, "Vic!"

"What?" Vic asked, turning to face her.

She looked at him with wanting and fear of rejection in her eyes. "Do, do you want me to stay here also?"

"Elena, I want you to be safe," Vic said, looking at her and feeling the tug of her beauty.

"I would feel safer with you," she replied, looking at him, seeing the skinned knuckles on his right hand where the pitchfork handle had hit him earlier. She knew he was a man that would protect her, if she were ever alone in a dark alley and a man whom she desperately wanted to be held by.

Vic remembered that Ralph had asked him to keep her close to him since she was the only lead back to Ithaca Exports. "Get in the Jeep," he instructed, then nodded to Padre and walked out of the church.

Pablo witnessed the verbal exchange between Elena and Vic and knew that Vic was in for trouble or at least was going to get very lucky, then shook his head and walked to the jeep.

Police Department
Perucho, Ecuador

Captain Garcia drove to the last address he had for Juan in Perucho, parking in the drive he walked to the door and knocked, then waited for several minutes. He saw Juan slowly open the door, his right forearm was tightly wrapped with duct tape over a dirty towel.

Captain Garcia explained he was investigating a crime perpetrated against Señor Cordova. That Eduardo Escamilla had murdered an employee; burglarized his business and destroyed his inventory of medicinal plants.

Juan told the captain he was kidnapped and held for ransom until he escaped, he also stated he was anxious to assist the police in finding Eduardo and told Captain Garcia that Eduardo had an accomplice. He didn't know the man's name, but he could describe him and that the man was staying at the Hotel Patio Amador.

Captain Garcia escorted Juan to the police station and assigned an officer, Inspector Perez, to go with Juan to Quito and stake out the hotel until Eduardo's accomplice could be identified.

Hotel Patio Amador
Quito, Ecuador

Pablo pulled into the drive and stopped, Vic told him to go home and take care of his family and they agreed to meet at the office the next morning.

Vic and Elena walked into the hotel; he placed his hand on the small of her back and guided her to the bar where they were seated by a hostess. He ordered two beers, then leaned back, closed his eyes and relaxed.

"It's been a hell of a day," he acknowledged to her. He drank half of his beer and ordered two tequila shots with a second round of beers while Elena sipped at her first beer.

Vic thought back to Curt's death and all the men he had killed. He remembered the Colonel in the Iranian army, whose family was in the house where had to make his kill. He thought back and wanted to forget everything.

Elena watched Vic as he seemed to be fighting some internal demon, noticing he would tremble slightly then shake his head as though he was screaming for help from somewhere deep in his memory.

She sat quietly, wishing she had the words to chase his demons away. He opened his eyes and saw Elena as a different woman; she was no longer the smuggling whore, but now a beautiful young lady, a woman with a new life in front of her.

"Elena, why don't we get you a room for the night?"

"Is that what you want to do, get me a room?"

Vic looked into her eyes; he didn't see a scared girl anymore, but saw the eyes of a woman who was comfortable being with him.

She leaned forward across the table and quietly replied, "I would rather stay with you."

"Why don't we go up to the room," he said scooting his chair away from the table.

Vic stood and placed his hand at the small of her back directing her to the elevator. She waited for him to remove his hand and felt a twinge of hope when she realized he kept his hand on her, guiding her to the elevator.

Northwest Hospital
Seattle, Washington

Commander Tom Sullivan with the Coast Guard walked into the room and saw Captain John Lytle sitting on the edge of the bed. He saw two nurses attending to his injuries, they were replacing the dressing that covered the stitches from flying glass on his forehead. His face was bruised and his left arm was in a cast from the shoulder to the tips of his fingers, bent ninety degrees at the elbow. Commander Sullivan stepped back out of the room and waited until they completed their work and watched the nurses leave, he walked back in and noticed Captain Lytle was now lying on the bed.

He introduced himself as the officer in charge of the crash investigation and explained that Pilot Musky was still in the intensive care ward and had not regained consciousness.

"Can you tell me what happened?" he asked.

Captain Lytle began with the uneventful cruise until Pilot Musky boarded the ship in the Strait of Juan de Fuca. He then relived that terrifying day, starting with the southerly turn into Puget Sound, explaining the inability to command the ship. He stated how the ship's speed did not seem to match the speed indicator on the instrument panel. He spoke of the failed attempt to close the fuel valves to the diesel generators and concluded with the morbid screams of the injured as the ship hit the pier. He asked about the number of fatalities. Commander Sullivan simply stated the wreckage was still being removed as he finalized his notes and left the room.

Hotel Patio Amador
Quito, Ecuador

Juan arrived at the hotel Patio Amador driving his old Chevrolet. He was driving behind the investigator who was assigned to the case. He slowly parked the car in the parking lot and quickly realized he was near the same parking spot the car was in when Vic had broken his arm. He started the car and parked across the street. He was shaking almost uncontrollably when he opened the door and walked to the police car parked in the parking lot in front of the hotel. He opened the door with his left hand and sat down, protecting his right arm, he knew the arm needed medical attention, but was afraid to ask Señor Cordova for the time to go to the hospital.

"Does he have a car?" Investigator Perez asked.

"No, I don't think so, but he has friends in a car that followed us," he said, swallowing hard and looking nervously around.

Juan fished his cell phone from his shirt pocket and pressed the speed dial for Señor Cordova.

"What do you want?" Señor Cordova asked, when he saw it was Juan calling.

"I am at the Hotel Patio Amador, with Investigator Perez. We are waiting for the American to walk out of the hotel where he will then be arrested."

"Get your ass in the hotel and search every floor, every room until you find that bitch or the American, do not call me until you have a name, or Julio will come to help you!"

"Yes sir, I will, but I hurt my arm and–"

"I don't want to hear about you or your arm, just get his name and call me back!" he said again and slammed his phone closed.

Juan opened the police car door and carefully got out of the car and walked in the side door of the lobby, being careful not to be seen by Vic as he crept along the wall to the front desk, eyeing a chair in a darkened corner with the full lobby in view.

Juan knew if he failed to discover the name he would certainly face Cordova's wrath, or worse, perhaps Señor Cordova would really send Julio to speak with him, that thought made Juan forget his arm for a few minutes.

....

Vic opened the hotel room door and watched Elena walk into the room ahead of him, watching her body slightly sway as she walked.

She walked to the foot of the bed and stopped, turning to face him, she asked, "Did you want something?"

Vic looked at her, seeing a beautiful young woman who trusted him to protect her. He walked to her and stopped a foot away, framing her face in his hands tilting her head back slightly; he leaned down and lightly, kissed her lips.

He felt her kiss him back and felt how she stood slightly onto her toes, as her hands found his belt loops; pulling him closer. She felt him as he moved closer and slowly moved his hands to the back of her neck, moving his arms down her back and tightening his grip on her, moving his lips to her left cheek. She sighed as she relaxed, leaning against him feeling his strong arms supporting her.

Joint Intelligence Meeting
Washington, D.C.

The president walked into the oval office with a deep furrowed brow and a frown on his face. He nodded acknowledgement to the individuals in the room and set down on the couch. He scanned the report he had received from the FBI once more and looked up at the group, clearing his throat.

"I want you to clarify a couple of questions I have regarding this report," he said, clearing his throat again, listing the bullet points of the report, beginning with the cryptic message received on Ed Tatum's computer, the Seattle ship disaster, the collapse of the oil rig in the Gulf of Mexico, the increase of the worm and viruses on the government computers, ending with the disappearance of the Plum Island vault, "What the hell is going on?" he asked the men in the room.

"Mr. President, we aren't certain yet. What we know for sure is that the CIA message was generated from China, and it appears the CSX work order change was generated from a computer at the Tsinghua University in Beijing."

The president stood and began pacing the floor between the couch and his desk. He heard a cell phone chirp and saw Director Pierce of the FBI open his phone, he heard one side of the conversation gleaning that the news was not going to be good.

"Sir," Director Pierce said interrupting his thoughts.

"What is it?"

"There were two major leaks in the gasoline pipe line running from Texas to Illinois and the leaks were definitely caused by software glitches." He then added that investigations were currently being performed, attempting to track and identify the hackers.

The men could see the vein in the President's neck bulging and saw his hands begin to tremble.

Hotel Patio Amador
Quito, Ecuador

Vic held Elena for a long time as they stood at the foot of the bed, he wasn't certain if he should allow his emotions to dictate his decisions. He wanted to continue holding her and even lay on the bed with her, but thought about all the things that might go wrong and how SatCom would suffer if he made the easy, but wrong decision.

He gently pushed her away, feeling her step back. He looked into her eyes and saw disappointment and perhaps fear.

He felt butterflies in his own stomach, felt the uneasiness and knew he needed a short break. "I'm going to the lobby for a paper or perhaps to the bar for a beer, I'll be back in a few minutes," he said as he stepped back away from her.

She looked at him wondering if he was genuinely going for a beer with intentions of returning to her, she wanted to believe that he would return to her. Vic walked to the door and opened it, then turned back toward her, winked and walked out of the room.

Elena ran to the bathroom, grabbing her brush, she straightened her hair and sprayed on more perfume, then put her hand to her mouth and felt the overwhelming tension of wanting to cry and leap for joy at the same time. She fought the urge and continued brushing her hair for a few minutes, then brushed her teeth.

She walked to the mini-bar, opened a small bottle of tequila and emptied it into a glass. She drank the contents in two gulps coughing several times, trying to regain her composure.

She set at the table and turned to look at the bed and wasn't sure if she had the confidence to be held by Vic. She wanted him to take and ravage her and at the same time she wanted to run away. She noticed her hands were trembling and walked to the mini-bar again, opening Tequila, she drank it straight from the bottle.

Vic walked out of the elevator when the doors opened and walked to the bar, he didn't recognize the man behind the magazine was Juan as he walked past him and purchased two Corona beers and returned to the elevator.

Juan walked to the bar and inquired about the man who bought the two beers, explaining he was at the hotel to return a book to the man.

"That was Mr. James," the bartender replied, Juan walked away, pressing the redial button and heard Señor Cordova's phone ringing.

"What now?" Señor Cordova demanded.

"I have his name."

"What is it?"

"James, his name is Mr. James,"

"That is excellent, Juan. Now go take care of your hand or arm or whatever," Señor Cordova said, terminating the call.

Juan walked out to the police car and told Inspector Perez how he had bravely discovered the man's name and that he was going to the hospital to have his arm looked at.

"I called Señor Cordova, he told me to go to the hospital, I broke my arm in a fight; the other guy won't need a doctor."

Juan watched Inspector Perez start the engine and drive away without saying anything.

Ithaca Exports
Perucho, Ecuador

Señor Cordova called the number he had for his contact at the Tsinghua University in Beijing, "Can I help you?" the voice asked.

"This is Señor Cordova I need to obtain information for a Mr. James, an American citizen currently staying at the Patio Amador hotel in Quito, Ecuador, how long will he be at that hotel and what travel plans does he have. I need the information as quickly as possible."

"I will call you," she said.

"Thank you," he replied, closing his phone.

Hotel Patio Amador
Quito, Ecuador

Vic returned to his hotel room door, then hesitated again, wondering if he was making a mistake. He opened the door to find Elena sitting at the table, he noticed she had brushed her hair; he slowly closed the door and walked toward her.

She was unsure of his intentions, seeing the two beers in his hand. He grabbed the bottle opener as he walked past the mini-bar and opened both bottles, then placed one on the table for her and took a sip of the other. She started to stand, but set back down and watched him as he walked to the television to turn it on, but turned toward her leaving the television off. He turned and gazed at her for a few moments; then slowly made his way across the room to her, feeling the strong impulse to kiss her again.

She waited for him to get closer, attempting to see if he wanted her or not, feeling her pulse increase as she waited and hoped he would reach for her.

Vic stopped at the opposite side of the table. He saw her watching him intently, then walked around to her side of the table and noticed her turn as she tracked him with her eyes. He leaned down and placed his right hand on the back of her neck. She tilted her head up toward him, he could see she had applied fresh lipstick and her lips were slightly open as she beckoned him with her eyes.

He leaned down and lightly brushed his lips across her left cheek and felt her tremble slightly, feeling her left hand as it touched his right leg; he kissed her lips.

She tried to stand, but was too close to the table and couldn't scoot the chair on the carpeted floor. He stepped back, sliding the chair a couple inches, helping her up. He put his hands on her shoulders and turned her, backing her three feet to the bed. She felt the edge of the bed against the back of her legs and set down. Vic placed his left hand against her right shoulder and felt her lay back.

He lay down beside her and held her tightly, feeling her shaking with anticipation. He slowly unbuttoned her blouse and felt her hot breath against his neck, making him forget the day's events as they made love.

....

Vic heard the sound of his phone chirping and quietly slid out of bed as he went into the bathroom, opening his phone, realizing that Lisa was calling.

"Ralph requested that you return home for a mission briefing,"

"What mission?" Vic squawked.

"I don't know. He is out of the office. He called me a few minutes ago and asked that I get in touch with you and ask if you could come in to the office tomorrow."

"Tomorrow! This is really short notice," Vic whispered.

"You are aware that I'm in Quito, Ecuador, right?" Vic whispered.

"You're not alone are you?"

"No, and I didn't expect to be traveling tomorrow either, or today, do you know what time it is?"

"I can tell Ralph that you are unavailable," she offered.

"Let me think about it for a little while."

Vic's thoughts started racing, thinking that since Cordova was neutralized he should be able to leave and that SatCom and Elena would be fine.

"No, never mind. I'll be there. Tell him I'll be there in two days, not tomorrow, there's not enough time to get a flight and make arrangements," Vic said.

"Thanks, Vic. I know he depends on you too much, but you are the best, I'll tell him you'll be in Dallas day after tomorrow, I guess that would make it tomorrow wouldn't it?" she asked.

"Yeah, right, I'll call later," he heard the connection terminate, then returned to bed. Elena made a dreaming sound and snuggled up close as he gently crawled back under the sheet. He placed his hand on her breast and felt her stir a little then turn to him and smile.

"I fell asleep after our wild ride," he murmured and kissed her neck.

"I did too. Oh, that feels so nice," she squealed and felt for him, pulling him on top of her. After making love, they lay side by side.

"Elena, I need to go to Dallas for a few days," Vic said, feeling her muscles tighten.

"Why?" she asked.

"It's business and I'll be back in several days, then we can pick up where we leave off today."

"No, we can't pick up then, I will not be alive then," she said, turning her head away from him.

"What? You'll be fine, I'll be back and we can start over."

"Señor Cordova will have me killed after he rapes me if you are not here to protect me, unless I give him his turtle."

"I am not giving you the memory card and I don't have time to explain it to the police. At least not enough time tonight and still catch a flight to Dallas tomorrow morning or the next day."

Vic thought that if he went to the Police now, she would be arrested. He didn't want that and tried to plan a way to deliver the memory card and not mention her name or implicate her in any way. He knew there was no way.

Elena lay quietly for a few minutes, wondering what else could go wrong. She thought she was so close to being freed from Cordova's grasp and now she would be at his mercy again. She felt the terrifying emotions of his threats again and knew if she confronted him again she would try to kill him. If she lived past his first beating, she remembered Rosita and her being led away by Julio.

Vic sensed how scared Elena was of being left alone. He didn't want to take a chance of leaving then returning and not being able to find her again.

"How would you like to travel with me to Dallas day after tomorrow?" he asked hesitantly.

"Why do you ask me to go on a trip with you?" she asked in the Spanish accent, he realized that she reverted back to the Spanish accent when she was very nervous or frightened.

"I think it would be fun to have you along," Vic lied.

"Is that the only reason?" she asked.

"Do you want to go with me to Dallas or not?"

"Yes, I, I want to go with you, no matter where you go, I want to go with you," she admitted.

"I'm going to jump in the shower," he said rolling out of the bed.

"Me too. If, if it is alright," she haltingly said, looking at him.

"Yeah, sure come on."

DIR Office
Plano, Texas

"DIR, how can I help you," Lisa answered the phone.

"Ralph here, did you locate Vic?"

"Yes, he will be in Dallas day after tomorrow."

"Great, I'm flying back to DFW tonight, schedule a meeting with Vic based on his flight arrival. When you have that information, let me know the time."

"I'll do that."

"Okay," Ralph said closing his cell phone.

Day Four
Hotel Patio Amador
Quito, Ecuador

"SatCom how may I help you?" Rachel asked as she answered the phone.

"Rachel, this is Vic."

"Hey, great to hear from you, I keep wondering what happens to you, then you call in and I can stop worrying for a few minutes, are you alright?" she scolded.

"I'm fine, listen I'll be flying back to Dallas tomorrow and I need you to schedule the flight."

"Sure what time, morning or evening, there are only two direct flights."

"Morning, make the reservation for two."

"Two, is Pablo coming with you?"

"No, it is a, uh, a new employee," he stammered and placed his hand over the satellite phone.

He snapped his fingers, "Elena, give me your passport," She retrieved her passport from her purse and handed it to him.

"Ready? Her name is Elena Torres, she is a citizen of Ecuador.

"Can you email me her passport information?"

"Yeah I'll scan it and email the information momentarily," Vic said.

"I'll check on the flight and get back to you."

"Call me as soon as you confirm reservations," Vic said as he hit the terminate button on the phone.

Vic retrieved his hand held scanner from his suitcase and connected it to his laptop, then scanned in Elena's passport. He emailed Rachel and sent the passport attachment. Next he dialed Pablo's cell phone and explained that he wanted Elena on Sat-Com's payroll.

"Oh she must be very good," Pablo smirked, imagining her in bed.

Pablo made several suggestions for a job title for her and Vic decided that he could choose one later. They discussed the possibility of Señor Cordova locating him in Quito or tying SatCom to the memory card and thought it wasn't worth the worry.

"Okay, consider her, a new employee."

"Thanks," Vic said and terminated the signal.

Vic walked with Elena to the restaurant and both ate breakfast empanadas. He wanted to know more about her, but wasn't certain how to ask, that didn't sound as though he was grilling her. They enjoyed their late meal and laughed together as both became better acquainted.

Ithaca Exports Office
Perucho, Ecuador

Señor Cordova's phone rang and he opened the cover.

"Yes."

"I have the information you requested," the voice announced. "The person you are inquiring about is Vic James, he is an American citizen and currently staying in room 447 at the hotel Patio

Amador. His reservations are for two more nights. He currently has no flight reservations listed."

"Can he be tracked?"

"He has a satellite phone which is not on the market, but I will inquire if it can be hacked."

"Thank you."

Cordova looked at his watch and realized this might be the perfect time to have Mr. James dealt with. He dialed Julio's cell phone, there was no answer. He dialed Juan's cell phone, it to rang with no one answering. He felt the rage building, but knew he alone would not be able to win a fight with an American. He called the police in Perucho and spoke with his friend Captain Garcia.

"The man who killed Ricardo is at the Patio Amador Hotel in room 447. I need his description so that I can confirm it is indeed the same gringo. Can you send someone to help me?"

Captain Garcia dispatched a special officer who was not on the city's payroll.

SatCom Office
Austin, Texas

Rachel dialed Vic's satellite phone, "What's up," Vic asked when he saw the call was from Rachel.

"There may be a problem with your traveling companion," Rachel said.

"I have your flight information and you are on the 8:10 in the morning. Who is this Elena Torres?"

"She is my interpreter while I am in Latin America this trip."

"Since when did you need a Spanish interpreter? You speak Spanish fluently, she said while looking at Elena's passport photo. "Well, she won't be traveling with you," Rachel announced.

"Why not?"

"Her name is on the FBI's 'no fly list!'"

"Shit! How do you know?"

"They called me and told me! I tried to get a seat for her and the ticket agent said to hold, then she said she wanted my phone number to call me back and then hung up on me!"

"So wha-"

"I'm not through explaining!"

"Okay," Vic swore under his breath.

"Some FBI agent called me and wanted to know how I knew this lady. I told him I didn't know her, but that she worked for SatCom and was traveling with you from Ecuador. He said she was not allowed to fly to the United States!" Rachel said.

"Well, I'll handle it,"

"I'm still not finished! Who is she?" Rachel demanded, realizing she was stepping out of bounds with Vic.

"Yeah, well, she is more of a hostess, very good with people."

"Yeah right, whatever!" Rachel said, feeling a heartache coming on. "I apologize, I have no right to question you, I'm sorry, Vic," she said, then hung up the phone.

"Trouble explaining me?" Elena asked.

"Yeah, a slight hiccup, no real trouble though," Vic said as he quickly started looking for a plan B.

Niagara Power Station
Niagara Falls, New York

Rocky Phillips, chief engineer for the power station, arrived at the parking lot and parked his car. He walked across the lot hearing the roar and feeling the gentle vibration of the water cascading over the falls. He heard a distant rumble form the north and looked up, seeing the morning sky and the dark rolling clouds coming from Canada. He reached the employee entrance of the multi-floored building of the generating station and took the stairs to the second floor where his office was located.

He was early, as usual, for his daily eight hour shift and stopped at the break room to fill his coffee mug on his way to the office at the end of the hall. He recently was assigned a project to study the feasibility of adding two generating turbines, increasing the number of turbines to fifteen from the current thirteen.

Rocky had calculated that 375,000 gallons of water flow over the dam per second and he was considering installing the two new turbines on the edge of the falls increasing the total potential of the Niagara Power Station to six million kilowatts.

He heard the loud clap of thunder and knew the lightening had struck very near the station. He was confident that even a direct hit would not affect the station, due to the outstanding lightening arresters which extended fifty feet above the building, and connected to cables that were buried thirty feet below the ground.

Rocky grabbed his mug and walked to the control room where he could monitor the operation of the station. He heard another loud clap of thunder as he walked into the large forty foot square room. The lights were dim and each of the gauges were digitized and glowed with the blue LED displays.

"It's raining really hard out there," Smitty said.

Smitty was the operator on duty and had run the continuity test on the grounding circuits when he received the storm warning from NOAA earlier that morning.

Rocky picked up a clip board with a "Storm Form" attached, and began the safety check-off procedure. He was on the second section, checking the turbine generator phases and electrical grid readings. He checked the satisfactory box and skipped down to the third section, the water chute force.

There were thirteen chutes channeling the water to a narrow six foot diameter opening directing the water at the base of each turbine blades. The chutes were controlled by massive gates made of concrete which opened and closed controlling the speed of each of the turbines.

He confirmed that each of the chute gates were opened wide, maintaining the same speed of each of the turbines ensuring the proper phasing of the generators.

Rocky heard another loud clap of thunder and noticed the lights flicker momentarily. He looked at Smitty, realizing either one lightning arresters was hit.

An alarm started clanging and buzzing, Rocky looked at the large instrument board and saw that chute gates number 11 and 13 were closing. He turned to his right to check that the generators were being isolated from the power grid. He noticed the generators were still operating and leaned over Smitty, typing the command to manually override the system to isolate generators 11 and 13 from the other generators.

Smitty saw the problem also and hit the emergency kill switch for turbines 11 and 13 and at the same time slapped the red push button switch to open the main relays for the generators. The main relays were large solid blocks of copper which allowed electricity to flow from the generators to the electrical grid. The relays are a 'fail-safe' to protect the generators. Each generator has the potential of creating 376,923 kilovolts of electricity and are phased to match the 60 hertz that electrical appliances in the United States use. The gauges registered connected or closed for both relays and the computer monitor displayed a green "connect".

Rocky typed the Gate Open command on the keyboard and waited for the system to respond. Each of the massive concrete gates weighed over twenty tons and traveled sixteen feet on two steel rails, taking a full thirty seconds to open or close. He waited for the monitor to register open and for the color to change from red to green.

When the system was operating normally all the icons on the monitor were green, if a problem was registered the icon would change colors to a red. The gates for 11 and 13 now were red. The gauge continued to display sixty percent open and the turbine speeds were now down to seventy percent speed.

"Take 11 and 13 offline," Rocky commanded as he continued monitoring the gates.

Smitty typed the command on his keyboard and watched his monitor as the turbine speeds continued decreasing below seventy percent and typed the command to open the line relays for both generators again. He watched the three phases of the generators as they reached the danger speed, indicating that generators 11 and 13 were now 180 degrees completely out of phase with the remaining 11 turbine generators. He confirmed the main relay indicators displayed green, indicating the relays were closed.

"Keep the other 11 generators at full capacity until the storm passes. We'll look at the problem then, just make certain we don't lose another one," Rocky said.

Rocky saw an instant message come across the monitor inquiring why the station had lost 700,000 kilowatts of electrical power and didn't respond since he had no answers.

Rocky noticed the main relays for 11 and 13 briefly changed to red and saw Smitty type the 'open command' again turning them back to green.

Smitty stared at the monitor and growled, "I didn't close those relays!"

Rocky watched the turbine speeds as they continued at 55 percent and the generator phases A, B, and C were still generating 200,000 kilowatts each, but completely out of phase of the remaining 11 generators. He saw the main relays close again and watched Smitty type the open command once more, noticing that this time the relays did not open on Smitty's command.

The voltage traveled across the closed relays of 11 and 13 bucking the line voltage of the other 11 generators. Rocky felt a strong shudder as the generators attempted to continue operating at maximum speeds. The two generators that were now 180 degrees out of phase were causing the other generators to attempt to cycle as six phase generators.

The electromagnets in the generators could not maintain the operations and began to vibrate uncontrollably. The shafts between the turbine and the generator on 1, 7, 9, and 13 each sheared. Pieces of the twelve inch solid steel shaft ricocheted and hit the turbine fins, destroying the generators and the turbines.

Generators 2, 3, 4, 6 and 10 shook so wildly that the main bearing races were ground to powder and stopped turning. Generator 5, 8 and 11 were damaged, but still operational at 40 percent capacity.

The 4.9 million kilowatts that is typically generated at Niagara Falls Power Station was reduced to 355,000 kilowatts.

"What the hell happened?" Rocky hollered.

The computer monitor went dark and all the electrical motors ceased functioning. The computer simply stopped and the disk drive motor started smoking. Rocky heard the emergency diesel genera-tor start up and saw the overhead lights come back on. He knew the entire northeast would be effected and that there would be massive brownouts and possible blackouts from Maine to Pennsylvania.

Hotel Patio Amador
Quito, Ecuador

Vic was still thinking about the conversation with Rachel, he explained to Elena that it might be better if she waited in Quito for him and that he would only be gone for a day or two.

She felt the fear creeping back into her stomach, feeling her throat as it began to close. "I understand. I will wait for you," she said, feeling the fear creeping into her chest.

Vic heard a knock at the door and looked through the peep-hole, seeing a uniformed police officer, he opened the door.

"Are you Mr. James?" the policeman asked.

"Yes I am," Vic said feeling the twinge of danger, looking closely at the officer, noticing the muddy boots that definitely weren't part of the uniform.

"Is there a problem officer?" Vic asked.

"No, no problem, I just need to verify your name," he said and made comments on the page in his notebook. "Thank you for your cooperation," he said and walked toward the elevator.

Vic closed the door and cussed silently, knowing he did not have the couple of days he had hoped for. He walked into the bathroom, reached down and locked the door, not wanting Elena to hear him talking to Lisa.

He dialed the number for DIR and explained the situation with Elena to Lisa. Vic remembered that Ralph told him the FBI might want to interview her, he then told Lisa that Elena was a SatCom employee and was needed in the states with him. He asked Lisa to attempt to sell the idea to Homeland Security and the FBI that the only way she would agree to an interview is to do it in Dallas with him present at the meeting.

"Vic, I'm sorry, but I reported your friend to the FBI. When you asked for her to be checked by the FBI I told them she worked for Ithaca Exports."

"Okay. Well at least now I know what's going on. Can you get her cleared for travel?"

"I'll try. This is very short notice Vic," Lisa cautioned.

Vic looked in the mirror and saw his lying face and shrugged, "I know, last minute decision, but it's imperative she travel with me."

"I'll try my best, but no promises."

"Like I said, your best is all I'm asking for," Vic said, slowly closing his phone.

Lisa placed a call to Rachel then started with a call to ICE 'Immigration and Customs Enforcement'.

....

Vic thought it would be wiser if they stayed in the hotel room until leaving for the airport the next morning. He was concerned that Cordova had not been stopped completely and would probably not accept his recent misfortunes lightly. He knew he was at a disadvantage, not knowing Cordova's capabilities, and that Cordova probably had many resources he could throw at him. Vic opened the room service menu and selected a steak and papas fritas.

She looked at him, staring until he looked up at her. "Why, uh, why do you want me to go to Dallas with you?" she asked tilting her head slightly.

"I'm not sure actually, maybe it would be better if you stay here in the hotel, you would feel safer and—"

"Is that what you want? You want to leave me again?" She purred as she stepped closer and placed her open palm on his chest. Vic placed his hands on her shoulders and pushed her back slightly, then slammed her against him.

"No! That is not what I want!"

"Oh!" she asked trying to catch her breath. "What, what do you want?" she begged.

"Damn it, I want you!"

DIR
Plano, Texas

Lisa dialed the number to the FBI office in Washington D.C. and asked for Sarah Mitchell in the fingerprinting department. They were roommates many years before and she was hoping their friendship could afford a favor.

Lisa told her the difficulty she was having with the Homeland Security Department not approving Elena to travel to Dallas. Sarah promised she would speak to her husband who worked for TSA and would get back to her before the next morning.

Hotel Patio Amador
Quito, Ecuador

Vic's phone chirped, he noticed the call was from Lisa and slowly slid away from Elena, then got out of bed and walked to the bathroom, closing the door quietly. Lisa gave him an update on Elena's flight status and told him she was trying to reach Ralph for his help.

"Ralph is traveling from D.C., and won't be back until late, I've tried calling him, but he doesn't answer. I called a friend in the FBI, but that is about all I can do, unofficially," she said.

"Okay, try this. Contact the local FBI office and tell them the single lead to Ithaca Exports will agree to their questioning if she is waived to fly to the states tomorrow. Between you and me, I'll be in Dallas tomorrow, whether she is cleared or not, but I really want her cleared, the counterfeit issue might get out of hand if I don't keep her with me."

"I'll not stop trying until you board the plane tomorrow morning, that's all I can do."

"I know, thanks."

He walked back to the bedroom and saw Elena sitting against the headboard holding a pillow in her arms. She appeared frightened and lonely, Vic walked around the bed and reached for the pillow, she held it tighter as he pulled it away from her.

"Elena, you're with me, I'll protect you from Cordova."

She looked up into his icy-blue eyes and sensed his warm compassionate nature and relaxed.

He set on the edge of the bed; she scooted over a few inches, "What else can you tell me about Cordova?"

Elena thought back to the conversations with Vic, attempting to remember any information she hadn't passed on. She knew he could keep her safe if there weren't any surprises.

"There is a man who works for Señor Cordova, his name is Julio. He is very mean, even vicious and likes beating people, especially women. Oh, also the man in Dallas did say one time that General Yi was growing tired of the delays."

As she spoke she reached for Vic's hand and pulled him closer, as though he were a security blanket. She scooted toward the middle of the bed and he lay down beside her.

"What delays was he referring to?" he quizzed.

"I don't know, he was speaking with someone on the telephone and had slammed it down hard, he was angry, but I don't know who at."

Vic thought about the General Yi statement for a few minutes; then reached for his satellite phone. He speed dialed DIR and asked Lisa to search China's military personnel for a General Yi.

Lisa was shutting down her computer when he called and clicked the cancel button. She accessed the main computer at Langley and typed in the name, she entertained Vic with idle chatter. A few moments later an image of a man appeared on her monitor with a bio.

"I have the information about General Yi."

She started reading the file, and told Vic the general was base commander at Chengdu Military Base and also senior officer of "Clandestine Operations" of the North and South American continents. He was thirty-seven years old and in excellent physical shape and had a ferocious sexual appetite.

"Sounds like China's 'man of the year'," Vic chuckled, closing his phone.

He rolled over and stroked Elena's cheek softly, pulling back when his phone chirped again, he noticed Pablo was calling, "What's up?" he asked.

"Are you going to be in the office tomorrow?"

Vic explained that he and Elena were flying to Dallas the next day and if time allowed he would drop by the SatCom office today.

"You're taking her with you?"

Vic got off the bed and walked to the bathroom closing the door. He told Pablo that he wanted Elena to be interviewed by the FBI in Dallas and that it was best if she traveled with him.

"There is an FBI office in the American Consulate here in Quito," Pablo offered.

"They'll do a better job in Dallas," Vic said closing his phone, feeling pissed that Pablo was getting too interested in his personal life.

Pablo began thinking how Vic had always been on the ethical and the right side of all things since he had known him and now was falling for a smuggler.

Ithaca Exports
Perucho, Ecuador

Señor Cordova opened his cell phone and dialed his contact in China, he asked if Mr. James at the Hotel Patio Amador could be monitored and added that he wanted to be alerted if rooms were changed or if he checked out of the hotel. The contact explained that if Mr. James used a cellular telephone, he could be monitored by tracking the phone and that phone conversations could be recorded if Señor Cordova could provide the phone number.

The contact briefly explained that if he could call Mr. James' phone he could capture the phone number, however he would have to know the number first, the contact also suggested using a CDMA or GSM interceptor to capture the number. Señor Cordova had no clue what the contact meant and promised to provide the phone number to her. He closed his phone and began thinking how to obtain Vic's phone number.

His phone chirped and he saw that Captain Garcia was calling. He provided confirmation that a man was in room 447 and gave the description.

His phone chirped again and he saw Julio was calling.

"Where have you been? I was trying to call you all day."

"I was busy with a, another problem, I can help you now," he said, feeling very hung over.

Señor Cordova looked at his watch and decided to wait until morning. "I want you to go to the Hotel Patio Amado in the morning, and get my turtle. The man with Elena is Vic James, he is in room 447. Get the turtle and kill both of them."

"What about Elena? Can I have her before I kill her?" Julio envisioned her begging him to stop.

"I want her to suffer, hurt the bitch. I don't care what you do to her, but make her suffer!"

"I can do that," Julio said and closed his phone, then lay back on the bed again.

Day Five
Mariscal Sucre Airport

Quito, Ecuador

The next morning Vic called a bellhop to come up to the room and carry their luggage to the front desk, so he could check out of the hotel, then he and Elena caught a taxi for the airport. He wasn't sure what to expect at the airport ticket counter, the standard cursory questions and inspections were a welcome surprise though. I guess Lisa waved her magic wand, looks like Elena is cleared, Vic thought.

Ithaca Exports
Perucho, Ecuador

Señor Cordova's phone rang and the contact from China announced that a Vic James had checked out of the hotel earlier that morning and had left a forwarding address at SatCom, 527 East Parmer Lane, Austin, Texas. Cordova called information and received a phone number for SatCom in Austin. He then called Julio's cell phone, "I am a block from the hotel," he said.

"The American checked out early this morning, go on up and have some fun with the bitch, then kill her."

"What if she has the turtle or knows where the American is?"

Cordova, was quiet for a moment, "Of course find out what she knows before you do anything," he said and closed his phone.

He dialed the number for SatCom in Austin and spoke to the receptionist. He explained that he had breakfast with Mr. James that morning before he left for the airport and that Mr. James had left his credit card by accident. Cordova told her that he was willing to run it to the airport if he could get the phone number to call him and arrange to meet before he boarded the plane. She provided Vic's satellite phone number, then Cordova called China back and provided the number to the contact.

Hotel Patio Amador
Quito, Ecuador

Julio walked through the front doors of the hotel, and took the elevator to the fourth floor. He looked around for anyone who might identify him and walked to room 447 carefully knocking twice. He waited and knocked again, then stepped back and kicked the door at the doorknob level, the wooden door splintered, he kicked again and reached in turning the knob; he slammed the door open. He looked around and realized that both James and Elena had checked out. He called Señor Cordova and told him that the room was vacant.

Ithaca Exports
Perucho, Ecuador

Señor Cordova's phone rang and he opened the cell phone, the voice reported that a trace was initiated on the number he had supplied. The phone was currently not active; apparently turned off. They would monitor and advise him when a signal was detected.

DFW International Airport
Dallas, Texas

Vic and Elena landed at the DFW airport and filed off the plane with the other passengers, they split up when Vic walked to the citizen line and Elena walked to the non-citizen line. He tried to watch her, but the crowds were too large. He was in line for thirty minutes shuffling his way to the man behind the glass, hoping she was safe.

His turn came and Vic handed the customs agent his passport, the inspector placed it under the bar-code reader and a message popped up on his computer terminal which stated, 'Special Ops X-19 Clearance' escort owner to conference room three upon arrival, with accompanying female passenger, Elena Torres.

The inspector peered around Vic looking for the female passenger and noticed the next person in line was a man with two kids. "Are you traveling with someone?"

"Yes, she is in the non-citizen line," Vic stated.

The inspector began typing on his keyboard while watching Vic. A moment later Vic heard the public address system crackle and a voice asked that Ms. Elena Torres please report to booth six in the U.S. citizen line in English and Spanish.

Vic leaned closer to the glass wall and asked if there was a problem. He began imagining ICE agents surrounding him and her. The inspector merely looked up at him giving no indication for the announcement. Vic looked through the glass wall and saw Elena walking toward him at booth six with a worried expression on her face. She walked up to the citizen's line, where Vic was standing, holding her passport and student visa.

"Please surrender your passport," the inspector said.

She handed the inspector her passport and visa. He scanned her passport, the message 'Cleared for travel with Vic James' appeared on his monitor.

"Please wait in conference room number three," the customs agent ordered and pointed to the doors behind him.

A guard walked over and escorted Vic and Elena to the conference room. Momentarily agents with the CIA, FBI and ICE walked into the conference room displaying their identification badges. The ICE agent walked past Vic to Elena.

She tensed when she saw the agent walking directly toward her. He handed her passport to her and she noticed Vic wink at her as the other men turned to face Vic in the conference room. She felt safer with him near her.

"Hey, Jake long time no see. How's the family?" Vic asked, watching the CIA agent close the door.

"They are fine. This is special agent Bob Pickering with the FBI."

"It is nice to meet you Bob," Vic said, noticing that Bob simply nodded without any friendly gesture. Vic wasn't sure how to interpret the cold attitude.

Vic motioned toward Elena. "This, is Elena Torres, she is traveling with me on this trip," he stated, hoping to somehow convince Pickering that she was no threat.

"She's cleared," the ICE agent said, turning and walking to Vic and the other agents.

Agent Pickering explained that the FBI wished to interview Elena before the day ended and Vic agreed to a meeting at the FBI office and would call when he finished his meeting with Ralph.

Vic looked at the three men and raised his eye brows. "I don't know the dance steps here, but she is with me and I need her while I'm in Dallas," he started fishing.

Agent Pickering looked at Vic, "Yeah, she was cleared a few minutes before your plane departed Quito; however, she is only cleared to be in your presence at all times though, okay?" he stated with raised eyebrows and looking over his glasses.

Vic nodded agreement, Agent Pickering then looked at Vic with squinted eyes, a furrowed brow and with a very serious tone of voice and asked if he was aware of the charges. Vic looked at him and shrugged his shoulders and looked to his friend Jake for support.

"Keep her with you at all times and have her at the FBI office this afternoon. Understand?" Jake strongly suggested with a nod toward Elena.

"Yeah, I understand, I won't let her out of my sight."

Jake leaned in so that only the agents could hear him and said, "Vic, it looks like you have friends in high places. She is on the 'no fly list' and is listed as associated with a terrorist organization; I know you will keep an eye on her, right?"

"I know how serious this is, and I know the hoops that people jumped through. Of course I'll keep an eye on her," Vic agreed, shaking his head as if to imply things were overblown.

"Okay, here is my card, if you need us," Agent Pickering said handing Vic a business card and opened the back door of the conference room, directing Vic and Elena downstairs to the luggage carousel.

They retrieved their luggage and caught the bus to the rental car lot, after renting a car he dove to the DIR office.

General Yi's Office
Chengdu Military Base

General Yi welcomed President Yang as he entered the office. Colonel Hon told one of the girls in the large room to pour three cups of tea and followed the president into General Yi's office.

"I want to know everything about Sun-Chang," President Yang announced, before taking a seat.

General Yi was wondering how he surprised him at his own base and began with the counterfeit operation in Ecuador and explained that there was a slight delay in that portion of the plan. The contact, Señor Cordova, assured him that the plan was still moving forward. The counterfeit images were stolen, but the thief was being monitored and was currently in Dallas, Texas and his cell phone was hacked and the information was being uploaded to the computers at the Tsinghua University. General Yi promised the culprit would be persuaded to return the images.

The economic trouble in Panama is working in our favor, just as you said they would. I'm certain you have more information on that issue than I do. I understand Minister Yon has negotiated a very pro-China contract, we will be able to close the canal to all United States shipping at your discretion.

He gloated about the shipping disaster at the Port of Seattle and bragged that the current death toll was over six hundred people and the local hospitals were overflowing with the injured.

General Yi slowly began talking about the Lab 257 virus disappearance, he knew the president had not been approached regarding the seizure and was trying to lay the plan out as a complete success.

"What are the plans for the virus?"

"The plans are to move the container to an Iranian Laboratory ship and develop a vaccine, then release the virus on the United States. If the virus is as potent as they believe a famine will ensue across the nation within six weeks, with the vaccine China will be protected.

General Yi continued expanding on the destruction of the livestock industry in the United States and Canada. He felt a smile on his face that he couldn't stop and turned to get a drink of tea.

General Yi informed President Yang about the massive oil rig disaster in the Gulf of Mexico, highlighting that over twenty people were killed during the rig collapse.

He stood up and walked to his desk, picking up a sheet of paper from his printer and handed it to the president. Here is the latest from the disaster at Niagara Falls Power Station. The city of New York is still dark as well as Buffalo, there are serious brownouts being felt all the way to Washington D.C. and Boston. Sun-Chang is a major success! He concluded, watching the president for agreement to his statement.

The president se quietly for several minutes looking at the empty cup in his hands, turning it around several times. He finally looked up at General Yi.

"Your virus was not approved. It is your responsibility to ensure it is successful, your responsibility alone," President Yang said, then quietly stood up without saying anything else and walked to the door.

"Yes sir, it will be successful," General Yi promised.

President Yang opened the door and walked through the outer office watching his aides quickly jump up and open the doors for him as he left the building.

General Yi looked at Colonel Hon and felt the added weight that was just placed on him, feeling his gut tighten and knew he desperately needed a girl whom he could threaten.

DIR Office
Plano, Texas

Vic walked in to the DIR office and saw Lisa sitting behind her desk, "Lisa you are as beautiful as ever," he said.

"I'll let him know you are here," she smiled and picked up the phone.

"Hey traveler, come on back," Ralph said as he opened the door to his office.

Vic walked in and closed the door, noticing the picture on the wall of President Reagan shaking Ralph's hand.

I wonder what sacrifice he made for that honor. I've got a picture like that with the President shaking my hand, Vic thought to himself. I was back for what two days, when he invited me to the White House, Curt should have been with me at that private ceremony. Vic's thoughts were interrupted when Ralph cleared his throat and Vic looked at Ralph, assuming he was reminiscing too long.

"Well, how was the trip?" Ralph asked, pouring two cups of coffee, seemingly fishing for something.

"It was okay," Vic said hoping to keep the meeting short.

"So how long are you in town?"

"Cut the chit-chat, I know you have some sort of mission for me. What is it?"

Ralph sat down at the small, round table and Vic took a chair across from him, Vic was nervous and didn't want to stay any longer than he had to. He was concerned that he hadn't brought Elena into the office with him, leaving her at the mercy of whoever might be around or more concerned with Jake's statement that she was cleared to be in the states if she was at his side, and he had made the decision to not follow that explicit command.

Ralph placed a manila folder with the words top-secret stenciled across the tab on the table and slid it across to Vic. Vic opened the folder and read a two-page report written by several people from different agencies. The first paragraph stated that China was attempting to infiltrate the operation of the canal, the second stated information regarding the counterfeit information, including Elena's name. The third paragraph listed various successful hacking attacks by China's government, and the last paragraph mentioned a lost container of deadly viruses.

Vic focused on the sentence stating the virus and bacteria in the container were extremely lethal and posed a bio-hazard of the worst kind. The report concluded with chemical structures and RNA of the products.

Vic turned the page and read that smallpox, hemorrhagic and other viruses which were listed will cause death to humans. The Aph-Zoot 27 is a new virus and has no vaccine. It is considered the worst of the viruses in the container. Cloven-hoofed animals have no antibodies to this strain of Hoof and Mouth disease. If the disease is loosed on a population, death to an estimated 90% of the susceptible animals will be complete; it is a new virus.

Hoof and Mouth disease virus has a range between 2 and 12 days. The incubation of Aph-Zoot 27 disease virus is considered to be less than two hours and death will be imminent in 12 hours from infection.

Due to the complex combination of the mixtures of the virus, and the Picornaviridae family of viruses Aph-Zoot 27 is highly contagious to humans, primarily children under the age of seven years. Vic finished the report and closed the folder, sliding it back towards Ralph.

Vic looked up at Ralph, "China is starting all of this?" Vic asked, not wanting to believe his eyes.

"Everything but the container, that one is ours and we lost it. The NSA is working on the hacking aspects of the war; I refer to war because we are under an orchestrated attack. We need you to work the lost container issue. Vic we are not certain how the bio-weapons will be delivered, if we did we could begin vaccinations possibly or perhaps issue appropriate protective outerwear for key personnel."

"Okay, so what do we do now, what is your plan?" Vic asked.

"Vic, I want you to find out if the container is on that ship. If so, determine if the locking mechanism has been compromised.

Now, you know you can refuse this operation, I wouldn't blame you if you did," Ralph said.

"So, who else do you have to do the job?" Vic asked and rapidly began thinking of Elena. What about Elena? I can't take her on this type of mission. Hell it could go bad, and if it does what would she do?

"No one is in the wings except you partner, at least not at this time. Vic, you are the only person in place to do this job. We could put a team together, but we are talking days, and we do not have days, hell we might be down to hours and not even know it."

"What if there is no shipment? What if the shipment gets through the canal before I get there or what if the container is dropped off in Havana or somewhere else?" Vic asked ignoring the option of refusing the mission.

"Then take a vacation in Panama, on my dime."

"What if the nasty stuff is there?"

"Vic, you will have additional assets at your disposal during this operation. These assets will aid you in neutralizing the stuff, but they are not as experienced in front line mission operations as you are," Ralph stated, thinking back to his own adventures as a CIA field agent.

"What does the container look like? Hell, how can I determine if the stuff in the container is genuine? Maybe they transferred the nasty stuff to an airplane and it is destined for China," Vic commented.

Ralph provided the description of the container and Vic set back in the chair and took a deep breath, then relaxed. He quickly started devising a plan, hell, I'll take her with me, with a little luck; I'll vacation on Ralph's dime, then be back in Quito to settle with Cordova or whatever is going on there, or I'll go on vacation in Latin America, he sighed and looked up at Ralph.

"Okay, I'm in, what's the pot ante?" Vic quizzed.

Ralph exhaled loudly. "That's my boy. I just knew you would not make me eat crow," Ralph said.

Vic's body tightened, he jerked forward with clinched fists, "What does that mean? Who did you promise that I would take this?" he demanded.

"The big guy knows and since we have no one else who can be on-site as quickly as you can, I really had no choice," Ralph admitted.

"Come on, Ralph!"

"Trust me, this is not a decision I made without forethought and sweat."

"Bull shit, you know me and you knew I would do this if you asked me to. Know this, the next time you ask me anything, the answer is hell no! I am an easy piece of ass and everyone knows it, 'ask Vic he'll do it'," Vic felt cheap and didn't want to discuss the mission anymore.

He scooted his chair away from table and tried to calm down, he looked at Ralph who had sweat beading on his forehead, "Okay, to change the subject here, did you receive my communications about the counterfeits?" Vic asked as he tested the coffee.

"Yes, I did. Are they secured?" Ralph asked.

Vic explained that the images were in the safe at SatCom and started explaining that Elena was with him on the trip—

"Yeah, I spoke with Lisa about her. I called in some favors to get her approved to fly to the United States," Ralph interrupted.

"Thanks for that," Vic said.

Vic explained how Elena and he met, that she was a mule for Ithaca Exports and that if they get their hands on her, she may lead them to the counterfeit Micro SD card and that would lead the police to SatCom and Pablo's office.

Ralph's eyes narrowed slightly. "Is she an asset? Can you trust her?" he asked.

"I truly don't know yet, I'm not thinking of her as an asset though."

"If you think it would be best for the operation we can eliminate her in Panama," Ralph said.

Vic jumped to his feet, knocking the chair over backward. "No!"

"Don't jeopardize the operation for a pretty piece of ass. Hell, I'll buy you one of those if that's all you want."

"Kiss my ass, you son of a bitch!" he said realizing he was set up. He picked up the chair and set back down.

"I merely wanted you to remember that any agent can be compromised. I didn't mean it the way I said it, I hope you know that. I have great respect and admiration for you and I want you to stop and think," Ralph said, leaning closer to Vic, he winked.

"No, I won't let her affect the mission," Vic replied, for his benefit as well as Ralph's.

"I passed the counterfeit information to the analysts in DC, they think Al Qaeda or China, perhaps both are behind the counterfeit ring and if Latin American governments collapse, the rag heads or China can then move in and secure the countries for China or for Allah; strange partners uh?" Ralph said as he shrugged.

"Okay, so then the Chinese can move in pop the rag heads and secure all of Latin America for China in the ruse of being good guys fighting world terrorists. Yeah, I think I understand now. The Chinese are playing for world domination; first by using bio-weapons of mass destruction to kill millions around the world. Then toppling legitimate governments in Latin America and replacing them with their puppet governments. This would be a big step towards invading and securing the United States for China," Vic said.

"You got it cowboy," Ralph said as he leaned back.

Vic realized he was in the office longer than he had anticipated and stood up. The two men shook hands.

"Listen, I know all about your friend. The FBI is expecting her this afternoon. I am supposed to tell them what time to expect the two of you."

"Tell them I am on my way, I guess thirty minutes will give me enough time to get there," Vic stated.

Vic walked out of Ralph's office and stopped at Lisa's desk and she smiled again, she leaned to her left, opening a safe in her desk, "Here is a packet of information you will be interested in," she handed Vic a large envelope.

He took it, winked at her and walked out of the DIR office. He walked to the rental car and noticed Elena was not in the car. "Dang it, where is she?" he said to his mirror image in the window.

He turned and noticed a convenience store a couple of storefronts down, Vic walked in and saw Elena selecting a soda from one of the soft drink coolers in the back. I have to test her somehow. I have to be able to trust her or, Ralph will have her hit. Shit, are we as ruthless as the other side? Vic knew the answer and wasn't comfortable with it.

Elena saw him and dropped two dollars on the counter as she walked past. "I got thirsty waiting for you, hace mucho color hoy, uh, it is very hot today," she said walking past him as she winked.

He smiled and followed her out the door to the car. Vic drove to the FBI office in Dallas and slowly pulled into the parking lot. He could tell Elena was nervous; she kept fidgeting in the seat, buckling and unbuckling the belt. He parked in a visitor's space near the front doors and turned off the engine. Vic turned to his right and looked at her, noticing she was shaking slightly and appeared as though she was trying to gain control of her emotions.

"Elena, I know you never wanted or even agreed to the smuggling and I will fight for you, you have to trust me."

She looked at him and calmed herself, hearing his words of support. She nodded slowly and watched him open his door, she watched him walk around the car to her door. "I just hope you can help me," she said, quietly and felt the tears wet the corner of her eyes.

She walked close to him as they entered the doors and stopped at the receptionist's counter. Vic gave her his driver's license and Elena surrendered her passport. They took a seat in the lobby and waited. Vic was thinking about the operation he was taking on and noticed Elena walk to the water fountain three times during the ten minutes they waited.

"Mr. James?" the receptionist asked.

Vic walked over to her desk, she handed him a clip board with a printed sheet of thumb-size photographs. The first one showed Elena standing outside a bar holding a pouch. The next one showed her handing the pouch to a man and the third one showed Elena taking a zippered bank bag from the man. Vic felt the slow pang of trouble in his gut as he reviewed the photographs. He heard the door behind the receptionist open and saw Agent Pickering from the airport standing there. He nodded and Vic walked back to Elena and tapped her on the shoulder, then they walked through the door.

Ithaca Exports
Perucho, Ecuador

Señor Cordova answered his phone on the second chirp and listened to the lady speaking Spanish with a strong Chinese accent as she advised him that Vic James' phone was activated.

"Please start the trace for numbers called to and from, also can the location of the phone be determined?"

"That can be accomplished on the smart phones. I will check if the location can be traced on his satellite phone."

Cordova heard the clicks as the phone line was terminated, then closing his phone, he felt a little better.

General Yi's Office
Chengdu Military Base

General Yi had set for over an hour after President Yang left his office contemplating several different scenarios for the virus, trying to find the plan with the least chance of failure. He knew if the plan was not successful he would certainly face execution, but the torturous days before the execution concerned him most.

He opened his email account and sent an email to Tehran requesting the laboratory ship, the Milanian, be reassigned from Havana to Panama. He would have the container transferred from the freighter before it entered the canal. Surely his team of scientists could discover a vaccine quickly, they had to. He sent an email to Dr. Qu, chief of staff for the Health Sciences department at Tsinghua University, in Beijing, China and copied Hon, requesting Dr. Qu to provide a team of scientists with biological expertise in vaccines to fly to Panama City, Panama, to conduct emergency work on a new disease. He chose to be as vague as he could, since he had no concrete evidence on Aph-Zoot 27.

He next sent an email to General Lam, the ranking general in the Biological Warfare unit of the Army. He briefly explained the situation, requesting that a team of scientists be dispatched to Panama, and suggested he contact Professor Szu for further details regarding the virus and the location of the ship. He pressed the send button, shuddering at the thought of the bullets hitting his chest if he allowed this to fail, hoping he had covered all the bases. He stood up and left the office.

FBI Office
Dallas, Texas

Vic and Elena followed Agent Pickering to the interrogation room, a room with bright white walls. The walls would contrast a person's movement and help to clarify facial expressions. Vic knew from his being grilled before, that the front legs of her chair would be an inch shorter, creating a feeling of falling to the person being questioned.

Vic noticed a stenographer had her steno machine ready for the first word spoken and a second lady was standing behind a video camera. He noticed the red light indicating the camera's status was already on and the camera was recording.

He didn't have a good feeling about the meeting, too much obvious 'doubting her deposition' before the meeting started, was tugging at his gut.

Elena was shown a chair on the back side of the six foot, rectangle table and Vic was instructed to sit at the end of the table. This positioned two empty chairs between him and Elena, forcing her to turn her head to see Vic's face. A movement easily picked up by the camera.

Agent Pickering closed the door and took his seat at the head of the table and nodded at the video camera. He started by swearing in Elena to tell the truth during the deposition and a statement directed at Vic warning him not to interject any verbal or nonverbal comments or signals to Elena.

Agent Pickering announced the interview was between Elena Torres and the FBI, stating his name and that it was being video recorded, the stenographer kept up with the conversation as well. He asked Elena to begin her story when she was in the orphanage and Vic wondered if they knew about the orphanage, what else did they know that he didn't know? He felt the old 'out-in-left-field' feeling creeping in.

She spoke about when her parents were killed in a mud slide following a terrible storm and how Padre Perez had found beds at the orphanage. She continued with how Eduardo had left to go to a job when he was fourteen and visited her often, but seemed to grow distant. She explained how she had a knack for languages and was awarded a scholarship at the Catholic University in Quito. She had graduated and needed a Master's Degree to be given a job at the consulate in the United States. She applied and was awarded a student visa to attend the University of Texas at Austin. She was traveling every six months from Austin to Quito when she learned of her brother's accident, or what she was told was an accident. Señor Cordova had threatened to kill Eduardo if she refused to deliver packages to and from an office in Dallas, and was instructed to travel monthly. She would deliver the packages, sometimes in suitcases and sometimes small enough to fit in her purse. Señor Cordova paid for most of her travel expenses.

Agent Pickering showed her the sheet of pictures he had, she looked at the pictures and explained that the man in the picture was Lupe. He was often at the Ithaca Exports office in Dallas, he had taught her how to sneak the packages past customs. Vic was impressed with her knowledge of clandestine operations.

Agent Pickering slid a folder across the table to Vic, he opened it and read that Elena was indicted for espionage, counterfeiting and smuggling drugs. He read the charges twice; then looked up at Agent Pickering. Elena sensed the severity of the situation and began wiping tears from her eyes again.

"What are your intentions?" Vic finally asked.

Agent Pickering leaned back and exhaled slowly while alternating his attention between Vic and Elena, he was hoping for some panic reaction from Elena, and finally said, "This is a very difficult situation. I understand that you will be instrumental in locating a very important item which was recently lost."

"Yes, I will be. Uh, I will be the primary instrument in the recovery process," Vic said feeling stupid.

Vic acknowledged that he was scheduled to leave the country as soon as possible and that the operation required her to assist him, hoping to play the she's-on-the-team-and-we-can't-win-without-her card.

"Who is your handler?"

Vic provided Ralph's phone number and name. Agent Pickering stood up and left the room.

"They are going to put me in prison, aren't they?"

Vic noticed the camera was still recording and the stenographer was recording everything she was saying. He motioned for her to be quiet.

Ten minutes later, Agent Pickering walked back into the room. He looked at Vic for a long moment. He then stated, "The charges remain open; however, she will be allowed to travel with you. You have friends."

Agent Pickering closed the folder and left the room. The stenographer picked up her machine and followed Agent Pickering and the video operator ejected the small 8mm tape and left the room, following the other two. Vic winked at Elena.

He opened his satellite phone and pressed the speed dial for the DIR office. The phone displayed the word ALERT in red. Vic closed the phone and powered it down.

"We're going to Austin, before leaving for Panama," he said, pulling Elena's chair away from the table.

Elena looked up at him and slowly stood to her feet, her knees felt wobbly and her stomach felt all knotted up.

"I just want to go home," she said. She thought about Cordova and realized that it was very dangerous for her at home. She reached for Vic's arm and felt a sense of protection.

They walked back to the lobby and Vic asked to use the phone at the receptionist's desk, he called Rachel in Austin and instructed her to send the company plane to Love Field in Dallas and not to call him on his satellite phone and to call Lisa at DIR and Pablo, and tell them not to call him either.

Rachel told him the plane would be in Dallas in a couple of hours and then said, "Oh, I forgot to ask earlier, did you get your credit card back, before leaving Quito this morning?"

"What? Credit card, I haven't lost my card," Vic quizzed.

"Tanya, the morning receptionist, told me that a man called for your number this morning, he said he was going to catch you at the airport."

"Son of a bitch!" Vic squawked.

"Is everything okay?" Rachel asked.

"No, but don't worry about it. I'll be at the office in a few hours," Vic said and hung up the phone.

They walked back to the rental car and drove to a steak house near downtown Dallas for dinner.

NSA Headquarters
Washington, D.C.

Steve Jenkins was working at his computer in the third level below ground at Fort Meade, Maryland. His team was assigned the task of tracing the email that Ed Tatum received. He knew the email had originated from the Tsinghua University in Beijing and was attempting to narrow the search to one of three possible locations within the university. The IP address he was searching for was 34.57.91.428. He had set a trap for that address. If the computer signs on to any of the popular search engines like Google or web pages such as MSN or AOL his trap would spring and load a worm onto that computer, he knew it was a waiting game now.

The worm program he had written would send back all passwords and logon information and would also send all user names and emails the computer had sent. Steve was hoping to correlate Ed's email with the user who was signed on at the time of transmission.

General Yi's Office
Chengdu Military Base

General Yi arrived at the office and told Colonel Hon to come to his office as he walked through the room, Colonel Hon grabbed a note pad and hurriedly followed the general.

"Where the hell is the freighter, the Tiangong Kaiwu?" he demanded after he was seated at his desk.

Colonel Hon made the comment that he was certain it was on schedule, but would get confirmation and an updated ETA to the canal. General Yi raised his head and looked at Colonel Hon for several minutes without saying anything. Colonel Hon began feeling very uneasy and suddenly realized that the general was acting more aggressive since the surprise meeting with President Yang, he wondered who would catch the brunt of his anger and hoped it wouldn't be him.

"I'll have the information momentarily, sir," Colonel Hon said, walking out of the room.

General Yi stood up, he was sweating and it was before nine in the morning, he felt the need to work off the nervous energy and extra aggression he was feeling. He knew the exact meaning of the words President Yang left him with. He thought back and remembered him saying, "Your virus was not approved. It is your responsibility to ensure it is successful. Your responsibility alone!"

He walked out of his office and looked out at the young ladies working at their desks, he scanned the room and found two of the three newest who were recently transferred into his command. He walked across the room keeping his eyes on the two ladies and didn't see the trash can that was in the aisle between two desks. He hit the can with his right foot and cussed loudly, demanding to know who left the trash can in his way.

A young soldier very timidly admitted it was her trash can as she dropped to her knees picking up the paper, he bellowed that she was incompetent and should be reprimanded for her actions.

"Follow me!" he quietly ordered walking back to his office.

Colonel Hon saw the disturbance as he printed off the freighter's location and scheduled arrival date to the Panama Canal. He saw Private Daiyu follow the general into his office and heard General Yi slam the door closed. He knew he should wait before delivering the sheet of paper.

Love Field
Dallas, Texas

Vic and Elena arrived at Love Field. He checked in at the courtesy desk and was told his plane was at the Business Jet Center. He led Elena through the terminal to gate 27 and walked down the stairs to the waiting van, flashed his identification and loaded their luggage into the van. The driver drove out to the business terminal and dropped them off at the stairs of the Learjet 31 airplane.

Vic climbed the stairs and saw Laura stowing Elena's suitcase. She was not only the flight attendant, but was also one of the receptionists at the SatCom office.

"Good evening, sir," she replied.

"Hi Laura, how are things?"

"Great sir," she replied eyeing Elena.

Laura helped load the luggage as Vic and Elena climbed the stairs and strapped into their seats, the pilot started the engines and was in the air within five minutes.

Elena noticed the jet's interior; the walls were paneled in a dark cherry wood, the lights were actually wall lamps, not the standard recessed lights she was used to on the commercial jets and the seats were wider than normal possessing a very plush feel.

She saw Laura bring a margarita to Vic and then asked if she would like a drink, she asked for a glass of white wine and noticed Laura's short, tight skirt as she returned to the galley. She wondered how much power and money Vic had if he could get her out of trouble with the FBI and owned a very expensive plane.

Vic was very concerned about the ALERT message on his satellite phone. He had programmed it with safeguards to keep it from being hacked or even monitored. However, he knew anything was susceptible to a really good hacker, so he had programmed the phone to display the ALERT message if any of the software or firmware was changed. He needed access to the main computer at the SatCom office to run a comparison to find what was changed. He knew Cordova had to be behind the hacking and the thought of him having that type of knowledge or strings scared him. I will have to deal with the son of a bitch, maybe before Panama. I need to let Ralph know the score, he thought.

Forty minutes later the plane landed at Bergstrom Airport in Austin. The Learjet pulled to a stop and the attendant opened the door and lowered the stairs, Vic saw a car pull up to the foot of the stairs and the driver get out holding a sign that read Sat-Com. Vic helped Elena into the limo and saw the driver load the luggage.

"Mr. James, I was sent to bring you to your office," he said.

Vic noticed it was past seven in the evening and was hoping that Rachel hadn't left for the day; he turned to Elena and noticed she was watching him.

"I never thought to ask, but where do you live while in Austin?"

"I have a dorm room at Castilian hall, many of the people there are exchange students," she replied.

Vic smiled and shook his head as though he understood and continued concentrating on the hacked satellite phone.

DIR
Plano, Texas

Lisa answered the phone and transferred the call to Ralph.

"Sir, this is Agent Pickering again with the FBI here in Dallas. I spoke with you earlier about Vic James and Elena Escamilla; you authorized the release of Elena Escamilla into Vic James' custody this afternoon."

"Yes, is there a problem?"

"No sir, only that. Well the proprietor of Ithaca Exports in Dallas was arrested an hour ago and he told us that she is not only the smuggler, but she is the leader of the counterfeit ring. We are considering having her arrested."

"Okay, I understand your concern and if I didn't know Vic James so well I might have the same concerns. I can promise you that he is working with the express directions from POTUS. Do you understand?" Ralph asked.

"Yes sir, we will hold off for now," Agent Pickering said and hung up the phone. He is connected at the very top. Well, if there is any trouble, I will not be hung out to dry, it is on video and the phone conversations were all taped, James, Ralph and anyone else even remotely connected will go down in flames with me.

SatCom Office
Austin, Texas

The limo pulled up to the SatCom office building and stopped. The driver retrieved the luggage from the trunk and opened the door for Vic.

Elena looked up at the tall building, seeing the spotlighted front doors and the manicured lawn and flower beds, "This is your office?" she asked as she awed the forty-three story building.

"Not the entire building, only the thirty-ninth floor. Our engineering and manufacturing facilities are located in Round Rock about thirty miles north of here. SatCom leases part of a closed military complex there."

They walked in through the front door of the building, the elevator stopped on the thirty-ninth floor and opened. Vic saw Rachel's purse on the desk in the hall and had a good feeling, he trusted her implicitly.

"Rachel, I'm home," Vic called out as they walked into the office.

Vic saw Rachel standing at the end of his office watering his plants.

"I'm glad you're home, it's been lonely without you," she said, introducing herself to Elena.

"With all your boyfriends, I'm sure you don't get too lonely," he laughed.

Vic grabbed a spare battery from his top desk drawer for his satellite phone and checked the in basket on the desk, nothing urgent he noticed.

"I need to access Taurus," he said, and saw Rachel get the key from her top desk drawer and unlock the tall metal cabinet which was standing against the far wall. She unlocked the door and pressed the 'power on' button of the large computer which was bolted inside the security cabinet.

Vic referred to the SatCom computer as Taurus. He had considered naming it Bevo, but knew UT would not like it if word got out, so Taurus was selected. The *HP* Supernova utilizing the Intel Itanium 2 processor was coupled with an unreleased Quantum computer which allowed an error correction scheme that was unequaled in the industry. The computer was not accessible from outside the office. He didn't want to allow the heart of the SatCom operations to be even remotely available to hackers.

He set down at the monitor and entered his password and hooked the mini B USB cable to his satellite phone, then uploaded the software package to the Taurus. The satellite phone's software package had over twenty million lines of code.

It would be impossible for a person to study the package and determine if a few of the lines were changed. Even though he had written the software package he hadn't memorized it line by line. He started the comparison check program which literally compared the current phone's package to the read-only file of the package in the Taurus. He watched the monitor which had three columns, the column on the left was titled Master and the center column was titled Phone and the column on the right had a green check if the comparison agreed. The comparison had a percentage box that displayed sixty percent complete and he started feeling better and thought that perhaps the ALERT message was a fluke. He knew that if he were hacked, it had to be by a government.

Vic turned his attention back to the monitor and saw a red check on three of the lines and had a sinking feeling that his phone was indeed hacked. The program concluded and displayed the message that twenty seven lines of code had been changed. He clicked on the print icon.

"Son of a bitch!" he exclaimed.

Vic scanned the printout and saw the lines of code that were affected, realizing that the worm or virus had forwarded the phone numbers he had called to an IP address including the conversations which were stored in a FIFO buffer in the phone. He activated the IP address locater program on the PC on his desk and typed in the address, and saw that the IP address was assigned to a computer in China at the Tsinghua University.

Vic looked at his watch and realized it was getting late and hoped Ralph was still in his office, picking up the office phone, he dialed DIR. He explained that his satellite phone was hacked and asked Ralph if he had any information on the Tsinghua University in Beijing.

"Let me check with Langley, I'll get back to you in less than twenty minutes."

General Yi's Office
Chengdu Military Base

General Yi was stroking the back of Private Daiyu's head while she serviced him and felt the ecstasy as he exploded into her mouth and heard her gag slightly. She stopped bobbing back and forth and slowly raised her head. She wiped her lips with the back of her hand as he handed her a tissue and smiled when he saw tears on her cheeks. The phone on his desk rang and he answered it.

"Yes," he growled.

The voice provided the information he had requested via email earlier. The Tiangong Kaiwu was traveling full speed and was currently eighty kilometers west of Cuba and three days out from the Panama Canal.

He hung up the phone and watched her putting her bra and tunic blouse back on, she looked at him after she was fully dressed and he nodded, she opened the door and left his office.

He called out for Colonel Hon and heard a chair slide across the hardwood floor, Colonel Hon walked into the office carrying a printout of the freighter's location. General Yi told him he wanted to know the status on the lost counterfeit images in

Ecuador. Colonel Hon reached for the phone and started telling General Yi the location of the Tiangong Kaiwu.

"You are late! I know where it is. Try to stay current with this operation," General Yi said with a disgusted tone in his voice.

Colonel Hon picked up the phone and dialed the number for Cordova's cell phone and asked Corporal Hong, the Spanish interpreter, to join them. He pressed the speaker button on his phone and placed the phone on General Yi's desk as she entered the office and stood facing the general.

They heard Cordova's voice when he answered and General Yi introduced himself and pleasantly inquired the whereabouts of the Micro SD card.

Colonel Hon sensed immediately that the news was not going to be positive by the stammering and pauses from Cordova. General Yi changed from his pleasant voice to his growling and gruff voice demanding that Cordova locate the lost memory card and contact him with a revised printing schedule within three days or he would not live past four days; he nodded to Colonel Hon that the conversation was finished.

Colonel Hon pressed the terminate button and nodded for the corporal to leave, seeing the frightened look on her face while she seemed to stare at General Yi, and backed out of the office.

General Yi indicated that President Yang was not going to be pleased with the delay. Colonel Hon placed the printout of the status of the Tiangong Kaiwu on his desk. General Yi looked at the sheet of paper and sighed, looking up at Colonel Hon.

SatCom Office
Austin, Texas

Vic started through the phone's software, looking for any type of changes that might be a way for the hackers to log back in. He found a line with a strange code which sent the operational system to different memory locations. He started writing the memory contents of each location and discovered it was 64 bits, the same as a number of two IP addresses. He wrote out the number and began a search on the internet and found the first IP address was a computer at Tsinghua University in Beijing, and the second was Chengdu Military base in China.

He remembered Lisa had said that General Yi was stationed at that base and his name was mentioned at Ithaca Exports. Maybe the university is tied in with him, he thought. Vic started devising an idea to really piss them off. He picked up the phone and asked Ralph about the two places.

"The university is suspected of hacking into government computers. General Yi is known to be a really bad dude. He is suspected of being behind the missing container, and might have been behind hacking into your phone," Ralph said.

"Okay, thanks for the info, I'll call you later," Vic hung up the office phone.

Vic moved the cursor over the reset option for his phone's software and clicked. He also scrolled down to the next worm detect and encryption algorithm and selected it to update his phone, then disconnected the phone's cable from the Taurus and powered on his satellite phone, he reached for a different keyboard which was connected to a desk top computer in his office.

Vic reached for a new Thumb Drive on the desk and plugged it into a USB port on the front of the PC computer and started typing code in visual basic.

He typed in the IP address of the computer which had hacked into his satellite phone, and labeled it the recipient, then pressed enter and waited for a response.

He knew if the computer was powered down he would not receive any type of response; however, if the system was on and it was a Windows or UNIX based he would receive a reply, either a list of active programs as he requested or a simple denial.

Vic saw a response appear on the monitor and realized the request was denied, but the computer had at least replied. Vic activated his password program and pressed enter. He was activating a program similar to PC Anywhere so he could access the remote computer. Vic had never attempted to break into a computer from China before and wondered if he would need to read Chinese.

The password program completed without finding the pass-word to access the system, he wondered if he should convert the passwords being attempted to Chinese characters and try again.

He turned and faced Elena, "Can you also read Chinese?"

"Yes I can read the language," she said looking up from the magazine she was thumbing.

Vic stopped the program and activated the language conver-sion program to Mandarin Chinese and restarted the program and leaned back to stretch his back. He noticed the program stopped with a success code and the password in Chinese displayed on the monitor.

"What does that say?"

Elena leaned over and read the words on the monitor and laughed. "Lin chong," she said.

"What the hell does it mean?"

Elena explained the term literally means lewd worm and is pro-fanity for a man who visits a brothel often, probably written by a younger man who wants to be thought of as well endowed.

Vic smiled and knew he was in, then rolled his chair back and let Elena type the characters in the password box. Vic rolled back up and pressed enter, the computer replied granting him full administrative privileges.

He switched back to Taurus and began writing a program that would lie dormant for two days then in 48 hours began sending out worms to any computer it was connected to, with additional commands for the next computer to pass on the exact same worm.

Vic next wrote a program for the worm to begin slowly mim-icking legitimate defragmentation of the hard drive, then pass on the worm to all other computers that would respond to emails it automatically sent out, then finally for the worm to go full blown, it would overwrite the hard drive of all computers and their rout-ers handling the online activities at 2:00 A.M. local time, he looked at a calendar on the desk, three days from now should be plenty of time for many of their computers to be infected, he thought.

Vic leaned back in the chair, and placed his right index finger over the enter key, but paused while deciding a wipe of the hard drive was not enough for the hackers, and definitely not enough for whoever hacked his phone. He quickly wrote a few lines of code in the hard drive speed control routine. The revised routine would now ignore every second index signal from the hard drive motor. That would generate a condition in the if/then routine and supply more amperage to the motor, causing it to overheat and burn out the motor within ten minutes of the worm's activation.

He asked Elena what would be a very insulting term for a Chinese General. Elena thought for a moment and replied with the words 'hong ri' and explained that it is the term for red ass, relating to an act when Japanese soldiers raped Chinese men and women. She explained that the term was very demeaning to a Chinese man, referring back to the invasion of China by Japan in the 1930's.

She explained that it was meant to imply that the Chinese man was a willing lover of the Japanese invaders. She typed the statement and Vic felt a smile come across his face, he gave a few more commands that would be written onto all the hard drives and then wrote a short program in Python language which would remain elusive on the computer's hard drive until the first program initiated.

The program was one of the best worms Vic had ever written and realized he might have missed his true calling. He reviewed his handiwork to ensure he hadn't missed anything. After all the hard drives were corrupted the computer's execute files would be erased, then the video RAM would control the monitor and the hard drive motor would burn up, rendering the computer useless as a boat anchor, he thought and chuckled.

Vic plugged the Thumb Drive into the online computer and uploaded the contents to the Chinese computer, then logged off the Chinese computer and logged off the Taurus and powered down the router.

He looked at Elena and said, "Let's go." He turned to Rachel. "Please check these emails and memos," Vic said, handing her a Thumb Drive from his pocket, "Then e-mail or snail mail them appropriately. Also, Elena and I are flying to Panama in the morning, can you reserve a couple of seats, have the limo driver take us back to the airport."

Vic dialed DIR and explained to Ralph that his phone was now active again and also told Ralph that he was concerned about traveling under his own name and asked for cover names for him and Elena, including passports and other identification documents to travel to Panama. Ralph asked where he would be staying the night.

"Hey Rachel, I need a room in Dallas tonight," Vic said, watching her access her computer.

"How's the DFW Marriott?"

Vic relayed the hotel to Ralph and was relieved to hear that a new identification would be delivered to him via special courier to the DFW Marriott hotel at nine o'clock the next morning.

Elena looked at him with a curious expression, but didn't say anything and was quiet as they drove back to the airport.

"Vic, I owe you more than I can ever hope to repay," she finally said, wondering who he worked for, but knew he was important if he could get her out of trouble and order a new identity over the phone, like she would order a pizza.

She was quiet as she thought during the flight back to Dallas.

Ithaca Exports
Perucho, Ecuador

Señor Cordova was still trying to regain his composure following the threatening phone call from General Yi, and dialed his contact number at Tsinghua University. He requested additional electronic security measures be initiated for tracking Vic James and was informed that the hacking tracers for his satellite phone were terminated and counter-espionage measures were implemented on the targeted satellite phone.

"I must know his location!"

"We will attempt other means for tracking," she stated and terminated the call.

President Yang's Office
Beijing China

"Mr. President, this email was received from General Yi," Gia said, laying the printed email on his desk.

>**President Yang**
>
>**Concerning Sun-Chang**
>
>**It is imperative that the Panama Canal be manned with Chinese personnel to aide with exporting counterfeit currency. Please approve Minister Yon to obtain this agreement from the Panamanian government.**
>
>**General Yi.**

"Gia, please forward a copy of this email to Minister Yon, in Panama. Make certain he understands it came through this office, also copy General Yi, so he is aware that his request has been approved."

"Yes sir."

NSA Headquarters
Washington, D.C.

Steve Jenkins was reviewing the latest reports on the hacking techniques of teenagers and was wondering if the email that Ed Tatum received was a hack job itself, when he heard the low level hum from his speakers. He had added a line of instruction code to sound at the mid C range the next time the computer with the IP address 34.57.91.428. logged on. He observed the monitor as it began mirroring the other computer's monitor, and saw the operator was signed on as Li and using the password Su Qui.

Steve dialed extension 3577 and reported that the computer was logged on, he was told to patch the feed to the conference room on the second floor.

Herman Hanks, the lead negotiator of the department ran to the conference room from his office and set down at the keyboard, the monitor was a large 37 inch display mounted on the wall.

Herman watched as Li typed in the words CIA and began entering the IP address for Ed Tatum's computer. Hank responded with a simple "hello" in Chinese, the system he was typing on converted English into Chinese. He waited hoping for a reply.

Two minutes lapsed as other people entered the room and several hushed comments were made that he should have started with, 'We know who you are' or a 'What the hell are y'all doing?'

Herman saw the monitor as it slowly displayed several Chinese characters. He turned around and asked who could read Chinese? Michelle Rawlins began translating the characters. "It reads, *what is your location?*"

Herman typed in the United States and I would like to speak with you.

The response was slow as it typed out; *Did you receive my message?*

Herman responded, Yes, can you help us?

Your Plum container will be at the canal soon and will be transferred to Iran's Milanian for vaccinations.

Hank typed in When? and saw the other computer go off line.

"Shit!" Herman said and typed several more responses, "They're gone," he said dejectedly.

Print the correspondence so we can try to figure out what they were talking about," he heard someone say.

PART THREE

Day Six
Marriott Hotel
Dallas, Texas

Vic woke and looked at Elena sleeping beside him. He slowly rolled out of bed, took a shower and dressed. He watched her walk to the bathroom and heard the shower running.

He sat down at the table and opened the large packet Lisa had given him when he left the DIR office. It contained the codes for his contacts in Panama and the code word was "Flying Fish". "Who the hell comes up with these phrases?" he asked the mirror. Hearing the bathroom door open, he closed the manila folder and slid it back into the large envelope.

She stepped out of the bathroom few minutes later, smiling broadly; she acknowledged that she felt free for the first time in almost a year.

He noticed she was wearing the mini skirt again, but with the pink blouse instead of the white one, she set down and put on her heels.

Vic heard a knock at the door. A man wearing a suit and tie asked to see his identification, verifying it matched the name and number in his book, he looked closely at Vic's face comparing Vic to the photo he had in his vest pocket, then handed a folded portfolio to Vic and waited for Vic to sign the receipt. Vic closed the door and removed the two passports including two visas in the names of Mike and Susan Roberts and a new Texas driver's license for him, the packet also included two first class tickets to Panama City.

He looked at her. "We are now married," Vic said and wasn't certain how to explain the new identities. He told her it was to keep her from Cordova and noticed she seemed to buy the idea.

"We have a flight today at noon and I don't have the answers you are looking for, I simply do not know, but I do know one thing. I, I want you with me!" Vic announced, grabbing her more force-fully than he meant to, holding her tight for a few minutes, feeling her body slowly relax.

Ithaca Exports
Perucho, Ecuador

Señor Cordova opened his cell phone and called the number for the Tsinghua University, waited for the call to be answered, then inquired the latest information regarding the location of the American citizen, Vic James.

The operator informed him that Vic James was in Dallas Texas at the Marriott hotel near the DFW airport. Cordova wondered if the information was accurate as he closed his phone and thought the gringo sure gets around.

DFW Airport
Dallas, Texas

They boarded the flight to Panama City without any problems and found their assigned seating in first class. The flight attendant stopped at Vic's seat and viewed her seating manifest, then confirmed that they were Mr. and Mrs. Roberts. She informed him that the flight was scheduled to be full. The flight took off without delay.

Vic reached down and pulled out the foot rest under his seat and reclined his seat back, then leaned back and rested his head, feeling himself drift off.

He awoke with a jolt and looked around, suddenly remembering he was on a plane, and noticed Elena looking at him. He recalled that the last time he woke like that, and hoped he hadn't said or done anything stupid; looking into her eyes for any indication.

"I guess I was more tired than I thought," he said wiping his eyes.

"Is it because you know you can trust me?" Elena asked, reaching out and taking his hand, then laid her head on his shoulder. He did not respond to her question but did squeeze her hand gently.

Tocumen International Airport
Panama City, Panama

The flight landed and they were processed through customs without any difficulties. Walking out of the terminal, Vic noticed a street vendor selling fresh fish on the sidewalk. He was holding a sign that read 'flying fish'. Vic imagined some pencil pusher sitting at a desk, having never been in the field, thinking that the code flying fish wouldn't catch anyone's attention, the son-of-a-bitch ought to be shot for stupidity, he stopped thinking about it, and walked over and asked how much his fish cost.

"They are three pesos Señor," the man replied, nodding knowingly at Vic.

Vic looked at the vendor and wondered if there was another vendor selling flying fish, "I would like to buy a flying fish."

"No the flying fish are two-hundred pesos Señor."

The vendor studied Vic intently for several moments, comparing his face to a photograph he had under the shelf of the vending stand. He then reached into his right jeans pocket and took out a small clear plastic vial. He looked up at Vic being certain he had Vic's full attention and then pushed the vial into the fish's mouth. He wrapped the fish in newspaper and handed it to Vic. Vic put the package under his left arm and walked toward the taxi stand, pulling his suitcase, leading Elena as she pulled her suitcase behind her. They took a taxi to the Riando Hotel. It was not the usual hotel Vic stayed at in Panama, but it was the hotel that had reservations for Mike and Susan Roberts.

Ithaca Exports
Perucho, Ecuador

Señor Cordova answered his phone and heard the sounds of Chinese in the background. The voice informed him that Vic James' room was vacated, and his name was not on the guest register for that night. The assumption was that he had checked out and was traveling incognito for the time being or had simply gone home. Tracers were active to locate his whereabouts. The call was then terminated.

Riando Hotel
Panama City, Panama

Vic and Elena got off the elevator on the fifth floor and followed the bell hop to their room. It was a suite with a bottle of champagne icing on the counter. Vic opened the fish he had purchased at the airport and found what he was looking for inside, then put the fish into the small refrigerator and read the note.

> **Use satellite phone only. Cell and local phones may be compromised. You will be contacted at the old city market by the train station at eight thirty tomorrow morning. Have a basket of bananas in left hand and a green melon under your right arm.**

Vic wet the note in the sink, then tore it into pieces and forced it down the drain. He placed his luggage on the stand near the closet and unzipped his suitcase. He looked up and saw Elena looking out the window; she turned and looked at him, her eyes were wet and her shoulders were sagging, when she said, "I feel as though I am in the way."

"No, you are not in the way and I want you here with me," Elena squealed and jumped into his arms. Vic set the alarm on the doorknob and joined Elena for a hot bath.

Joint Intelligence Meeting
Washington D.C.

"I'm short on time, fill me in on Jupiter, gentlemen," the President said.

"We know the Tiangong Kaiwu is somewhere in the Atlantic Ocean. We also know that no United States or Latin American port is scheduled to receive the ship. We have requested all shipping to be on the lookout for that ship and contact their offices if she is spotted. Other than that we have no idea where she is," Director Waters announced.

"The NSA was in contact with someone at the computer who generated the message to the CIA. That operator alluded to an Iranian Milanian and said the ship was steaming for the canal, but we can't figure out what Milanian means, it infers it is a ship, but why give us that information?" Director Greene said, shrugging his shoulders.

"That doesn't blow smoke up my skirt. Keep looking boys; she has to show up somewhere. With luck she will dock at North Korea and kill everyone over there," the President said.

"Everyone is looking for the ship, sir," the Chief of Staff said.

"We will reconvene at a later date. Sorry to have to cut this short, but I have other pressing matters to attend to. Keep me posted," he stood to signal the end of the meeting.

Itahaca Exports
Perucho, Ecuador

The cell phone chirped and Señor Cordova looked at the caller ID and saw it was an international call. He answered it and started writing the message. Vic James and Elena Torres were traveling with new identities to Panama City, Panama. They were now Mike and Susan Roberts, he wrote the new passport numbers on his note pad and wrote Riando Hotel and that he worked for SatCom. He called Julio and told him to meet him at the airport.

Day Seven
Riando Hotel
Panama City, Panama

Vic woke early and dressed, then walked out of the hotel room, quietly closing the door behind him. He took the elevator to the first floor, walking outside he noticed the sun was bright and a few billowy clouds in the sky. The streets were noisy with traffic and street vendors were setting up their carts for the day. He noticed the streets were still damp from the rain during the night. He hailed a taxi over to the old city market by the train station.

The market was old, hence the name 'Old City Market'. The roof was made of wooden timbers covered with palm leaves and cane branches which had turned dark from the almost daily showers, the sides of the market were open except for the large tree timbers that supported the roof. The smell was a blend of fresh fruit and the pungent odor of sweet and over ripe fruit blended together.

He picked up a basket that was weaved from reeds, he saw bananas on a narrow bench and picked up a bunch; glancing at his watch it was eight–twenty-five. He walked around the market as though he were inspecting other items and discovered the green melons on a table. He selected the smallest one and wedged it under his right arm, and continued meandering around the market.

A few minutes later he felt a nudge from behind him and turned around. A lady pushing a shopping cart with a broken left, rear wheel was behind him attempting to get past him. Vic stepped back to his left against the table with the cocoa beans in burlap sacks, to let her pass.

"Meet me at the coconuts," she whispered, moving slowly past him.

Vic slowly walked around for a couple of minutes before inspecting the coconuts.

"I'm Rosa; exit the north end of the market in two minutes, then turn right and walk on the sidewalk with one banana in your left rear pocket. Get in the first whore taxi that offers you a 'special gringo price'," the old lady said slowly pushing her cart past him.

He watched her walk over to the papayas and inspect one by squeezing it. He put the melon on the nearest table and purchased the bananas in his basket. He walked through the north door handing his sack of bananas, minus one, to a kid standing just outside the door. He turned right and walked down the sidewalk, putting the banana in his left rear pocket. The traffic was heavy with a thick automobile exhaust hanging in the air. Pornographic shops were open and the ladies were offering anything a man wanted.

He heard a car slowing, hearing the driver tap the horn once, he then pulled to a stop a few feet in front of Vic. The taxi driver leaned to his right, "Need a taxi?" the man asked yelling out the passenger window.

"No, gracias," Vic said, walking past the stopped taxi, hoping he hadn't misunderstood the old lady.

He walked two more blocks when a small, white, four door Toyota with a taxi sign on the front door squealed its brakes as it passed him and stopped at the curb a few yards in front of him. Vic saw the driver scooting across the seat to the passenger window then lean out the window. "Hey gringo, I have a best whore for you; a special gringo price."

Vic stepped off the curb as the whore in the backseat opened the door for him. He noticed she was very attractive, perhaps in her late twenties.

He got in and closed the door, realizing the door did not close securely and the driver took off so fast around the left corner, the door opened; Vic grabbed the back of the front seat to keep from falling out and the whore grabbed him by the shirt, pulling him back in.

"Don't leave me yet!" she laughed loudly as Vic slammed the door.

She leaned against him, grabbing the front of his shirt with her left hand and said, "Do you like fishy smells?" she asked.

"I only like flying fish."

"Vic James?" the whore asked.

"Yes, I'm Vic James," he responded.

She leaned back against the door and spread her legs, revealing red panties. "Unzip your pants and pull them down and get rid of that damn banana," she instructed.

Vic threw the banana out the window then reached down and unzipped his jeans and pushed them down to mid-thigh and watched as she opened her blouse.

"Come to mama, big boy."

She grabbed his shirt and pulled him on top of her putting her arms around him and pulling him tighter against her.

"Can you hear me?" she whispered into his ear.

Vic nodded yes, but wasn't sure how to respond to the whore, he decided to play along.

"Yes, I can hear you," he said.

"Don't talk, just listen. Meet your contact at nine o'clock tonight at the north base of the 'Bridge of the Americas'."

Vic repeated Bridge of the Americas as he lay against her. He could feel her hands on his back as she seemed to be feeling for something, perhaps she was trying to find a hidden gun in his jacket.

"They will be driving a dark green Toyota van with the right headlight out. Don't hesitate to hop in, they will not wait for you. Be alone. Now start your business."

Vic reached down to open his boxers when she planted a big kiss on him and bit his upper lip.

"Ouch!" Vic hollered pushing up from her.

"What! You have no money!" she hollered out the open window.

"Get out of my taxi you pindejo, stingy Gringo. Go to hell," she yelled several more obscenities at him as the taxi pulled to the curb and stopped as if the driver was waiting for her signal.

Vic set up and opened the door as she pushed him with her feet knocking him to his knees on the street by the curb. The taxi sped off with her head hanging out the window still yelling. Vic felt very conspicuous sitting on the curb with his jeans down to his knees.

He stood up and pulled his jeans up, then hailed a taxi who returned him to the hotel. When he entered the room, Elena was preparing to step into the shower. She turned around looking at him, her eyes dropped to his waist.

"Where have you been? I was worried."

"I was just walking," Vic said.

She looked into his eyes, and raised her eyebrows. "Do you always walk with your jeans unzipped?" she asked.

"Uh, no, I guess I forgot to zip them this morning," he said looking down at his open fly and noticed part of the boxers material was sticking through the fly.

"Uh, uh sure, get in the shower with me. Let me see if you have been a naughty boy."

President Sanchez's Office
Panama City, Panama

Minister Yon set down in one of the visitor chairs and looked across the large desk, "President Sanchez, The People's Republic of China is very interested in the viability of the Panama Canal. We wish to offer the Panama Government our manpower without additional charges. Your government will continue to collect the ship's fees for traversing the canal; this will ensure that the sovereign country of Panama can recover financially from the devastating corrupt hold the United States held you under for years. We, our two countries together, can halt the United States' influence on the people of Panama and allow the population to regain the pride they once had in themselves and their great country."

"Minister Yon, that is not necessary. That was not in our agreements. China providing the salaries for the canal employees is all that is needed, and that is only for two years, we will be able to support our employees after that time."

"Mr. President, I do not believe that you understand my offer to you, we will provide man power for the canal."

"I understand, however, I do not want the man power."

"We are here to help Panama and to ensure that the world does not discover the true financial difficulties that you are facing."

"We agreed this would not be made public, you gave your word!"

"And I will keep my word, however, I can't control all prying eyes," Minister Yon responded.

"No, please, I must meet with my cabinet advisors before I make a decision such as this," President Sanchez said.

"I will return tomorrow, we can make decisions then," Minister Yon said as he stood and walked out the door without shaking the President's hand.

Research Lab
Tsinghua University

Professor Szu and General Yi were both watching the large monitor on the wall. They overheard several of the students and the hackers from General Chang's group, having discussions on the best way to initiate the trap door to keep the virus detection from sensing the invasive maneuver.

The decision was made to create a diversion by attempting massive login attempts via the server, sufficient attempts to crash the server and open the trap door when the system reinitiated the server.

The login program was started and slowly ramped up to a level of 400 login attempts per second. General Yi watched and was amazed at the overall operation of the system he was responsible for.

He saw the screen freeze and knew that the Pentagon's computer had crashed. He saw the hackers feverishly typing commands then smiled as he saw encrypted codes as they began to spell out ongoing operations of the United States military. He was looking for any sign of aggression on the freighter the Tiangong Kaiwu.

General Chang nodded, informing General Yi that no aggression had been initiated, General Yi pointed his finger at the monitor and pulled his index finger across his throat indicating to crash the computer system at the Pentagon and to back out.

SatCom office
Panama City, Panama

After the shower Elena and Vic dressed and being too late for breakfast, they ate a piece of sweet bread in the hotel restaurant. Later they walked into the SatCom office at eleven-thirty, a few moments later Manuel came bounding through the door.

"Vic mi amigo, your secretary Rachel emailed me that you were coming, "What emergency do we have?"

Vic explained that the trip was a non-business trip as he winked and introduced Elena. Vic told him that he would need a company car while he was in the city and that he wanted to keep his trip low key.

"We have a spare Suburban. Keep it all week."

Vic and Elena drove back to the hotel, he gave her a quick history on the Panama Canal. She seemed to be reserved even quiet.

"What is wrong?"

"I am scared that Cordova might find me, he is very resourceful."

"You don't have to worry about him. Hell, we are in Panama and he is in Ecuador, crap we even have new identities."

"He will find me."

"It's going to be alright. I'll protect you from big, bad Cordova," Vic promised.

He held her tightly for a long while, until she relaxed. After they made love Vic got up and took a shower, the water was nice and warm when the shower curtain slid back and Elena stepped in with him.

After the shower they dried off and got dressed. Vic pulled a clean pair of jeans from his suitcase and hung them in the closet. While putting on his clothes, Vic noticed Elena put on the same clothes she wore two days earlier. Vic attempted to have Elena put her clothes in a dirty clothes bag so the hotel could do their laundry and was startled when she refused and even more bewildered when she put her underwear in the sink and rinsed the bra and panties.

"Here, put your dirty clothes in the bag. We can drop it off at the front desk on our way out," Vic said holding the hotel laundry bag out.

Vic watched as she sat down on the edge of the bed, looking like she lost her favorite stuffed doll. He thought back to what he had just said, now what the hell is wrong, what did I say that made her upset this time and continued thinking what he said to upset her while he walked toward her.

She looked at him and said, "I don't have but three changes of clothes Vic."

"It's okay, sometimes I don't pack enough clothes either, or sometimes I pack the wrong clothes. You know I packed summer clothes one trip and ended up in the snow. Here, put the other clothes in the bag."

"I can't Vic. It's not that I packed incorrectly; I have nothing else to pack. Vic, I only own three changes of clothes, that is all I own."

"Why do you have only three changes of clothes?"

"I can't afford more clothes! Okay?"

"But you said Ithaca Exports pays or paid you very well."

"Yes they do, uh did; but I must pay them for rent and food and pay for my tuition and dorm at UT, then I have no money left."

Vic felt the anger build inside him, realizing that she was a slave to Cordova, an indentured servant to his demands and threats. He stood up, feeling anger welling up inside him for Cordova or anyone else that caused her pain.

"Sweetheart, would you like to go shopping? I'll buy you new clothes."

"Oh! Vic you don't have to do that, I don't want to owe you anything more."

"Honey, I'll buy you anything you want and you won't owe me anything, I want to do this for you. Come on let's go."

Vic called the concierge and received directions to a women's clothing store. They walked in and spent two hours while she tried on clothes, selecting the clothes she thought he liked her in best.

Vic looked around the men's section, picking out a black jogging suit and a pair of tennis shoes. A few more boxers as well.

"I'm ready now," she giggled.

Vic looked up and saw her holding three dresses and new underwear. He wondered if she would ever fit in as an American. "Only three dresses?" he asked, and saw her smile as though three were plenty.

Tocumen International Airport
Panama City, Panama

Señor Cordova and Julio walked off the plane and down the jet-bridge, grabbing their luggage. Then they hailed a taxi for the Riando Hotel. Cordova had reserved two rooms earlier that morning before catching the flight and during the plane ride between Quito and Panama City, he re-played the general's comment in his mind, 'you will not live past four days if you do not find the memory card and get back on schedule'.

The taxi pulled up to the hotel door and the two men walked in to the lobby. He suddenly realized that they must stay hidden from Elena, if she saw either of them, he would lose James again and be farther behind on his three days. He picked up an apartment locater flier and held it close to his face as he walked to the front desk. He noticed Julio was eyeing several of the ladies near the bar entrance and walked to where Julio was standing, "Stay with me and keep your face concealed!"

Julio promptly turned and followed him to the desk, picked up a brochure and buried his face in it. Cordova asked the clerk if Mike Roberts, an American was staying at the hotel.

The clerk checked the computer, "Yes Mr. Roberts has a room here. If you will pick up that white phone I can ring his room."

"No. I mean I will meet him later," Cordova said.

He checked in and requested the two rooms be on different floors, he handed Julio one of the folders with his keycard in it, then handed Julio a newspaper that covered his face as they boarded the elevator.

"I do not want her recognizing you," Cordova hissed.

Julio lifted the paper to his face and pressed the sixth floor button, "Not in here stupid!" Cordova said, shaking his head.

"Find her, but do not let her see you; keep her in your room."

"What should I do with her?" Julio asked.

"Anything you want, just do not kill her, not yet."

Señor Cordova got off at the sixth floor and Julio took the elevator back to the third floor and went to his room.

Panama City, Panama

Elena was so happy with the new clothes Vic had purchased for her, she couldn't decide what to wear while sightseeing, so Vic made a decision for her and they drove toward the canal. He drove over the bridge of the America's and selected a spot where he would wait at the north side base of the bridge. They drove to the east side of the canal and stopped at Fort Sherman where he used the tourist binoculars to scan the area for the Tiangong Kaiwu.

Vic gave Elena a history lesson of the Panama Canal, noticing that she was interested, asking many questions as they drove around and watched several ships being processed through the locks.

Vic wasn't sure how to tell her he would be busy, since she seemed to be sensitive to the idea of not returning to Quito soon. He started, "Elena, I have a meeting with some associates tonight and you will not be able to join me, you can either stay at the hotel alone or perhaps I can ask Manual to find someone to stay with you."

"What! No, I will be fine alone."

They returned to the hotel at six-thirty, Vic dressed in the black coveralls that he had purchased at the clothing store and activated his transponder on his phone, then put on the new black tennis shoes and kissed Elena good night before leaving the room.

He exited the hotel through a side service door and walked a couple of blocks before hailing a taxi, telling the driver to take him to the old city market, once there he changed taxis and repeated changing taxis several more times.

Each change of taxi was nearer the bridge than the previous one. When Vic was satisfied there was no tail he told the last taxi driver to drive to the Bridge of the America's, when the driver was a mile south of the bridge Vic leaned forward.

"Driver stop here, I think I'll jog for a while," he said opening the door. He got out and watched the taxi disappear, he could smell the sea breeze blowing in and felt the moisture on his skin. He jogged the mile to the bridge then ran across the bridge and reached the north base at nine twenty-five.

He stopped and looked both ways as though he was going to cross the highway. He bent down and retied his right shoelace, noticing a vehicle with the right headlight dark, coming across the bridge. He couldn't tell the make of the van with the one light glaring in his eyes, he watched it get closer. Vic began wondering how many one-eyed vans were out that time of night when the driver slammed on the brakes, causing the tires to skid in the gravel.

Vic then saw the Toyota emblem on the front fender in the lone streetlight, but couldn't tell if it was green or black. He ran to the van, the sliding door opened and he hopped in, landing hard on the floor. There were no seats in the back. Someone slammed the door and the van sped off. Vic couldn't see anything in the dark, but could hear faint noises and hoped he wasn't being set up for a robbery or worse.

Riando Hotel
Panama City, Panama

Señor Cordova and Julio met in the restaurant for dinner and discussed a plan to monitor the hotel lobby and restaurant, attempting to find Elena. Señor Cordova would monitor between 9:00AM to 2:00PM and Julio would be on duty from 2:00PM to midnight. "Find out which room she is in, but don't let her see you," Señor Cordova said.

They were discussing the possibility of not seeing her at all when Julio looked up and saw her walk into the restaurant and pick up a menu. He watched as she placed an order and set down at a table near the cash register and nodded to Señor Cordova while looking at Elena indicating she was near. Señor Cordova mouthed for Julio to walk to the elevator and follow her to her room when she left the restaurant.

Julio left the table and waited in the lobby, with a newspaper covering his face, he saw her exit the restaurant with a Styrofoam container and get in the elevator. Julio watched as the light stopped at the fifth floor, he ran up the stairs, bounding two at a time.

He opened the fire exit door just as she was putting her key into the door to room 527, then he took the elevator back to the lobby and met Señor Cordova and told him the room number.

"Now, it is my turn," Señor Cordova said.

Green Toyota Van

"How are the fish biting in the canal tonight?" a voice asked.

Vic recognized the whore's voice and replied, "The flying fish are biting well."

He felt a hand reaching from the front passenger seat and tap him in the chest, he felt the hand and noticed it was outstretched; he shook it.

"James, I am John Hawkins," the man owning the hand said, withdrawing the hand.

Vic's eyes slowly adjusted to the dark interior of the van and he could now tell a curtain was closed behind the driver and front passenger seat.

"So do you know anything about a test for the contents on board the ship?" Vic asked.

John explained that his group was informed that the agent coming from the states would have the required information needed to complete the operation.

Vic felt very conspicuous sitting on his ass in the darkened van, realizing they were expecting him to have answers to their questions and resolutions to their problems; knowing he didn't have shit.

He explained that Langley was to notify him via his handler or pass the info directly to them when it was available.

"I have not been advised of any type of test. Actually I haven't received any correspondence at all since we were told about you," a voice somewhere in the van said.

"Are we still on then?" Vic asked.

"We are on, until we here different. They know how to communicate with us," John replied.

Vic told the group he had reconnoitered the area earlier that day, but had no luck spotting the freighter. He admitted he wasn't certain what to be searching for other than the name and a photograph of a freighter with four large cranes.

"We know what to look for and have made daily boat trips to the area where ships that have been assigned a slot wait. The Tiangong Kaiwu isn't in that area."

Someone turned the dome light on, and he noticed the whore from earlier that morning and another man, all on the floor and dressed in dark sweat suits.

"Who would be the first to know that the ship is coming? Hell, I was told that the ship might be in Fiji."

"Fiji!" the whore said, readjusting the pillow under her ass.

"I think it was more of a sarcastic statement implying that no one really knows what the ship's destination is. It wasn't meant to be informative," Vic said.

"All transit schedules are set at the Panama Canal Administration Building on Balboa Avenue and we have no way of getting that information."

Vic started formulating a plan to locate the freighter, perhaps utilizing SatCom he thought. Vic attempted to fold his legs under his ass to lift his butt off the van's floor. It was starting to hurt when the van made a sharp turn to the left and Vic felt himself falling to his right, falling against the whore.

"Get off me! We're not in the whore taxi," she said.

Vic wanted to apologize, but thought any apology would not be appreciated, he merely set up straight and found a strap behind the passenger seat to hold on to.

"I have an idea that might offer some intelligence on scheduling," Vic said.

"Fair enough, use your satellite phone to call me."

"I don't have the number," Vic said.

Vic heard John's voice sounding nearly friendly as he said "Oh yeah, this is Sheila, your local whore and Martin there beside you, Henri is driving, we are all company agents and in need of information that you are supposed to have," John said, ending the introduction with an aggravated tone.

"Nice to meet everyone," Vic said.

John told Sheila to provide his phone number and she cited it three times as Vic memorized it.

"When you call me, mention the code, I will get in touch with you, but do not leave sensitive information on the voice mail," John instructed.

Vic heard John tell the driver to stop the van at the next corner. Vic grabbed the strap again, and braced himself as the van screeched to a stop causing everyone in the back to tumble forward, then John reached behind him and opened the door, Vic tried to hop out, realizing his left leg was asleep, instead of hopping he fell out and rolled away from the rear tire, before the van sped away.

Vic stood up working the blood back into his legs. He walked about two hundred yards, before hailing a taxi to return him to the hotel. He entered the hotel through the service entrance and took the elevator to the fifth floor. After knocking lightly on the room door, he heard Elena moving in the room before she opened the door.

"Oh, I was worried for you," she said stepping back.

Vic walked in, "it's not that late, only eleven-forty-five," he said looking at his watch.

"I know, but I didn't know what to think, I didn't know when to expect you," she said hugging him tightly.

President Yang's Office
Beijing China

"President Yang, please excuse me, I received an email from Minister Yon a few minutes ago, I printed it for you," Gia said placing the email on his desk.

President Yang looked at the printed email;

President Yang
Concerning Sun-Chang:

Sanchez will not accept the manpower offered.
Requesting further instructions.
Minister Yon

President Yang read the email twice then called for Gia, "Gia, please call General Yi for me."

"Yes sir," she said dialing General Yi's office phone.

"General Yi's office, may I help you?" Colonel Hon said.

"I have a call for General Yi from President Yang, is he available?"

"Please hold," Colonel Hon said then knocked on General Yi's door.

"What?" General Yi growled.

Colonel Hon opened the door, "There is a call for you from President Yang holding on line two."

He felt the twang of fear as he said, "I'll take the call," and picked up the phone.

"General, I forwarded your request for China to provide manpower for the canal however; President Sanchez is refusing the offer."

"Refusing? It is a very good offer for him, how can he refuse? We are offering twenty workers, who all speak fluent Spanish. The workers have been briefed to move printed counterfeit currency in their possession to ships as they transit the canal. We are depending on this, Minister Yon must sell the idea to President Sanchez," General Yi said, feeling sweat forming on his forehead.

"I knew there was a good reason for the offer, I will encourage Minister Yon to sell the idea. Thank you General Yi," he said hanging up the phone.

"Colonel Hon," General Yi hollered through the open door.

"Yes sir?"

"I want to dictate a letter, ask the taller of the two new recruits to come in here," he ordered.

"Sir, you want to dictate a letter?" Colonel Hon asked, hoping for clarification on the statement.

"Get her in here, now!" he growled, slamming his fist on the desk.

Day Eight
Panama City, Panama
SatCom office

Vic and Elena arrived at the SatCom office the next morning. Vic spoke with Manual about the SNOOP microphones. Manual told him the system was still activated. Vic then instructed him to relocate the microphones to the Panama Canal Administration Building on Balboa Avenue and set the filter to key on the name of a specific ship, a Chinese freighter, the Tiangong Kaiwu.

Manual looked at Vic for a reason for the cloak and dagger actions, but accepted Vic's silence for him not needing to know. "I can have the equipment set up by 9:00 this morning and operational by 10:30," he said.

Vic walked out of the office and back to the suburban and called DIR on his satellite phone and informed Ralph that he was attempting to locate the freighter using SNOOP.

Vic asked if he had received a testing protocol for the virus. Ralph admitted he had not, but was expecting a phone call any time with the information.

Joint Intelligence Meeting
Washington D.C.

"Does anyone have anything on Jupiter or more specifically the Tiangong Kaiwu today?" the President asked.

"Sir, this is Ralph, the latest I have is that the program SNOOP is being utilized to locate the ship."

"The same program that got everything started, uh?"

"Yes sir."

"Is there anything else regarding this issue?"

He grimaced and slowly closed his eyes, "Umh, I'll take the silence as a no. Okay, we will reconvene tomorrow," the President said and stood up.

General Yi's Office
Chengdu Military Base

General Yi stepped away from his desk and buttoned his trousers.

"What is your name?"

"Su Li," she whispered.

"I want you to come back to my house with me, plan on staying the night," General Yi said.

"Sir, I have plans for tonight," she whispered, wiping away the tears.

"There is a girl there; Choon-Lei who I think will like you as much as I do."

"But-" she pleaded.

"No! Your plans are to accompany me. My driver will take us to my home. You will be my guest, you do not want to disappoint me do you?" he asked.

"No, I do not want to disappoint you, General Yi," she said.

Riando Hotel
Panama City, Panama

Vic rolled off of Elena as she squealed loudly in his ear, he commented it was the best vacation he ever had, and admitted it was the first vacation in several years.

President Sanchez's Office
Panama City, Panama

"President Sanchez, Minister Yon is here early to see you this morning, sir," the secretary said.

President Sanchez felt the feeling of disgust grab his stomach, "Show him in," he said.

Minister Yon, started talking before he set down, "President Sanchez, I apologize for not calling ahead, but time is of the essence that I see you."

"Is there a problem?"

"Yes there appears to be a problem looming over the horizon," Minister Yon said taking a seat.

"What is the problem?"

"I have received a letter that will be forwarded to the news press today," Minister Yon said, placing a folder on President Sanchez's desk.

President Sanchez opened the folder and read the letter;

Panama's Corrupt Government.

President Sanchez has guided his country into bankruptcy. President Sanchez has signed contracts between China and Panama for cash.

What did President Sanchez do with the nation's wealth? What will President Sanchez do with the new cash from China? Why wasn't President Sanchez honest with the people of Panama?

"What? Why is this letter being sent?" President Sanchez demanded slamming his fist on his desk.

"You ask why? I made a simple request to offer a few Chinese personnel to help with the operation of the canal and was summarily dismissed and embarrassed."

"But, that is not part of the contract!"

"It can be an unwritten clause in the contract. China is here to help you and this is the best way to help you."

"But the letter-"

Minister Yon held up his right hand, interrupting him, "The letter need not be delivered, if you agree to the generous manpower," he said.

"Do I have a choice?"

Minister Yon smiled and leaned forward. "Of course you have a choice, but I recommend that you make the wiser choice."

"Yes," President Sanchez whispered.

"Excellent, your manpower, provided by the Chinese Liberation Army will be on an air transport, which will land at the airport tomorrow. There is a Chinese freighter the Tiangong Kaiwu, which should be arriving at the east end of the canal sometime today. Please have that ship processed for transit no later than two days from today."

"Leave that information with my secretary," President Sanchez said resting his head in his arms on his desk.

"I will and thank you, I will see my way out. You have made a wise decision," Minister Yon said leaving the office.

Riando Hotel
Panama City, Panama

Vic heard his satellite phone chirping and rolled out of bed and walked into the bathroom, closing the door. He turned on the shower and opened the phone. Manuel informed him that the freighter arrived at the east end of the canal this morning and also told him that he had forwarded the email with the conversation to him.

"Thanks, Manny, I'll take a look and get back to you sometime today," Vic said closing the phone and turning off the water.

Vic walked to his computer and powered it on, watching Elena's nude body as she walked into the bathroom while the computer completed the power up sequence. He opened his email account and found an email from Manny, opening it, he clicked on the attachment and heard two voices.

"Yes sir, I will process the Tiangong Kaiwu this morning."

"Let me check. Currently, there is a five day wait."

"I will assign a priority to that freighter and prepare for transit as soon as the next slot becomes available."

"Perhaps two days."

"Shit, we are on!" Vic said, feeling concerned for Elena.

Vic opened his satellite phone and dialed the number he had memorized for John. He listened to a pre-recorded message asking for a voice message to be left. "Vic here, the flying fish have arrived. I have the details."

Vic next dialed the phone number for DIR and told Ralph that the freighter had arrived and was scheduled to transit the canal within two days. Ralph explained that he still hadn't received any testing protocol, but was demanding assistance from Langley.

Vic was silent for a moment, clinching his fists. "That's what I expected. I'll let you know what our plans are once we have a plan," Vic said, terminating the connection.

He walked to the bathroom and stepped into the shower, the warm water and her inviting body helped relieve some of the stress that he was feeling.

He wasn't certain what the outcome of the mission was going to be. He felt guilty about having her with him and knew if something happened to him, she would be stuck in Panama for a long time.

He took all the cash and his credit card from his wallet, put everything into an envelope and wrote her name on it. He thought about explaining everything in a letter, but knew he couldn't reveal the details that would be required in a letter. He wrote Sat-Com's phone number for Austin and Quito on it and placed the envelope in her suitcase.

After she dried off he explained he was going to be busy for the next couple of days. He saw the confused look in her eyes, but offered no details.

He took a taxi to the 'Old City Market' then spent ten minutes window shopping at one of the strip bars. He started walking along the street where the whore taxi picked him up the first day. A few minutes later a taxi squealed its tires as it stopped just in front of him, he noticed it was the same taxi.

Henri leaned out the passenger window and yelled loudly, "Do you want a ride? I have a special gringo price for you."

Vic stepped off the curb and climbed in the rear door of the taxi.

"A little foreplay first," she said leaning against the door and opening her blouse.

Vic leaned over on top of her and whispered, "The Tiangong Kaiwu is either already here or will be here very soon. It has been given priority and will transit within a day or two, three days at the most."

"Meet the van at the same place, same time tonight. I'll tell Henri to pull over," she said pushing him off her and setting up.

Vic attempted to keep from being pushed out of the taxi as it veered to the curb and squealed the brakes, stopping abruptly, causing him to slide into the floorboard between the seats. He scrambled to regain his composure and opened the door trying to get out before he was kicked out on his ass again.

The taxi sped off, he tried to assess where he was but wasn't familiar with that part of the city, waiving at the next taxi, he paid the driver to take him back to the Riando hotel.

Vic walked through the lobby and turned to the hotel bar instead of the elevator and ordered a beer.

Joint Intelligence Meeting
Oval Office
Washington D.C.

Ralph opened the meeting with, "Mr. President, I received verification that the Tiangong Kaiwu is in the area awaiting canal transit," he said.

Director Waters of the CIA leaned forward from his comfortable position on the sofa, "Sir, I believe we have figured out what the Iranian Milanian is. There is an Iranian ship called the Milanian, it is a laboratory ship and was recently sighted near Jamaica heading south. The general consensus is that the container will be transferred from the freighter to that ship where they have equipment to handle the viruses and bacteria."

"What is our plan?" the president asked.

"Sir, plans are still being formulated and assessed, we would want to know where the ship will be before we devise a plan for it," Director Waters answered.

"Do your boys at Langley have any suggestions for testing the virus or bacteria? Do we even know if the container on that ship is the same container that was heisted?" Ralph asked.

"Excuse me, my name is Dr. Lewis. I am the Chief of Staff at Plum Island," he said, feeling intimidated by the personnel in the room. Dr. Lewis then continued by explaining the safeguards that were taken to secure the incubator inside the container. He explained that the walls were made of silica and carbon steel, rated as blast proof with an aluminum outer shell. The incubator was self-contained, utilizing a propane powered, temperature controlled environment to protect the contents. Each of the viruses are in individual plastic trays and labeled. Each of the bacteria are in Petri dishes and secured in small ovens.

The incubator is secured with a keyless electronic lock that requires six digits. If the code is not entered correctly the keypad goes dormant after the second attempt and stays off for three hours. There is also a timer that disables the keyless lock for twelve hours after the door has been opened and closed.

Ralph cleared his throat loudly and said, "Dr. Lewis, what we need to know now, is how to verify if the viruses are still active, or alive, or whatever they would be. How can we confirm that the danger still exists?"

Dr. Lewis started explaining that the only way to be certain is to open the incubator and perform a test. For smallpox, the definitive laboratory identification of variola virus, or smallpox, involves growing the virus on a chorioallantoic membrane and examining the resulting pock lesions under defined temperature conditions using a microscope. There is no general test for the general contents, but a specific test for each virus or bacteria.

Ralph sighed loudly, "Doc, what we need to know is… is there a test for perhaps a specific virus that would confirm if all the viruses in the incubator are still alive. Hell, we don't even know what they plan to do with the stuff, something bad I suppose," he said.

Dr. Lewis began explaining the life expectancy of a virus and the fragility of its outer envelope. Some viruses can live on counter tops for several days and others may die within hours outside of a host body. The outer envelope of the virus may have surface tubules allowing it to adhere to the surface of a cell. There are usually several layers of the internal layers. The core of the virus is where we target the vaccines to fight the virus-

Director Waters took the handoff from Ralph by asking, "Excuse me, Doc. We're not looking for a biology lesson here, what we need to know is how to determine if the viruses are alive and how to kill them!"

Dr. Lewis set back in his chair for a few minutes, looking up as he contemplated that statement and realized his life's work was going to be destroyed. He knew the decision he had to make as he started again. The virus you want to look at is a strain of the Avian Flu. The tray is labeled H1N67C. This virus is a manipulated strain that is lethal to birds within minutes; however, it is lethal to humans also, the incubation period for humans is three days.

"That is what we need. How can we test it?"

Doctor Lewis continued and stated that testing required a strong microscope and a vent hooded lab, then he broke into his teaching personality again and informed the group that viruses are 100 times smaller than a typical red blood cell and he was not aware of a test for the virus unless a laboratory was available.

Ralph felt his blood pressure hitting the danger level and interrupted him by saying, "Doc, our agent in Panama doesn't have a lab. Hell, he doesn't even have a gas mask that I know about!" he finished by slamming his fist down on his desk.

"Then I would not recommend attempting to open the incubator without proper safeguards."

Director Waters shook his head in amazement, then stated, "That avian thing, the H1CNF or whatever the numbers are, is the virus deadly to birds?"

"Yes it is deadly to many avian species, but not all. We tested it on several including crows and sparrows; it was fatal on the canary within thirty seconds and the crow after two minutes.

"Are you saying that the smaller the bird, the quicker it will die after exposure?" Ralph asked.

"You can assume that, but until the species is tested it would be just an assumption," Dr. Lewis said.

"Thanks Doc, we will take your advice to heart as we attempt to retrieve the container," the president sighed and waived his hand indicating the doctor could leave the meeting.

On board the Tiangong Kaiwu
Panama Canal

The ship's captain placed a call on the ship's secure telephone to General Yi's office.

"General Yi this is Captain Zoeng," he said.

"Yes Captain, what is your status?"

"We are at anchor in the staging area, we have been assigned a priority for transit scheduling and I anticipate notification in two or three days."

"Why the long wait?"

"That is normal, sir," the captain replied.

"I have received verification that the Milanian is two days out from the canal and I want you to prepare the container to be transferred to the Milanian when the ship arrives," General Yi ordered.

"It will be ready," Captain Zoeng reassured the general.

"Excellent. Contact me when you start the transfer," General Yi said, hanging up the telephone.

Panama City, Panama

Vic reached for his watch on the table beside the bed and saw that he had an hour to meet the van at the bridge. He told Elena he would be gone, perhaps all night long, but would return as soon as he could. She cried slightly, sensing that whatever he was doing was dangerous.

She reached out and lightly stroked his bare back with her fingernails. "Okay, I will wait here for you," she said.

Vic quickly showered and dressed in his black coveralls and tennis shoes again, walking out of the room as his satellite phone chirped, he looked at the caller ID and noticed it was from Ralph, then closed the door behind him.

"What's up?"

Ralph stammered a couple of times before stating that Langley had a protocol for testing the virus. He also gave Vic the code for the keyless lock, with a caution that he had two chances to enter the correct code before the lock would power down for three hours. Ralph reminded Vic that the container was a typical 8.5 foot by 20 foot container, painted gray and the numbers 52973 were stenciled in black on both sides and on the door, unless it had all been concealed or painted.

"So what's the testing protocol?"

Ralph was silent for a moment then informed him that the test had to be performed on a bird.

"What! I'm supposed to take a bird with me?"

"I don't know how to get the bird there, but that virus, the H1N67C, is deadly to Avians and humans. Small birds are supposed to die almost immediately following exposure to the virus and that virus is in a tray." He then repeated the tray's label and suggested using a canary if possible.

"I still have no authorization to sink the ship," Ralph said, feeling his guts churn as he clinched his right fist.

"I'll let you know how it went tomorrow," Vic said and closed the phone.

He caught a taxi and got out close to the north end of the bridge, then walked about fifty feet when he saw the van with the headlight out, he waited then jumped into the van when it stopped.

"We spotted the ship at anchor; it's about a mile out. How did you know it was in the area," John asked.

Vic briefly explained SNOOP to the group in the van as they drove, realizing everyone was quiet and were looking at him intently as he concluded telling them how the voice patterns could be detected as they bounced off buildings. He and John began discussing possible plans to determine if the container was actually on the freighter and it appeared that John had the beginnings of a plan when he asked Vic if he could scuba dive.

"Yeah, I am certified, but it has been several years since I went below fifty feet though," Vic replied.

John explained he had a diving boat three miles off shore waiting to take the four of them to the freighter.

"Four of us?" Vic interrupted.

"I'll explain specific duties as needed, but for now, there will be four of us," John continued as he told Vic that they would swim to the freighter; then he would sneak aboard.

"Hopefully the accommodation ladder will be down," John said.

John suggested only one person should actually board the freighter, while the other stand guard, the person aboard will determine if the viruses are hot. If they are perhaps he can destroy them tonight, if not we return tomorrow night and dispose of them, if they are not hot we go home. Sound like a plan to you?" John asked.

"I received information a little while ago. I'm supposed to test a specific virus on a bird."

"A bird?" Sheila exclaimed.

Vic told the group about the phone conversation he received from Ralph, but wasn't certain how he was supposed to get a bird, but would play it by ear as the plan progressed during the night.

Shelia said she would be the entertainment for the boys in case they were boarded by the Canal Authorities, bachelor party type thing, she explained.

Vic looked at her in the dim light and wondered if she really was a whore or just a very talented agent. He knew she certainly had him convinced that she knew that business well.

"What would happen if I'm discovered aboard ship?" Vic hesitantly asked.

John explained that the Panamanian government was not overly sympathetic to U.S. citizens and the Chinese would probably tie his feet and hands, then hit him in the head and throw him overboard. The diving boat would leave quietly and report his death to Langley.

"You're never heard from again," John quietly concluded.

Vic didn't say anything and it seemed that everyone was quiet for a very long time. He thought about Elena waiting at the hotel and wondered how she would get home if he didn't survive the night. Would she be able to go home with Cordova waiting for her there? He knew he had to survive, if nothing else, to protect and take care of her.

He told John about Elena and asked that he look out for her if something went wrong and make certain she was somehow delivered to DIR in Plano, attention Ralph. John reluctantly agreed to Vic's request.

"Sounds like a cake walk," Vic finally said, not feeling much hope for the mission.

John told the group that the moon would rise at four-thirty that morning and the dive boat must not be in the area when it did.

"Doesn't give us much time," Vic said.

"Nope, so we need to get started."

The van screeched to a stop, the door slid open and everyone, but the driver hopped out. The van took off and the four of them were standing near the shore.

There was a dense jungle fifty feet inland and twelve foot swells pounding the shore and a warm wind was blowing inland at perhaps twenty miles an hour. The surface temperature seemed to be in the mid-seventies and Vic could feel the cool ocean spray hit his face, as it began to wet his hair.

"Let's do it," John said.

He flashed a small red laser light southeast; it was answered with a similar flash of green light. A few minutes passed, and then Vic saw John looking through night goggles. He handed the goggles to Vic, and Vic put the goggles to his eyes and saw a bright light in the distance, he focused his eyes on the light and realized it was an outboard motor on a boat. He handed the goggles back to John.

A few minutes passed and they heard the small outboard motor and saw the silhouette of a small pontoon boat coming toward them; the boat had difficulties with the swells but landed without breeching.

The captain jumped out of the boat and each of them grabbed a corner of the small boat, picked it up and turned it around, then clambered aboard as the captain headed back out to sea. When they reached the heavy swells the pontoon boat was standing at a sixty-degree angle on its ass. The captain leaned forward and shouted, "Everyone move forward as far as possible. Put your weight in the front of the boat now!"

Vic lunged forward and landed on Sheila, and John landed on him, he saw Martin on the other side, hanging on to a lanyard running the length of the pontoon. Vic grabbed hold of the lanyard on his side, to keep from sliding back to the rear of the boat. He looked beneath him and saw her face pinned against the bottom of the boat.

Shit, I may suffocate her, he imagined her unable to breathe beneath his weight and pushed himself up a few inches and saw her turn her head to the side and breathe deeply.

"Sorry," Vic hollered.

She coughed and breathed deeply, "Thanks," she muttered and spit out a mouthful of water.

Vic was convinced the Chinese could hear the little motor even though they were five kilometers from the freighter and he began to feel seasick. What if I throw up on the whore? He thought to himself, shit don't let that happen, hold it, hang on, it has to get easier.

The motor was straining against the weight in the boat and against the oncoming swells. The motor would have a muffled, low pitched, strained sound, then as the boat would fall before hitting the next swell the sound would be very high pitched and loud sounding like a bumble bee.

If the Chinese don't hear us they must be deaf he thought as he felt the heavy pitching of the boat began to subside and the little motor began to steady out as they got further out to sea.

"Distribute your weight evenly; there is too much weight in the front," the captain yelled.

John crawled to the rear of the boat close to the captain and Vic followed him and stopped in the center of the boat. They were soaking wet and shivering from the cold, their wet clothes and the boat's head wind was the enemy now. Vic tried to keep his body as low as possible to avoid the wind, but it still whipped around him and sucked the heat from his body. He noticed the captain was wearing a wet suit, and thought he was the only smart one in the boat. The motor stopped abruptly, now what he wondered.

"Everyone up", the captain ordered quietly, "Climb aboard the diving boat, hurry up, move your sorry asses."

Vic looked up and saw a boat painted black, the small pontoon boat had tied up to the rear of the diving boat and the dive boat captain was pushing them up and someone was leaning over helping each of them aboard. His turn came, he was so cold Vic thought his arm would break as the helper grabbed him and yanked him aboard.

They were shuffled below into a small heated cabin at the front of the boat, one small red light bulb cast eerie shadows on their faces and the walls. He noticed the portal holes were painted black and a small electric heater was on and the fan was making a whining sound.

"J-J-John how long b-b-before we g-g-go?" Vic stammered.

He was so cold he was shivering and shaking uncontrollably. The temperature couldn't be below eighty degrees, but the water and headwind in the little boat dropped their core temperatures below a safe level. Vic remembered during scuba training that hypothermia could kill even when the surface temperature is above seventy degrees.

"Get out of those wet clothes," the dive boat captain ordered, as he threw down some dry towels.

Everyone stripped completely naked and they began to warm up almost immediately, the dry towels felt so good he wanted to curl up in his towel and go to sleep. The cabin was so small that they were crammed against each other. Sheila turned slightly pressing her breasts against Vic's chest.

Vic felt her movement and realized even when he was not interested he started getting an erection.

She turned her head and looked up at him and snarled, "Don't even think it! I will cut that little thing off."

"Sorry, it was an accident, it just happened," Vic whispered.

After warming and drying, Vic and John were each handed a wet suit to put on and Sheila was handed a bikini swimsuit to wear.

It was so cramped they took turns putting on the suits; fortunately no one lost their balance.

Vic felt himself start to have severe second thoughts, he thought about swimming two miles, then boarding a ship with possible overwhelming odds against his favor as he continued wiggling into the wet suit.

He noticed it getting really warm and stuffy in the little cabin. Finally the dive boat captain opened the hatch and leaned into the hole, announcing that whoever was diving to get their asses into their scuba gear.

"Stand by John, we're two kilometers from the freighter, exactly where you wanted us to be," the captain whispered loudly.

Vic knew he was a strong swimmer, but didn't want to get half way there and discover he couldn't complete the job. He leaned closer to John and said, "Two kilometers is a long way to swim to the ship."

"Don't worry, we have that covered," John replied.

Vic followed John up the short stairs to the main deck. A light warm breeze was blowing toward land and it actually felt good after the cramped stuffy cabin they were in.

John and Vic strapped on their gear and tested the regulators and facemasks, after a couple of adjustments they fit fine. The captain started the engines, what a welcome sound of the deep rumble of the twin inboard engines compared to the high pitched, outboard motor of the pontoon boat; the dive boat began to move slowly toward the freighter.

"Here, use these to look at your ship," John said, handing Vic the night vision goggles.

Vic could see the freighter's dark silhouette against the night sky. He kept the goggles against his eyes as he turned to the front of the boat and saw a scuba scooter hooked to a crane. He lowered the goggles and started to feel better.

"Here, familiarize yourself with this," the captain said handing Vic a nylon zippered bag.

Vic unzipped the bag and saw several tools; a pair of slip jointed wire pliers, a six-inch crescent wrench, a screwdriver with a Phillips at one end and a slotted blade at the other, a small flashlight that would rotate the lenses from clear to red. There was also a leather-man's tool, a water proof nylon bag with draw string and Velcro closures, a small hacksaw and a length of nylon cord wrapped around a roll of duct tape and four gallon size zip-lock plastic bags completed the assortment. He strapped the bag around his waist.

"Think I'll need all this, Captain?"

"Who the hell knows, I just hope you can do this without getting caught. If you get caught there's a good chance that all of us will be found out and then, well it won't be much fun," he said, looking at Vic with doubtful eyes.

"John, are you ready?" Vic asked.

John shook his head affirmative, a few minutes later the dive boat engines were killed; Vic felt butterflies in his stomach.

The captain lowered the scuba scooter into the water using a small crane on the side of the boat. The scooter resembled a torpedo, round and sleek. It was painted black and twenty feet long and had two sets of handlebars with a low curved windshield in front of each one. The front seat was located in the center and the rear set of handlebars was located five feet behind the front.

John slid into the water and Vic slid in after him. John opened the ballast valve slightly to allow water into the scooter's ballast tanks and the scooter began to sink as they positioned themselves on the scooter. Vic was at the rear set of handlebars and straddled the hump that served as a seat, he positioned his feet into the stirrups and leaned forward to hold the handlebars; this put him in a prone position. He calculated they sank below the surface approximately twenty feet when John hit the throttle and the scooter began angling away from the dive boat, Vic heard the twin screws of the dive boat as it pulled away.

The low purring and swishing sound of the scooter's electric motor seemed very loud as they sped toward the freighter. Vic began wondering if the scooter's GPS compass was accurate and hoped he didn't lose his grip on the handlebars. The ocean was pitch black, he could not see John's fin's that were no more than six inches from his face in their stirrups. Vic hoped John could see the scooter's controls, he noticed the strange thoughts one had as he headed for possible death.

As if on cue the scooter slowed until they were barely moving forward then John stopped the scooter completely. Vic heard the faint whirring and gurgling as John began pumping water from the ballast tanks to allow the scooter to surface slowly. Even though Vic thought he knew what to expect he was startled as they surfaced; he looked around and saw the freighter twenty yards to their right.

Shit, that is larger than I thought it would be, he thought.

Riando Hotel
Panama City, Panama

Julio waited by the kitchen for the first kitchen staff to respond to a room service call. He saw an employee, carrying a covered tray, walk out of the kitchen door and followed him to the elevator, he stepped in as the room service attendant smiled and pressed the button for the third floor. Julio remembered to keep his face covered and quickly brought the newspaper up to his face. The door opened and the attendant waited for Julio to exit first.

"You go first," Julio said.

He watched the man take two steps into the hall, and then hit the attendant in the back of his head, knocking him to the floor. The man went down, dazed.

Julio quickly picked up the tray and stepped back onto the elevator and pressed the button for the fifth floor, stepping off when the elevator door opened. He walked down the hall and stopped at room 527. He knocked on the door and quickly lifted the tray to cover part of his face, waiting for the door to open, he positioned most of his weight on his right foot and stepped forward slightly with his left foot to force the door open when she turned the knob. He waited and heard her grab the door knob.

"Who's there," she asked.

Julio froze. He wasn't prepared to speak, only to push the door open, he heard her ask again. Realizing his mind was a blank, he hollered that he was there to check her water.

"The water is fine, gracias," she said and walked back to the bed, turning the channel on the television.

Julio tried the knob and confirmed it was locked, then put the tray on the floor and returned back to room 334 cussing himself and knowing that Cordova was going to be upset.

Freighter Tiangong Kaiwu
Caribbean Sea

Vic slid off the scooter and unhooked his tanks; removing his fins and facemask, he handed the equipment to John. John cinched the equipment to the utility straps on the scooter and Vic began swimming silently toward the freighter.

He saw the ladder secured horizontally high out of the water, he swam around to the starboard side of the ship and saw the anchor chain. If the anchor chain was any indication of the ships cleanliness it must be filthy, the chain was covered in a black slimy goop.

Vic grabbed a chain link to begin his climb, pulling himself until his knees were out of the water; he couldn't hold onto the slimy links with his hands, slipping, he splashed back into the water. He stayed under water for as long as he could, and then slowly surfaced; listening for any sounds aboard the freighter.

He decided to try a different approach to the long climb and reached his right arm through a link, then bent his elbow pulling himself up six inches. He repeated the maneuver with his left arm, then his right arm again, bending his arms at the elbow to lock the grip each time. He wrapped his legs around the chain to relieve some of the strain from his shoulders and back.

Thirty minutes later he looked down and discovered he was only half way up the chain and decided to rest for a minute or two, then panicked when he felt his legs losing their grip on the chain. He tried to wrap them tighter, but lost their grip completely. He now was holding his entire weight on the inside of the elbows, and his body was dangling at a forty-five degree angle to the anchor chain.

He took a deep breath and swung his feet to the left then hard to the right, pulling his right arm out of the link and slipping it into the next link, locking the elbow. He repeated the maneuver with his left arm and continued until he developed cramps.

He dangled for a few moments, catching his breath. Looking up, he saw he was three links from the hole where the chain fed through. He started to swing again and was hit with cramps in both arms. "How the hell do rats ever get aboard ships?" he cussed softly and cussed the Chinese for not having the ladder down or at least providing him with a cleaner chain.

Vic knew that he could not hang still long, cramps or no cramps, and knew he was going to fall back to the water, causing enough noise to alert the Chinese and perhaps even the canal guard, getting himself killed, but worse being responsible for getting the team killed.

He gritted his teeth tighter and swung up reaching the next link, then again until he could reach the hole with his right hand. When he stretched his right arm out to grab the ship's deck his arm felt like it was being pricked with a thousand needles at one time, he forced it to extend fully, as the muscles kept trying to tighten, bending his arm.

Vic felt the deck and a bolt that the chain pulley was guided on; grabbing the bolt he pulled himself up and through the small opening. Finally he felt solid footing and waited for several minutes listening for voices. He looked for guards and waited for the pain in his arms to subside, no sounds and no one in sight, but a lot of pain.

He crawled and duck-walked along the ship's railing until he was even with the first ship's hold opening, he saw a faint glow emanating from the open door and dashed to the door, cautiously peering into the opening. Not seeing any sailors in that area of the ship, he started down the ladder stopping when he heard voices, knowing people were walking toward him. He hurried down the ladder to the next level and heard the voices pass the opening he had come from above and continued on. His pulse slowed somewhat, but still felt as though his heart might explode.

Vic continued down the ladder to the third level below deck, he thought about Ralph telling him that intelligence said this is the most likely area to store the container. The lights were brighter on this level and he heard voices again and peered around a large, rectangular, shipping container. Three sailors were walking toward him; he looked around and saw nowhere to hide; he noticed a ladder on the side of the container and climbed to the top, lying down in the cramped two feet between the top of the container and the ceiling.

The sailors walked past the container and to the other side of the ship then continued their route toward the rear of the ship. They must be the guards for third deck, he thought. Why have guards if you have nothing to smuggle or hide, he continued thinking.

Vic climbed down the ladder and began searching for the container with the numbers he was searching for. He read the numbers from seventy-three containers before finding the container that had 52973 stenciled on the side. The door had a padlock; and a green tamper-proof cable weaved around the lock and hasp, all the other containers had a simple tamper strip attached and no lock. Now why didn't I just look for the locked container, he wanted to kick his own ass, but knew he was too tired and tried to laugh at himself to relieve some of the stress.

Vic slowly and quietly unzipped his fanny pack of tools and took out the small hacksaw and began sawing the lock hasp and realized the hacksaw blade would not etch the lock. He stopped sawing and used the leather man's tool which had a file to etch a notch on the lock so the hacksaw blade would stay in one groove. Ten minutes later he heard the guards making their rounds again and he climbed the container ladder and slid on top in the cramped space. He watched the guards continue past and climbed back down and continued sawing on the lock.

Hearing the sound of lone footsteps walking toward the container, he climbed the ladder again when his left foot slipped on the rung and he clanged against the container. Vic heard the lone guard say something and hasten his footsteps, Vic grabbed for the Leatherman's tool and dropped the tool on the deck with a loud metallic bang, he bent over and grabbed the tool then he wedged between two containers and waited for the guard to arrive.

He remembered what the dive boat captain said, if you get caught there's a good chance that all of us will be found out. Vic knew he had to be prepared to take the fall and thought, shit they are depending on me to get this done and keep them from being discovered. If he sees me I have to take him out! I can't let them be killed for my clumsiness.

The guard walked to the container and pointed the beam of a bright flashlight on the lock. "Uh," the guard exclaimed and reached for the lock, noticing the filing dust on the floor beneath the lock and kicked at it with his right foot. Vic had the knife blade open, as the guard inspected the lock closer.

Vic jumped from the top of the container and plunged the knife into the left side of the guard's neck. He pulled the knife out and plunged again, one more time and a fourth time. Vic noticed the guard's knees buckle, leaving the knife in the guard's neck; he grabbed the guard to keep him from falling onto the deck. Vic was shocked that the guard was heavier than he looked and laid the guard on the deck.

He started cutting the lock again. As Vic sawed the lock his mind began to wonder, as he thought, what the hell do I do with him, it's not like he might have gone on a drunk and not returned from a weekend pass. This is a ship! Where the hell would he have gone?

Vic felt the blade saw through the metal and removed the lock from the hasp and slowly opened the container door. The door squeaked loudly and he heard sounds of guards beginning to talk again. He grabbed the body and shoved it inside the container and stepped in, pulling the door closed behind him, hearing it squeak again.

He could hear the guards walking around searching for the squeak, then after a few minutes they were apparently satisfied and returned to their end of the deck compartment.

They must be stupid, Vic thought, or maybe they are not aware of the importance of this container, hell this stooge was looking for the lock he wasn't just inspecting containers. Vic turned on his flashlight and looked down at the guard, shit he thought, now what do I do with him? Vic considered leaving him in the container, hoping they wouldn't look in a locked container for a body, it's no longer locked and I don't have a lock.

I'm not getting out of here he thought and could see Elena's face and knew he had get back to her. I'm here; I might as well just destroy this shit and stay until the job is complete. Hell, I don't even know if they are hot! What a fouled up plan, why couldn't they just send in one B2 and sink the ship, he continued cussing the pricks in DC.

There was just enough room in the container for Vic to turn around, and he rotated the flashlight lens from clear to red and noticed that the container was loaded with a second large container, the incubator he surmised. He saw the keypad and a second lock, like a long ass bicycle lock.

Vic started filing the shaft on the lock, it took a full hour to saw through the metal, he twisted the shank and removed the lock and laid it on the container floor. Vic remembered he had two chances to enter the code correctly or wait for the rest of the night in the cramped container.

He felt himself getting a little light-headed, shit he thought, now I'm running out of air. He opened the door an inch and pushed his face to the crack and breathed deeply several times, then turned around and turned on his flashlight again. He released his breath and pressed the six numbers slowly. Nothing happened, so he waited for another two minutes in case it was on a timer, but still no release.

Vic inspected the sides of the lock and felt a small slide switch on the side, he maneuvered around and looked at the switch and saw that it was in the lock position. He slid the switch to the unlock position and entered the six numbers slowly again, holding his breath, hoping the electronic mechanism didn't count his first attempt.

He saw the green LED light come on and heard the triple bolt of the lock releasing, he took a breath and realized he was out of air again. He moved back to the container door, gulping a few breaths of air before turning back to the incubator.

Vic tried to open the incubator door and realized there wasn't enough clearance to open the incubator door with the container door closed. He opened the container door half way, stepping out trying to lift up on the door as he swung it open to silent the screeching.

"Ugh."

Vic heard the dead guard breathing and coughing.

The guard's eyes were open and he was making guttural sounds, trying to speak, Vic grabbed the Leatherman's tool and opened the blade again. He stabbed the guard in the throat below the larynx and worked the blade back and forth several times then pulled the blade out and cut the right carotid artery. Vic pushed the guard towards the side of the container as far as possible to keep the blood from pooling near the door and waited until the guard stopped bleeding.

Vic opened the incubator door and noticed a light turn on. The bulb was so intense it blinded him momentarily. He stepped back and slipped in the blood on the floor of the container, catching the edge of the door to keep from falling. He then stepped out of the container and realized the light from the incubator cast a very dim shadow on the ship's deck, reminding him of the moon at 4:30. He knew he had to hurry to get out before it came up.

Vic walked back into the incubator and noticed that there were rows of trays from top to bottom of the incubator. He looked for a labeling system and found that each column was numbered sequentially from the left rear clock wise around the incubator. He found the H column and the H1N67C tray in the second row. He slid the tray out and saw that it was a small plastic box 4 inches by 8 inches. He placed the box in the nylon dry bag and tightened the drawstring. Then used the piece of cord as a belt and secured the dry bag to his waist.

Vic closed the incubator door and saw the green light on the keypad turn red. He stripped the dead guard's shirt off and closed the container door, hearing it squeak again. Vic used the shirt to wipe up the drying blood and closed the container door. He heard the guards speaking and began walking toward his container. He put the lock back on the door and tried to make it look secure, then noticed metal dust on the floor. He knelt down and swept the dust under the container with the shirt and climbed on top of the container again.

The two guards were talking and their conversation sounded more like normal conversation between two sailors rather than alerted guards. They walked past the container without looking at the lock. Vic waited until the guards were at the other end of the compartment, then climbed down and walked towards the stairs and quietly climbed up. It was slow getting up the stairs quietly, while holding the bag, trying to keep it from banging against the railing and holding the guard's shirt. He made it just as the guards walked past the container, then he looked at his watch, it was 3:30, he had an hour to get back to the dive boat before the moon came up at 4:30. He made his way back to the deck of the ship and began climbing down the anchor chain, using the guard's shirt as gloves. It was easier and faster going down than climbing up. He finally reached the water and started to swim in the direction where John was supposed to be.

The bag weighted him down so that all he could do was dog paddle while trying not to drown. Vic swam for about fifty feet due West of the ship's rudder when he heard a noise and stopped swimming. He felt himself losing the battle of trying to keep his head above water, he wanted to call out for John, but knew if he did the noise would be heard aboard ship and the spotlights would find him and probably John also, then both would be killed. Vic's legs couldn't kick any more, he felt himself sinking. Suddenly a hand grabbed his right arm. He looked up, but saw nothing. Then feeling the scooter; he knew it was John.

John secured the dry bag to the scooter and helped him into his scuba gear, the ride back to the dive boat was a blur and it seemed as though only a few moments had passed when he felt himself being pulled onto the dive boat and his gear being removed. Vic became fully awake in the small cabin of the dive boat.

He opened his eyes and saw a body leaning over him, it was Sheila.

"What the hell?" Vic said, jerking back from her.

"It's okay, don't be frightened. It's me, Sheila."

"Where's John?"

"He's topside, everyone is waiting for you to come around."

"Damn, it's cold," he said shivering.

"Here, I'll help you get warm," Sheila said as she unbuttoned her blouse and loosened her bikini top.

Vic realized he was nude and that someone had removed his wetsuit when they put him on the bunk.

"Sheila lay on the bed beside Vic and pressed her body against his.

"Yeah that feels better."

"Just relax for a few minutes, allow your body to recover," she said nuzzling his neck and pressing her breasts against his chest.

"I'll be okay, I need to get up and let John know what I found."

"John looked in the bag you brought from the freighter. Are the contents hot?"

"I don't know. We have to test it somehow."

"Do you have a plan?"

"No, but you feel very good," Vic said.

"Then you are ready to get dressed. I wasn't going to have sex with you if that is what you thought. I am married and love my husband."

"But you are a uh, I thought you were a, err-"

"No, I am not a whore. This is my job, I work for the same government you work for," Sheila said, as she stood, putting on her bikini top.

"You are very good at your job."

"Screw you."

"No, I didn't mean it that way. I just meant that you go the extra mile to do your job."

"Get dressed, asshole. I'll tell my husband you are ready," Sheila said while putting on her blouse. She turned back as if to say something, then opened the hatch and walked out on the deck.

"John, he's ready."

"Hey Vic, how are you feeling?" John asked poking his head through the hatch.

"I'm feeling much better now," Vic said, trying to put his coveralls back on.

The captain and the ship's mate helped everyone back into the pontoon boat. The captain started the outboard motor and they raced to the shore, it was not as cold traveling with the wind as the trip earlier that night.

He heard the crashing of the surf against the beach getting louder, when suddenly the little motor revved up as they dropped at least ten feet and hit the sand hard. Vic and John were both thrown out of the pontoon boat and struggled to stand up just as a large wave hit Vic and knocked him down. He felt the backwash beginning to pull him out to sea, he started swimming toward land and on the next wave he landed on the beach about ten yards from the boat.

John walked over and offered his hand, Vic grabbed it and stood. They walked over to the group just as the pontoon boat headed back out to the dive boat.

John flashed his laser pointer and the Toyota van flashed its one good light and started toward them. They got into the van and it sped off when someone turned on the dome light.

"I have not tested the box yet," Vic announced.

Everyone looked at Vic as though he had the plague.

"There was no time to test and I don't know how to test without killing someone or me. I'll test later today. I received something about a bird or something, anyone have any suggestions?" Vic asked.

John turned and looked at Vic and explained that he would be expected to test the virus or whatever was in the box and do it with enough time left in the day for a return trip to the freighter if one was required. Vic acknowledged it was his responsibility and would figure out a plan to determine if the box of shit was lethal or not.

"How much time do you need?" John asked.

"I'll try to have the testing completed by, say three o'clock this afternoon."

"Walk east on the sidewalk outside your hotel at five-thirty this afternoon, Sheila will pick you up in the whore taxi," John said.

The van dropped Vic off five blocks from the hotel. He looked at his watch, realizing it was almost six o'clock. He entered through the service entrance in the back and took the elevator. He tapped lightly a couple of times on the hotel room door and heard Elena unlock the door.

"Where have you been? I have been so scared all night."

"I can't tell you where I've been. I just want to go to bed, I'm exhausted."

Vic took off his clothes and started the shower. After a long soothing shower he dried off and walked out of the bathroom and saw Elena laying on the bed, she smiled and opened her arms, "Come here baby," she said.

Day Nine
Riando Hotel Restaurant
Panama City

Julio met Señor Cordova for breakfast and explained how he was almost in her room, but admitted he panicked and she wouldn't open the door.

Cordova was so angry he pressed the flat side of the knife through his sweet roll. "Today is day two, try again!"

Riando Hotel, Vic's room
Panama City

Vic heard muffled voices and wasn't sure if he was dreaming or not, he heard a door close and opened his eyes. Elena was standing beside the bed and he realized he was still very tired. Perhaps he was getting too old for the all night operations, he thought as he swung his feet out of the bed and set on the edge.

Elena explained that she had let him sleep and had ordered breakfast. She smiled when she announced that she had ordered fried eggs while lifting the cover off of the plates. She noticed he was moving slower than usual as she set down beside him and ran her fingernails across his back and attempted to convince him that he was working too hard.

Vic leaned forward and let her scratch his back and felt himself starting to drift to sleep, then forced himself off of the bed and set at the table, eating his breakfast, watching her nibble at a banana. They ate in silence and he could sense that she wanted to ask questions. He did respect the fact that she knew when to be quiet, thinking that she probably learned how to be quiet from her activities as a mule for the Ithaca Exports Company.

He took another hot shower and put on a pair of khaki shorts and a tropical shirt; noticing Elena was again having difficulties selecting her apparel for the day. He pitched a very short sundress onto the bed and asked her to wear it so he could see her legs all day.

He grabbed the dry bag containing the box, stuffing it into a small duffle bag, exited the room, telling her he needed to make a phone call, closing the door behind him. Vic dialed DIR and waited for Lisa to transfer the call to Ralph and told him that he was aboard the freighter and had returned safely with the H1N67C tray.

Ralph wanted to know if the virus looked as though it were still active.

"How the hell would I know? Do you have a protocol or suggested testing procedures? Hell, I'll take anything right about now, just give me something!"

CIA HQ
Langley, VA

Director Waters took the call that his secretary transferred to him and listened as Ralph told him that the H1N67C tray had successfully been removed from the freighter, but without a testing protocol, it would be difficult to ascertain if the virus was still active.

"Ralph, we have no protocol written at this time, but the guys in the lab are hoping to have something by the end of the day."

"Damn it, Waters, Vic can't wait until the end of the day. I have to provide him with something," Ralph pleaded.

"Okay, tell him it is supposed to be deadly to a bird; that is all I have."

Ralph squeezed the receiver so tightly it creaked, and he terminated the call without saying another word.

Panama City

Vic grabbed his phone before it completed the first chirp and opened it seeing that the call was from Ralph.

"Vic, negative, no testing protocol or other information available; they haven't provided anything specific at this time. It is supposed to be lethal to birds within minutes. The Dr. said that canaries would die within a minute when exposed to the stuff. That's all I know."

Vic tensed up and wanted to hit something, he felt anger building and realized he was being hung out to dry. He told Ralph he would attempt to play it by ear for the day and would most definitely be available if Langley had a testing protocol they would share and slammed the phone closed. He returned to the room and told Elena to go with him and hurried her when she started brushing her hair. He ushered her out the door and to the elevator.

Vic shook his head in anger as he said, "They call themselves analysts, they are nothing but pencil pushers! Maybe there is nothing to be had, well hell, I guess that is why I am here." Vic realized that he was talking out loud. He looked at her and wanted to say something or perhaps apologize, but just shook his head.

Vic watched Elena walk out of the elevator and guided her to the gift shop, he asked the concierge for directions to a pet store and a car rental agency, and then they took a taxi to the car rental office and rented an SUV.

He drove the rented SUV to the pet store, where Elena fell in love with the puppies running around when they walked into the store. Vic pulled Elena's arm and walked her to a counter in the rear of the store.

Vic started asking questions about the birds and asked if they sold canaries, the clerk showed him the avian section of the store and answered his questions. Vic selected four canaries, and then the clerk asked about feed and accessories. Vic looked at Elena as she was cooing to the birds; he selected a cage and feed for the birds. The clerk helped him carry everything to the rented SUV.

Vic next swung by a hardware store and a gas station to pick up a few items he would need later. He then swung by the hotel to drop Elena off.

"Why can't I go with you? I can help you," she pleaded.

"No, you can't help. I don't want you to help me. I promise I won't be gone too long."

Vic pulled to the front lobby doors and Elena reluctantly got out of the rented SUV, she stood holding the door open, as if she couldn't make a decision to get out or in.

"Stay in the room. Do you understand?"

"Yes sir. I will stay in your room all day!" she said and slammed the door, running through the front doors of the hotel.

Riando Hotel
Panama City, Panama

Señor Cordova was in the lobby when Elena ran to the elevators. He watched the door close and called Julio's cell phone explaining that she was going to her room and he had to make the grab before James returned.

Julio ran up the stairs and opened the stairwell door just as the elevator door opened, he saw her walking down the hall toward her room, he hid behind the open stairwell door, knowing that if she saw him she would scream and he might miss her again.

He saw the fire alarm box on the wall and considered pulling the alarm. He reached for it, just as the door across from where he was standing opened and a man walked out of his room and closed the door. The man nodded to Julio as he stood with his hand outstretched to the alarm, he didn't want any witnesses and decided to wait for a better time.

He started for the elevator and watched the man step in when the door opened, then Julio ran back to Elena's door and listened, he heard the television, and walked to the fire alarm box and pulled the handle.

Immediately the alarm started warbling and the lights began flickering, he stepped back and noticed doors began opening as people started walking to the stairs, a few walked to the elevator and pressed the button. He saw Elena's door open and quickly turned away so she couldn't see his face, he waited and as she walked past him, then he followed her to the stairs.

She waited her turn at the stairwell door until a man waited for her to go ahead of him. Julio pushed the man out of the way and started down the stairs immediately behind Elena. When she reached the landing at the third floor Julio reached around her and opened the door. He then grabbed her arm with his left hand and shoved her through the doorway. She attempted to turn around and tripped then fell to the carpeted floor.

Julio slammed the door closed and reached down and grabbed her left arm and started dragging her down the hall. She was finally able to lift her head enough to see his face and tried to scream. He leaned over and slapped her face and jerked her to her feet. He slammed her against the wall, holding his hands under her arms. He saw a man and woman open a room door, then start down the hall toward Elena and him. He looked at Elena and saw that she was dazed and stood her up, pinning her against the wall, trying to act as though they were making out.

He growled in her ear, "If you scream, I will kill you!"

He continued holding her arm as they walked past people trying to get to the stairs, noticing they were ignoring him while they hurried to safety. When Julio reached his room he unlocked the door and opened it. Elena tried to run, but he caught her hair and jerked her back. She fell to the floor and he kicked at her shoving her into his room and slammed the door behind him.

"Sit in that chair and shut-up!" Julio ordered as he ripped the electrical cord from the base of the table lamp and tied her hands behind her back and looped the cord around the leg of the chair and took out the slack. The cord was digging into her wrists causing her left wrist to begin to ooze blood. She quit fighting and set still, looking at him as her eyes were wide with fear and darting around the room, silently praying for Vic to rescue her.

Julio walked over close, leaned down and placed his left hand on her right breast,

"Where is the turtle, bitch?"

She could smell his foul breath and felt her gagging sensation starting to kick in. She looked into his hard, brown eyes and knew he was a killer, perhaps even enjoying his job. She saw the many pock marks on his cheeks from earlier years, perhaps as a teenager and the long ugly scar on his right cheek, that made his smile crooked. His black hair was greasy looking from not bathing and she felt the fear in her stomach, knowing that he would rape her before killing her if she didn't tell him what he wanted to know.

"Well bitch, where is the turtle?"

She wanted to tell him to save her life, but she also knew that Vic would be killed if she told him. She thought for a moment, the turtle and Micro SD card had to be at the SatCom office in Quito, unless he took it to the office in Dallas, she thought. Perhaps he had given it to the FBI and that is why they released her, she was so confused and scared.

Julio saw her eyes working as though she was thinking that perhaps he would accept any lie she could conjure up. He stood up and hit her in the face with his right fist. The impact was so hard it knocked her backward, she landed hitting her head on the floor and felt herself blacking out.

Julio set her chair up and realized that she was unconscious and cussed himself, remembering Cordova told him not to hurt her, yet.

Panama City, Panama

Vic drove the rented SUV north, away from the city, up into the mountains. He was looking for a secluded area to park and was driving slowly on a dirt road, when he saw a narrow trail leading off into the thick brush. It did not appear to have been used in a long time. He turned and followed it until it narrowed to mere tracks.

He pulled up under a large tree and killed the engine. He thought back to the identification card he carried when he was a Special Agent with the OSI, which informed anyone who found his body to contact the embassy and not to touch the body or remove the ID card.

He decided to leave a note for the authorities, tearing off a piece of paper from the pad he was carrying and wrote that the American embassy should be contacted before moving his body or the vehicle and placed the note under the driver's side wiper blade. He removed the full gas cans he had purchased at the gas station, then crawled inside the SUV and closed the door.

He reached over the back seat and hit the lock button on the driver door to lock all four doors. This is it he thought as he removed the container from the small bag he had brought from the freighter and inspected it for cracks. It appeared to be well constructed and had a hinged lid with a plastic catch. He peered through the opaque box and noticed there were four small round containers perhaps three inches diameter and about an inch deep.

He held his breath and opened the box, realizing the round containers were secured in the bottom of the box in plastic molds. He picked one of the containers up and saw it was actually two pieces that were screwed together. He slowly unscrewed the two halves of the container and stopped. The bottom half contained a dark gooey looking substance which appeared to have moss growing on the top. Vic decided that must be the virus and tightened the top again.

He gently placed the container in the bottom of a canary cage. Next he slipped one of the large plastic trash sacks over the cage, then leaned over the front seat and hit the unlock button and crawled out the rear door. He lifted the trash sack up just enough so he could tell if the bird fell to the bottom of the cage.

Vic took a deep breath, then reached in and removed the top of the small container dropping the lid on the floor of the cage, then slammed the cage's door and backed up, closing the rear door of the SUV.

Vic watched the bottom of the cage and saw the bird fall to the floor. He looked at his watch, realizing the bird was affected in less than a minute.

"Damn, that shit is potent!" he said.

He reached under and pierced the gas tank using the screwdriver, then sloshed gas on the roof and sides of the SUV. He stuffed a gas soaked rag down the gas tank as far as he could and struck a match and lit the rag. It began to burn; he struck another match and dropped it into the puddle of gas under the leaking tank. He started running back to the main dirt road.

He reached the road just as the SUV's gas tank exploded with a whoosh! He noticed black smoke rising over the thick green jungle. He began walking toward Panama City. Looking at his watch again, he saw it was now half past eleven. Looking back at the smoke he noticed it was becoming a lighter color and dissipating quite well.

Vic dialed Ralph and informed him that he had tested the contents in the box he had taken from the freighter. He wasn't certain what was in the box, but whatever it was killed a canary within a minute. He explained how he had tested the bird and had then burned the car he had rented.

"Now what do I do?" Vic asked.

"Let me pass this information on and I will get back to you sometime today. I imagine that the ship needs to be neutralized though," Ralph said.

Vic said, "No shit, Sherlock! Ralph, I need some help here."

Ralph promised he would get clarification on the next step and would contact him. Vic explained that going back aboard was not a good idea, since he had left a dead guard in the container.

"They are going to miss him and it doesn't look good for me to return to that ship, I mean they are going to be looking for him. Hell, they may have already found him and if they have all bets are off."

"Do you think they might believe it was accidental or maybe killed by another sailor?"

"Ralph, I cut his throat and stuffed his body into the container. No, they won't believe accident and being in a locked container rules out being mad at your bunk mate."

Ralph promised to call him back within two hours and terminated the call. Vic continued walking and fifteen minutes later he heard a vehicle behind him, it was a passenger bus. He waved his arms and the driver slowed and pulled up beside him. He hopped in and paid ten pesos for the ride into Panama City, as he boarded he looked over where the SUV was and noticed that only a faint wisp of smoke was rising now and no one on the bus seemed interested in the smoke.

The bus dropped him at the edge of the city; he hailed a taxi and hopped out two blocks from the hotel, then walked the rest of the way. He saw a fire truck in the street in front to of the hotel, fearing the worst he walked through the front doors, directly to the clerk at the front desk.

She informed him that there was a false alarm and all was safe and back to normal, he took the elevator up and walked to the room. He used his key to open the door and noticed Elena was not in the room, thinking she was still waiting for the all clear signal or perhaps was still pissed and had taken a walk.

Research Lab
Tsinghua University

Professor Szu walked into the research lab and touched the mouse to wake the computer and noticed the large flat screen monitor flicker twice before initializing, seeming take longer than usual to wake up. He looked back at the monitor and froze when he saw a different screen saver display than ever before.

There was a Japanese flag displayed on the top half of the monitor and was in animation mode as though the wind was blowing across the flag. Under the flag in large Mandarin characters was the phrase "General Yi has a Red Ass!" scrolling across the bottom of the screen.

Professor Szu heard snickers from the open door of the lab and looked up to see several of his students standing and gazing at the monitor, he pressed the Esc key to exit from the screen and realized the next screen listed several commands and he heard the hard drive start spinning. He pressed several keys and quickly realized that the keyboard was locked out, after pressing the Control-Alt and Delete keys simultaneously to restart the computer, he wondered why the keyboard was still locked out and ignoring all his commands, he reached for the power button and pressed it, holding it down for ten seconds until the computer powered off.

Someone does not like General Yi, he thought to himself and quickly realized that he would be blamed for the hacking. He instructed the students to power up the Play Station systems and to begin testing the other computers in the lab. He then continued trying to successfully reboot the computer He heard Li inform him that the PlayStations were operable but that each of the other computer systems they tested had the same problem as his computer. He instructed that all systems be powered off and rebooted to attempt to find a Windows based system that was operational. He was advised that all the computers were affected.

Professor Szu grabbed his cell phone and called the Engineering lab and asked that they test their computers, he was informed that every computer had a strange display and that all the computers were inoperable. He immediately felt ill and knew that General Yi would blame him for the problems.

General Yi's Office
Chengdu Military Base

General Yi arrived at his bunker and walked through the anteroom toward the door to his office. Colonel Hon was standing near a computer at the far end of the large room with a very strange facial expression. General Yi ignored him and set down at his desk and powered up his computer.

He instructed for someone to bring him a cup of tea as he waited for the system to boot up. When the girl walked into his office with the tea he noticed the Japanese Flag on the monitor and his name with the rude statement below the flag, he yelled for Colonel Hon to get into his office quickly.

Colonel Hon alerted him that it appeared that every computer on the base and perhaps all of China had the same displayed message. He also told him that all the hard drives were destroyed.

"That Szu!" General Yi yelled at the top of his voice.

President Yang's Office
Beijing China

President Yang heard the commotion outside his door and stepped into the hallway and saw the fear on the faces of the people in the building.

He was advised of the situation and the statement regarding General Yi including the Japanese flag and also the terrible devastating news that much of the data from the military computers to even the smallest personal computers at many of their homes were destroyed.

He slowly picked up his cell phone and pressed the speed dial and said two words when the phone was answered, "Find him!" he said and slammed the receiver back into the cradle.

Riando Hotel
Panama City, Panama

Vic walked in the hotel room, thinking that Elena was still waiting for the all clear. He took a hot shower and washed off the gasoline smell, he was rinsing the shampoo out of his hair when he heard the bathroom door open.

"The concierge told me it was a false alarm. Were you scared?" Vic asked.

He hopped out of the shower and noticed a man, wearing white slacks and a brown Panama shirt with large pockets at the bottom, standing in the doorway looking at him. Vic tensed and quickly hit the man in the chest with a karate jab, his right foot slipped in water that had splashed on the floor, keeping him from putting much force into the jab, causing him to slip and fall.

The man merely laughed and stepped back as he lifted a .38 caliber pistol, pointing it at Vic's chest as he lay on the floor. Vic waited for the man to make the next move, but he simply looked at Vic and smiled.

"Mr. James, you have something that belongs to me and I have Elena. I will trade."

Vic got to his knees and reached for a towel on the rack, then slowly got to his feet and quickly dried off as he slowly walked out of the bathroom toward the man who was backing into the bedroom.

"Who the hell are you?"

"My name is Hector Cordova and you have my turtle. I want it back now or she will be, how do you say, made love to?" he gleefully replied, in his broken English.

Vic felt the anger growing and attempted to find a stalling ploy, trying to find a weakness in Cordova. He demanded to speak with Elena to verify that she was not hurt. Cordova refused the request and repeated that he wanted his turtle.

"Where is she now?"

Cordova again ignored him and demanded that he hand over the turtle. Each step that Vic took he noticed Cordova took two and kept at least five feet distance between the two men.

Vic told Cordova that the turtle was in the safe at the front desk and that he would go and get it. Cordova demanded that he use the telephone and have the turtle brought to the room. Vic realized he was quickly running out of time and that Cordova held all the cards, and the pistol.

Vic walked to the phone beside the bed, then dialed the operator and asked for the front desk. Vic noticed the phone's LED display was displaying the words Operator and knew Cordova could see the display also and rethought the idea of trying to trick Cordova. When the desk clerk answered Vic told him to please bring up his valuables from the safe and gave his room number. The clerk said he would check, and transferred the call to the hotel manager's desk. Vic saw the LED display stating Hotel Manager. He again asked for the safe contents for room 527 be delivered to the room and hung up the phone.

Vic turned to face Cordova and stated, "He said he would send it up."

"If the turtle is not in my hands in fifteen minutes I will make a phone call, then Elena, no Julio will have some fun!"

The phone rang and Vic looked at the display, it listed the caller ID was from room 334, Vic looked at Cordova and then back to the phone. He noticed Cordova stepping closer to see the caller ID on the display.

Vic picked up the receiver and listened. "Hola? Can I rape her now?" Vic heard the caller ask.

Vic turned and noticed Cordova was now about three feet away, trying to see the caller ID on the phone. He tightened his fists and rotated his body to his left and stepping forward with his right foot, he dropped his right elbow two his waist then released his shoulder, bringing his right fist around with his elbow parallel with his fist.

He felt the perfect executed judo hook when it caught Cordova's left jaw and travel through to his right jaw. Vic saw Cordova's eyes roll back before he even hit the floor and heard the pop as Cordova's finger clinched on the trigger as he lost consciousness, feeling the heat from the gun's barrel as the round was fired.

Vic grabbed his boxer shorts and put one foot in as he opened the door and ran down the hall to the stairwell hopping and getting the other leg into the shorts. He slammed the door open and took the stairs three at a time to the third floor, then slowly opened the door and looked down the hall. He saw room 334 on his right and ran to the door.

He banged on the door and heard Elena crying, and a man's voice telling her to be quiet. Vic stepped back and lowered his right shoulder and ran the four feet, hitting the door, he repeated the linebacker move twice more and saw light between the metal door facing and the sheetrock of the wall. He tried once more and felt the entire door and facing give way as the door swung open leaving sheetrock and bent metal door facing dangling from the wall.

Vic raced through the door and saw Julio standing beside Elena, her blouse was ripped open and her bra was cut and was hanging down at her sides.

Julio took two steps toward Vic, holding his knife in an under-handed grasp. Vic jumped as high as he could and kicked the heel of his right foot straight out, catching Julio at the base of the nose, shoving it deep into his head.

Vic landed and felt extreme anger against the coward who was now staggering backward in the room. Vic felt that old feeling return, when training assumes ownership of the soldier's body. He felt his right elbow snap back placing his fist under his shoulder, hand open as though he were going to pick up a can of beer then pivoted his upper torso while thrusting his hand forward, his thumb went to the left of Julio's esophagus and his fingers went to the right. He squeezed then ripped outward as hard as he could, feeling Julio's throat rip and heard the loud gurgling sound as Julio attempted to breath.

Vic looked at his hand and realized he was holding Julio's bloody throat and threw it to the floor. He fell to his knees in front of Elena.

"Are you hurt? Are you okay?"

"Vic, help me!" she screamed.

He reached around and untied the cord and helped her to her feet, pulling the blouse around her for modesty. He saw two hotel employees standing at the door, with blank stares as though they were in shock.

He told them to call the police and noticed that neither of them moved. Vic walked Elena to the bed and helped her sit down. She clung to him so tightly he had to stretch, to reach the phone between the beds. He dialed the hotel operator and asked her to call the police.

Vic realized his satellite phone was still in his room with Cordova and that Cordova would get away if he didn't get up there. He placed a hand on each side of her face and tilted her head up.

"Elena, I need to go to the room," Vic said.

He realized she was stiff. Her muscles were rigid and knew he had to get her medical attention to keep her from going into shock. She screamed and grabbed him tighter around the waist forcing him to lose his balance and topple onto the bed. Vic was still trying to get up when the hotel manager arrived. He was on a cell phone with the police

Vic heard sirens in the street below his window and a few minutes later he heard policemen in the hallway running toward the room. He provided a brief explanation about the guy in the room and that Cordova was in room 527 and would get away if someone didn't get up there and stop him. Two officers hurriedly left the room and three others stayed as more policemen arrived.

"Elena, do you know who he is?" Vic asked, pointing at the dead man on the floor.

"Julio, his name is Julio. He is very mean, he works for Señor Cordova!" she said and began sobbing again, pulling him against her.

Two EMT's arrived with a gurney while a third EMT confirmed that Julio was dead. Vic heard the room phone ring and saw an officer answer it. He nodded several times, and placed the receiver back in the cradle.

"Your other attacker, that Cordova hombre, is under arrest," he stated and turned his attention to the EMT crew, informing them that a second man will need their gurney in room 527.

"Hurry, he is alive, but needs your help."

Vic began thinking back when he was an OSI agent, it was forbidden to be married or even have a serious relationship with girls back then. He knew he was in trouble as he continued holding Elena.

A doctor arrived and noticed Elena was still hysterical, he opened his small medical bag and took out a syringe and a small bottle, then loaded the syringe and gave her a shot in the arm.

"That will help her relax and sleep for about twelve hours," he explained to Vic.

The hotel manager walked into the room, offering Vic a different room, explaining that his personal affects would be delivered to room 256 and handed Vic a key.

Vic helped Elena down the hall to the elevator, into the new room, noticing all the luggage, clothes and his satellite phone were laying on the bed. He picked up his watch and realized he had less than twenty minutes to meet the whore taxi. He laid his coveralls on the bed as Elena began undressing. She slowly took off her jeans making certain that he was watching. She pulled the blouse and what was left of the bra off. She then started weaving as though she were drunk.

Vic helped her onto the bed, her eyes closed as soon as her head touched the pillow.

Vic knew he was falling in love with Elena and there was nothing he could do about it. He quickly dressed and walked downstairs at 5:20. The whore taxi squealed to a stop before he got to the end of the block.

"Hey gringo, you want fun with my fish?" Sheila yelled, leaning out the rear passenger window.

Vic climbed in and slammed the door. She pulled him near and asked, "Hot or not?"

Vic unzipped his jeans and pushed himself up on top of her as they lay there faking the real thing as he whispered.

"It is very hot!"

"Same place, same time, tonight," Sheila whispered.

Vic was ready to be pushed from the taxi, but Sheila just continued with the ruse. They drove for another ten minutes, then Sheila reached out with her left hand and tapped Henri on the shoulder. He pulled to the curb and stopped. Vic pulled his jeans up making certain the zipper was zipped and exited the cab, he watched Sheila drive away. He flagged down a taxi then returned to the hotel.

Elena was still in bed asleep, he set his alarm for half past eight and snuggled back under the covers with her.

He fell asleep next to her and dreamed of Elena and him on a merry-go-round. He kept reaching out for her to get on his horse with him, but she seemed to always slip away before he could grab her hand, no matter how hard he tried he couldn't get her on his horse. The alarm sounded, Vic awoke and kissed Elena one last time.

"I have got to go babe," he whispered.

She lay there without moving. Vic finished dressing and grabbed his phone then walked out the service entrance onto the street.

DIR
Plano, Texas

Vic called Ralph again and pleaded for direction, knowing he did not want to return to the freighter and was distraught over the fear that Cordova had other friends in the hotel. He felt terribly guilty for leaving Elena unconscious and alone in the hotel room. Ralph assured him that he was applying as much pressure as he could to force an Air Force attack on the freighter. Ralph promised to call him in less than an hour with the time of the attack, but to continue with the original plan until he was told otherwise. Vic slammed the phone closed.

Panama City

Vic began jogging toward the bridge, when he felt confident no one was following he hailed a taxi and rode around awhile. He got out of the cab on the south end of the bridge and jogged over to the base at north end, just as he stopped the Toyota pulled up and he hopped in.

John and he were alone in the van except for Henri who was driving.

"Sheila told me the shit is hot," John said.

"Yes, I tested the box it had a couple of glass dishes in it. I opened one of them in a bird cage and the bird died in about a minute."

"Okay, we either sink the ship or somehow destroy the container," John said.

"I was expecting a call from my handler about this, but I haven't heard anything," Vic said, then grabbed his satellite phone and called DIR.

"Hold a moment Vic. He has been on a conference call for the past three hours, I'll sneak in and let him know you are on the line," she said.

Lisa walked to Ralph's desk, Vic could hear Ralph screaming at someone on the phone. Lisa wrote 'Vic is on the line for you, can you speak with him?' on a note pad.

Ralph shook his head yes and held up one finger. Lisa returned to her desk, telling Vic to standby. Ralph pressed the hold button and told Vic that he was on the phone with the Joint Intelligence meeting.

"I need direction here. You were supposed to call me! Are they flying some jets in to sink the ship?"

"No, Vic. This has to be done covertly and without military intervention," Ralph said, shaking his head with disgust.

Ralph explained that another ship was believed to be near and that the container was going to be transferred ship to ship either that night or the next day. If the container was transferred they would lose all hope of a possible covert operation and very possibly lose the location of the container forever. He continued with a pep talk trying to boost Vic's morale when Vic mentioned that he was ambushed and had killed one person and injured a second and that the attack was related to the counterfeit operation not the ship.

Ralph breathed hard and told Vic to do the best he could to destroy the container. Vic felt his ass pucker knowing he wasn't getting any assistance from Langley and closed the phone.

Vic turned to John, "Sounds like another boarding party tonight."

Vic explained that Washington wanted the contents in the container destroyed, but to salvage the ship and also added he had no idea how to accomplish that safely. John instructed Henri to continue driving while he and Vic discussed how to perform the operation.

The two men considered several options, throwing out every idea they came up with. "There is one way, maybe, but it will require timed explosives and a hell of a lot of luck," Vic said.

John told Henri to swing by the storage facility the CIA rented in Panama City.

Joint Intelligence Meeting
Washington, D.C.

"This is Ralph, our man will destroy the container and save the ship if possible" he said to the men in the Joint Intelligence meeting.

"Did he give you a plan?" Director Watson asked.

"Listen Waters, I've had enough of your questions and absolutely no support from Langley. I didn't ask him what his plan is, or if he even had a plan! Vic is the best agent I have ever known. I have complete faith in his ability to get the job done. I told him to destroy the container and save the ship, I know that is what he is going to do! So all of you can just kiss my rosy red ass!" Ralph yelled, slamming the phone back into the cradle.

Lisa walked back into Ralph's office, looking at him and realizing that his relationship with Vic was closer than she thought or he had ever let on.

"Are you alright?" she asked nervously.

"No, I am not alright! I may have just sentenced my friend and best damn agent to a horrible death and probably ruined my retirement to boot," Ralph put his head on his desk and cried.

East coast of the canal
Panama City, Panama

Henri drove the van for another ten minutes turning and backtracking to ensure no tails, he then pulled into a gated storage facility. He inserted his magnetic card into the card reader and the gate rolled back, then they pulled up to storage door number one-nineteen. John hopped out and motioned for Vic to join him, then John opened the storage door, Vic walked in and John entered and closed the door behind him, Vic heard Henri drive off.

John turned the lights on, there were several metal shelves against the wall on the right, locked metal cases were on the shelves, each case was labeled with the type of explosive or weapon it contained. A full-length mirror and a clothes rack were on the left side of the facility, a gun safe with a combination lock was at the rear of the facility. Three M-16A2 rifles, two Remington pump action 12 gauge shot guns, two Colt.45 caliber automatic pistols and four M4 assault rifles completed the arsenal.

"What will you need to do the job tonight?" John asked.

Vic was formulating a plan to destroy the contents of the container as he gave John his grocery list, starting with eight ounces of C4 explosives, two detonators with a time delay, and four grenades, he also asked for thirty or so magnesium burn sticks.

John opened a locker and pointed, Vic stepped over and counted out thirty burn sticks and put them into a canvas bag.

"Here is a one pound block of C4, cut off what you need," John said.

Vic put the entire pound into the bag and noticed the timers John was preparing were the old style five minute per click timers. He saw a pad lock on the locker and asked if John had the key. John pitched it to him and he removed the lock and stowed it in the bag with the arsenal he was preparing.

"I'll need a weapon tonight also."

"What do you prefer?"

"Light weight, semi-automatic, medium caliber, magazine fed."

John opened the gun safe there were three M60 machine guns, ten LAWS rockets and a wide assortment of handguns.

"What about this one?" John asked as he pitched him a nine-millimeter Bursa automatic assault weapon.

"It's made in Argentina, not traceable to the Company."

"John, there is no way in hell I'll be able to climb aboard with all this. If the ladder is not down, I will not be back. Please take care of Elena, the girl I told you about."

"I will," John said and squeezed Vic's left shoulder.

Vic grabbed a vest sling for the weapon and John opened the door and Henri pulled back to the storage door. They loaded the gear and hopped back into the van.

Henri drove around for fifteen minutes verifying there was no tail. Vic took advantage of the time that Henri was checking for tails by setting up his explosives. He turned on the dome light and constructed two bombs with four ounces of C4 each and set them for fifteen minutes, he taped the timers to the block of explosives. Henri stopped the van at the same place as the night before, then he and John got out and Henri sped away.

John flashed his laser out to sea and his signal was answered with another laser light, a few minutes later they heard the little motor on the pontoon boat start up. Vic immediately felt seasick and wanted to sit down. The wind wasn't blowing as hard tonight as last night, actually it was almost calm, but that did not make him feel any better.

The pontoon boat glided up on the beach rather than flying the last ten feet. They grabbed it, turned it around and pitched the packs of gear in, then all three men jumped in to the boat.

The little motor was not laboring as hard tonight without the headwinds and fewer passengers on board. He was almost enjoying the trip, realizing it was much easier; the pontoon boat seemed to glide on the waves tonight. The dive boat came into view as the captain cut the power to the little motor, and then all three crawled aboard the dive boat as the deck hand secured the pontoon boat.

"Welcome back," the captain said.

"Thanks, it's almost nice out here tonight," Vic said noticing that he was barely wet.

He followed John down stairs to the little cabin and felt the heat in the cabin, noticing it was much more comfortable tonight compared to last night, they slipped out of their clothes and put on the wet suits.

"Get your tanks on and check your gear," the dive boat captain said.

John and Vic stepped up to the main deck and put on the fins and tanks and adjusted their goggles and regulators. Vic transferred the explosives and the Bursa nine millimeter to a dry bag and inspected the tool bag that he used last night; he noticed someone had replaced the cord that he had used.

"I'm ready when you are," Vic said.

The dive boat's crew readied the under water scooter while John and Vic slid into the water, Vic put on his safety belt and patted John's leg and felt the scooter start off for the freighter. Vic kept going over in his mind how he would sneak on board and where he would set the charges in the container. He was still pondering these thoughts when the scooter slowed down and they surfaced. There was the freighter; it looked larger tonight than last night. Vic noticed the ladder was down and pointed it out to John.

Vic took his gear off and John secured everything to the scooter, then Vic swam to the ladder and checked his gear for noise and realized the explosives pack was rattling a bit. He used some of the duct tape to compress it, which stopped the rattling. Just as he started up the ladder he heard splashing, he turned around to faintly see slight frothing on the water, and realized someone was pissing off the side of the ship from above, he stopped and waited until they were through.

He made it up to the door at the top of the ladder and stopped to listen, but did not hear anything out of the ordinary. He pushed on the door to see if it was locked and felt it open easily and peeked in noticing the room was empty. The only light was one small red light around a corner thirty feet towards the center of the ship. Vic slipped inside and closed the door. Getting a bearing on his location he knew he needed to be two decks up and near the front of the ship. Vic found a stairs going up to the next deck and began climbing.

Suddenly bright lights were turned on, he was blinded for a moment and heard voices behind him and quickly bounded the stairs two rungs at a time, more or less feeling his way, until his eyes adjusted to the sudden illumination.

The next deck was empty, and he knelt on one knee and turned to look down at the deck below where the bright lights were turned on and saw three men walking toward the door he had come in through. He saw them close and secure the door. He heard clanking against the side of the ship as the ladder was raised. Vic sprinted for the stairs leading to the next deck up, making the stairs in two jumps and felt the ship shudder and heard rumblings.

The next sound came from the front of the ship, loud clanking; the anchor was being pulled up. He was glad that he was not hanging onto that anchor chain right now. Vic was now on the deck he needed to be on and began making his way to the container. The lock was as he had left it, he saw two guards walking toward him; they were talking and laughing. He waited for them to make the corner and walk back to the other end of the room.

Vic removed the lock from the door and pulled it open. It seemed to be louder tonight than last night, after opening the squeaking door he stepped inside and closed it. Then turned on the flashlight and rotated the lens to red. He noticed the dead guard was still where he had left him and smelling very ripe. He opened the bag of explosives and took out the magnesium burn sticks and the four-ounce bombs. He looked at his watch and noted the time was a few minutes after one o'clock.

He turned the dial on the timers to the second white dot. He flashed the light on the keypad and entered the six digits and saw the LED turn green and heard the triple bolts move. Then taking one of the bombs and all the burn sticks, he opened the container door then opened the incubator door. He was ready for the bright interior light and shielded his eyes, then walked to the rear of the incubator and started placing burn sticks on the trays. He placed one of the timed bombs in the rear of the incubator and the second near the front. He could feel the ship beginning to move and knew he had better hurry and pressed the arming switch on the remaining explosive, then taped it to the inside of the incubator door and the last one was taped to the outside of the door near the electronic lock.

Vic stepped out of the container and started to close the incubator door when he heard a voice behind him and realized a guard was standing there. He didn't turn around, but continued as though he was completing a job for the Admiral. The guard spoke and Vic could only hear one person talking and breathing behind him.

Vic quickly turned 180 degrees and brought his left foot up with a round house kick and hit the guard in the right side of his face. The guard dropped, out cold. Vic left the container door open and started walking toward the bow of the ship. He heard a clanking sound as though the anchor was being secured knew with the ship preparing to get under way. He knew he couldn't exit the door he entered the ship through.

Vic found the stairs that he had used the night before and climbed up to the next deck. No activity on that deck so he climbed the stairs to the deck below topside and saw a light shining in from the main deck, people were busy on deck.

He climbed up to the main deck and noticed a scurry of activity. Several crewmen were washing down the anchor chain with a pressure hose and he noticed armed military sentries walking around the deck. Vic wondered why the guards were armed; noticing most of them were carrying assault weapons not the typical pistols. He wondered if they were expecting him? Is that why the ladder was down, he convinced himself that it was a trap.

"Well they're invited to my little party!" he said softly.

Vic looked at his watch; he had eight minutes before the container blew up wondering what his next move should be. He realized that he could either make a run for the rail and dive off, probably getting shot in the process or stay below and take his chances. Staying below did not seem like a good option either, a pound of C4 can be very damaging, he considered, not to mention the hot stuff that might be released from the incubator. He pulled the bolt back on the Bursa and ensured the safety was off then opened his dry bag and took out three of the grenades. He positioned himself just below the hatch opening, then pulled the pin on a grenade and threw it as hard as he could towards the rear of the ship. He heard the clang of the grenade hitting against the metal of the ship and the loud explosion of the grenade, then he threw a second grenade in the same general direction. He heard men yelling from the deck below him and threw a third grenade down the stairs opening. Vic heard men running past him topside and yelling in Chinese, looking out the hatch, he saw fires about mid ship.

Vic knew John was waiting for him on the starboard side of the ship. He did not want to bring attention to John so he grabbed the Bursa in his right hand and the dry bag in his left hand and began sprinting for the rail on the port side. Vic heard sailors screaming and saw one of them pointing at him. He saw one sentry was running at him from his left on an angle that would have prevented him from jumping overboard. Vic pointed the nine-millimeter across his chest aimed at the sentry and fired. The slugs hit the sentry in the chest; the force of the slugs knocked him on his back he set up grabbed his chest, then fell back and was silent. Vic heard shots and heard the crack as bullets came too close to his ears, he knew the sounds of bullets breaking the sound barrier, that snap sound they made when they were an inch or so from your ear, that sound always fascinated him.

Vic was five feet from the ship's rail when he felt something hit him in his left shoulder, it felt like someone hitting him with a baseball bat. He saw stars the pain was so intense. He knew where the rails were, but could only see white stars, he judged the distance by the number of steps he took and jumped, hoping for a perfect leap over the top rail.

His momentum did not carry him as far or high as he expected due to the slug in his shoulder. He felt the rails hit him in the shins just below the knees and fell backward onto the deck of the ship.

Vic rolled over and fired several times, not actually seeing what he was firing at and knew he would be dead or captured within a few seconds if he didn't do something. He fired the weapon until the magazine was empty. He pressed the clip release lever and ejected the empty magazine and attempted to grab a second magazine from his pack which was on his left side. His left arm would not respond; he couldn't move it. Vic crawled between a row of barrels and the rail, his sight was returning and he could here Chinese sailors still firing at him and knew it would be only a few seconds before they realized he was not returning fire.

Vic noticed his dry bag was only two feet from the barrels and reached out and grabbed it, they responded with a volley of fire that ricocheted off the deck and the barrels he was hiding behind. He grabbed the last grenade from the bag and pulled the pin with his teeth and threw the grenade over the barrels. It landed in the middle of a group of sailors who were starting to advance toward his position. It exploded, the firing stopped as the Chinese sailors retreated farther back toward the center of the ship.

He hobbled the three feet to the rail and jumped or more or less fell overboard. Vic landed in the water on his back. The impact knocked the breath out of him, his left shoulder felt like it was on fire and had a deep pain that was throbbing so that he could hardly think. He struggled to resurface and gulped in a breath of air dove, trying to go as deep as he could and felt the ship with his right hand, then began swimming away from the ship. He was under water for a few seconds and realized he had to resurface for air, but wasn't certain which way was up and could not move his left arm.

Total darkness surrounded him and he was underwater, dark water and was disoriented. He felt his right hand cover his mouth feeling for bubbles. Was he conscious of what he was doing or was it the training taking over. He was feeling for the bubbles to determine which way was up? He could hear someone in the distance screaming underwater and he knew that they were in trouble and in great pain, perhaps one of the sailors he shot.

Vic realized he was swimming parallel to the surface. He arched his back and swam up using his right arm. He could not seem to propel himself with his legs. Finally he surfaced and realized the screams were loud and close, then he realized the screams were his own.

Vic forced himself to stop screaming and couldn't seem to breathe deep enough; his ribs and back hurt from the fall and he had difficulty just breathing shallow. His left shoulder hurt and throbbed and he realized that both legs were injured, but he could not determine to what extent.

DIR office,
Plano, Texas

"Raleigh Chemicals, how can I assist you?" The telephone receptionist at the CIA headquarters in Langely, Virginia asked.

I need to speak to Director Waters. This is Ralph with DIR in Plano, Texas." Ralph said.

"He is not in the office at this time."

"This is an emergency. I must speak to him as soon as possible. Please have him call me at my office, he has the number."

"I will try to reach him, sir."

"Oh my God," Ralph said as he placed the phone back on the base.

"Lisa, how late are you going to work tonight?" Ralph asked.

Lisa stood up and walked into Ralph's office and leaned against the door sill.

"I thought I would stay and catch up on some filing."

"That's bull shit and you know it."

"I just thought I would wait until we heard some news from Vic," she said, nervously running her hand over her hair.

"Yeah, me to."

Lisa returned to her desk.

Caribbean Sea
Panama

Vic looked around for John, but did not see him, then remembered he was on the opposite side of the ship from John. He saw bright lights moving on the water, at first thinking the lights were for him; that somehow John was searching for him, perhaps coming to rescue him.

Vic was waiting for the lights to find him, slowly realizing they were for him, but not for rescue, rather for death or worse. He moved closer to the ship hoping the lights would not find him there.

He heard shouting from the top deck and gunfire began, the Chinese were firing randomly into the water. He saw tracers hitting and knew they were firing a heavy caliber machine gun and heard the tracers sizzle as they hit the water. After what seemed an eternity the weapons ceased firing and all but one of the lights were switched off. He knew lookouts were still posted because cigarette butts hit the water every once in a while.

He was knocked into the side of the ship with every other wave and sometimes he hit his left shoulder; he saw stars each time that happened and thought he could not continue this, then he felt the ship start moving slowly which increased the frequency that he banged into it hitting his shoulder.

Suddenly he heard or maybe felt more than heard an explosion inside the ship. He began to swim or more or less dog paddle using his right arm only, away from the ship, afraid to attempt underwater swimming so he paddled as quietly as he could.

Vic saw the moon just over the horizon and oriented himself so he was facing away from the moon and continued dog paddling in a westerly direction. He would swim for as long as possible then turn over and try to float on his back for a while trying to rest his arm.

Vic turned back over to swim again and caught a glimpse of the outline of land and began swimming in that direction. He was swimming for approximately thirty minutes when he heard the freighter behind him. He thought it was heading for the Panama Canal, he tried to increase his slow speed with the one arm stroke, attempting to veer to his right to get out of the way of the ship, but could not keep up with the pace, reverting back to the floating when he tired.

He was startled awake with the ship's lights moving crazily on the water and loud screaming from the crew, he could see silhouettes of crewmen stumbling on deck many were jumping overboard. He also heard the clanging and warbling sounds of what appeared to be fire alarms on board. What the hell is going on Vic thought, maybe a mutiny, no it must be the virus shit. I've got to keep my head or I won't make it to land Vic continued thinking each time he regained consciousness.

He would black out then awake as he was sinking below the water, which would make him choke and cough while attempting to breathe. He noticed the sun rising in the east behind him as he swam for shore and with daylight he noticed blood in the water around him and wondered if it would attract sharks.

The pain in his left shoulder and legs had subsided somewhat and the sea currents were helping; however, with each wave that he crested he seemed to sink farther below the surface and it seemed to take longer to resurface.

The waves were getting bigger and louder, then after what seemed an eternity he felt sandy ground under his feet and knew he just might live long enough to get ashore without drowning. He tried to walk when the water level was shallow enough and the sand was level enough, but his legs were too sore to hold his weight. He crawled to the shore line and passed out.

He awoke several hours later as the tide was coming in, and knew he had to get off the beach. If he were caught on the beach wearing a wet suit after a freighter was sabotaged he would be the prime suspect and no hope of assistance from Washington. Vic crawled past the beach and into the thick jungle before collapsing.

Day Ten
DIR office,
Plano, Texas

"Lisa, wake up," Ralph said standing at her desk.

"Uh, what. Have you heard anything?"

"No, but that just means he is too busy to call," Ralph yawned nervously.

The office phone rang and Lisa grabbed the receiver, "DIR, can I help you," she asked.

"This is Director Waters, is Ralph in the office?"

"Yes sir, one moment please," Lisa said, putting the call on hold.

"Ralph, it is Director Waters."

Ralph walked back to his office and took a deep breath, then set down and Lisa hit the transfer button.

Director Waters explained that an email was received earlier that morning from an agent in Panama. Your man didn't return from the freighter last night he explained.

"What the hell does that mean," Ralph asked, watching Lisa walk into his office and set down in one of the visitor chairs.

"That is the only information we have right now. Don't read more into this than what is here. We have a satellite feed monitoring the Tiangong Kaiwu and it appears the ship is out of control. The feed is active for another fifteen minutes. We will notify the

Panamanian government and report a rogue ship, but we can't officially do anything until they notify us. There was a smaller ship, perhaps a frigate, which was nearby earlier in the morning. It has since vacated the area."

"Call me as soon as you hear anything," Ralph demanded and gently hung the phone up.

Lisa inhaled, putting her right hand to her lips and silently prayed. Ralph told Lisa what Director Waters had told him and added that Vic is a survivor. He felt wetness in his eyes.

"Oh God!" Lisa whispered, "No, he is too good to-, I have faith in him," she said, getting control of her emotions.

Director Waters', CIA office
Langley, Virginia

Director Waters walked out of his office and stopped at the secretary's desk.

"I want you to notify the Panama Canal Administration Building in Panama City that there seems to be a ship that is out of control. Tell them it is a Chinese registered freighter, the Tiangong Kaiwu and it narrowly missed hitting a freighter registered to the United States. Tell them the location is currently two miles east of the canal entrance, turning in tight circles at a slow speed."

"Yes sir, I will call immediately," she said, picking up her telephone.

General Yi's Office
Chengdu Military Base

"What do you mean the Tiangong Kaiwu was attacked?" General Yi asked.

"General Yi we do not have all the details, but it appears the ship was attacked last night or today while waiting to enter the Panama Canal. The entire crew was either killed while aboard or jumped from the ship and drowned," President Yang's chief of staff said.

"That does not make sense. Who or what attacked them?"

"The last communication we received from the ship was that one of the crewmen went berserk and started attacking the crew. The ship was preparing to relocate to deeper waters to make your cargo transfer then make the passageway through the canal. Just as they lifted anchor and started their engines was when the attack begin. There was an unconfirmed report of an explosion somewhere below decks."

"Where below decks? Where was the explosion reported?"

"I do not have that much detail in this report."

General Yi began sweating; how did they know? How did they find out? He felt sick to his stomach; he knew his family would soon receive a letter regarding his treason with an invoice from the government for 23 yuan to pay for the bullet that executed him."

President Yang's Office
Beijing, China

President Yang was reading the "Sun-Chang" plan that was delivered from General Yi's office the day before. He reread the line stating, the computers at the Clinch River Breeder Reactor Plant in Oak Ridge, Tennessee was to be wormed the next day. He knew that someone in the United States was able to outmaneuver Professor Szu, General Cheng and General Yi and all their programmers at the Tsinghua University including the Zhongda Bram programmers.

He turned to his computer on his desk to email the professor and remembered that all the computers were destroyed or at least hacked and could not be trusted now.

He picked up a cell phone and dialed the university, then told Professor Szu that Sun-Chang was to be cancelled immediately and for all documentation related to the program to be destroyed. He then made the same phone call to General Cheng and Colonel Hon, deciding to have General Yi notified in a different manner.

President Yang then called and ordered that General Yi be arrested and placed in solitary confinement until further notice, adding that if he resisted he should be executed immediately.

Near the beach-
East coast of Panama

Vic awoke and saw that the sun was setting. He tried to stand and get his bearings, but had difficulty keeping his balance. He couldn't tell where he was, just thick jungle.

His legs were badly swollen just below the knees and his left shoulder was throbbing and felt as though it were bleeding again, he walked twenty minutes away from the shoreline before stumbling onto a dirt road, the jungle was thinning and he could see the faint glow of city lights.

An hour later he realized the lights were Panama City and knew that he was close to help, but what kind of help he thought. He passed a house with laundry on the clothes line and attempted to remove the wet suit, but couldn't get his left arm out of the tight sleeve. He realized he still had a knife on his utility belt and cut the suit starting on the left collar across the shoulder and down to his stomach. He slowly stripped off the wet suit, he inspected his shoulder and found what looked like an exit wound in his chest, it was a ragged hole and the skin was a deep red with green lines leading from the center of the wound.

He dug a small hole with his knife and buried the wet suit as best he could in their garden. He put on a pair of cotton pants that were too large at the waist and found a piece of nylon rope to hold them up. There was a shirt on the clothes line that was too small, but at least covered his right shoulder. He could not lift his left arm to put the shirt on properly and just draped the shirt over his left shoulder, hoping to get away from the house before the owners saw him in their yard.

He started walking along the road again toward the city. Several cars passed him, but no one stopped to help. An hour later he noticed a larger gravel road that led directly to the city. His feet began bleeding from the rough gravel.

He hailed a taxi once he reached a paved road and convinced the driver he was in a boating accident and needed to get to the city. The driver insisted on taking him to a hospital, Vic was too drained to argue and fell asleep in the back seat.

Vic awoke when a nurse opened the door of the taxi and began helping him to his feet into a waiting wheel chair. She rolled him into the emergency room where a doctor was waiting beside a gurney. They put Vic on the gurney and started emergency procedures, he passed out again.

Day Eleven
DIR office,
Plano, Texas

Lisa picked up the receiver before the first ring ended, "DIR, how may I help you?" she asked. Then buzzed Ralph's phone and walked into his office, leaning against the door.

"This is Ralph," he said holding the phone to his ear, he listened to Director Waters then hung up.

"Lisa, he's alive, he is alive, in a hospital, but he is alive!" Ralph yelled and watched Lisa smile and return to her desk with tears in her eyes.

Hospital,
Panama City

The next morning Vic awoke with fire in his left shoulder, he saw Elena sitting beside by the bed and saw her crying. He saw her look up and he asked how she knew to come to the hospital. She said a man, whose name was John, came to the hotel room and told her. A lady drove her in a taxi.

Vic adjusted himself in the bed and sat up against the pillow, he looked at her and knew she was more loyal than he deserved. Vic realized he could use his right arm fine even with the left arm in a cast from his shoulder to the tips of his fingers.

He saw a telephone on the table and told Elena to get an outside line, then he gave her the number for the SatCom international operator and gave her the number for DIR in Plano, she handed him the phone when it started ringing.

Lisa answered the phone and almost screamed when she heard Vic's voice. She quickly contained herself and transferred the call to Ralph's phone. Vic briefly explained that the container was destroyed and that he was wounded and was in the hospital. Ralph told him to take a vacation with his lady friend and that he would fly down to visit him in a day or two to get details. Vic heard voices in the hall and told them he would call again later.

Ralph slowly replaced the receiver on the base and looked up and noticed Lisa was standing there with tears flowing down her cheeks. Ralph started crying and got up and walked to Lisa, the two hugged as they cried and laughed.

"I told you not to worry, Vic is a survivor and the best damned agent this country has and I don't even pay him."

Ralph made it to the table and poured two cups of coffee, they talked for a while and decided they both wanted to see Vic as soon as possible, then locked the office and went home, agreeing to meet at the DFW airport that evening.

Vic reached for a glass of water when the door opened and two doctors walked in, one had a clip board and they were speaking quietly. Vic looked up and greeted the men and waited for the bad news about his condition.

They informed him that he should take a couple of weeks to recuperate before attempting to return to his job on the sea. Elena turned to them and announced she would help him.

The room phone rang and Elena answered, she listened for a moment and handed the receiver to Vic.

"Hello," Vic said.

"Vic, Lisa and I will be in Panama City in the morning. What room are you in at the hospital?"

Vic provided him with the room number and handed her the receiver, "I guess we will have visitors," he said, looking at her.

General Yi's Office
Chengdu Military Base

Colonial Hon saw the military police arrive at the door and walk through the room into General Yi's office. He heard the voices and heard General Yi's demand that he be treated with the respect his rank demanded. He then heard the single gunshot and saw the military police walk out of the office.

He felt his gut tighten and wondered if he was next while he watched the police walk out of the office, leaving the body where it fell, feeling relief when he realized they were not interested in him.

Day Twelve
Vic's Hospital room
Panama City, Panama

Vic woke when he heard the door open, he saw Elena sitting in the chair next to his bed and saw Ralph and Lisa walk into the room. Elena stood up as though she was going to defend him if necessary, but relaxed when she saw Vic smile at the two visitors.

"Hey Vic," Ralph said, walking to the edge of the bed and extended his right hand. "You must be Elena," he said, looking at her, and smiling.

Elena acknowledged and smiled at Lisa. Ralph then told Vic that all was forgiven and that all charges against her was dismissed by the FBI. Vic saw Elena smile and recognized the obvious relief in her demeanor. Ralph continued with a statement that he needed details on the mission and asked that Lisa step out with Elena. The ladies left the room and Vic then filled in any holes of Ralph's known story.

After he closed his folder Ralph told Vic that he was needed in Dallas for a new situation which was brewing in the Middle East after he recuperated. Vic nodded and announced that he would need several weeks of loving TLC from Elena and winked at Ralph.

Ralph acknowledged his understanding and stated that Lisa had never seen the canal, then informed Vic that he was a hero in DC and Langley and left the room. He held the door open, letting Elena back in to the room, then Vic informed Elena that he would need some serious loving as he heard Lisa laughing and saw Ralph escorting her out of the room, turning and saluting Vic as the door closed behind him.

THE END

Footnotes

[1] Cyber War, Richard A. Clarke published by Harper Collins, page 56

CSX Corporation is an international transportation company offering a variety of rail, container-shipping, intermodal, trucking and contract logistics services.

HP is an American multinational information technology corporation

www.ingramcontent.com/pod-product-compliance
Lightning Source LLC
Chambersburg PA
CBHW071108250626
47159CB00002B/654